THE GODCHILD

ISBN-13: 979-8-9899340-3-4

THE GODCHILD

S.C. TERLECKY

Also by S. C. Terlecky

American Relic
Canticle of the Spear
Author website: https://scterlecky.wordpress.com

For Ravenna and Evanna

PART I
Discovery

Humanity failed miserably in the previous world. They executed their familiar playbook of conquest and competition for control, and in the end, they destroyed everything they held dear. From their ashes, the few remaining survivors united to form the last community of our species. If we are to endure on this planet, we must play under a new set of rules. Life is but a game, and we are all Teammates in this endeavor. The sum of us all equals TEAMMATE.

—excerpt from introduction of the TEAMMATE Rulebook

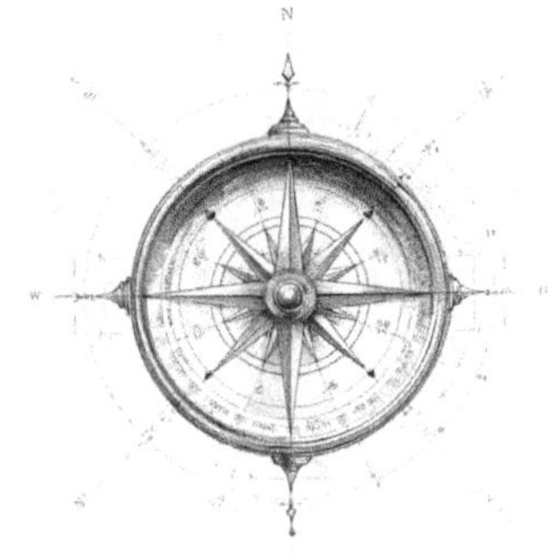

CHAPTER
ONE

The sweet scents of autumn permeated Ellie's nostrils as she waited for her school bus. It was unusually warm outside for the dim hour, though the sun was now beginning to kiss the horizon with its balmy red glow. Soon, the radiant orb would fully crest above the eastward track of road, creating a byway leading to illumination on her right and darkness on her left. Standing between this battlefront of darkness and day, the gentle breeze spurred Ellie's olfactory attentiveness westward. It harbored fragrant notes of ornamental fruit, flowering goldenrod, and crisp grasses, mixed with fresh dew. The initial rays began to fall on her mother's lavender chrysanthemums, bringing the first splash of color to the gray, ashen landscape. She inhaled all of the fall's offerings with a new appreciation for the changes of season. Her final school year would determine a new direction for her contributions to the sector, and she was equally excited about discovering her future path as the butterflies that were taking flight in her stomach.

"Achoo!"

The morning's tranquility was destroyed by the snotty-nosed intruder beside her.

"Please cover your mouth, Molly," she repeated for the zillionth time to her seven-year-old sister. "And use a tissue for TEAMMATE's sake!"

"Sorry," said the watery-eyed youngster. "I was fine until we came outside."

Ellie shot her a look of annoyance as the girl wiped her nose on her sleeve. *Kids are so gross.*

"You really need to work on your manners this year, Molly. You're not in first-grade anymore."

The rebuke upset her younger sister. "Mommy says you need to work on being nice to people," she shot back.

Ellie rolled her eyes. "Let me rephrase, dearest Teammate Molly. Thank you, my dear, for sharing all of your germs this morning with me. I really appreciate the extra shower, especially on the first day of school."

"That wasn't real."

"No kidding."

"I'm telling mommy."

"I'd be more surprised if you didn't."

Her sister crumpled her nose, looking at her. "What's that mean?"

Ellie caught sight of the bus, silently rolling down the street. She glanced sideways at her sister. "It means you're a tattletale."

"I am not." She stood with her arms folded, threatening to cry.

The bus brakes screeched in protest as the large and otherwise silent machine rolled to a stop at their driveway. She stepped in front of Molly to make sure the silly girl didn't get too close before it completely stopped.

"Achoo!"

She felt the damp impact of the violent wind reverberate against her back. A wave of rage erupted from Ellie, and she growled her next words out of earshot of the bus driver. "I am so done with you! Just when I thought I couldn't be any more stressed, you ruin my morning. I'd be better off without both you and TEAMMATE in my life!" She roughly yanked Molly ahead of her before pushing the girl up the stairs of the bus. Her sister looked over her shoulder at the top of the steps before sticking out her tongue in defiance of her older sibling.

Ellie deposited her sister with the other younglings in the front of the bus and headed as far away from them as she could get.

Her best friend Judith was sitting in the very last seat, motioning for her to join. It was an unspoken rule that the oldest students on the bus sat furthest away from the driver. This helped keep teenage conversations private and kept the younger children supervised. Were a youngling to attempt to take a back seat, they would be politely told to move quite far away.

Judith slid over, and Ellie plopped down beside her.

"So, get this," started Judith, who looked to be nearly bursting to get her onslaught of words out. "This summer, my cousin and his wife had a baby, and I got to hold it. He was the cutest little baby ever. Oh, you should have seen how tiny his fingers were. I could have just died right there and been happy holding him. But then, of course, he had to ruin the moment and throw up on me." She crumpled her face in revulsion and pushed her palms outward. "So, I handed him back to his mommy. I suppose I'm not ready for kids yet."

Ellie smirked at her dramatization. Then she raised her eyebrows. "I sure hope you're not ready for kids. You could never be granted a child permit at your age anyhow."

"But what if I somehow got pregnant?"

"I'm pretty sure there's a bunch of steps prior to just becoming pregnant." She paused thoughtfully. "And if your body somehow slipped into a fertile state, your bracelet would not stop alarming until your hormone levels were adjusted. But if it somehow still happened, TEAMMATE would take your baby. I remember overhearing my parents talk about a high school girl in that same situation when we were in second grade." Everyone knew that the rules of TEAMMATE were set in stone. Disobedience was not an option if they wanted to enjoy their prosperous world. A proper permit was required to bring another Teammate into the game.

"Well, what if like...I didn't tell anyone? I could totally hide it until I gave birth."

Ellie rolled her eyes. She glanced up the dark aisleway of the bus, which was illuminated every few seats by the glowing bracelet of its occupant. A few children spoke in hushed conversations, but many tried to sleep during the long ride. Ellie hoped their conversation wouldn't be overheard. "That could never happen," she said with her voice in a whisper. "But if it did, TEAMMATE would find out and put you in jail."

"That's all expected, but my question is...what would they do with my baby?"

Ellie sighed and shrugged her shoulders. "I don't know. Just take it? Why does this even matter?"

Judith gave her best friend a very serious look. "Ellie, you realize I need to find these things out for when I have my love child with Andy Jacobs."

Ellie arched her brow. "The boy who doesn't know you exist?"

"Oh, he knows I exist. He just chooses not to acknowledge it... yet."

Ellie shook her head and nervously looked around again. "You shouldn't joke about things like this, Judith."

Judith giggled. "Oh, I'm totally not joking about having Andy Jacobs's love child. I would absolutely have his baby tomorrow, if possible." More giggles followed. "But...enough about my love life. What about you? Anything interesting happen over the summer?"

"No," said Ellie. "I'm not actively seeking anything like what you're insinuating."

"Oh, come on, Ellie. Don't you even want a boyfriend?"

Ellie thought for a moment. "I suppose someday. I'm just not boy-crazy right now. They all seem interested in other girls in our class anyway."

Judith glanced sideways out the window. "Tell me about it. But you need to put yourself out there. Make yourself more available, Ellie. Open up and talk to more people than just, well...me. Not that I mind being your only friend," she smiled sweetly. "I think I'm like...the only one who gets you. People think you're selfish, but you're not. You're just reserved and totally smart. There's some perfect boy out there waiting to meet you. I really hope it happens this year. You know me. I'm always rooting for the home team."

Ellie laughed off her friend's concerns. "Thanks, Judith, but I'll be just fine. I'm more worried about a whole lot of other things this year." Who had time to brood over boys when the biggest test of her life was just around the corner? The thought of it made her queasy. The path of her future would be paved by the results of this one test. Added to that, she'd be receiving her driving permit next spring. Why, she needed more time than she presently had to study and practice driving. The time for boys could come after she had her life regimented and on track. She wasn't there yet, but perhaps in another year or two.

THIRTY MINUTES LATER, ELLIE AND JUDITH WERE WALKING through the doors of TEAMMATE High School. Ellie followed Judith into the auditorium and up the steps where most of their class already perched confidently, like the renowned upperclassmen they were, on the verge of learning their true purpose within TEAMMATE by year's end. Ellie cringed in pain when the overzealous volume of a man's voice boomed from the speakers.

"Good morning on this sunny Sunday," Principal Flannery's loud words assaulted their eardrums indiscriminately. The loud roar of chatty children quickly toned down. Flannery was a tall man, middle-aged with glasses and a formality about him that screamed administrator. "I would like to extend a very warm welcome back to all our Teammates-in-training. I hope you had a nice summer break and are all excited for this year's instruction to begin. As always, I will be dismissing you by grade to your homerooms." He turned to his side to acknowledge the teachers on the stage. "I'd also like to welcome back your teachers. And let's give a warm reception for our newest addition to the staff, Miss Conway, who will be taking over the sorting class, tenth-grade."

The young teacher stood from her chair and smiled with a wave to the mass of students.

"We are excited to have Miss Conway back here as an instructor, as she returns to us with the highest qualifications. Not too long ago, I remember her sitting where you all are now. With that said, I'm releasing the sorting class first to your homeroom. It's a big year for your group, and I want to make sure you have every minute of your six-day school week available to further your learning."

"I wish it were Saturday already," groaned Judith, with a roll of her eyes.

Ellie and the rest of her classmates rose to their feet, adjusting coats and belongings, and made their way down the aisle to where Miss Conway now stood. She, in turn, led them from the auditorium into the hallway and down to their classroom.

"Everybody may sit where you like this year," began Miss Conway. "We will not require assigned seats in sorting grade as long as we all can handle that responsibility."

Judith quickly eyed an open desk and pulled Ellie along with her so they could sit near each other. After taking a seat, Ellie looked up the row of desks and saw, without surprise, that Andy Jacobs would be sitting in their full view from this vantage point. If Judith had any defining characteristic, it was perseverance. *She'll be lucky to pass while studying him all day.*

"Welcome to the sorting class," began Miss Conway. "We have a large amount of material to cover this year to prepare you for the Teammate Placement Test, or as you will commonly hear it referred to as, the TPT. Now, don't be scared or intimidated— you've all been preparing for this year since kindergarten. The test will simply discover which profession your skills are aligned with. We will review for the spring exam all year. However, you will actually take the test twice. Your first attempt will be at the end of next week. Although it's theoretically possible to use the fall score, everybody improves in the spring, and only the higher score counts."

A hand shot up in the front of the room.

"Yes, dear..." Miss Conway glanced at her handheld screen containing pictures and names of the students in her class. "Um, let's see... Alice? Yes, Alice. Question?"

The bright-eyed girl with blonde hair and big eyes nodded. "But what if the test is wrong? What if it puts me in a career I don't want to do?"

Ah, there it is, thought Ellie. We've nearly reached the culmination of a lifetime of obsessive studying, and her own fear was just as irrational as Alice's. Could the test be flawed? Could she hate what she'd be destined to do the rest of her life? Had she wasted her life with meaningless preparation?

Miss Conway smiled. "I think the greater risk would be allowing us all to choose what we want to do. How could we contribute to the team effectively if we don't all play to our strengths? We each have a purpose in society, my dear. This year, your abilities are the key to discovering what that purpose or "job" is. The TPT is merely the tool to unlock that mystery. Some of you may already recognize what type of work you are best suited for, but others may be surprised at themselves. We must all trust the process."

The process was exactly what Ellie had misgivings about. If there was a "trust" measurement built into the TPT, Ellie knew she'd score dead last, behind every other stooge in her class. And what would that poor result even mean? Would it punish her to a lifetime of performing menial tasks for being a lesser Teammate than her peers?

Judith raised her hand next. Before Miss Conway could locate her on her screen, she began talking. "Hi, I'm Judith. My strength is talking...at least that's what everyone says. Sorry...sometimes I overshare. Anyhow, my question is...how hard is this test?"

Miss Conway smiled while reading the notes next to Judith's name. "Yes, I can see in the past notes you have quite the gift of conversation." She lowered the screen and stared upward in thought. "I wouldn't say to think of it as difficult. It's not meant for Teammates to be able to get every question correct. In fact, the creators of the test state that it's impossible to get a perfect score these days. Sure, you've all heard that a long time ago, one student was able to get a perfect score in the spring, but they changed the test significantly to make it even more diffic...let's say more challenging. As everyone knows, that particular student, by rule, ended up on the TEAMMATE Council."

Miss Conway glanced around the room. "Are there any more questions? No? Well, then I guess it's my turn to ask you questions. Don't be shy. I'm just trying to get familiar with each of you while reviewing your material for the year." She studied her screen closely. "Blake?"

The boy in the last row shyly raised his hand. Blake Weirton was nearly as awkward as Ellie in social situations. She would feel worse for him, but at least he was attractive, if not weird. Some people claimed he had social anxiety. At least he wasn't labeled selfish, like she was.

"There you are," she said warmly. "Now, can you tell me what years The Last War took place?"

The boy was frozen in his seat, trying desperately to think. "Was it 2090?" he guessed in a hushed voice.

"Hmm," said Miss Conway. "I think Blake is thinking of the year TEAMMATE was established. Can anyone help him out? How about...Ellie?" She searched the room for the girl pictured on her screen.

Ellie raised her hand. "The Last War was fought from 2061 through 2064, or years four through zero BLW." BLW encompassed all history, "Before the Last War." Of course, most of that time frame was littered with the messy mistakes of numerous failed societies. The previous numbering system for that time period was quite antiquated, originating from some obscure event that had occurred two millennia before.

"Excellent," remarked Miss Conway, looking up from her screen now that she'd identified Ellie. "And can you tell me who won, Miss Wilder?"

"No one," said Ellie. "Everyone lost."

"Correct. Let's try someone else." She glanced downward again. "Jordan?"

"Yes, ma'am," the reply came from the front row.

"Jordan, what was the war fought over?"

He scrunched his face in thought, as if the action induced pain. "Uhhh, there were many problems with the old world. There were multiple contributors, including resources, arbitrary boundaries, and power-hungry leaders. But the biggest contributor was the differing beliefs throughout the world, or what was known as paganism."

"Precisely spoken. Thank you, Jordan. To summarize, we had too many different *teams* competing against each other, which led to conflict, which led to grand-scale destruction, which almost led to the end of humanity. But on the brink of extinction, we finally got it right. And so, we joined one team and changed our foolish ways." She looked around the class thoughtfully. "We should all be thankful to have been born in a time such as now. You all will have long and meaningful lives and careers to look forward to. Life is but a game, and we are all Teammates in that game."

Ellie knew it was wrong, but the familiar slogan made her want to gag. She glanced shamefully at the floor.

Miss Conway paused for effect. "Now then, let's turn our attention to our readers, and spend the next few minutes reading in silence the first twenty pages of today's lesson. Then we'll discuss. Please begin."

The students reached quickly for their screens, and the learning began.

CHAPTER
TWO

Sunday afternoon was the assigned market time for the Wilder family. Going to the TEAMMATE market was a job that every Teammate took seriously. Ellie's mom had begun to rely on her help each week over the past few years to help her increase her efficiency. Her sister, Molly, would have been more of a hindrance at the market, so she was normally left at home with her father, Kirk. TEAMMATE was very stringent on assigned market times and allowances. Teammates who entered the doors unprepared would find the end of each month very difficult, as their allowances often dwindled quickly, leaving them with unsavory meal choices such as bran and oats for breakfast, lunch, and dinner. It was all by ingenious design, of course. The result of the fixed allowances was the preservation of the sector's food stores, as well as the near elimination of diet-induced illnesses.

Anne Wilder and Ellie, still wearing her school outfit, stood outside the building, waiting for their turn. They were fortunate that their time slot was on the first day of the six-day work week.

"Two minutes to go," Ellie said to her mom. She was already exhausted from one day back in school. Some people said that long ago, there had been a mere five-day work week with two whole days off for the weekend. Ellie wondered if some parts of the old world weren't so bad. She brought her attention back to her mother's list and read it through one more time. Her mother stood with eyes closed, likely envisioning their pathway through the market. She'd admitted to her daughter that she usually got butterflies before they started.

"Four thirty-two appointment," spoke the man at the entrance to the market.

Anne stepped forward and held out her bracelet. The man scanned her device, confirming her appointment.

"Anne Wilder and daughter Ellie are redeeming supplies for a family of four. You have twenty minutes. The team celebrates your contributions."

"Praise TEAMMATE," returned the two shoppers. Into the store they hurried.

Ellie pushed the buggy while her mom read through her list aloud. Shoppers were allowed in every two minutes, but they had to leave before their twenty-minute time limit expired, otherwise they forfeited their cart of food. It was a very efficient system, leaving ten carts in the store to compete with. "We need extra eggs for that pie topping I wanted to try this week," said Anne. "Now, we got a dozen last week, so this will put us at the limit for the month."

Ellie grumbled. "Can't we do a crust topping instead of meringue? I wanted to make brownies next week."

Anne shook her head. "We won't have enough sugar anyway. I'll tell you what, honey. Next month we'll make brownies, okay?"

"I wish Dad could just raise some chickens to go along with his secret garden."

Her mother flushed a deep shade of red and looked around. "Ellie!" she whispered harshly. "Keep your mouth shut and go get the eggs. I'll be in the produce section. Not another word from you until we're in the car."

Ellie mumbled under her breath as she scurried away to do her mom's bidding. Ellie knew better than to create a scene at the market. She also realized her mother couldn't reprimand her at this delicate moment for being selfish. After all, what if a Teammate overheard her? Then their family would have real problems. She turned her thoughts back to food as precious time ticked away. For a brief moment, she considered grabbing extra eggs for the cart, but the credit penalty would wreck her mom's entire meal planning for the next month. Plus, her mom would say she needed to accept the rules like everyone else.

Ellie returned with the correct number of eggs.

Anne glanced at her bracelet. "We're cutting it close. Get a tablespoon of salt, ten cubes of sugar, and two cups of flour. Meet me in the dehydrogenated foods aisle. We'll try the bakery last, if there's enough time."

Ellie had learned that her mom put the bakery last to make them both move faster. Putting asparagus or brussels sprouts last did not evoke the same effect. Ellie raced off to follow her instructions.

They made it to the checkout with two minutes to spare.

"Excellent teamwork," greeted the cashier with a smile as mother and daughter unloaded their cart for scanning. No payment was required, of course. The scanning was merely to deduct store inventory and to keep track of family allowances.

Once the food was loaded in their vehicle, the doors were shut, and it was time for Ellie to apologize.

"I'm sorry, Mom. I lost my temper, and I apologize. I'm not always a great Teammate. It's just so irritating to see plenty of supplies in that store and realize we can't have them. It's not fair."

Her mother took a breath before replying. "Is it fair to put your family in jeopardy with a careless comment? You need to dispel these selfish feelings you experience. It's time to grow up. You're in the sorting class this year. You have strong abilities to contribute much to the sector, but I'd hate to see your placement be downgraded due to your attitude. It's happened in the past, I assure you. No one technically likes the market limits, but they are necessary to keep distribution fair. Imagine if people could purchase whatever they wanted. By the time we got our appointment, there'd be nothing left. We have to follow the rules. We are all in the same game."

Ellie frowned. "I just see plenty of other people playing by different rules. Dad plants vegetables in the woods. Our neighbors burn extra trash at night when they exceed the limit. Everyone knows the Hendersons' grass is so green because they collect rainwater to water it at night. Practically everybody on our street breaks the rules every week. All I wanted was brownies. How is that a crime?"

Her mother was taken aback by her accusations. "Criticizing your neighbors is not becoming of a young Teammate. If their actions begin to hurt the team, TEAMMATE will intervene. By the way, it's not a crime to want brownies. As you are aware, the penalty for the extra eggs would just ensure we wouldn't eat the last few days of the month. That hurts *our* team. That's why it's selfish and you know it. You're a very intelligent girl, Ellie...but perhaps instead of looking outward at others' flaws, you should look inward and concentrate on your own. The team becomes better when you do better. Pointing fingers is not how the game is won."

"I just want the ability to do what I want someday, Mom."

"Maybe someday the TEAMMATE Council will figure out a better way, hon."

"I'm tired of waiting. And yes, I realize that's selfish too."

Her mother looked at her and smiled. "Realization is the first step toward transformation.

A GUEST LECTURER STOOD AT THE PODIUM OF ELLIE'S CLASS THE next afternoon. He was from the Energy branch of TEAMMATE. He would be the first of many this year, each speaking on their respective role within TEAMMATE and imparting wisdom and fielding student questions. The man had identified himself as Reginald Neidhart, and it was evident that the man knew his trade. However, what he didn't grasp was how to relate those concepts to a roomful of teenagers who'd spent the entire morning being drilled with facts for their TEAM-MATE Placement Test.

"And so, mankind, looking outward, had left no stone unturned in our endless quest for energy. Everything we use requires some type of power. Power does not come without cost. Our history of energy use is well documented as violent and polluting. From chopping down forests, to harpooning whales, to drilling deep in the ground, to splitting the atom, it took just one man to finally think outside the box. And to step out, he simply looked inward." Mr. Neidhart pointed to his chest as he walked around the room. "Anyone remember the man's name?" He made eye contact with Judith. "You there. Yes, you. I think you know."

Judith looked around confused. The man had simply wandered in front of Andy Jacobs and therefore directly into her gaze.

"Was it you?" She asked with uncertainty.

A few students groaned.

"Ha! Hardly, my dear... although you should know I'm flattered to be mistaken for Henry Needlebaugh, the father of modern energy." The man smiled now with excitement. "Now, how did he do it? I'm sure you're all dying to find out." He paused for effect, then cleared his throat for the rehearsed lines. "There has never been anything close to approaching the degree of complexity and efficiency of the human body. We are made of systems within systems, ensuring hemodynamic stability for an average lifespan of a hundred and ten years. There is the heart that never stops beating, the neurological conductions, storage of a lifetime of memories and learning, the production of heat, the immune defense system...why the human body is a self-contained world of its own. It's absolutely spectacular."

Ellie found herself daydreaming about discovering something meaningful like Needlebaugh while her tablet's screen automatically filled with the typed transcript of Neidhart's spoken words.

"It sure is spectacular," whispered a boy in the front row a little too loudly with his eyes resting on the perfectly postured girl sitting next to him.

The subject of the boy's soliloquy turned toward him and wrinkled her face in disgust at his comment. "I'd prefer it if you didn't look at me," Alice replied, not in a whisper. The boy looked down at his desk, turning red while a few classmates snickered. Neidhart ignored the sideshow and continued on with his presentation.

"After identifying the best source of potential power, the next logical step was harnessing all the plentiful energy." He held up his left wrist. It was, of course, adorned the same as everyone else's in the room. The material was somewhat flexible and soft, but the color was shiny and metallic. "These little beauties brought life to Needlebaugh's imagination. Unfortunately, his vision wouldn't be applied until many years after his passing. But as a result of his unique thinking, we can now harvest energy from a variety of the body's systems that would normally be...for lack of a better word...wasted. There's the thermal energy from our sustained body temperature, the hydro-electrical power from the pumping of blood, cells polarizing and depolarizing, and of course, that's not even mentioning kinetic energy... all of which can be captured, transferred, and stored in our sector's collecting cells wirelessly. As you all have learned, the conducting cable allocates power everywhere it encompasses in our quite large sector of life. And hence, as long as your device has a receiver and is within the proximity area, you get power. As a result, for the past fifty years, we have been entirely self-sufficient for energy." This was the proud climax of his lecture, where Reginald Neidhart finally brought his eyes back down to the classroom to witness...perhaps the same illumination on the teenagers' faces that he now possessed. But where was the applause?

A hand darted into the air from the back of the room. Neidhart smiled eagerly. "Yes, young lady? Did you have a question?"

Becca looked sheepish in her quest for information. "Yes...Can I get a pass for the restroom?"

His eyes fell downward. "If you must."

Andy Jacobs slowly raised a hand.

"The young gentleman with long black hair," he pointed. "Do you have a question or insightful commentary?"

Andy hesitated, as if he didn't want to ask his question before the entire class. "What else can our wristbands do?"

The guest speaker smiled, happy to have a question pertaining to his field. "Why...everything, young man. They store credits, they access the communication cloud, and they can diagnose thousands of medical conditions. Why, the band's invention alone can be credited for raising life expectancy by thirty more years for our citizenry. There really is no limit."

"Can it be used to track you?"

The man was silent for a moment in thought. "Well, I suppose if you're near a collecting module, it's theoretically possible to triangulate movement from module to module. I can't say that it's ever been needed to the best of my knowledge. Of course, my expertise is limited to the energy application of these devices. That may be a good question for the Security branch representative when they come in to speak. But why do you ask?"

Andy shrugged his shoulders. "I dunno, I've always wondered about that. Like you said, there aren't many limits to its capabilities."

"I can only assure you this," began Neidhart. "If it could benefit our Teammates in any way, it would be used to do so." He glanced around. "Now then, if there aren't any more questions..." he glanced at his own bracelet, "I have another half an hour to impart as much knowledge on power as possible. If you think you might want to score higher for a career in energy, buckle up."

The collective groan was ignored, and Reginald Neidhart taught on with unbridled enthusiasm.

—Article 17 of the TEAMMATE Rulebook

CHAPTER
THREE

That evening, Ellie was supposed to go with her parents to watch Molly's soccer match. Participation in team sports was a requirement for younglings per the TEAMMATE Council. It wasn't without merit. To understand how the community functioned, it was necessary to have experience on multiple teams starting at a young age. Ellie remembered her own experiences, particularly the games they won. Now that it was no longer mandatory in her grade, she did occasionally miss the excitement. Despite her pleasant memories, she did not feel like accompanying her parents to the event. There would be a large gathering of fans to cheer on the youngsters, and there was always the expectation of socialization with other siblings and parents present while watching. Ellie was never comfortable in such situations due to her lack of friends and, frankly, lack of care for small talk.

"Oh, come on, Ellie. You don't want to stay home by yourself, do you?" asked her father.

"Dad, that's literally what I just said I wanted. I'd prefer not to deal with any more Teammates today. I was around them all day in school the last two days."

Her dad sighed, a look of disappointment in his eyes.

"Leave her be, Kirk." Anne Wilder, often the voice of reason, walked through the hallway while getting ready. "She's been to all of Molly's games so far this season. She's fifteen years old now. If she wants a night off, there's nothing wrong with it."

"When do I get a night off?" asked Molly. She was wearing her uniform and holding her soccer ball under her arm.

Kirk laughed. "Hey, this is all for you, Moll-doll. And remember, your soccer Teammates are counting on you. They need you to try your best, even if you don't feel like it."

"I'm going to score two goals for them tonight," said the young girl. "Ellie is going to miss it."

"That's pretty ambitious for someone who hasn't scored any goals this season," said Ellie. She saw the wince in her sister's eyes at the comment and changed course. "But I hope you do. I know you've been practicing awfully hard."

Her sister nodded with renewed enthusiasm.

"Kirk, we're going to be late if we don't leave now," said Anne while digging in her purse.

"Okay, everybody in the car. Ellie, get some rest and remember, no parties here while we're gone." He laughed as he said it.

"Right, Dad," returned Ellie. "I'm avoiding one social gathering just to create another one here with my imaginary friends."

"Tell them we said hello," he laughed as he led the way to the garage port.

"Good luck, Molly," shouted Ellie as an afterthought. "I hope you get those two goals."

ELLIE SPRAWLED ACROSS THE COUCH, EMBRACING THE SILENCE of the empty house. She activated her bracelet, which illuminated into a readable hologram above her arm, and scrolled to see what her Teammate contacts were up to tonight. Judith's status read *visiting my sweet nephew tonight.* Ellie would be seeing pictures on the bus tomorrow of her friend's newfound baby infatuation. She scrolled down and found herself unexpectedly stop on Andy Jacobs' post. *Cycle racing this evening,* she read with interest. Now that sounded fun. She had never seen the bike racing contests, as they were generally looked down upon by TEAMMATE. It wasn't a true team sport, but that didn't bother Ellie. Andy Jacobs was the type of boy who didn't care what others thought. Sometimes Ellie wished she could be more like that. Even though staying home was exactly what she wanted, she was essentially a prisoner in her own house. The TEAMMATE transit buses didn't offer routes as far out as where Ellie's family lived, and it wouldn't be until her birthday in the spring that she could apply for driving privileges. However, it wasn't like she had anywhere to go even if she could drive.

Ellie pulled herself off the couch with a sigh. What did she want to do with her free evening? She walked around the house looking for something to occupy her time. The dishes were done, and the kitchen was already spotless. She felt a craving for something sweet right now, like ice cream or brownies. Unfortunately, the only options included bland bread and starchy leftovers. Back up the stairs she went, past her parents' bedroom. She paused in the doorway of her own room. There was nothing sweet in there, and it was way too early to go to bed. She turned toward the natural disaster of Molly's room for a brief second. Ellie didn't want to set foot in that petri dish of germs.

Perhaps she could find something sweet stashed in the storage room. Occasionally, her dad would hide sugary tidbits in the often-overlooked space. She flipped on the light switch and studied the windowless interior room. There was an airtight container of excess flour, boxes of outgrown clothes, and stacked boxes that held every toy or game that was no longer used. Kirk Wilder insisted his family's waste remained minimal, a goal for which all good Teammates strived to meet. On wooden shelves sat glass jars. The contents of these jars were considered contraband by TEAMMATE. Kirk had preserved vegetables from his secret garden, in addition to his practice of canning extra market produce since before Ellie was born. On occasion, they'd had to use it when the market produce yields were lower than anticipated. Kirk had also been known to give some to neighbors for nothing but a wink and a nod.

Ellie's eyes were drawn to the ceiling above those jars. Why did the tile look different above them? Had she ever noticed that before? Perhaps it had broken, and her dad made a replacement tile out of scraps. But then, who would have broken it? She made her way under the spot of interest and realized that the wooden shelving against the wall created a natural ladder for a closer look.

Upward she climbed until she could reach and touch the discolored ceiling. It lifted easily from her touch and slid partially over, on top of a neighboring tile. Curious, she set her bracelet to flashlight mode to reveal a small crawlspace above her. It was about four feet high and looked to follow the interior wall of the storage room. A metal bar appeared to have been installed to pull oneself into the passageway. Ellie grabbed on and pulled herself into the ceiling cavity.

Immediately, Ellie's glowing bracelet illuminated the dark space. The hidden compartment looked untouched for years, as there was a thick layer of dust upon everything. She shivered with excitement. If her father had known this existed, there would no doubt be boxes of his hoarded treasures up here. This could be her very own secret place. Why, if she ever needed to have a break from her family, she could hide away up here for as long as she wanted. They would never guess. Ellie smiled proudly at her discovery. Feeling emboldened, she decided to follow the corridor to figure out which rooms it passed over. On all fours, she bear crawled until she reached the area above the hallway. The crawlspace intersected another walkway, which followed the hallway. This one was almost tall enough for her to stand. She was giddy with excitement. It was almost big enough to be another room. She looked up to see the apex of the roof above her. This was designed to be a hidden room, she realized. At the far end of the walkway, she noticed something else.

There was a wooden chair facing something near the wall. An old-style lightbulb hung on a wire from the ceiling. Ducking while walking over, she pulled a string from the lightbulb housing, and the room illuminated beyond her bracelet's glow. Behind the chair, she noticed a dusty wooden chest.

She had seen such constructed boxes in museums, along with other relics from days long past. Made of wood and thin metal trim to strengthen the edges, it had a locking mechanism to protect its contents. There were handles on either side, made of a peculiar, rough, cracked material, the likes of which Ellie had never seen. It wasn't rubber or even vinyl. It stretched slightly when she tried to lift the box. Whatever was inside, it was too heavy for her to carry back downstairs.

The metal lock appeared to be engraved. Many nicks and blemishes disguised what the inscription read, so Ellie decided to try to open the heavy box. To her dismay, it was locked. However, she was far too intrigued now to accept defeat. She sat in the chair and inspected the chest closely. A small cloth bag hung from one of the rough handles. She grabbed the attached bag, feeling something solid inside. Upon loosening the drawstring, a small iron key fell into her hand.

Excited, she quickly inserted the key into the locking mechanism and turned until she heard a *click*. Lifting the top of the old chest revealed a foreign smell. Where had she smelled the odor before? It wasn't unpleasant, just unusual. She carefully opened the lid fully to reveal the secrets inside.

She instantly realized what she laid her eyes upon was very old and very much against TEAMMATE rules. On top of it was an enormously thick book, as Ellie had seen pictures of such things in history class. There was a metallic necklace adorned with a symbol that looked to be a lower-case *t*, a smaller book with an unmistakably pagan depiction, and also some type of handwritten notebook. She realized the smell must have been from the old material that comprised the books. She recalled from school and from fieldtrips that it had been called paper in the old days. Writing on such material was considered wasteful, and any resources using the substance had been banned before Ellie's parents were born.

While removing the larger book and the notebook first, a single piece of folded paper floated to the floor. It was faded, like artifacts she had seen under glass protection at the TEAMMATE museum. Envisioning herself as an archaeologist, she opened the note to read without hesitation.

To my dearest godchild,

It falls upon me to bring light into your life. With this grave responsibility, I pray I do not fail you. No doubt, by the time you are able to read this, you will be faced with a decision. You've been taught that you should turn this chest into the officials. But I ask you this—what right do they have to destroy it? You will never know of me, except through what I write in this notebook. I will be long gone by the time you enter this world. You're wondering how I know all this, I'm sure. This will take a little bit of what we once called faith on your part. I have a gift to see important things before they happen. My task was to prepare the way for you. Your way will be difficult, much like mine was. Now would be a good time for you to close this chest back up and think very hard before making your decision. I cannot make you do anything. The choice is yours. I recommend you ask for guidance, silently. I realize you do not understand these things yet, but there is One who will hear you, and aid you. I'm sorry to lay this burden at your feet, and yet my heart rejoices that you may soon discover the truth that's been hidden from you for so long. One last part for you to ponder...you shall inherit a powerful gift much greater than my own. While I can see what may come to be, I can't see a way out of the predicament I'm currently in.

    Faithfully,
    G.W.

CHAPTER
FOUR

Ellie felt the sensation of small spiders racing down her back, their tiny legs not stopping until they reached the soles of her feet. Nerves, she understood, and yet she was powerless to stop shuddering in fear. What had she read? What kind of conspiracy had she implicated herself in? What was she going to do?

She heard a warning beep from her bracelet and saw her heart rate had exceeded 140 beats per minute. *I have to get out of here, now.* Focusing on her objective, she placed the note back inside the wooden chest and turned off the old light. She tucked the notebook, along with the thicker book, under her arm.

Back down the secret compartment she crawled, turning down the smaller alleyway and slipping down into the storage room. She slid the ceiling tile back into place and hurried into the safety of her bedroom. Once inside, she closed the door and locked it, concealing the journal under her mattress. She sat upon her bed, unsure of what to do.

She hugged herself tightly and rocked back and forth in thought, allowing the conflicting emotions to roll over her. Thankfully, she would have plenty of time until her family returned. What were her options? Three main choices came to her mind. First, she could pretend she never saw it. That was a very attractive option, although she knew her curiosity would be hard—if not impossible to fight. Second, she could turn everything over to the officials. That was the correct answer. TEAMMATE could sort it all out, give her whatever treatment was required for what she had read, and she could move on with her life. The third option, of course, was to continue reading what G. W. had written.

The risks were high. If and when the officials ever found out about the chest's existence, they could hook her up to their machines and question her until they uncovered the exact date she'd found the relics and the names of everyone she'd shared her secret with. There was no way to tell her family without implicating them. However, they couldn't answer incriminating questions if they had never been told. But TEAMMATE *could* find out about her father's secret garden. And if they did, it could be very bad for him. He could be taken away. And he'd surely be questioned if she turned over the chest. They all would. She was stuck.

After a few moments, Ellie slowed her breathing and tried to be more logical. Panicking wouldn't help anything. She could fix this. She *had* to fix this. Ellie had been taught about the dangers of paganism her entire life. Never in a million years had she thought she'd encounter it in her own home, but was she not smarter than an ideology? Words might have more effect on a younger, unsuspecting Teammate, but did she really need to be concerned with all her years of learning? She asked herself, what did she really know about it? She racked her brain, trying to remember anything important that she'd learned in school.

The intricate details of organized paganism had been destroyed long ago, so they'd been taught, at least. Ellie rubbed her temples, deep in thought. There were, however, some main themes that overlaid all the various sects. Such education was deemed vital to recognizing any resurgence and making sure it was ended promptly. On the surface, the teachings would seem harmless. Each would prioritize appearing good and charitable to pull in more people. Most required gatherings on a certain day of the week for more education. All taught of a reward after death. Various groups had different interpretations of this promise. In all cases, the ideology eventually would shift from helping neighbors and peaceful gatherings into forcing the ideology on others and ultimately killing those who rejected the belief. As all Teammates learned, The Last War was brought about when the main sects set upon each other, ultimately destroying the previous civilization.

But Ellie would certainly never hurt, let alone kill, anybody. She wouldn't even want to suggest people behave a certain way if they didn't want to. So, how dangerous could it really be for her to read this secret journal? Her mind was quite capable of reason, after all. She felt a thirst for answers growing inside her. No one knew all the secrets her journal held, and Ellie was very good at keeping secrets. Who would she ever tell if she gained insight into the mind of an authentic pagan? She could root out their tricks and recognize them for what they were. She'd already seen the first example. The promise was that she'd have some sort of power. It was laughable. Perhaps it would be believable for a young child, but certainly not for herself.

And what had her mother been telling her about it being time to grow up? This was her moment to do exactly that. She could analyze and learn as well as anybody else from TEAMMATE. This was not the proverbial monster in her closet that she needed to tell TEAMMATE about, like some frightened child, incapable of her own reason. These were merely words in a journal. Written words, apparently...well, supposedly written for her. They probably could have been written for anyone, though. She thought about that for a moment. That was likely another part of the deception. The author cast a wide net so that whoever found it would think it was for them. Ellie almost laughed at herself for coming close to actually believing it was written for her. No one could tell the future. If nothing else, further reading would be entertainment.

Still, she would need to be careful going forward. It was a prudent precaution any adult Teammate would agree with. And thus, it was settled in her mind. She would keep the journal she'd found. She could read it and gain insight. And when she was done, she would burn it. And no one would ever know, no one could ever prove, and no one should ever suspect it ever existed. Her problem, which she'd just agonized over for the better part of an hour, was solved. She alone was in control. There was minimal danger as long as she kept quiet.

ELLIE KNEW HER FATHER WAS TIRED THAT EVENING. SHE'D OVERheard him tell her mother about his exhausting day at work while she lay wide-awake in her bed. Although Ellie had made up her mind regarding the journal, it hadn't subdued her adrenaline, and she was no closer to sleep than a cat thrown in cold water. Apparently, Kirk's caseload had been higher than usual. Reports were starting to build up. He'd said he would get caught up eventually, that he just needed to get some rest. The house had grown silent quickly as Molly had crashed after her soccer game, and their mother habitually turned in for bed early. So why had her dad slipped on a light jacket and walked into the cool night air? Watching from her upstairs window, she decided to take action. Silently, Ellie slipped from the house and followed him through the backyard and into the wooded land behind their neighborhood.

The land was reserved for lumber, but it wouldn't be due for harvest for another five years. Ellie was privy to this information because her dad's office had access to most of TEAMMATE's records. She kept a safe distance behind her dad in the dark, cool air. There was just enough moonlight for her to pick her way through the forest. The night was mostly quiet with a slight breeze occasionally rustling leaves. At one point, Kirk turned quickly around after Ellie stepped on a branch. She froze in panic at the cracking sound, hoping he'd think it was a wild animal somewhere behind him. And it could very well have been a deer, as they were plentiful in the unharvested woods.

After trailing him for fifteen minutes, he stopped at a clearing and checked the sky. He waited a moment, likely to make sure no lights blinked up above. From her vantage point, Ellie saw stars and the moon but nothing else. The danger would come in the form of a drone patrolling in the area. After he seemed satisfied that he was alone, Kirk stepped into the small opening in the woods. He pulled back on a rusty wire fence and entered into his secret garden—the one place Ellie had never been allowed to visit. It was only now that he chanced a little light. He produced a small flashlight from his pocket, likely because he didn't trust using his wristband. His shadowy figure crouched low to the ground and opened a small umbrella to block direct light from being noticed from the sky above. With an unmistakable illuminated smile, he began filling his cloth bag with his harvest of tomatoes, peppers, and carrots. Once he had all he could carry, he stashed his flashlight and umbrella away and closed up the wire fence to protect it from the deer. When he turned around, he nearly dropped the bag when he realized a shadowy figure had been watching everything.

CHAPTER
FIVE

Kirk seemed frozen by indecision. Ellie wasn't sure what he might do in a panic situation, so she revealed herself.

"It's just me, Dad."

He let out an audible breath of relief. "What in the world are you doing out here?"

She began to move toward him.

"Wait there, Ellie," he said sternly. "Don't come into the clearing."

He made his way to where she stood at the edge of the woods. After they were under the cover of the overhead canopy, he set down his bag, preparing to give her a thorough verbal reprimand for following him and for leaving the house at dark.

Ellie clung to him in a hug, knowing full well it was harder to yell at someone when they greeted you with affection.

"Ellie, what do you mean by sneaking out of the house at night? This is reckless and dangerous."

She straightened herself up. "I couldn't sleep. I heard some noise, and when I looked out the window, I saw you in the backyard. I wanted to see where this was. You never let me come."

"And there's good reason for that," Kirk shot back. "The less you know, the safer you are. Now you've put yourself at risk, and I'm seriously upset with you."

"Why are you doing this, Dad?" she countered. "Because there's no need for you to be out here, either. We have all we need. You're putting yourself at risk for no reason as well."

The reflection of the moon in his eyes betrayed a brief look of surprise. Then his eyes narrowed. He inhaled slowly and deeply, as if reminding himself that there was so much she didn't grasp. He sighed. "I will tell you why, but not until we're in the safety of our own yard. Follow me, but keep quiet."

Ellie crossed her bare arms in the cool air, but did as she was told. And she was quiet, too—probably just as quiet as her dad. The truth was she wasn't sure why she'd followed him. She knew better. Maybe she was being selfish again, she supposed. The exhilaration of discovering the contraband in her house had likely fueled her boldness. Some people were addicted to adrenaline rushes. Could that explain her thoughtless actions?

She could tell her father was deep in thought the whole way home. *Would he tell Mom? Will I be grounded?* She couldn't say yet.

Finally, they reentered their yard. Kirk led the way to the basement door. Once inside, he gently set down his sack of produce and gestured for Ellie to sit in the old armchair they kept in the basement. It was apparent that he'd be standing for this talk. He cleared his throat. He spoke clearly but quietly enough not to wake Molly or her mom.

"Ellie, there's a whole lot you don't understand yet," he began.

"But Dad, I know…"

Kirk held up a hand to cut her off. "This will go a lot easier for you if you listen instead of arguing. Got it?"

She sighed but nodded.

"I take this risk because I remember a time when there wasn't enough food. You were just over a year old when the last shortage happened. Our canned supply kept you healthy until the next harvest season."

"But Dad," she said, "someone could turn you in."

Kirk smiled at his daughter's worries. "Who would turn me in out here, dear? The Hendersons? They sure didn't ask where the canned beans came from when their child got sick. They knew and they appreciated. I've helped out nearly everyone on our road when I could spare it." He grimaced. "No, we're all on the same team with our neighbors. We help each other out around here. They would never turn me in. It would be like turning themselves in. And what would they do when the next shortage happens?"

"But TEAMMATE fixed the output problem after the last shortage. Our teacher said it could never happen again. They've learned from their mistakes and increased agricultural land and permits."

Kirk sighed. "I hope they're right, Ellie." He crouched down so that he was eye level with her. "But if there's one thing that you can always count on, it's me taking care of our family." He made a fist and gently tapped his chest. "I owe it to the collective team to make sure I provide for my family. That's my job. I take it seriously, and I don't trust anyone else to do it, no matter how good their intentions are." He paused and looked away. When he turned back, he seemed distant, as if caught in a memory. "Things are much better now, and I'm glad. But I can't forget the hard times…after my mom was taken away." His voice threatened to grow weak, but he slowed his words and struggled on. "But it became my job to take care of myself after that. I learned to use a needle and thread when I grew out of my clothes too fast. I learned what I could eat from the woods when the pain of emptiness in my stomach wouldn't go away."

"Dad, you do a great job," she interrupted before he completely lost himself in the past. "I just don't want what happened to her to happen to you."

He smiled back, fighting the lump in his throat. "It's a minor thing, getting reprimanded for agriculture without a permit. On a first offense, I'd only be away for a week or two with reeducation."

Ellie saw her chance to gain some information. "I'd really like to learn more about your mom...my grandma. Why was she taken away when you were so young?"

He frowned. "She was sick, Ellie. I didn't understand it at the time. Still don't, I suppose. I was told she could come back someday. She just had to get better. She had to make a choice to get better...to come back and see me."

"But she never tried to contact you again? Was she even sad when she said goodbye?"

"No, she never attempted to reconnect with me," he said quickly. "But she was devastated to leave me. She wailed loudly and screamed for me to come to her when the officials knocked down our door and chased her. I was...I was too scared as a second-grader. They said she was dangerous...I didn't know what to do."

"She was sent to the other society."

"Yes."

"And this was her house?"

Kirk wore a look of confusion. "No, this was never her house."

Ellie sat in confusion. "I thought you told me that this house had been in our family before?"

Kirk nodded. "Yes, it was. But it belonged to my aunt. When your mom and I took our TEAMMATE vows, it was vacant because Aunt Ruth had to go to the TEAMMATE retirement home a month before. We had petitioned for birthrights, and so we qualified for a home with extra bedrooms. We were very fortunate to end up here." He glanced around. "So close to the woods and with good neighbors. Aunt Ruth would have been delighted, if only the dementia hadn't set in so quickly. She barely lasted a few weeks after moving out. My mom's sister was a lovely woman."

He looked around for a moment, as if trying to remember what he had wanted to say. "There's no need to worry. Worst case scenario, if I were caught, which I won't be, I'd get a slap on the wrist." He looked at her in concern. "But you are in a delicate time. Being in the sorting grade, your future remains unclear. A blemish on your record could ruin your ability to contribute to TEAMMATE. Let's forget tonight happened, okay? You know nothing of my activities, and let's keep it that way."

Ellie sighed. "Fine. But I may have more family questions to sort out."

Her dad smiled. "I'd love to tell you everything, but it's currently past midnight, and we should both be sleeping. Now get back in your room, and no more of this sneaking out. Got it?"

"Yes, Dad." She realized she needed one last question answered tonight. "But what was grandma's name?"

He furrowed his brow. "I'm sorry. I can't tell you because it's no longer an approved name in the sector. It's better that you never hear it."

Ellie was disappointed, but she gave him a hug and quietly made her way up the stairs and into her room. She was exhausted, but that didn't stop her mind from circling back to her grandmother and her aunt. To be expelled from TEAMMATE, her grandmother had to be considered very dangerous. If she were a pagan, that would be a logical explanation. But this wasn't her house. She had to have been the one to write the diary, but how could she have known Ellie would even be born, let alone that she'd come to live here? And what were the chances of her finding the book versus someone else? She needed to read more...but her eyes wouldn't allow any further use tonight.

Any form of paganism is contrary to TEAMMATE policy. All violators shall be excommunicated.

—Article 33 of the TEAMMATE Rulebook

CHAPTER
SIX

It was a quiet Tuesday morning in class. The only sounds were the breaths of Ellie's classmates and the occasional tap at their reading tablets, swiping to the next page of their assignment. The reading involved the history of the early years of TEAMMATE. The beginning had been very difficult because not everyone envisioned the same goal. Too many people wanted to return to the old, familiar ways. But these were the ways that had failed and left the planet mostly destroyed. The sector was the last surviving pocket of humanity. But even after their ancestors had emerged from the massive cavern that had spared their lives from the grand finale of The Last War, the battle against extinction was only starting.

Ellie read diligently.

Teammates knew something had to change in those early years. Despite a general consensus that more change was needed, they weren't gaining enough traction to move the process forward. Five years had come and gone, and humankind was not thriving. There was just as much division as before regarding distribution of the meager supplies the refugees of the past world possessed. Groups were threatening to fracture off from the whole. Something had to be done by the First Council.

Ellie stopped to look around the class. Everyone else read the well-known history intently, as if they hadn't gone over the formation of TEAMMATE every school year before this. She scowled at the absurdity of it all when her eyes met Miss Conway's. The arch of her teacher's eyebrows was all she needed to be redirected back into her reader.

The Council eventually realized they could not force people to stay in their new society. Their job was to ensure that the Teammates wanted to join the new societal structure that they were creating. Therefore, they moved their headquarters to a better geographical area, where their architects rendered enough room for a self-sustaining population to thrive in safety. Those who committed to building or working for TEAMMATE were granted entry upon taking the TEAMMATE oath. Others were screened more carefully, especially Teammates with a history of beliefs opposing TEAMMATE ideals. Unfortunately, the new society could not accept everyone. This was a hard lesson to be learned. Little by little, more people petitioned the Council to join the community, which provided new homes and schooling and produce to all who would work. This continued at a steady pace until the original area was left with only the undesirables. These survivors of the previous world would have a very dark path ahead. They did not work together. They did not plan well. Ultimately, this original civilization would fail.

Ellie heard a series of sudden gasps originating further up the row of desks. Her classmates heard them as well, and the sound of tablets collapsing against desktops echoed in unison. A boy in a black shirt slumped forward and slammed his head against his desk before falling to the floor. Judith screamed in terror. It was not just any boy. It was Andy Jacobs. Whatever was happening wasn't over. His bracelet was beeping wildly, and his arms and legs began to flail against the floor and desks, knocking the row into disorder and sending neighboring students scrambling from their seats in fear.

"Call the nurse!" Ellie heard someone yell.

The entire class backed away from the boy who could not seem to control his body movements. Miss Conway ran toward him but was rewarded with a sweep of her legs that sent her to the floor before she crawled away to safety.

Some classmates screamed while others stared in horror as the boy started to bleed from thrashing against the metal desks. Judith was crying.

"He's dying!" someone screamed. His bracelet was turning purple in color, a signal that oxygen levels were dropping.

Ellie rose shakily from her seat to take everything in. Seeing the boy thrashing helplessly did something to her. She wanted desperately to help him. She *had* to help him. The words from the journal popped into her mind like a whisper at that exact moment. *Ask for help, it will come.*

She closed her eyes and she asked, she wasn't sure of whom, to help this boy who looked to be dying on the floor. She found herself walking toward him, calmly.

"Stay back!" yelled Miss Conway when she saw the girl heading into harm's way. "Ellie, no!"

But Ellie sidestepped a kick and dropped to her knees to place her palm on the twitching boy with deep purple now upon his wristband. She pleaded for help in her mind, and she felt...something. A prickle. Was it heat? Static electricity? Whatever it was, Andy must have felt it too. He immediately stopped moving. He sucked in a lungful of air to her relief. His eyes, which had been twitching wildly and rapidly as well, rested on Ellie. There was blood on his normally pearl white teeth where he must have bitten his tongue or cheek. He stared at her in shock. Everyone in the room watched them in silence for a moment.

Ellie felt a hand grab her and pull her away from the boy. It was Miss Conway, with a look of terror on her face.

"Are you alright, Ellie?" she asked with a gasp.

"Yes," whispered Ellie in wonder.

"What did you do?" she asked.

"I...I'm not sure," Ellie said with confusion. Her hands trembled. "I just wanted to help."

Miss Conway gave her a look that mixed a little awe with a hint of disapproval. "You're lucky he didn't knock your teeth out."

The boy was attempting to get up from the ground.

"Lie still, Andy." The teacher looked at her bracelet. "The nurse says she is on her way. Tell me, if you can...has this ever happened before?"

Andy rubbed his hand through his long, dark hair. "Never," he said.

Just then, the school nurse hustled through the door.

"Is he conscious?" asked the middle-aged woman, still breathless from her run.

Miss Conway nodded. "Whatever it was seems to be over."

The nurse stooped down and read his medical bracelet. "That's strange," she murmured to herself. "Everything is reading normal."

"That thing was going crazy three minutes ago," stammered Miss Conway.

"He seems absolutely fine now," said the nurse. "Can you stand?"

Andy got to his feet, but not without some wincing from pain.

"Come with me, good-looking," she grabbed his arm and winked at Miss Conway. "We'll download his bracelet data and get to the bottom of this." She looked around the room. "Did he just stop seizing on his own?"

"I'm not sure," said Miss Conway, glancing at Ellie. "It all happened so fast, I'm just not sure.

THE REST OF THE DAY PASSED WITHOUT ANDY IN CLASS. IT WAS difficult for everyone to concentrate on schoolwork. Judith was so traumatized that her mother had to pick her up early from school. Ellie kept replaying what happened again and again in her mind throughout the day. She had experienced something special when she touched Andy, but what had she actually done? She couldn't comprehend how it had happened, which was as frustrating as it was terrifying. Miss Conway seemed suspicious of her as well. But it was the journal that kept popping into her mind as she tried to reconcile the events from that morning. When she finally got home, the need to learn more did not recede. She waited impatiently for the hour when everyone in her home was asleep for the night. When at long last the time had come, she read with the voraciousness of a hound gifted table scraps.

If you've read this far, then it seems you've made your decision. There is so much to tell you and so precious little time. I trust by now you're aware of the importance of complete secrecy. This is not just for your protection, but also for the ones you love. Their time to learn will be soon enough, but not yet. The best place for me to start is the beginning, so that is what I'll attempt to do now.

TEAMMATE has done its very best to erase our history. The accounts had been written and passed down for generations until after The Last War. From its beginning, TEAMMATE sought to destroy every version in print, but as you have found in the chest, it failed. You will need to begin to read the accounts from the separate book in the chest. I have marked where to start. You will read about the birth of a baby boy, unlike any the world has ever seen since. He was viewed as a threat in his day, just as his very name is viewed today. You've never heard it, I know. His name was Jesus. He was human in form, but that's where his earthliness ended. Your reading will reveal his teachings, his works, and what ultimately happened to him. If you follow his words, you cannot go wrong.

Ellie stopped reading. She desperately wanted to learn everything about this strange cult, but where would it end? She had to read the journal. That wasn't even a question anymore. But now it was giving her other reading assignments? What other things would it have had her doing before she realized she was being controlled? Yet it was still her choice to do or not do. The written words had not come with threats...yet. Still, if nothing else, the reading was a new perspective on TEAMMATE history. Surely, she could be objective about interpreting the slanted history it presented. Her eyes were drawn back to the journal.

Historians blame our people for The Last War. TEAMMATE has taught you that the absence of our beliefs helped end all wars for good. This is a fallacy. Unfortunately, it has been true throughout history that humankind has the ability to manipulate nearly any strong belief into aggression. This has been true with countless examples before our new civilization emerged. Nationalism, politicism, familialism, tribalism, and yes, religion have been used by people in power to do bad things in the past. TEAMMATE sought to eliminate all these differences in their quest for unity. But even with their collective brain power, they did not understand that it was merely the human element that sullied the reputations of all these collective groups. Soon, you will learn many truths, and the first one will be that TEAMMATE is just as susceptible as any other ideology.

I again urge you to ask for help as you begin your journey into history with these texts. The child that I spoke of before is the one who will help guide you. Perhaps you've already asked for help. If you have, I trust that your needs have been met. I would advise you not to be afraid, but I know it to be impossible in the current circumstances. So instead, be brave. You were created to bring back what has been lost in this world. Many have tried and have seemingly failed before you...except they did not truly fail. They protected the diminishing light of truth by blowing on the dying embers enough that its radiance could not be completely extinguished from our world. And they all did so, hoping someone like you would come along. Well, here you are, my godchild. You are the last of many, and your time is at hand. I wish I could be there to help guide you, but my written words are all I can offer you from where I am. But

before you read any further into my imperfect narration, I ask that you at least begin to read the text I mentioned.
Faithfully,
G. W.

Only the wisest of Teammates may sit on the TEAMMATE Council. The best of the best in each Teammate's field may become eligible to retake the TEAM-MATE Placement Test after ten years of service in a management position. The highest achievers are the only Teammates considered for the Council.

—Article 36 of the TEAMMATE Rulebook

CHAPTER
SEVEN

Ellie stayed up to read her assignment most of the night. When she dropped her tired body into the bus seat the next morning, Judith wasted no time in filling her in on the updates regarding Andy.

"Well, he totally wasn't responding to my messages, so I had to get my info directly from his friend, Blake. Speaking of which, do you think he blocked me? I mean, I used to get at least a one-word response from him. And now...nothing. Isn't that weird?"

Ellie shrugged. "It's kind of suspicious, I guess." She yawned loudly. "How often were you messaging him?"

Judith giggled. "Three times a day?"

Ellie narrowed her eyes. "Every day?"

"Well, that's more of an average...you know...some days less, some days more."

"Yeah, he definitely blocked you," said Ellie. "I would block you, at least."

"I was afraid of that. Hopefully, he's just ignoring me. I need him aware that I'm worried about him. How's he going to know if he doesn't get my message? Anyway, Blake said they took him to the medical center for tests, and guess what?"

"What?" asked Ellie, with annoyance in her reply.

Judith wrinkled her nose. "You're a grumpy pants this morning. Anyway, the tests show that he's completely fine. They ran a scan of his electrical brain activity or whatever, and he's not sick. Sooo, it was probably a one-off thing, which is great news. Otherwise, if it was something ongoing or genetic, we might have difficulty getting that child permit we were talking about."

Ellie gaped at her friend. "You're not right in the head, you realize that? On a side note, I am relieved to hear he is okay. Your stalking techniques are top notch."

Judith rolled her eyes. "Thank you, thank you—I think. I must admit I'm a little jealous you got to touch him yesterday. He was definitely staring at you when he stopped doing his...you know...shaky body thing."

"I'm pretty sure it was a seizure."

"Whatever you say, smarty pants. Sounds like you're ready for the big test next week."

Was she ready, though? Ellie wasn't sure if she'd ever be ready for the TPT. Instead of studying every night like she'd planned, she was engrossing herself in the history of paganism—something that surely would not be on the test. Ellie stared guiltily out the window, past Judith's mocking grin. The bus had stopped again to let on a first-year student. The boy lived in a modest home, like most of the other older cookie-cutter styled residences on her road. Ellie studied the thick woods behind the child's house. She wondered if they might be close to her father's secret garden. Hadn't he traveled east after heading deeper into the forest?

"Hello, TEAMMATE to Ellie." Judith interrupted her thoughts with a giggle. "You're zoning out like Henry Needlebaugh. Didn't that lecturer say he'd often daydream about inventions in the middle of a conversation?"

"I must have been daydreaming through that part," Ellie quipped. "I suppose I'm ready enough." *I probably should have slept last night.* "Not that it matters," she yawned. "Everyone does horribly on the first one. It's the spring version we need to worry about."

"Well, I realize I can't outscore you, Ellie. Hopefully, we can end up on the same training track for a while. I'm sure you'll probably end up in something with math or science, like engineering or medicine. I don't want this to be our last year as friends. I'm so worried I'll do too well or too poorly and won't have any friends with me."

"Judith, it's not like we wouldn't still be friends. Also, you make friends more easily than anyone. Just do your best and let TEAM-MATE take care of the rest." She said the last part mockingly.

"Yeah, and TEAMMATE will probably place me somewhere awful. I realize you're not particularly worried about the lack of a so-cial life, but I actually need one. Maybe you've never noticed, but I don't function well in solitude."

Ellie laughed. "I noticed. But if you can befriend me, the possibili-ties are endless. We both know I'm not easy to be friends with."

"True, but you're loyal. And also, there's no tough competition for your friendship."

"Ouch."

"Sorry, didn't mean it to sting."

"No worries, my feelings died a long time ago."

Judith laughed. "See, this is yet another reason why I love you. Your jokes are so terrible."

"Can I unfriend you?" asked Ellie.

"Sorry, no returns."

"Good morning, Teammates," sang Miss Conway's cheery voice. "I trust you all completed your homework assignment from last night. Let's all hit that send button now so you'll get your credit." She glanced over to see Andy back in his seat. "Don't worry, Mr. Jacobs, you'll be credited for this assignment due to medical reasons. Can anyone tell me where we left off yesterday?" She walked among the rows of students as they tapped at their readers to send their homework before pulling up where they left off.

"No one at all can remember? Clint, what's the last thing we discussed yesterday?"

The boy straightened up in his chair and brushed his hair from over his eyes. "I dunno...I guess The Last War?"

"Oh, so close, Clint. We were talking about what happened *after* The Last War. The new beginning. I guess you're partially correct, though. It was that final culmination of destruction that forced us to change for the better. And how did the first gathering of survivors pick their new leaders in the post-war years? Jordan?"

The boy jolted upright. His eyes were wide.

"Did you not do your homework assignment, Jordan?" She glanced at her own tablet. "I see you turned something into me. I sure hope you completed the assignment yourself and didn't do something foolish like copy someone else's work?"

He cleared his throat. "Well...they just picked the people."

"Yes, but how?"

The boy's face flushed red. It was clear she wouldn't be getting much out of Jordan.

Miss Conway sighed. "Perhaps Alice could help you out?"

The girl was all too eager to answer the question. "The First Council was composed of the smartest thinkers left in the world. The goal was to rid the governing body of the people who were well connected, wealthy, and willing to be bought and sold for office." Alice smiled proudly. "And it was their wisdom that helped rid the world of the divisiveness caused by things like paganism."

Ellie accidentally snorted at the word-for-word textbook response.

Miss Conway's eyes narrowed at her reaction. "Miss Wilder seems to disagree, class. I'd be most interested to hear exactly where you find fault in your Teammate's answer."

Now I've done it. Don't blush. Don't act embarrassed like Jordan.

"I'm serious, Miss Wilder. We're not continuing until you enlighten us with your wisdom."

The eerie silence with stares upon Ellie made her uncomfortable. *These sheep don't even comprehend what they are, what we all are.* The realization made Ellie smile to herself. "Sure, I'll enlighten all of you. What makes our textbook's answer amusing is that it implies paganism is dead."

There was a collective gasp heard throughout the class.

"That's because it is, Ellie. It's been dead for a hundred years."

Ellie straightened up. "I disagree, if I'm permitted to apply my own logic. We've merely been taught it was dead our whole lives. It's simply not true. In fact, a new form of paganism has simply evolved, and it is very well and thriving and..."

"That will be enough foolishness, Miss Wilder. You know the punishment for promoting anything considered pagan. Quit being a silly girl and recite what the textbook..."

"There it is," Ellie interrupted with excitement. "Recite what the text says. Follow the rules of TEAMMATE. Give everything to TEAMMATE. Trust in TEAMMATE. Can't anyone see the hypocrisy? Paganism hasn't been killed, it's been replaced with TEAMMATE, and it's thriving."

Glossy stares and gaping mouths surrounded her.

"TEAMMATE is the one world religion now. We've all been forced into the same camp. There are no wars because we have nothing left to fight over. We've given up our right to nearly everything. It's all divided up and given away by TEAMMATE!"

Now there was an uproar from the class. Using logic to criticize TEAMMATE was not something anybody did openly. While a few kids may have looked to be on the verge of agreeing, most rushed to the defense of TEAMMATE and denounced Ellie loudly.

"Quiet class!" her teacher screamed. "I will not permit such hysteria in my classroom. Ellie Wilder, you take your things and head straight to the office. Do you hear me? Move it, young lady! Get out!"

Ellie couldn't help but smile at the effect she'd created. Where had it all come from? She glanced over at Andy on her way out. He was staring at her intently with his dark eyes, the start of a smile threatening on his lips. Under his desk, she noticed movement from his hands, hidden from everyone else. He was silently applauding her outburst. *It's possible I'm not the only one who sees things differently.*

CHAPTER
EIGHT

Ellie sat in silence in the car. She'd been sent home with the infraction of inciting disruption in the classroom. Her dad had left work to pick her up. She felt especially bad about this because she'd already overheard him confide in her mom about how stressful work had been just a night ago. But that wasn't something that Kirk Wilder would add to his daughter's plate. In truth, he didn't appear as mad as he seemed baffled on the car ride home.

"I just don't understand what would make you have an outburst like this. Is there something going on that your mom and I should know about? You're a good student. Next week, you will take your initial TEAMMATE Placement Test. Are you acting out in defiance for some reason? Talk to me, please."

Ellie tried to cage her frustration. "I don't understand why no one else can see it."

"See what?" He took his eyes off the road for a second, furrowing his brow in her direction.

"That there is no safe way to question TEAMMATE. Everything has been set in stone our whole life, and it's against the rules to suggest it be challenged." She was more careful in her wording this time. "If our society is so much better than any other before, why am I in trouble for sharing my logic with the class?"

Kirk cleared his throat. "I understood that you interrupted another student who was giving an answer."

Ellie sighed. "Miss Conway asked me to explain what was funny. I did as she asked, and she just didn't like the answer. I'm sorry you had to leave work because of all this."

"I only spoke with your teacher for a few moments. She cares about you and your future. You're lucky she's reporting your outburst as a simple disruption in class. Had she filed it under hostility to TEAMMATE or as pagan sympathizing, the record would follow you forever. It would absolutely ruin your chances of any meaningful employment placement in the future. Do you even realize how dangerous your words can be? Even now, you're still not out of the woods. What if someone in your class tells their parents and they address their concern to TEAMMATE?"

She shrugged. "I messed up. I mean, usually I can just bite my tongue instead of being argumentative. But today I just couldn't hold it in for some reason." She looked out the window and sighed. "Everyone acts like they're so wise, but all they do is repeat the history text. They're not actually thinking for themselves. I don't understand what's wrong with saying what I'm thinking. It was the truth, at least as I see it. I do know better than to have an outburst. It might have slipped because I'm tired from staying up studying this week. I really do want to score well on next week's test. I do want meaningful employment and to contribute. I think I was just frustrated and reacted stupidly. I'm sorry, Dad."

Kirk nodded knowingly. "Well, you won't be in school tomorrow either. Your teacher sent me something for you to watch and learn from. Sometimes it helps to have a little time away to reflect on our mistakes."

My only mistake was saying it out loud. "I'll be more careful next time."

Her dad took his eyes off the road again for just a second. "Ellie, there can't be a next time. It is beyond selfish to even suggest to other impressionable Teammates that you're wiser than the Council. You cannot comprehend having the greater good of everyone resting on your shoulders. You can't understand because you've never had to truly worry about anyone else but yourself." He swallowed. "I love you, Ellie. I can't bear to see your future ruined. Okay?"

"Of course, Dad. Like you said, there won't be a next time."

Ellie took dinner alone in her bedroom that evening. It wasn't a punishment from her family. She just wanted to be by herself. She realized that the journey and learning she had undertaken would have to be traveled in solitude. Everyone around her had been ingrained with the philosophy of TEAMMATE. Perhaps they just weren't selfish enough to understand her point of view. Her mom might have been onto something. She couldn't dispute that everything had been given up for the greater good. And the world seemed to be a much better place than it had been described before the unification. Everyone seemed to agree it was far better to sacrifice the little day-to-day choices than to revert to the old ways.

Ellie began to wonder if she had been different from everyone else her whole life. Perhaps she didn't belong in any society. Was she defective? It couldn't be ruled out. But from now on, no one else was going to know. She would learn to play the game safer. And she would definitely finish reading that diary.

Ellie heard a soft ding from her bracelet. The text rolled across her screen.

I never got a chance to thank you today.

Her chest fluttered when she saw the sender. It was Andy Jacobs.

She tapped on her bracelet to illuminate the keyboard hologram. But what should she type? She didn't think the boy knew she existed. She took a breath. *Just be yourself.*

After a few minutes of thought, she began to type. *You won't get to tomorrow either. Apparently, I'm still "contagious."*

That's too bad. They're just afraid you're right. I thought you were spot on today.

Ellie couldn't believe what she was reading. He agreed with her?

Thank you, she said. *It's probably safer if you didn't agree with me, though.*

Now, where would the fun be in that? I guess I'll have to thank you when you're out of jail. Goodnight, Ellie.

Thanks. Goodnight.

Ellie let out a breath of relief. Her bracelet showed an elevated pulse. She was slightly unnerved that she was behaving this way. *Maybe something is wrong with me.*

When the lights went out, she concentrated on her accepted task. She pulled the diary from its hiding spot. She no longer had any hesitation in reading its contents. Perhaps one day she would regret her choice. But the alternative would be the regret of never reading the author's words. Then she would always have to wonder, what had the writer been trying to teach her? No one should have the right to take that away, she decided.

The first truth you must learn is that our world has good as well as evil in it. It always has and it always will. The source for both comes from within us. It does not originate from an object or an idea. It is people who manipulate things for better or worse. What I'm trying to tell you is that the things that have been taken away, things that you have never known, were not bad things. They were and still are just things.

We have been classified as pagans by TEAMMATE. It is not accurate in the least, but that is the classification they use for all beliefs different than their own. You come from a family of Christians. I realize you have never heard the word, and it is inherently important you never speak it out loud, at least not yet. Be careful with your words, both spoken and written.

"There's an understatement," she muttered to herself. Wasn't that almost exactly what her father had mentioned earlier? It was very similar, at least. She recalled his warning. *Do you even realize how dangerous your words can be?* Oh, she was definitely learning. However, she wasn't stopping from reading more of them either. A slow smile pulled the corners of her mouth at the small victory.

Our family is just one of the three sects that took part in The Last War. There were other sects in addition to the three, but these were the siblings who couldn't get along. The original teaching foretold the birth of the one who would save the world. We, as Christians, believe Jesus to be that man. Actually, as you have already read, he was much more than just a man.

And so, in time, the original teaching was divided into three. Throughout history, it is true that the three factions did not get along well. There was bloodshed. Belief is a powerful motivator, and people were willing to die for it. You won't read that Jesus instructed to kill those who didn't believe the same, for that decision was a man-made manipulation. The sects were not evil in any perceivable way, yet there were evil people who misused their influence over others.

One thing that each of the three sects believed in was an evil being. Known by many names, he is often referred to as Satan. He is the very opposite of God. And he tries to lure people away from God. I tell you of his existence not to scare you, but to prepare you. He will take a special interest in you in the future. Be strong, for he will appear at your weakest moment. Charles Baudelaire once wrote, 'The greatest trick Satan ever played upon the world was convincing it he didn't exist.' If you're keep-

ing score, he's winning in this world of ours. But you, my godchild, are the one person who can change that.

The last part gave Ellie a chill. It was irrational. Monsters of all kinds had been made up throughout history to scare children and the feebleminded. Fear was needed for obedience. She closed the book for the night. Her objectivity must be preserved at all costs. She would not allow herself to be frightened into reading more while she was tired. And that was the real problem, wasn't it? Fatigue. Lack of sleep had lowered her defenses, and now she'd experienced physical chills from this simple journal entry. She chuckled softly in disbelief. It had been a good effort by G.W., but now it was time for sleep.

—Article 1 of the TEAMMATE Rulebook

CHAPTER
NINE

After a few hours of sleep, Ellie was again drawn to the journal in the early morning. She was a fluttering moth, determined to dance with the alluring flame. She'd already sidestepped another pagan trap and was all too anxious to continue her study of their curious behavior and beliefs.

The greatest power in the world is often the most underestimated. Love. That is what Jesus taught. This is what Christians believe. It's written that you can have everything in life, all the knowledge in the world, the ability to prophesize, and the power to move mountains, but if you do not have love in your heart, you have nothing. Likewise, you can give your gifts away, donate all your possessions, and even hand over your very life, but without love, you gain nothing. What did all the power seekers of the world throughout history gain in the end? Nothing that lasted. What do we love in this present age? The only thing left by

TEAMMATE for us to love is our family. And that's why I want to share and entrust with you this gift that I leave.

Ellie heard hushed voices from downstairs. She put down the journal to listen.

"I think it might be my fault," her father's voice confided to her mother downstairs. "With the secret garden and my family's history, I've put our child in danger, Anne. And I'm worried she still doesn't grasp the risk of questioning TEAMMATE. I should be the one staying home to fix this mess I've helped create."

Ellie heard a shush from her mother. Then she continued in a low voice. "Just let me handle it, Kirk. She's immature and selfish. This is not your fault. I'll straighten her out. You already missed work yesterday."

"I feel sick to my stomach over it. What if someone turns her in? I can't bear to think of it. I tossed and turned all night."

"I'm aware," replied Anne's voice, no longer in a whisper. "And now I'm tired too. Please, just go to work. Some things are better handled by her mother. You've done all you can."

"Not everything. I'm going to talk to Miss Conway again. She obviously cares for our daughter since she omitted an important part of the suspension reasoning. I need to tell her about our family history. This teacher can help guide our daughter, and she's given us reason to trust her."

"Are you sure that's a good idea?"

"She told me she wants what's best for Ellie, and I believe her. No one understands the danger to our daughter better than me. I was fortunate to be provided a central TEAMMATE job with my mother's history. But my background was thoroughly investigated before I was accepted. My teachers were interviewed, all past communications were subject to search, and I even took the KSM test. I'm telling you it was awful. There's no way to bend the truth answering questions when TEAMMATE has all the answers beforehand."

"Let's not relive that unpleasantness, Kirk. No one's asking our daughter to take the KSM test. If it makes you feel better, talk to Miss Conway. Do it in person, though. And leave Ellie to me today."

There was a sigh from her dad. "Then that's the game plan. Are you sure Molly is okay with getting on the bus herself?"

"Everyone will be fine. Now, get going before you're late."

The door shut, and the house went silent until Ellie heard her mother wake Molly for school. Ellie tried to fall back asleep but found it impossible with all the noises her sister made getting ready. She lay in bed, pondering getting up until finally she'd had enough waiting. She found her mom making breakfast downstairs.

"Nice of you to finally show your face in the kitchen." Ellie's mother was one of those parents who took pride in her dinners. There were no distractions allowed during mealtime. It was the one time of the day when everyone in the family was required to be in the same room, at the same time, engaging in discussion. Bracelets were even required to be in silent mode. Ellie knew her mother would not be happy about her absence from dinner the night before. However, it didn't change the fact that she hadn't been ready to be the topic of the previous evening. Selfish as it was, she regretted nothing.

"Good morning, Mom. Sorry about last night. I just needed some time alone."

Her mother raised an eyebrow in a gesture of disapproval. "I guessed that." She pursed her lips, thinking of the right wording she needed to continue. "I decided not to press the issue last night. But now you've had plenty of time to reflect on the reason you're not in school today."

"Did Dad tell you everything?"

Anne Wilder pursed her lips again and nodded. "You should know your father is taking this quite hard. He sees it as a reflection of failure on his part. But I have a different theory."

Ellie's ears perked up at her hint. Perhaps there was a way to slither out of more punishment if she listened attentively. "What's your theory?" she asked with genuine curiosity.

Her mother set her breakfast plate down and pulled out a chair, beckoning her to be seated. "I think you're after attention, whether you realize it or not. Is there something you'd like to tell me?"

Ellie couldn't guess where this was going. "Mom, I'm not after attention."

"Well, I think you're hiding something."

Is it that obvious? Ellie's face flushed redder than Blake's had in class. "Hiding something like what?"

Her mother smiled gently and took her hand. "Is there a boy I should know about?"

Ellie had not expected this tactic from her mom. She tried to respond, but couldn't without tripping over some words. "What...well... I'm...I'm obviously not around any boys...besides at school."

Her mother smiled, her eyes piercing her daughter's look of surprise. Then, those hard eyes softened. "I was your age once, you realize. I remember what it's like. Is there a boy you like at school? It's perfectly natural at your age. Are you trying to get noticed by him?"

Is this my bailout? Should I play along? "I didn't think so in the moment..." *that's not a lie,* "but maybe it's possible?"

Anne nodded with appeasement as if she'd just solved the entire puzzle. "What does he look like? You don't have to tell me his name if you don't want to. I just wish you'd share more with me...and come to me with questions. You're going through a lot of changes."

"Mom, you're making me uncomfortable."

Anne put up a hand to stop her. "Just tell me this. Am I wrong?"

Ellie shrugged her shoulders. "Maybe there is a cute boy in my class. But he'd probably never be interested in me."

Ellie's mom smiled. "He'll wake up soon enough. You'll see. Until then, no more disrupting class. Got it?"

Ellie nodded quickly, happy to see her mom less angry than she'd anticipated.

"Good. Now eat your breakfast. We might as well not waste any more time. I have to play the four-hour documentary that Miss Conway sent us from school. It's very important. I expect you to take it seriously, which means this will be the last time you ever speak out about TEAMMATE, whether it is for a boy's attention or any other reason your fifteen-year-old brain can dream up. Are we clear?"

"Crystal clear."

"Excellent." She flipped on the monitor.

A man in a bright orange polo shirt appeared on the screen. He seemed youthful, energetic, and happy. Music played lightly in the background as he walked along outside, conversing with the camera as if it were a friend accompanying him on a leisurely stroll.

Hello there, Teammate. I'm Melvin Johnson. If you're taking this walk with me, then we need to have an important discussion. What I need to teach you today involves working on becoming a better Teammate for your family, your friends, and all the other members of TEAMMATE. As you should know by now, the world we live in today wasn't always so wonderful. Over a hundred years ago, the world had many, many problems. In fact, you might say it was in chaos. Tell me, have you eaten anything today? I'm sure you have. Can you believe that millions of people used to go hungry every day? Are you wearing clothes? Haha, I certainly hope so! Well, many people used to go without clothing or even housing! Can you imagine no indoor plumbing, no power for your devices, no heat or air conditioning? Well, this was reality for a large part of the world's population. It certainly wasn't because they weren't invented at the time. No, it was because we used to be a completely divided world. Some people had all of these things, while others had some or even none of them.

Ellie considered the man's words as she chewed her pancake while sitting at the kitchen bar. A glance at her mom, who now sat on the love seat closer to the screen, confirmed she was nodding her head in agreement while intensely watching the program. Ellie couldn't fathom the past world described by the man wearing the orange shirt. How could one house have an overabundance while the next-door neighbor crawled about naked and famished? It seemed nonsensical. Was the world really that unfair before?

Why? I'm sure you're wondering. It was simple, random luck. Some people were born into good circumstances, while others were not. Do you think this sounds fair? Of course not! There was no equality, no fairness in the distribution of goods and services. No wonder we had nonstop wars, full prisons, sweeping famines, prolonged droughts, and economic collapses. Some people amassed fortunes, and some people had no money at all. Some families had one child, and other families had ten. Some people worked 80 hours a week, and some worked far less. There was absolute chaos because everyone did what they wanted without rules. Everyone was on their own. There was no unified team.

Now look around today. When was the last war in our current world? How about the last economic collapse? You can bet it wasn't even in your parents' lifetime. Why? Because we are unified. Thanks to TEAMMATE, we have true equality for the first time in history. We have removed nearly every reason for discontentment. What's the result? We are all free to enjoy our lives. We can still do everything we want, but we simply don't have to worry about the terrible situations in which people once found themselves trapped.

Now, from time to time, some Teammates forget what a wonderful world it is that we now enjoy. Some people become selfish and feel that they deserve more than everyone else does. This thinking is especially dangerous. We've been down this road before, and we've seen where it leads. These selfish views lead to foolish thinking. It's vitally important that if anyone you are in contact with starts to talk or behave in this manner, you report them to TEAMMATE quickly. They need prompt attention so they can relearn the importance of equality. Even if the person is a friend or family member, the danger is real. Remember, if you put the team first, you can never go wrong.

Now, in our next segment, we'll take a look at the lives of people who can't assimilate into our world. Their society is kept completely separate from our own because their logic and thinking are far too dangerous for a perfect world such as ours. You'll hear from some of the inhabitants who were offered retraining and a better chance at life but chose to be exiled in the false belief that they could do better. Many of these inhabitants include the darkest Teammates that once lived among us. You will see the faces of murderers, rapists, thieves, and pagans. But first, let's pause and discuss what we've learned so far.

The screen cuts to a country landscape with just the soft music playing. A caption came on the screen with a message to pause the program for discussion. Mrs. Wilder followed the prompt.

"What did you learn so far, Ellie?"

Ellie shrugged. "What you've been telling me. Don't be selfish. Don't doubt TEAMMATE," Ellie lied.

"I can only hope it's sinking in now." She glanced at her wristband, obviously reading notes provided with the program. "This next part might be a little scary, but it's reality for the people who leave our society. Remember, they chose this way of life after multiple offers from TEAMMATE to be welcomed back into society. Unfortunately, TEAMMATE cannot save people who do not wish to be saved. Again, this might be disturbing, but it's important to understand the consequences. You need to know the truth."

Yes, the truth as TEAMMATE sees it, thought Ellie.

The second segment was a stark contrast to the first. For starters, the scenery was gray and windy. Gone was the greenery and sunshine that had accompanied Melvin Johnson. The music had even turned somber. Melvin's enthusiastic smile had been traded in for a look of sorrow as he narrated the footage both on and off the screen. As promised, the segment depicted the people living in a separate society. They all wore rags for clothes, and most were missing teeth. Melvin interviewed an older woman who begged him to take her back to TEAM-

MATE. She kept insisting how foolish she had been so long ago when she left the safety of her former life.

The footage depicted dwellings that were all in disrepair. People tried to grow gardens, but the few plants they could produce in the dusty soil would usually be stolen by others with no food. There was even a brutal fight caught on the program between two men who had gotten into an argument. No one broke it up. Some watched sadly, while others cheered for the entertainment. It ended when the bigger man crushed a rock over the smaller man's skull, and he fell to the bare ground, bloody and motionless. The victor casually took something out of the fallen man's pocket and walked off. No one checked on the hurt man. They all kept their distance and eventually shuffled off.

The scare tactics continued for quite some time before Melvin broke up the disparity with his appearance back in the lands of TEAM-MATE with lush grass and sunshine. All Ellie could think about was that the woman who wrote in her journal—likely her grandmother, she'd decided, had probably ended up in that very camp. Perhaps she was even still there if she had survived. It bothered Ellie so much that she found her throat grow dry.

The program was far from over as it reverted back to all the wonderful opportunities offered by TEAMMATE. Ellie watched in silence for the remainder of the program, feeling numb. How could she complain about living such a wonderful, carefree life while others lived in squalor? *It was their choice,* she kept reassuring herself. *But what if I got sent there for reading the journal? What have I gotten myself into?*

With the final music playing, her mom turned off the program. She too looked affected by the documentary. "Well, Ellie, at least that's over. Very unpleasant business, I must say. Just look at how different our lives would be without TEAMMATE." She shivered. "But let's be thankful we're here and make sure we're both better Teammates from here on out. Don't ever forget what we saw today."

Ellie stood up with her arms crossed. "I'll never be able to forget that."

"I guess the point was taken then," said her mom. "Why don't you start on your homework so you'll be ready for school tomorrow?"

Ellie nodded, but first gave her mother a hug. She needed to sell her sincerity, and this was a good first step. But it wasn't entirely an act because she felt herself tremble ever so slightly in the warmth of their embrace.

CHAPTER
TEN

When her bracelet chimed later that evening, Ellie's familiar fluttering friends took flight from the pit of her stomach as she read Andy Jacobs's name yet again. Why had this boy suddenly noticed her? Why did he now care that she existed? Was it because of what she said in class or because his seizure stopped at her touch?

How was your day of exile? She read it in a whisper.

Ellie wasn't sure if she wanted to be funny, honest, or sassy in her response. She settled on sarcastic. *Apparently, I'm considered rehabilitated and am no longer a threat to my fellow classmates. Praise the team!*

His response promptly chimed softly. *That's disappointing. I would love to pick the brain of the girl who spoke up in class. It's too bad she had to go.*

Despite her nervousness, Ellie smiled to herself. Was she starting to enjoy the banter between them? Maybe a little bit. She didn't need to overthink what she quickly messaged next. It seemed Andy might understand her more than she'd have previously guessed.

She's not gone. She's just evolved. She would NEVER speak out in class again or in messages prone to being surveyed by TEAMMATE. She'll likely live out her days burying her thoughts into flippant TEAM-MATE responses oozing with sarcasm.

The team must always come first. His reply was accompanied by a laughing emoji.

We are all in the same game. Her reply was accompanied by an emoji of someone throwing up.

Contribution is love.

Life is a game. We are all Teammates.

All for one and one for all.

Trust the game plan...or you will be beaten into submission. She had added the second part to the familiar slogan.

Well, in light of this update, I've decided what I have to do now.

She waited for a moment before typing the obvious question. *And would you care to enlighten me as to what that would be?*

I need to talk with you in person.

Ellie felt her heart stumble in its elevated rhythm. *That could be dangerous in more ways than one...*

That's not a problem for me. Is speaking in private too risky for you?

Ellie tried to think quickly. Would Judith be jealous to hear about this? Yes. However, was it fair to never speak with someone because of her friend's craziness? Probably not. And she was already talking to him on her bracelet, so...was there even a difference? After a pause, she shakily typed her response. *What harm could come from exchanging a few words?*

Good. Meet me tomorrow, after school. I'll be in the library.

Okay, I can manage that. But how will I get home?

I'll drive you home. Thanks for agreeing to it. I'll see you tomorrow. Goodnight, Ellie.

Goodnight.

She collapsed breathless onto her bed, unable to suppress a smile. What was happening?

"WE'VE MADE IT TO FRIDAY, TEAMMATES," BEGAN MISS CONway. "I want you all on your best behavior this afternoon." She smiled warmly at the uniformed official standing at the front of the room beside her. "We're continuing our guest lectures today with someone who's likely familiar to many of you. Official Wayne Weirton is one of the Chief Officials employed by the Security branch of our sector. Most of you likely know him as the father of your fellow Teammate, Blake Weirton."

There was silence in the room as most of the kids shifted their gaze from the official to Blake, who seemed embarrassed at being mentioned by their teacher. "It's okay to clap, Teammates. Please give Official Weirton a warm welcome to our classroom."

The momentary hesitation of the teens receded, and they clapped loudly, giving rise to what could almost be considered a smile on Chief Wayne Weirton's very serious-looking face.

"Thank you all for that warm welcome," he began, as he adjusted the tan-brimmed hat that matched his tight, creaseless uniform. He was tall and muscular, with an imposing, rigid posture. "Today, I have the privilege to tell you about the different career paths available in the Security branch of our sector. Can anyone here explain what my primary job description includes?"

A hand shot up from Alice in the front row.

"Yes, you there in the front. Ready to take a crack at it?"

She nodded. "You catch people who break the rules."

Wayne glanced upward in thought before bobbing his head from side to side, as if he were having a conversation in his head. "You're not wrong," he said. "But that is one of many duties of my service to TEAMMATE. Why do you think I'm titled as an official?"

"Because you're important?" asked Judith out of turn.

He chuckled. "I'm no more important than any other TEAMMATE. My role is just different. I'm sure you're all familiar with the saying, *Life is a game. We are all Teammates?*" He glanced around and noted all the head nods. "Well, if life is a game, and we're all on the same team, don't we need someone to make sure the game is being played fairly and by the rules? Someone like a referee in your soccer match? Well, that's essentially my job. I'm still a Teammate to all of you, but I help make sure the game runs smoothly. That's my role. Not everyone in my department is visible on the street and in public, like me. We have many different roles that help us do our job. We have dispatchers, TEAMMATE defenders for court cases, recorders of proceedings, and many other important duties handled by our area. Now, oftentimes, we work closely with other TEAMMATE departments."

Miss Conway interjected. "Yes, we actually had a visit from the Medical branch yesterday. Paramedic Larson was our guest lecturer."

Chief Official Wayne nodded in approval. "Paramedic Larson has a very important job. He helps people who are injured. We help him complete his job safely. Often, traffic might need to be diverted around an accident, and sometimes, under the stress of an emergency, Teammates might begin to act unpredictably and dangerously. We step in to make the situation safe so he can do his job to help people." His gaze encircled the room. "Are there any questions so far?"

No one raised their hand.

Miss Conway's voice interrupted the brief pause. "Andy, didn't you have a question from when the energy department was here? Didn't Teammate Neidhart refer you to the Security branch?"

Andy winced at being called out. "I forgot about that. Yeah, we were talking about our bracelets. My question was if you can use TEAMMATE's bracelet information to help you do your job?"

Official Weirton looked confused for a moment. "What kind of information are you asking about?"

"Things like location and messages sent. Are those reviewed by your department?"

"A very insightful question. It sounds like you're wondering if the Security branch spies on you?" He glanced over his left shoulder in thought before turning back. "I would tell you this. I don't have access to any bracelet information myself. As a Chief Official, I can make requests from time to time if the information may help the team. My requests are reviewed and either accepted or rejected by the head of our Security branch, who also sits on the TEAMMATE Council. I'm sure you've all heard of Councilmember Thurman. He's been on the Council for a very long time. Ergo, to answer your question, TEAM-MATE does not spy on anyone if the rules are being followed. With that said, it's prudent to realize there is a trail left behind for almost everything we do, including myself. Data is stored securely, though, so only appropriate people under appropriate circumstances could review the things this young gentleman is asking about. Most of this conversation is moot, however, because the development of the KSM test answers just about any questions that arise in, say, a criminal case."

"Can you really read people's minds?" asked Judith out of turn again.

"That's actually not in my job description," said Weirton with a smile. "So KSM stands for Key Stored Memories. I've never personally seen it given, but from what we are told, it highlights memories that have occurred. Therefore, it's very useful in investigations to deter-mine if rules were broken. But no, it can't read your mind per se. Only significant memories are subject to KSM."

"Is it painful?" she pressed further.

"I'm fairly certain it's not. But remember, this is not a technique used for small violations. KSM is only to be used in very important circumstances. We're talking mostly about cases that may involve exile as a punishment. We're lucky that such occurrences rarely happen in our sector."

"What do the letters on our bracelets stand for?" asked a boy on the far side of the room. The wild-haired boy was the notorious Ernie Barfton, renowned school-wide for his superpower of disorganization. "Mine says DCLX-VI on the underside of the strap."

"I believe it may involve the transmission frequency that the bracelets connect through, but again, that's really not my area of expertise," said Official Weirton.

"I have a question for you," interrupted Miss Conway. "I can see my class is getting off topic a little bit as far as careers. Could you explain what type of skillset the TEAMMATE Placement Test would highlight for a career in the Security branch?"

"Absolutely. We're looking for Teammates with strengths in areas like rules and procedures, as well as students who score high in human psychology and sociology. Remember, in a role like mine, you deal with Teammates all day long. You have to understand human behavior. Oftentimes, Teammates don't even realize where their strengths lie at your age, and that's okay. The TPT results may surprise many of you. It's important to take them seriously and put all of your trust in the game plan you are provided. The TEAMMATE Council and test creators have everyone's best interest in mind."

Ellie managed to suppress her inner reaction to Weirton's advice. She noticed Andy steal a glance in her direction before Weirton began to talk about the types of rule violations that he dealt with on a daily basis. Her goal was to remain invisible after the events from two days prior. She was also more than a little nervous about how things would go after school. Messaging with Andy Jacobs was one thing, but to talk with him in person? Alone? What if she froze and couldn't think of anything to say? And more importantly, what if Judith found out? Ellie had sold her an excuse about not riding the bus home. Her best friend had bought the tale of her having an appointment right after school. It wasn't exactly a lie, but Ellie knew it was wrong. She just felt like she couldn't tell Judith. Not yet, at least. Especially considering that Andy seemed mostly interested in her negative opinions of TEAMMATE. Someone else in the sector might actually think the same way Ellie did. He just so happened to be the most sought-after boy in school.

When the final bell rang for the day, Ellie inhaled a deep breath. Everyone rose to their feet, their readers in hand. It was too late to chicken out now. She'd given Andy her word, and she'd already told Judith she wouldn't be joining her for the ride home. She had to go through with the plan. Ellie took her time, waiting for nearly everyone else to leave before she started for the door. She had nearly reached it when Miss Conway, who was standing beside the doorway, cleared her throat.

"Miss Wilder, I'd like to have a word with you before you go."

CHAPTER
ELEVEN

As the last student filed out ahead of her, Ellie did not fail to notice the urgency in Miss Conway's eyes as she closed and locked the classroom door.

"We need to talk, Ellie. If you're riding the bus home, I can give you a ride."

Ellie had to think fast. "I...I've got a ride home today already...but thank you." She could now recognize the worry etched on Miss Conway's face. Or was it fear?

"Ellie, I spoke with your father about the events from two days ago. He is very concerned about you, as am I. He also told me in confidence about your family's history. I need to be certain that the occurrence in my classroom will never be repeated again."

Ellie could almost hear a tremble in her teacher's voice. Why was she so stressed?

"Miss Conway, I am really sorry about my outburst. You won't have to worry about it happening ever again. My outburst was both foolish and selfish, but I definitely learned my lesson. I did the training and I understand better now." *I understand I can't get caught again, at least.*

Her teacher looked deep into her eyes. Was the first-year instructor buying it?

Miss Conway exhaled. "I know the behavior was unlike you. There was never mention of hostility toward TEAMMATE in your prior records, just occasional selfishness that seemed to be resolving." She had a grave look on her face. "There won't be a mention of it now, either. Do you understand what that means?"

Ellie nodded. "It never happened."

"That's right. No one in class reported it, thankfully. And I'm not going to. Which is not in my best interest because if said occurrence were to come to light somehow in the future, I would be in very big trouble, just like you. However, if I had reported it, your future work opportunities would become...quite bleak. Do you understand?"

Ellie swallowed but nodded again.

"As far as your family history, I had no idea your grandma was ex-communicated. Please tell me you are not going down that path."

Ellie quickly shook her head. "I'll be good."

Miss Conway nodded. "If you have questions or just need to talk, you can come to me in private. Okay? Whatever we discuss can be confidential."

"Thank you," said Ellie.

"You're welcome. Now, are you sure you don't need a ride?"

Ellie glanced at her bracelet. *As long as he doesn't think I left already.*

"I'm sure but thank you so much for everything. I realize I messed up, but I promise I won't let you down again."

"That is very comforting. You're free to go. I'll see you next week."

As soon as Ellie closed the door behind her, she sprinted down the hallway. What if Andy thought she stood him up? Not that it was a date, but...it would be rude. She had wanted to have a quick look in the mirror beforehand and stop by her locker, but there was no time now. She raced to the other side of the school until she burst through the door of the library, her face flushed from exertion.

The library was deserted. It wasn't unexpected for a Friday. The room, of course, did not contain any paper-bound books as it might have in the old days. It carried extra readers for students to borrow, and there were many nooks and crannies with soft seating for comfortable, quiet reading and studying. But where was Andy?

She looked at her bracelet and saw no notifications. She decided to type him a message. Hopefully she could catch him before he left. Then another thought crossed her mind. What if he had come to his senses and decided he wanted nothing to do with her?

A tap on her back made her jump before whirling around.

"Nice reflexes," said Andy with a devious grin.

"Where did you come from?" demanded Ellie, still caught in flight-or-fight mode. How had he snuck up on her?

"Sorry," he replied through a growing grin. "I have an annoying habit of thinking I'm funny. I'm glad you showed up."

Think fast. Don't be weird. "I'm glad you showed up too."

He laughed. "Of course I did. It was *my* idea. Anyways, where have you been?"

"I got held up by Miss Conway after class." She glanced around. "It looks empty, but we probably shouldn't talk about it here."

Andy checked his bracelet. "You're right. It should be safe to head to the parking lot now. The buses have left, and most everyone else should be gone."

"Where are we going?" asked Ellie nervously.

"Uh, home?" said Andy. "Just maybe the scenic way, so we can talk."

"Why did you want to meet in the library?"

He shrugged. "I thought you'd rather not have to answer questions from Judith if she saw you talking to me. Your friend's a bit of a stalker."

Ellie nodded. "Oh, I'm aware. More than you know. But she's my best friend. I'm definitely breaking friend code right now just to talk to you."

"Well," he started. "You could just casually tell her I drove you home."

Ellie thought the scenario through. "That probably wouldn't go well either."

They reached his car. The gray-colored vehicle had seen heavy use with more than a few scratches and dents. Ellie didn't perceive its condition as a reflection of Andy's driving since it was common practice to issue new drivers the worst possible transportation while they were learning.

He opened the door for her, but she hesitated.

"Having second thoughts?" he teased. "It's a good car, trust me. And I am a very good driver. I've had my permit for six months already. But I've been driving for years if you count bike racing."

She lowered herself carefully into the seat. "As long as you don't use any of those racing skills with me in the car."

"No worries," he said. "Not with precious cargo. It is a shame my modifications under the hood won't be noticed, but I'll survive."

How many rules does this boy break?

He walked around to the driver's side and strapped himself in.

"Where do you live, Ellie?"

"I'm pretty far south of the capital on Sector 78 road. Not so far south as the agricultural lands, but it's basically in the middle of nowhere."

He smiled. "Good. Like I said, we'll take the scenic route."

As they drove, Ellie began to relax a little bit. Andy seemed to be a very good driver, which put her more at ease. He was also true to his word about the scenic route. He had started out going north, putting them in the busy capital within minutes.

After a little small talk about their classes, Ellie felt a little more at ease. But the superficial conversation, mostly about teachers and homework, was skirting the real reason she was sitting in Andy Jacob's car. In a moment of braveness, she turned toward him, unintentionally cutting him off. "So, what did you really want to talk to me about?" She owed it to Judith to be direct, she decided. This was, after all, an appointment she had told her friend.

He paused his review of everything she'd missed in class while at home and met her eyes, smiling again. *Why did he smile so much? It's as if he has a secret that no one else knows.*

"Okay, do you want the truth?'

"Of course," she said. "I want the three TEAMMATE T's—truth, trust, and team."

He chuckled. "That's exactly what I want to talk to you about, your humor."

"You think I'm funny?"

"No...well, actually yes—but not just funny. You're...interesting, Ellie. I had no idea all this time until the past week. You're not one of them." He gestured around them as they slowed to a stop at a traffic light in TEAMMATE square. Teammates stood in line, waiting to cross the street. Many were going in and out of the various TEAMMATE agency buildings that surrounded the square, while others walked the open grass in the center. "You think differently. You don't buy all the slogans and rules without question. You didn't wait for the nurse to help me the day I was convulsing. I still don't understand what you did, but you stopped my episode. And I want you to know I am grateful for it." He turned with a look of sincerity towards her.

Ellie's heart raced. *But no one's ever found me interesting.* "I'm selfish, I've been told."

He looked at her, confused. "Selfish? You're not selfish. You're just too smart for the dog-and-pony show that's put on by TEAMMATE every day. People just don't get you, do they?"

She smirked. "I never thought of it that way. I guess most people don't, except possibly Judith."

He shrugged. "Well, I have to give her credit for that. I have an idea that might help with her, by the way."

"She needs help?" asked Ellie.

"More than you know. But seriously, I think she needs a boyfriend."

"Isn't that where you come in?" teased Ellie.

Andy actually blushed. "Not me," he said. "But I've been thinking about setting her up with someone. What do you think about that?"

Ellie considered the implications. *It actually makes sense. Instead of wasting so much energy on someone clearly not interested, what if she found a boy who treated her well?* "Did you have someone in mind?" she finally asked.

"I do. In fact, I have had someone in mind for a very long time. I have to admit, initially the idea was just to get her to leave me alone, but actually, I think it might help her out a lot."

"Who?" asked Ellie with curiosity.

"Blake Weirton," he said with certainty.

"You think that could work?"

"Totally," he said. "He seldom talks, she never stops talking. He's shy, she's outgoing."

"But he's too awkward and nervous. How would they even start talking without Judith initiating the conversation?"

"I'll take care of that," Andy said confidently. "Do I have your permission to try?"

Ellie had doubts about the idea. *Was it wrong to do without Judith's knowledge?* "You don't need my permission to try. But if you do, it has to be real. No fake interest or bogus relationship that's going to hurt Judith."

"It will be completely real. I told you I've been thinking about this for a long time. I think she needs this. TEAMMATE itself would probably match them as compatible for marriage. Their blending of diverse traits and strengths is exactly what TEAMMATE requires in applying for a match."

Ellie sighed. "Okay, you can try. If it's not meant to be, I suppose it won't work out. But I have another question for you."

"Throw it out there. Whatever you want answered."

"Is there another reason you want to help her?"

He paused for a moment. "Truthfully? Yes."

"And what is it?"

He smiled again. "You haven't figured it out yet?"

"Not yet. Maybe I just have to hear it to make sure."

He looked at her again. "I think we're more similar than we realize. I can't believe I never realized it after all of our years of school. Everything you said about TEAMMATE was right. But it's not just that I agree with you. I like you, Ellie. Is that what you wanted to hear? I think you are far more interesting than any other girl I've ever met. I want to talk with you without time and subject restraints. I want to learn about you. But I also want to protect you."

Chills rose up her back to her neck. She took a breath, but no words came.

"Are you okay?"

She nodded, still no words.

They drove in silence for a few moments, now heading south. The skyline of the capital was visible in the rearview mirror. They had now entered the suburbs, and most Teammates were completing their normal afternoon rituals. A younger man walked his dog down the sidewalk. An older couple sat on their front porch swing, watching the afternoon activity pick up. An attractive woman in a halter-top jogged along the sidewalk. Ellie watched Andy closely to see if the alluring sight would catch his attention. His eyes remained on the road, but when he realized she was staring at him, he caught her stare and smiled warmly back, making Ellie feel embarrassed.

"I'm sorry if I said something wrong, but it's true, Ellie. I don't know if you did something to me when you stopped my seizure or if I'm just going crazy right now. I am drawn to you, for some reason, ever since. There's just so much mystery, so much intelligence behind your beautiful brown eyes. I want access to all of it." He shifted his eyes to the sign for sector 78. "Are we getting close to your home?"

"Yes," she replied weakly. "My road's a mile down on the left. Then, two miles down on the right is my house. House number 4280."

After a few more minutes of awkward silence, he pulled into her driveway. "I hope you'll be willing to talk to me again," he said softly. "I didn't offend you with anything I said, did I?"

She stiffened and reached for the door handle before getting out. Her heart raced frantically, causing her bracelet to alarm.

"Ellie?" he asked. "Are you okay?"

"It's just…" she muttered, confused. "I think…I…like…you too." The words squeaked pathetically out of her now dry throat. Embarrassed, she scrambled out the door before he could reply. She slammed the car door behind her and ran into the house, fighting back tears the whole way. Only one question lingered in her mind. *What kind of friend am I?*

—Article 40 of the TEAMMATE Rulebook

CHAPTER
TWELVE

Ellie was beginning to struggle under the weight of her secrets. Furthermore, she realized she could no longer deny her selfish desire for Andy Jacobs. It was terribly wrong, of course, but the way he had been looking at her, his smile, made her want to melt into a puddle. The revelation that he had strong feelings for her had turned Ellie into moldable clay. *I'm much closer to mud than to clay.* After all, she'd barely been able to form a sentence in his presence. Her reaction to his admission that he liked her despite her selfishness had ensnared her in quicksand, comprised of heavy guilt and suppressed glee. Judith would be absolutely destroyed if she found out.

Ellie still had to cover for why she wasn't on the afternoon bus ride home with Molly—otherwise, her sister would definitely cause more questions to be raised by her parents. Ellie hadn't gotten permission to have the boy drive her home, and she was already on thin ice with her parents after her outburst in class. Once again, Ellie bent the truth. Miss Conway *had* caused her to miss the bus, and she'd also offered to drive her home. Ellie was very careful with her wording to only say her teacher had offered the ride home. The assumption by her parents was that she'd taken it. No one had been home when Andy dropped her off, and she'd fallen to pieces in her room for twenty minutes.

As a result of her carefully curated half-truths and omission of details, she was able to make it through the remainder of the evening at home until it was late enough to safely pull out the diary. It was strange that these forbidden pages had begun to feel like a refuge at the end of each day. When did this transformation take place? She realized she was too tired to care. She needed more.

I pray that as of this reading, your faith is growing stronger. It will be tested time and time again. Do not let it slip away. Trust in the plans He has for you. I hope you've been reading the passages I've instructed. I now have a few questions for you to think about. Why did so many powerful people fear such a simple, peaceful man so long ago? Why does TEAMMATE fear his teachings today? I am confident you will find it very difficult to find examples of him calling for violence, trying to incite rebellion, or clamoring for wealth, goods, or power. So, what made his message so dangerous and terrible that it needed to be silenced?

You won't read this from your history books, but Christians have been outlawed before. The followers of Jesus were beheaded, stoned, and tortured for their beliefs a long time before the present. We arose, more numerous once before, and it can happen again, peacefully. As always, I urge you to ask for His help. He is with you, always.

The words were reassuring, but no part of Ellie, including her faith, felt strong at present. In fact, she felt quite the opposite that night as she lay in bed mentally reliving her struggle to form a simple sentence after Andy admitted he liked her. How could someone like her be the one to start any type of movement? This diary had to have been meant for someone else. Foolish as she was, she'd almost begun to believe it was destined for her. The one question that continually gnawed at her was also eating at Andy. If the journal was all myth and lure, how had she stopped his episode? Clearly, he'd admitted he felt something, the same as she had at the time. Perhaps it was time to see if there was anything else she could do. After she failed at another attempt, she could kick this sliver of belief to the curb. But what should she try? Opportunities to help in emergencies did not happen very often. If only she could come in contact with someone else who needed help. That Friday night, alone in her room, she silently asked for help, for opportunity, and for the strength she did not believe she had. It felt silly and was entirely forbidden by TEAMMATE, but on the other hand, what actual harm could prayer impose?

"GOOD MORNING, ELLIE." HER DOOR OPENED, AND HER MOTHER slipped into her room. "I'm sorry, but we have to leave a little earlier for your sister's game. Your dad will take Molly there, but I need to swing into work beforehand to resolve a medication discrepancy. I thought you might like to come with me since you're learning about careers this year.

Ellie sat up and rubbed her eyes. "But I'm so tired," she groaned.

Her mother looked perplexed. "I can't understand why. You've been in your room early every night this past week."

Of course, the only reason for that was to read contraband all night, but her mother didn't need to know that.

"How long do we have to be there?" Ellie always felt uncomfortable at her mother's workplace. Her mom's job could be stressful, and you could never guess what kind of day she'd have or what time she'd get home.

"It'll be a quick in and out. It's not as if I'm on the schedule today. Don't worry, I promise we won't get stuck there."

Ellie sighed. "Guess I don't get a choice in the matter, do I?"

Her mom smiled. "No. But I did make you some breakfast downstairs."

Finally, some good news. "Okay, I'll be down in a few," she said a little more pleasantly.

After a quick breakfast, the two were off. When they got to the hospital, they took the elevator to the sixth floor, which was the cardiac monitoring unit. There was a central hub with seats for nurses and physicians to enter notes on their tablet devices. The unit was comprised of two long parallel hallways, the outside of each lined by patient rooms. In between the parallel hallways were the central hub and what looked to be storage and supply rooms.

"Good morning, Anne." The greeting came from a middle-aged lady with short blond hair. "I didn't expect to see you today." She looked Ellie over quickly. "Is this your beautiful daughter?"

"Yes, it is. Ellie, this is Marie, one of my work friends." Anne looked around quickly. "Have you seen Laurie yet today? I needed to chart something I forgot yesterday with all the craziness."

Marie gave a look resembling pain. "I did. I don't think she's having a great start to her day. She's in her office. How about you leave Ellie with me while you take care of that?"

"That's exactly what I was hoping for. Can she shadow you for a few patients?"

"Absolutely," Marie flashed a grin. "I can always use a second set of hands."

Ellie followed the nurse as she popped in and out of each room, recording blood pressures, drawing blood, and passing the morning meds. The patients seemed to like Marie and her peppy nature.

The third patient's room had a lot of beeping devices going off, although no one seemed concerned about the man.

"What's wrong with him?" whispered Ellie.

"Oh, this is Mr. Jones," Marie replied, not in a whisper. They walked through the door. "Mr. Jones has a heart arrhythmia that won't convert, hence these beeping monitors. How'd you sleep, Mr. Jones?"

The man looked uncomfortable. "Not at all, I'm afraid. I still have to wait until Sunday for the ablation?"

"Yes, unfortunately," said Marie. "I'd do the procedure for you if I could, but trust me, you wouldn't want me for that."

Mr. Jones chuckled. "Maybe your helper could then." He winked at Ellie, although he was still wincing with discomfort.

The comment gave Ellie an idea. It wasn't an emergency, but perhaps she could try to help this man. She focused on remaining calm as she walked next to his bed. "Where is the pain?" she asked softly.

"My dear, it's not terribly painful, more uncomfortable—like there's a fish flopping around in my chest. They're trying to get my heartbeat to slow with these infusions because I've been refractory to everything else so far. Over the last week, my bracelet's delivered me more shocks than I'd care to remember. Thankfully, they were able to disable it from attempting to help me further."

Ellie stepped closer. On a whim, she reached for his arm, which had tubes and monitors connected. She closed her eyes and silently asked for him to be healed.

Ten seconds of silence passed. She slowly opened her eyes. "I hope you feel better soon," she said to the man.

"I suppose I will," he said. "Come tomorrow, at least."

Marie handed the man his medication and a glass of water. "Okay, Mr. Jones. You know the drill."

After taking his meds, the man seemed the same, but as Marie and Ellie exited the room, the erratic beeping stopped.

Marie turned around and looked back at Ellie. "That's unusual." She walked back in and looked at the screen EKG. "Mr. Jones, how do you feel?"

He looked at them both in surprise. "Why, the flopping stopped."

Marie seemed surprised. She looked at Ellie. "I'm grabbing the resident."

She led Ellie to a younger woman sitting in the central hub, staring intently at another patient's chart on her screen.

"Dr. Ford, room nine just converted for the first time since he's been here."

The resident looked up. "He's not scheduled until tomorrow." She quickly stood. "Okay, I need to see this."

She entered the room to find Mr. Jones sitting up and smiling. No evidence of discomfort was apparent on his face.

"Doc, I think I'm healed," he said with eyes full of excitement.

Dr. Ford listened to his chest with her instruments and reviewed the EKG strip. "You've converted to sinus rhythm, Mr. Jones. I'm not sure why now, although it can happen anytime. You hadn't responded previously to drug or shock therapy, which makes this even more surprising. I'll have to talk to my attending about this. It's very possible that you could slip back into the arrhythmia at any time, so we'll have to continue to monitor for now."

"Do whatever you need to do, Doc. I can't tell you the last time I felt this relieved. It's like the weight of the world's been lifted off my shoulders."

Just then, Anne stuck her head in the room. "There you guys are. Come on, Ellie, it's time to go."

Ellie looked at Marie, who still had a look of surprise on her face. "Thank you," she said to her mother's coworker.

"I think it was you who cured me, young lady," Mr. Jones said in a serious voice.

Everyone in the room chuckled lightly.

"If that's the case, I'd love to borrow her for a few more patients," said Dr. Ford with a wink at Ellie.

"You might have a future in health care," said Anne proudly. "We have to leave now to catch her sister's soccer game. I'm so glad to hear you're feeling better, Mr. Jones."

"Thank you, Ellie," the man said. He ran his hand through his white hair. "I don't suppose I'll be forgetting that name anytime soon."

—Article 42 of the TEAMMATE Rulebook

CHAPTER
THIRTEEN

When Ellie collapsed into her bus seat Sunday morning, she couldn't get a sigh out before Judith filled her in on the unfolding events.

"So, guess what. A boy messaged me Friday night, telling me I was beautiful and wanted to find out if I had a boyfriend." She barely paused enough for half a breath before continuing. "And I'm like, who is this? No, I don't have a boyfriend. Why do you want to know?"

"Who was it?" Ellie's question showed genuine interest.

"Well, I wasn't sure. He'd blocked his bracelet identity. Naturally, my first reaction was Andy, but that's not really his style. Also, he specifically said it wasn't Andy." She blushed. "I had to ask, right? But apparently, I have a secret admirer." She stuck out her lip in a pouty manner.

"Isn't that a good thing?"

"Well, like yes, of course it is, but I still don't know who it is."

"They aren't going to tell you?" Ellie asked.

"He said I had to guess. With his bracelet identity scrambled, I have no hope of tracing whoever it is."

"Are you sure it's not Ernie Barfton?"

Judith's reaction was akin to being offered a glass of vinegar to drink. "Eww. No, it couldn't be."

"How can you be so certain?"

"Well, after guessing Andy, I began to ask descriptive questions, but not too descriptive because he wanted it to be difficult. Anyways, we talked again Saturday morning and Saturday night, and I think I have it narrowed down. He's tall, dark, and handsome. So that rules old Ernie out, right? He wants to take me out, so he has to have his license to drive. On top of that, he's in at least one of my classes this year, so that really narrows it down."

Ellie hugged her friend close. "This is so exciting, Judith! I wish I had a secret admirer." Now it was her turn to fake a pout.

"Don't worry, girl, maybe he's got cute friends!"

"Let's not get ahead of ourselves. Anyways, how are you going to find out?"

Judith shrugged. "I'm still not clear on that. He said there would be clues throughout the day. I can't lie; I'm nervous about finding out, but it's so exciting. We literally chatted for hours over the weekend. After we stopped, I couldn't sleep. I can't remember the last time I felt this excited."

Ellie was happy for Judith, but she also felt guilty at the same time. Andy had said it would be a perfect fit. She wondered if he was the one really talking to Judith now. She felt a warm sensation in her chest. Was she jealous? Was she doing the right thing to allow whatever this was to continue? Her best friend was absolutely glowing when they walked into the school building. Judith looked extra cute today. Her hair was curled with red ribbons to match her form-fitting uniform sweater. She even walked more confident than usual, and did Ellie detect extra perfume today?

When they arrived at Judith's locker, an alert on her wristwatch binged, and Judith illuminated a message against the dark backdrop inside her locker. Glancing at the bottom shelf, they saw a vase with a colorful bouquet of flowers.

Dear Beautiful,

Have you found me yet? I have always gazed at your beauty from a distance, but I just can't bear it anymore. Every day without your acknowledgement is like a day without sunshine. Like a flower can't live without sunlight, I simply cannot stay in hiding much longer. I enjoyed our chat last night. Your inquisitiveness is endearing, just like your eyes, mouth...and I have to stop there...for now.

With Love,
Your Secret Admirer

Both girls glanced around to see if anyone was watching their reaction. No one appeared to have any interest. The boy seemed far more forward than Ellie would have imagined. Was there more to Blake than on the surface? Every class throughout the day, she watched Judith eyeing each boy with suspicion. In Miss Conway's class, she hardly even glanced in Andy's direction. Maybe this really was what Judith had needed all along. Someone to appreciate her so she could stop daydreaming about Andy.

At one point, Ellie caught Andy's eye watching her when he pretended to turn around to stretch. He casually winked at her and smiled, unbeknownst to Judith. Ellie now found herself beginning to daydream about him. And why not? For some reason, he genuinely liked her, as plain and selfish as she knew herself to be. He was everything she should have wanted all along, and yet, she'd never allowed herself to even imagine them together. Was it out of fear or out of friendship? She really wasn't sure anymore. Is this what it felt like to be beautiful? To have boys begging for your affection and attention? Why did it feel so good and yet so wrong?

When lunchtime finally came, Ellie was able to catch up on the unfolding events of the morning.

"Did you figure out who it is?" asked Ellie as she sat beside her friend at the small square table.

Judith nodded with confidence. "I've narrowed it down to two people," she said, sounding scientific. "Based on who's in my classes, their current girlfriend status, the physical clues he gave me, and my own strong intuition, it could only be Clint or Blake. Both are intriguing prospects."

Ellie raised an eyebrow. "I think they're both good choices. I've barely ever spoken with either one, but are you leaning more towards one over the other?" Clint could have very well been a good candidate if Andy thought he could sway him. He was handsome but not nearly as quiet and mysterious as Blake.

"I think I am. But I'm not sure what to do. I stared at both of them throughout the morning, and neither one gave off a strong vibe, you know? It's so strange that he could lay his heart on the line two nights in a row in messages and yet be so distant in person. I feel like if I talk to both of them in person, maybe I could slip in a reference from our talk and catch their reaction. I'm just not sure how to talk to them."

"Oh, come on, Judith. You've never had a problem talking to anyone before."

"But what if it's awkward?"

"Hello, look at me, your best friend. I'm the queen of awkward, and you have zero difficulty talking to me on a daily basis."

Judith laughed. "But this is different. This could be embarrassing. We've talked a whole lot about our feelings. He's very deep, which makes me think there's more to Blake than meets the eye, but he's also kind of forward, which makes me think of Clint."

"Why won't he just tell you? Didn't he say if you guessed, he'd tell?"

Judith looked at her uneaten lunch tray. "I can't guess wrong this far into it. It would doom our relationship before it even started. Imagine him always thinking I chose someone else first. Plus, to make things worse, I think they are kind of friends. Imagine if someone chose me over you. How would you feel?"

Ellie had to admit she wouldn't like that at all. But it would also depend on whether she really liked the boy in the first place. "Well, do you like both of them?"

"No," she said stubbornly. "I only like the boy who's talking to me. We have a connection, Ellie. We're made for each other. I just know it."

"So long as TEAMMATE approves, of course. But wait, what if you're wrong and it is Ernie Barfton?"

"Then I will have his babies," said Judith matter-of-factly. "He would, of course, have to take my last name. I refuse to have barf in my name. I'd have to take him somewhere for a scrubbing and a haircut. We'd have to change his wardrobe and get him a gym membership. There are terms that would make it work, though."

"You sound serious," giggled Ellie.

"I am," stated her best friend without a grin. "The boy I'm talking to would do anything I asked of him. I forgot to tell you he slipped a teddy bear into my locker between classes. How romantic is that?"

"If he'd do anything, he should tell you who he is when you ask."

Judith shrugged. "Well, almost anything, I suppose. I think I'm just going to have to go with my womanly intuition and confront him this afternoon. I'll need to be extra crafty."

"Wait, which one does your intuition say?"

"I'm not going to say yet," said Judith. "That way, you can be in suspense, just like me." She giggled with excitement.

Ellie forced a smile. She really needed to talk to Andy. This could go south very quickly.

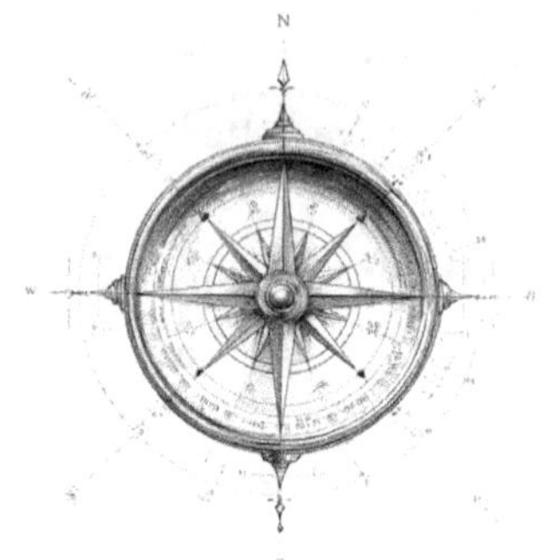

CHAPTER
FOURTEEN

As the two friends waited in line to board the bus, Judith beamed with pride.

"Who is it?" Ellie asked.

"Not until we're in our seats," said Judith with a firm voice. Her wry smile betrayed the truth, which was that she enjoyed holding her knowledge captive, in addition to Ellie's curiosity. "You need to be sitting down for this."

Once they were seated, Judith glanced around for would-be emissaries of espionage. Ellie might have laughed if the implications weren't so entangled with her own conspiratorial aspirations. Instead, she hung on her friend's every word and facial expression, trying to decide if Andy's plan had gone awry.

"After eying both of them all afternoon, I noticed one starting to stare back at me. I was obviously suspicious. But was he just noticing me noticing him? Then he smiled at me, which was a dead giveaway, right? I never said a word to him until just before we walked out to our bus line. I just couldn't hold it in anymore. Then, I asked him in a joking manner if he had gotten me flowers. That way I could play it off as a joke if he acted surprised. But he wasn't! He said I deserved more than just flowers. So, I said, *like what else?* And he said I deserve my very own field of flowers, like a queen from ancient times, with a gardener to tend the blossoms and a boyfriend to accompany my walks through them. That's when I asked, *do you know anybody that could do that?* And that's when he said, *I don't know any gardeners, but I could take care of the second part.* Then he asked me to go to the party after the game Friday night."

Ellie was feeling nauseous. "I've never heard of Blake attending any parties. He's so antisocial."

"It wasn't Blake. Eww, no. It was Clint all along." Her eyes did not fail to register Ellie's initial reaction. "Why do you have that look on your face? Shouldn't you be happy right now?"

Ellie blinked a few times and swallowed. Her throat felt as if it was swelling. "I'm...just surprised it was Clint, I guess." *I have to talk to Andy immediately.*

"Why are you so surprised? I should have known all along. But now we need to shift our priorities. You're going to have to come with me to the party, of course. We need to get someone to come with you, so it's not awkward. I have a fantastic idea." She smiled deviously. "Blake might be available. You said he was cute, right?"

"Yeah..."

"I'll talk to him. Just to feel him out for you. I'm thinking a double date would be fun."

"Please don't."

"Why not? Is there someone else you've got in mind? We have already established a need to get you out more. You stay home too much,

Ellie. It's not like you have to have his babies or anything." Judith laughed at her own joke.

"I'll...I'll find someone on my own," blurted out Ellie. "Please don't ask anyone for me."

Judith rolled her eyes as if offended. "I just want to help you. We both know you aren't going to ask anyone, and I hate to see you come along by yourself. I want to be a good friend to you, Ellie. Won't it be awkward if you come alone? Hey, wait a minute." She narrowed her eyes. "You don't have a crush on Clint, do you?"

Ellie cleared her throat. "No. I'm just surprised and...happy for you. Don't worry about me. I'll figure something out so we can both be there."

Judith smiled and grabbed her friend's hands. "I'm so excited! I can't believe this is happening right now. We're becoming the cool girls!"

Ellie could not believe it either.

As soon as she was off the bus, Ellie tapped her bracelet and commanded, "Call Andy." She would normally have been nervous about calling him, but she was past that feeling at the moment. Their whole plan was about to implode, and things could escalate very quickly.

"Hey, gorgeous, I've been wanting to talk..."

She cut him off. "She thinks it was Clint. He just asked her out to a party Friday night. She now thinks Blake is gross."

"Whoa," said Andy. He was silent for a moment. When he finally did reply, he didn't seem frantic or worried at all, for that matter. "This development changes things...but it's not necessarily bad."

"How can it not be bad? Clint will find out she's been talking to someone else. Blake will find out what happened when he messages her tonight. They were literally falling for each other after talking for not even three whole days. What are we going to do? She's going to end up hurt...and probably alone again."

Andy inhaled slowly. "It's going to be fine. She never talked to Blake. It was me all along, trying to make Blake look more appealing, more intriguing. It sounds like it had been working. Right now, Blake is only privy to the fact that I was in the process of setting him up with someone. I never told him who it was in case something went south."

"So, Judith has been falling even more maddeningly in love with you? She told me she didn't care if she was talking to Ernie Barfton on the other end of her messages. I can't believe I let this happen." She started hyperventilating. "I think we have to come clean about this now. Clint won't have a clue about your previous conversations. Judith is too smart not to figure this all out."

Her state of panic was taking over. She should have just told Judith from the start. If she'd been honest, this wouldn't be happening. Her friend might have hated her for liking Andy, but she wouldn't have to pretend and lie this whole time. Andy had even suggested honesty from the start. Now she'd wrecked everything. Would Judith ever forgive her?

"Take a deep breath and relax," said Andy coolly. He was so calm that it irritated Ellie. "I will take care of it. Nothing will fall back on you. I promise."

"What are you going to do?" asked Ellie in a helpless voice.

"I'm going to finish what I started. I'll make sure everything continues smoothly with Clint. I guarantee he'll thank me later for my help. Now I just need to find a girl interested in Blake so I don't let him down."

"Judith wants me to go with him to the party Friday."

There was a pause. "That may be a perfect opportunity to tie things up."

Ellie was confused. "You're going to set me up with Blake?"

"No, no, beautiful. You can tell Judith you'll go with Blake as friends to this party. Blake is going to owe me after I set him up with a girlfriend, who just won't happen to be Judith now. He doesn't need details. In return for my aid in getting him a girlfriend, I'll have him lead us together by accident at the party. Just act surprised when we meet, okay?"

"More deception?" *How far am I willing to take this?* "Andy...I have some reservations about..."

Now he cut her off. "How were you planning on telling her when we decided to actually go on a date? Or, assuming things progressed well with us, would we need to remain in secret for the entire school year? It doesn't matter because whatever you say would not be honest. But now she can watch it happen with her own eyes. And it's possible, she'll be happy that you aren't alone and neither is she."

Ellie bit her lip, considering his words. But he wasn't finished yet.

"There's another angle about all of this that we haven't discussed openly yet."

Ellie's eyebrows rose. "What other angle besides Judith's matters?"

"The most important angle, perhaps." His voice grew darker. "The angle of TEAMMATE."

"I don't understand."

"I wish I could say more right now, but I'll explain Friday. It has to be in person."

Ellie could now add frustrated to her current state of guilt-fueled anxiety. Was this the price of being together? Not even together really—just to go on a date? Was Andy worth all this trouble? Of course, he was. Any other girl in school would do the same thing if they were in her shoes. Even Judith. But why did her friend have to be beyond obsessed with him? Why couldn't this just be easy? Why couldn't she have just told Judith that Andy liked her and wanted to take her on a date? Ellie never admitted it to herself, but she had been attracted to him too. Just because she didn't stalk him didn't make her feelings less valid, did it? And what could TEAMMATE possibly have to do with any of this? Obviously, it was something Andy felt could be dangerous if overheard.

"I guess we have no choice but to tiptoe around whatever obstacles arise," Ellie said with an air of resignation. "I just wish it didn't have to be this way."

"Well, you're worth it to me."

Damn him for knowing what to say. Now he was making her feel guilty. The truth was, she was the one who'd forced him into this situation. *Am I worth it?* It wasn't his fault that he was so desirable to every girl in school.

"I'm sorry," she said.

"You'll never need to say that to me as long as we're together."

"I only wish you were right. Just make sure you save me from my date on Friday."

"Trust me. I've got this."

CHAPTER
FIFTEEN

Ellie was relieved when Friday finally arrived. The school day felt as if it would never end. The TEAMMATE Placement Test took nearly the whole school day. It was a very difficult test, but Ellie was confident she'd given it her best attempt. More important than the TPT was that everything else seemed to be falling into place. Ellie kept running over the plan in her mind, trying to keep the intricate details straight. Judith was going to the party with Clint, her new beau, as she'd now started calling him. Ellie would be accompanying them with Blake, but just as friends. She'd made all parties particularly clear regarding this detail. Andy had already explained the setup to Clint. He was now aware that Andy had been secretly trying to set up Judith with Blake when he'd accidentally assumed the role of secret admirer. Andy explained that neither knew about the setup and that he was merely pleased to see Judith happy. However, it was now Clint's job to help find a date for Blake as payback. Ellie was the means to get Blake to the party only, as she'd made it clear that she was not interested. At the same time, Blake thought Andy was finding him a replacement for his date with Ellie, whom he was indebted to relinquish to Andy at some designated point that evening. Everyone was on board, although none of them understood the true extent of the plan, save Ellie and Andy. By night's end, Judith would still be with Clint, Ellie would be with Andy, and Blake would be with whoever Clint came up with. They were all pawns in a greater scheme of deception, but their participation and their reward for helping ensured their silence. It was made extremely clear that all previous arrangements were to be forgotten after tonight.

Ellie was so excited that she developed chills when she thought about it. Finally, she could talk to Andy in public, and no one would have a reason to be upset. She could now bury her mistake of not telling Judith about Andy for good. It was a lot of groundwork, but the energy expended to keep her best friend happy and to land herself a date with the hottest guy in school was justified. Andy was one of a kind. He was the only classmate to support her ill-fated decision to criticize TEAMMATE. He was so mysterious and interesting; she couldn't wait until they could talk more in private. She wanted to learn more about his inner thoughts. The other boys involved tonight were single because they didn't have the guts Andy did. They didn't think or act for themselves. Andy liked Ellie for who she was and came out and told her to her face. The other boys were nice, but just too immature. They had to be set up with who they liked, without putting in any preparation beforehand. It was lucky they were so unconfident, though; otherwise, the plan would never have worked.

The other hurdle that Ellie had nearly mishandled was getting her parents to allow her to go. She didn't go to parties or social gatherings...ever. Both her mother and her father gave her what she'd describe as KSM-style questioning before they would let her go. She explained that Judith liked Clint and needed someone to go with. Blake was just a friend. Didn't they tell her she spent too much time alone in her room? This was her chance to be more sociable. The gathering was merely a birthday party for a set of twins from her class. They all needed to unwind after the stress of TEAMMATE Placement testing that day. She even agreed to check in with her mother every hour and be home at a decent time. And...she might finally kiss Andy. Of course, that information was not to be shared.

Clint arrived at six o'clock with Judith sitting up front and Blake in the back seat.

"Hey, love!" yelled Judith out the window as Ellie exited her front door. Blake immediately scrambled out to hold the door open for Ellie.

"Thank you, Blake." He blushed and smiled, scurrying back around the vehicle after she was seated.

"Blake, you are such a gentleman," said Judith. "He is such a good guy, Ellie. I'm so glad you two are going together. I think you're adorable." She was still trying quite hard to sell Blake.

Clint turned over his shoulder to back out of the driveway. His arm "accidentally" went around Judith. "I love you, baby," he said with a wink.

She immediately kissed him on the cheek, distracting him. "I love you more. We were so made for each other."

Ellie wanted to barf. But this was exactly what Judith had needed. Finally, someone was on her level of enthusiasm. She looked across her seat at Blake. The poor boy had no clue what to do with his hands, so he sat with them in his pockets. He didn't know that Ellie had absolutely no interest in him. He only knew that she was for Andy, and his job was to sell his part to everyone else, including her.

"So, um...Ellie, how do you like living out here?" He finally managed to speak.

"I love it," she responded politely. "I just hate how long it takes to go anywhere. Not that I really go many places, especially since I don't drive yet. Where do you live?"

"I'm about five minutes from downtown. Dad has to be in a proximity that allows him to get to the station quickly." He paused a moment before shaking his head. "Just two weeks ago, there was a burglary at the TEAMMATE Market in the middle of the night. Whoever it was got away with it, too. That's the third one this year, which means we've now surpassed last year's number. I don't understand what's wrong with people. Everyone is allotted the same stock of groceries, and yet people still want more."

"I guess TEAMMATE can't control everything," Ellie let slip. "Err, I mean...there's always someone ready to break the rules," she tried to correct her response.

Blake looked her way and shrugged. "Just because my dad is an official doesn't mean you have to guard everything you say around me."

"In that case, I've got a whole trunk of hot cupcakes and homespun clothes for sale," joked Clint from the driver's seat. "Who's ready to party?"

Judith snorted at his joke. "I have a briefcase full of knives for sale, too."

Blake laughed nervously. "Guys, I wouldn't care even if that were true. I realize it's not, but just saying."

"You would if I cut you," teased Judith.

"Some people like that kind of thing," he said without a smile.

"Judith probably would, right, babe?" asked Clint, laughing.

She raised an eyebrow at him and returned a devilish smile. "You know I'm crazy but not like that, Clinty."

It was a half-hour ride to the party. Most of the chattering continued between Judith and Clint while the other two listened in a reserved manner, occasionally laughing or shaking their heads at their friends in the front. They arrived at their destination fashionably late, which led to parking along the road behind a long line of vehicles.

It was twilight when they walked up to the two-story, older brick house. There were lights and a good amount of noise coming from the backyard. Clint led their little group around the house. They found their classmates sitting on a large deck, illuminated with torches on its outskirts. In the middle of the structure was a built-in fire ring where some kids were either sitting or hovering closely in conversation. The sliding glass door to the back of the house could repeatedly be heard opening and shutting as people came in and out of what looked to be the kitchen.

"Clint! I see you brought some good-looking friends," said a stocky boy with long brown hair. "You even got Blake to come out, too? What's the occasion, other than me and Becca's birthday?"

Rodney Forman, the classmate's house they were at, was good friends with Clint. He also had a twin sister named Rebecca. While Rodney seemed like a nice guy, neither Judith nor Ellie knew him or his sister very well.

"Well, we just wanted to celebrate with you, is all. I think you've met my girlfriend Judith," said Clint. "She's beautiful, but she is taken," he added with a wink. "And of course you know Blake and Ellie."

"Girlfriend?" asked Rodney in surprise. "Sounds like things are progressing well, and I'm glad to hear it. I must have been out of the loop."

"It's pretty recent. But we're here to celebrate with you, my friend. Oh, and Becca, of course." Clint pulled Rodney in for an engulfing bear hug.

"Everyone, make yourselves at home. We have a cooler with all kinds of drinks; unfortunately, none are alcoholic. My mom and dad are watching like hawks for that. Anyhow, I've been drinking plain water for a month to build up a soft drink supply, so I hope everyone enjoys it. There's food inside the kitchen, and the bathroom is at the end of the hall if anyone needs it."

Rodney got up and walked into the house while the group set to pulling together the three empty chairs they could find.

"Clint and I can share a chair, unless you two would rather share," said Judith with a grin.

Blake and Ellie exchanged a quick glance before each grabbed their own chair.

"I'll get everyone some drinks," said Clint. As he walked away, Judith let out a sigh.

"I just love that boy. Isn't he so funny and handsome? It already feels like we've been together forever. And we're perfect for each other. Don't you think?"

"He seems very nice," said Ellie. Blake just smiled and said nothing.

"I'm so glad we got you two to come out. Isn't this fun? It's so much better than sitting home on a Friday night. Especially after that test today."

"Yeah," said Ellie with a yawn.

"We'll have no more of that tonight, Missy."

"Sorry. I'm worn out from this week." The truth was, she was tired from staying up every night to message with Andy. Where was he anyway?"

"Please don't be lame tonight." Judith glanced at Blake, who was trying to figure out what to do with his hands again. "I mean, not that you're normally lame. Just loosen up and try to have fun, okay?"

"I'll do my best, guys. I'm sorry if I turn out to be a party pooper."

"You're not a party pooper," said Blake.

Clint came back with the drinks. "Judith, you took my chair!" he joked. "It's alright, I can take a hint." He proceeded to sit on her lap while she laughed hysterically until she squeaked that she couldn't breathe.

The conversation turned to classes and questions from the TPT, along with other boring daily events. Ellie found herself daydreaming even though it was turning to nightfall. Without warning, a hand appeared on her shoulder that made her jump. She looked up to see the two most beautiful objects against the night sky, Andy's sparkling eyes in the firelight.

"We need one more person for our game out back," said Andy. "Ellie, you look like you might be fast. I need a girl on my team. Would you want to play?"

"Me?" asked Ellie, trying to sound surprised. She was actually surprised to learn of a game. This part had not been specifically planned. "Uh, sure?" She looked over to get approval from Judith and Blake.

"Is it alright if I borrow her, Blake?"

For Blake's part, he was nearly too gracious to let his date slip away. It was obvious he wasn't much of an actor. "Absolutely fine, Andy. You guys have fun. Don't worry about me."

"I'll make it up to you, Blake," said Andy with a grin.

Ellie shrugged her shoulders as she made eye contact with Judith. Her poor friend's jaw seemed to be dropping downward quickly. "I guess I'll be back when the game's over?" Ellie tried to sound confused as to what was going on. For once in her life, Judith didn't seem to have a reply.

Walking away, Ellie felt a little bad for Blake. He'd played his part as well as he could. She glanced over her shoulder as she followed Andy and realized her seat would not be vacant long. Already placing a hand on the back of Ellie's former chair was Becca Foreman, and she was asking Blake if the now-empty seat was taken. Becca looked extra done-up for her birthday, and she was wearing a sparkly, form-fitting dress that was sure to catch anyone's eye tonight. Ellie smiled, relieved. Andy's plan seemed to be falling into place quite nicely so far.

CHAPTER
SIXTEEN

"So...is there really a game back here?" Ellie voiced her doubt as she followed Andy's outline ahead of her. "I don't think I can handle any more stories to keep straight."

He stopped and looked around before carefully taking her hand. "I think it's safe now." There was a hint of growing excitement to his words as they hung in the night air. The anticipation of this moment and all the groundwork it took to be here made Ellie shiver with excitement. "No more stories. Do you trust me, Ellie?"

"Of course."

He gripped her hand in both of his. There was no doubt he could feel her racing pulse in his hands. Why was she so nervous? Was this normal? They walked hand in hand nearly a hundred yards before they stopped again. They were in an empty field, but the dim torches and firelight from the party seemed to be another world away from the hums of insects and other night sounds that now engulfed them. Andy handed her a helmet with a pull-down visor. Ellie nearly jumped in fright when two other people appeared beside him.

"Okay, we have our fourth. Ellie will be on my team. Here are the rules. The perimeter of the field is marked off with cones that won't let us leave the field with our helmets on. We don't start until both teams have walked to their respective opposite ends of the field. After three hits, that player is 'dead' for the game. They must remove their helmet and walk to the sidelines beyond the cones. The objective is to capture the flag and make it back to your home end of the field without getting shot or captured. The last rule goes without saying, but I'll still say it. You cannot speak a word about this game to anyone because it's definitely contraband. Any questions?"

The opposing boy and girl grinned at each other but neither said a word. Ellie thought she recognized one of the two from the previous school year, but she hadn't known many upperclassmen, and it was difficult to make out their features in the dark.

"Once we reach the two back cones, the game will begin automatically. Start walking!"

Andy put on his helmet and again took Ellie's hand.

The reality of the situation began to settle in Ellie's stomach. As exciting as the surprise was, did they really need to break the rules to have fun? "Why did you want to play this?" she whispered nervously. "TEAMMATE expressly forbids unsanctioned gaming."

Andy laughed off her concern. "It's only a little hide and seek in the dark...with some enhancements. It's fun, Ellie, just give it a try. You, of all Teammates, realize how ridiculous the rules are."

"There's nowhere to even hide, though."

"Stay with me and you'll be fine. I promise it'll be fun. You'll need to put on these sensory gloves." He handed her a pair of ordinary-looking gloves—until she slipped them on and a tiny pulsing green light appeared on each of her palms.

They had now reached their end of the rectangular field. He carefully pulled Ellie's visor down until it clicked securely. She heard him do the same, but it was not possible to see anything in the night. He gently pulled her another step back until they were in between the two back corner cones. That's when everything changed.

It was now daylight. Ellie looked at Andy and was shocked to see him holding some type of weapon. Yes, they would definitely be in very big trouble if they were caught with these helmets. She looked downward and was startled to see an elongated metallic object in her own hands. She felt its weight in her sensory-gloved hands with amazement. They'd read about these instruments of war in history class, but she'd never known what they looked like. Any rendering of the artifacts of the past was punishable by TEAMMATE, and yet here they were. There was no denying it now. She was scared.

When she turned around, a red flag waved in an artificial breeze. This was the object that the other team would be coming after. Looking ahead, she could see no more than ten feet in front of her. On the previously flat field stood towering trees with thick brush along the ground level. Footpaths led into the tangled mess, but the paths did not provide any long-range visual aid as they turned and curved about.

"We better get moving," Andy's voice whispered from the speaker in her helmet. She nodded and followed him forward, surprised that it felt like she was pushing through the high grasses popping back up in his wake.

"What's our plan?" she whispered into her helmet, wondering if he could hear through the swishing of grasses.

"We're going to scout the halfway point first." He didn't bother to turn around as he spoke. "If you see any packages on the ground, tell me. We need to find some camouflage. If we're lucky enough to find some body armor, you get it first."

She tried to follow closely behind Andy, but it was becoming more difficult to keep up with him. Imaginary branches were now smacking her helmet as she pushed forward. There was nothing she could feel beyond the helmet and sensory glove weight, but the sound would whip in her ear, causing her vision to go out for a second. She sped forward and reached out to touch Andy, but immediately saw her weapon pressed against his back.

He turned around.

"Sorry," she said.

She couldn't see his face through the mask. Was he annoyed or amused? "Relax," her speaker projected his soft, cool voice. "I promise you'll get used to it in a few minutes."

"We must look ridiculous if anyone is watching without helmets."

"They aren't. Here's what we're going to do. I need you to hide off this path and wait in that thick grass." He pointed to her right. "If anyone but me comes through, keep pulling your trigger until they remove their helmet. Close your left eye, and the sights will appear to help you aim. I'm going to sneak a bit closer until I find a good lookout tree."

Sure, I'll babysit myself. This sounds like a great time. Although she was annoyed, she followed the plan and hunched down.

The ground was cool beneath her, and she realized it might be a while before she was able to move. Ellie had never experienced any game like this before. The only game that mattered to TEAMMATE was life. Any other rogue games available on the black market were deemed a threat against the teachings of TEAMMATE. Making and playing such games wasted resources, including time and innovation, for mere entertainment. To make things worse, many, including this particular game, contained violence, banned items, and goals contrary to the TEAMMATE Rulebook. These types of games were something that only outlaws participated in, as far as Ellie knew. The question was, how big of an outlaw was Andy Jacobs?

On the other hand, it was only a game. Ellie didn't see the actual harm in pretending for fun. It was really more of an exercise in using your imagination. It wasn't against the rules to think or dream, was it? Of course, that may have only been true because there was no way for TEAMMATE to monitor thoughts, except memories. Ellie was thankful for that. Otherwise, she'd be on another level of trouble. If she had ever typed out some of her thoughts, especially since finding the journal, it could be enough for excommunication. She'd eventually have to do something about the diary and chest, but she wasn't ready to give them up yet. It felt wrong to destroy what had been meant for her, and she was now convinced it had unlocked some type of ability within her to help people. She desperately wanted to continue to help more people...if only she could avoid getting into trouble. She wished she could talk to someone about it all. Someone she could trust with her secret. Could Andy be that Teammate?

"Ellie! They got behind us! I can't see our flag from up here!" Ellie looked around but couldn't see anything through the patch of grass. She slowly stood up.

"I didn't see anyone come this way," she said.

"Stay still. We have to put three shots on them before they forfeit the flag. Don't let them reach the midpoint. I wish I knew where..." Ellie heard shots ring in her ear. "Crap. I'm dead."

"Andy!" Ellie dropped back to the ground. But she heard nothing back. His microphone was shut off, and he was likely now walking to the sideline, helmet in hand. The partner of their opponent with the flag must have taken out Andy. Ellie thought about that and also about Andy Jacobs now watching her cower uselessly on the ground. She was hopeful he couldn't see her in the darkness, but it still didn't sit right with her. This was her chance to show him how brave she could be. She began crawling towards the sideline. Since the other team had snuck by once, they'd likely try the same path again. It could only be left or right since they hadn't come her way. She guessed left.

Snap! A branch broke to her right. She should have stayed where she was. The enemy was coming up the same path she and Andy had used. Ellie crawled as quickly and quietly as possible. The branches and grass moved first. She had a second to position herself behind a fallen log for protection. Then she saw her, creeping forward with the artificial flag image wavering from the top of her helmet. Ellie closed her left eye, and a red dot appeared.

Pop! Pop! Pop! Ellie kept her finger on the trigger. She heard a muffled curse. The flag fell downward, disappearing before hitting the ground. The girl removed her helmet and disappeared. Ellie could hear her exit the field, still grumbling towards the sideline. Ellie realized the flag must be programmed to reappear in its original position near the end markers.

She felt a rush of satisfaction now that the game was even. Maybe she could win this barbaric contest. It would be fitting that she'd be good at something that TEAMMATE expressly forbids. Now that she'd improved her odds, she had another choice to make. She could wait and try to guard the flag or go on the offensive. All she would need to do was grab the flag and sprint back without getting shot more than twice. Remembering how she'd foolishly told her mom she'd check in every hour, she realized she needed to go all in on getting the flag. Waiting could take too long if her opponent went defensive as well.

She continued crawling all the way to the left sideline. The terrain continued on in the same pattern, seemingly without end. There were five laser lines, resembling a fence that signified the side boundary. She continued forward, staying on her hands and knees. Her arms were beginning to hurt, but she ignored the ache. Every snap of vegetation made her want to stop for good, but that wasn't an option. Surely the remaining player had heard her by now. It was too quiet.

Crawling under the vegetation, she pulled herself forward. The distance seemed so much longer than it really was. *It's just a mind trick. Whatever you do, don't stop.*

After what seemed like forever, she could see the boundary ahead. All she needed to do was crawl to the center and grab the stupid flag. After that, it would be a footrace to the midpoint. It almost seemed too easy as she gazed upon the flag, seemingly unguarded.

Her decision was made by opportunity as well as necessity to end the game quickly. She snatched the flag and started running. There was nothing quiet about her sprint towards victory. The undergrowth shuddered. Imaginary birds scattered and scorned her, leaving no doubt that her position would be easy to pinpoint. She stayed on a trail leading near the center of the course. Branches were whizzing by her ear, but she thought she could hear movement ahead. *It's too late to stop now. I'm so close!* She barreled through a tuft of grass and was immediately hit with the first shot. Her helmet vision went black for a second before returning with a fuzzy resolution.

Thwack! Her helmet surged in brightness this time before going black again. She was so disoriented that she closed her eyes and tried to recall her last visual of her surroundings. There had been a log to her right. She heard more shots fired as she dropped and rolled until her sensory gloves felt the protection of a large object between her and the unending gunfire. She opened her eyes to find her helmet's vision had returned. The enormous log was blocking the volley of shots. Abruptly, the firing stopped, and she could hear metallic clicks. *He must be reloading.* She popped to her feet above the log and found her attacker standing in the open, fussing with his weapon.

Ellie didn't stop pulling the trigger until her firearm was empty. No one else remained.

CHAPTER
SEVENTEEN

"How's the party going?" In an effort to hear her mom's voice and particularly her tone, Ellie cupped a hand around her bracelet and ear to block some of the background noise. She now paused a moment before answering. Presently, she was sore, her clothes were grass-stained, and she'd worked up a sweat during the events of the game. But the boy who sat beside her had his arm around her and didn't seem to mind at all.

"It's a lot of fun. I'm glad I came."

Her mother cleared her throat. "Well, I suppose I'm happy to hear that. I thought you were supposed to check with me every hour, though."

Ellie's stomach dropped. In the excitement of winning and being hoisted into the air by Andy's strong arms, she'd forgotten all about the promise she'd hastily made. "I'm sorry. I was having so much fun, I must have forgotten to link you. You know, no one else has to check with their parents every hour." She felt a pinch on her arm and barely suppressed a screech and giggle. Andy mocked an innocent smile.

"I'm sorry, Ellie, but you broke the very rules you agreed to, which means you'll have to come home early. As you are well aware, no Teammate is above the rules."

Ellie's heart sank. The night had been going so well. They were now back at the party, sitting on the deck, and the plan had been nearly executed to perfection. Judith sat in Clint's lap, Becca leaned inward in deep conversation with Blake, and she and Andy sat on the deck floor listening to Judith and Clint jabber on like an old married couple. She could tell that her group didn't buy their hide-and-seek story, but Ellie wasn't really concerned about that right now. She couldn't stop smiling at the fact that she'd actually won, and Andy had praised how well she'd done.

"But Mom, they aren't ready to leave yet."

"That's not a problem. I can leave now to come get you."

Andy nudged her. "I can take you home if it's okay," he said.

"Hold on a second, Mom." Ellie covered her microphone on her bracelet. "Don't let me ruin your Friday night. It's really okay."

He smiled. "It would only be ruined if I stayed here by myself. Tell her you're leaving now. I insist."

Ellie uncovered the microphone. "Okay, Mom. I have a ride and we're leaving now. I'll be home in just a little bit."

"That's more like it, Ellie. There will be more parties, so long as you follow the rules. Now, make sure your ride drives safely. It's dark out and there's no need to speed."

ELLIE WAS ALMOST EMBARRASSED BY THE LOOK OF SHOCK ON JU-dith's face when she'd told the group Andy would drive her home. But she took solace in the fact that her friend was happy for her, if not astonished by the sudden interest that Andy had taken in her at the party.

Andy was such a gentleman that he even pulled his car around front to pick her up.

"Thanks for treating me like a lady, especially since I don't look like one at the moment." She slipped gracefully into the passenger seat, and Andy gently closed her door before walking to his side.

As he opened his own door, he cleared his throat. "Well, you've never looked better to me—so free, so wild, so beautiful. I'm embarrassed I got taken out of the game so quickly. I could have at least gotten shot protecting you, or something heroic like that." He put on his seatbelt. "I told you this already, but I can't get over how impressed I am. I mean, you literally won the game by yourself. And I'm pretty sure I was right, but tell me—did you have fun?"

Ellie hadn't thought it was fun, initially. But winning changes a person's view. Andy backed out of the driveway and started down the road.

"I don't think I've ever been so nervous and excited in my life. I didn't think I was going to like it, but it was by far the most exciting game I've ever played. I wish it weren't contraband. I mean, what harm did we cause to TEAMMATE? Anyways, where'd you get the helmets from?"

Andy grinned. "I traded for them from a guy at a stunt bike competition. He got them from some rogue computer programmer. Aren't they lifelike? Actually, there are a few other games we could play."

"Like what else?"

"There are all kinds of military games. You can play against the computer, too. I'm partial to the racing games. We should try them next time."

She raised an eyebrow at him. "You're certain there'll be a next time? What if I'm grounded for the next year because I forgot to check in?"

"I guess we'll just have to wait," he said soberly. "But I doubt that's the case. The plan worked so well. It would be a shame not to see each other outside of school again."

"That would be a shame. You know what else would be a shame, though? If we got caught with your helmets."

Andy laughed. "It's practically impossible. You have to enter the password to activate the cool games that TEAMMATE wouldn't like. If anyone else took them, the only game they could play is tic-tac-toe. Luckily, there's no rule against that yet."

"Well, at least you never have to worry about me turning you in," Ellie said slyly. "Any chance of getting the password?" She asked the question innocently, but it was really a test.

"Sure, I trust you. After your outburst about TEAMMATE, I know how you really feel."

Now Ellie laughed. "You still don't know that much about me."

"You're right, and I have a theory as to why that is." He took a deep breath before turning toward her. "Remember I said we couldn't talk about it over the bracelet...about the angle of TEAMMATE?"

Ellie nodded, intrigued by what the boy might be thinking. In the excitement of the evening, she'd forgotten he'd mentioned there was something he needed to tell her in person. She was thankful the drive wasn't a short distance. There were so many things she wanted to ask Andy.

"I've been thinking about you quite a bit lately. How is it, after all these years of school, that I've never known the real Ellie? I think I may have figured something out. By all the equations and factors, our system weighs our future jobs, our future spouses, our future circle of friends—I'm certain the algorithm will do everything it can to separate you and me. In fact, I think it's already been doing it for most of our lives."

Ellie couldn't suppress her look of surprise. "What? Don't you think that sounds kind of crazy? We both agree TEAMMATE is overbearing, but you believe it's been actively trying to keep us apart our entire lives?"

Andy turned onto a main road before continuing. "Think about it. How many obstacles have been between us in school? Your best friend has overshadowed you since kindergarten. Have you ever had a class without Judith?"

"Well, not that I remember."

"Right. And since she is with you nearly every moment of the day, if I were to approach the two of you to talk, who would respond?"

"That's not fair," said Ellie.

"No? Well, how many classes have we had? Have we ever been part of a group project?"

"Very few classes," said Ellie. "And Judith has kept track every year. But that is all coincidence. Why would TEAMMATE care about two elementary students?"

"I should think it would be obvious. We were identified early on in school. We're not blindly obedient to the TEAMMATE Rulebook. We have the ability to think for ourselves, and that can be dangerous."

"Why not excommunicate us if TEAMMATE is so worried?"

"Because there are too many like us, Ellie. They can't remove us all, but they can dilute our influence. Mark my word, we will be consistently steered toward partners who are rule sticklers. We will be separated from each other within this society."

"But how could they do that?"

"You think test results aren't capable of being manipulated? What about homerooms in school? What about career paths? What about partner compatibility tests? Look at your own parents. I'm guessing your dad takes liberties with some rules while your mom takes more convincing."

Ellie swallowed. Andy had hit closer to home than he imagined. Her mom constantly worried about her dad's gardening activities.

"The game plan has always been to divide and conquer. I must admit I'm not sure if it's the TEAMMATE Council or just the

TEAMMATE program that runs scenarios, but if you pay attention, you'll see the pattern too."

"You're saying, not only is my best friend an obstacle, but our entire society is an obstacle designed to keep us apart?"

"Yes, and do you know why I think this?" He hesitated before continuing. "It's to keep discussions like this from happening. I like you, Ellie. And I believe you're smart enough to figure things out."

Ellie had to catch her breath. As ridiculous as Andy's explanation sounded, if TEAMMATE was half as sophisticated as everyone claimed, it could definitely steer them apart. Not merely them, but others like them too. And if it had been successful thus far, how much further would it go once their attraction was noticed? And was it planning a way already?

"What you're saying is technically possible, but it's also a conspiracy."

He nodded. "Which is why I couldn't mention it over the bracelet. Because...as always...the Rulebook." He gestured with one hand forward, keeping the other on the steering wheel.

"Okay, if we're assuming this is all true, what should we do?"

Andy smiled. "We could give in, and let the sector control our destiny...or we could fight the algorithm." He glanced sideways before grinning. "You strike me as a fighter."

Ellie couldn't suppress her own grin now. "And that's why you like me, right?"

He chuckled. "As I've already said, one of the many reasons." He unexpectedly took her hand in his. "The two of us together feels right to me, even if I don't know you that well yet."

Ellie liked the feel of his hand around her own. She nearly pinched herself that this was happening. He'd already shared so much with her that could get him in major trouble. She felt herself wanting to confide in him as well.

"Actually, I have a secret that's much worse than your conspiracy and the contraband game." She hesitated, studying his reaction closely as he drove. "Does that worry you?"

He licked his lips. "I don't doubt that. I feel like most people have something over their heads if TEAMMATE accessed our thoughts. But the truth is, I'd really like to be someone you felt like you could trust with that sort of thing."

"Time will tell," Ellie said slyly. "But I'm beginning to think you could be that person."

"Thanks," said Andy. "But just out of curiosity, what makes you think so?"

That's a bold question. Think Ellie. Think! "I guess...because you said you already trust me. And you haven't given me a reason not to yet. Although I still don't really know you that well."

"I'm an open book. Ask away."

"Are you sure that's a good idea?"

"Yes. But be careful what you ask. I have a dark history of being honest."

"I like this game."

He smiled. "I'm glad you do, but this isn't a game."

That response stung Ellie a little bit. Fine. No easy questions.

"How many girlfriends have you had?"

"Counting grade school, six."

It was more than most by their age. But on the other hand, she might become lucky number seven.

"I don't think grade school counts, but that's still a lot. Have you ever been...intimate with anyone?" *How did I really just ask him this?*

"No."

"Really?" She felt a rush of relief.

"Yes, really. Got any more?"

"Why do you really like me?"

He paused a moment and smiled. "I thought we talked about this before."

"Yes, but you weren't an open book at the time. I want to understand the sudden interest in me after years of being invisible. Even if your theory about TEAMMATE is right, you were still aware that I existed. You weren't blind the last fifteen years of my life. How long have you felt the way you do? I want it all."

Now he laughed. "You don't pull any punches, do you? We've always been casual friends of friends in class, right? You were never invisible, but you were an unknown entity. So quiet on the surface, but what was going on underneath? I've always been curious. Maybe I got tired of waiting for you to come out of your shell. The other day in class, I saw you emerging. I think it was a preview of the real you. And make no mistake, you've always been cute in my eyes, but that's superficial. But that's not all. When you did...whatever it was the other day in class, you touched me, and not only do I believe that you saved my life, you awoke something else in me. I told you before, I haven't felt the same since. But to go back to before that, I can't deny I've always seen potential in your eyes. You never seemed to care for what everyone else does. Everyone recognizes that you're super smart, but there's a determination in your eyes that's going to make you great someday. I can't fathom what that greatness is going to turn into, but I also can't sit back and pretend I don't see it anymore. TEAMMATE can't hide you from me any longer. I want to be a part of a future that includes you."

Ellie swallowed. "That was quite a lot, but I guess I asked," She nervously laughed. "Thank you," she said awkwardly. Then, in a moment of realization, she said, "But I'm not really that great at anything...unless you count capture the flag." She smirked.

"That's exactly what I'm talking about...your potential. You didn't curl up in a ball when I made my early exit. You stayed in and won the game. You made me jump through a lot of hoops to go on this date. It was all worth it for this night. And when you spoke your mind in class the other day, you were right about TEAMMATE."

"You're saying you like me for my potential?"

"Not just that. I admire you for who you are. Introverted? Yes. But I want to help you completely emerge from that shell. It's like everyone else is asleep and you and I are the only ones with our eyes open. You get me...I think. And someday I feel like you're going to open a lot of other Teammates' eyes."

"For all this talk of having my eyes open, it sure feels like I'm dreaming." *That was so corny, Ellie.*

"When your eyes are open, you have control over the dream instead of the dream controlling you."

"Who are you, Andy Jacobs? That was pretty philosophical." How could this boy be so calm, so confident all the time? What was it he thought he saw or knew that no one else did?

"You've known of me your whole life. Who do you think I am?"

They were, unfortunately, now pulling into Ellie's driveway. *Quick! Think of something witty!*

"I think I'm still not sure yet, but I like whoever you are."

"That sounds like an opening for a second date," he said.

"Because it absolutely is. You'd better link me tomorrow."

As she grabbed for the door handle, he caught her other hand.

"The password is *Nightranger,* for the helmets." He kissed the back of her hand.

She was taken aback by his honesty and trust, and of course, the kiss.

"Thank you...for trusting me. You promise you aren't scared of my secret?"

He nodded his head. "I promise, but you don't need to..."

"I want to," she said. "But you won't feel the same way about me after I tell you." She stepped out of the car to see Andy's expression. "Imagine the darkest secret ever kept. Think about that a little while before our next date. If you still think you're ready, I'll tell you next time."

His jaw fell for a second. "I...think you're trying to scare me away, Ellie. It's not going to work, though. I can't deny what I feel. Nothing you've done in the past will deter me. If anything, it feeds into your mysterious element."

"Good," she said. "But you still need some time to think about it first. I'm far more dangerous than you realize. Good night, Andy. Thank you...for everything."

"Good night, Ellie. You can trust me. I'm on your side no matter what."

CHAPTER
EIGHTEEN

Ellie was relieved by Andy's response to the bomb she'd unexpectedly dropped on him. He seemed undeterred, at least for now. She couldn't believe she'd nearly told him everything. *What was I thinking? I should have kissed him instead. But he deserves to know before things go further. And he was honest with me. Was I too honest with him?* Weighing all these thoughts in her mind as she walked into her living room, she was surprised to find her parents, as well as her sister, still awake.

Molly was performing a puppet show, crouched behind a blanket that had been hung between two pieces of furniture. Of course, you'd have to count her teddy bear and a baby doll as puppets to classify the show accordingly. Ellie was about to say something when she saw her mom put her finger to her lips. There would be no discussion right now about not checking in.

"Why, hello there, Ellie," said the bear in Molly's voice. "What are bears without bees?"

Ellie rolled her eyes. "I dunno, Molly. Hungry?"

"Nope. They're ears!"

Her parents roared loudly with what could almost be classified as genuine laughter. It wasn't all that funny, but at least Molly was keeping them in a good mood. Ellie decided to remain civil.

"So how grounded am I?" she asked.

Kirk looked at his wife before answering. She nodded in unspoken agreement, signaling it was already settled.

"Because you got home early and haven't pouted—yet at least, we aren't going to ground you. Do you think next time you can keep your part of the agreement?"

Ellie couldn't stifle her smile of happiness now. "I won't ever forget to check in again, I swear! Thank you!" She ran and hugged them both at once. Then, seeing an opportunity to score bonus points, she engulfed Molly in a hug as well.

"Thanks for the bear hug," said the bear.

"Molly, your jokes are almost *unbearable*," Ellie said, petting the puppet.

Her mom and dad seemed to love her corny joke as much as her sister's. Seeing a chance to end the night on a high note, Ellie excused herself for bed and ran up to her room. She had more reading to do, and she wasn't ready for the night to end. Everything had turned out perfectly regarding her master plan. The future was finally looking bright.

WHEN THE BUS ROLLED TO A STOP BEFORE ELLIE AND MOLLY ON Sunday morning, Ellie had to resist the urge to run back to her bedroom. She had been dreading this moment since Friday. Perhaps it would've been better if Judith had linked her that night or even anytime on Saturday. However, she had not done so, and Ellie hadn't been in a hurry to start the conversation that lay ahead. She slowly followed her younger sister up the steps and down the bus aisle. She found her best friend in their usual seat. Judith's bulging eyes reflected the brilliant morning light until her all-knowing grin grew wide enough to tug their corners.

"I need details, my friend." There was growing excitement in Judith's voice. "I need to know everything. Where did you two go? What did he smell like? What did you guys do? How did this all happen so quickly? I mean, one minute we're all together, and the next he appears out of thin air and plucks you from the deck like the pretty flower you are. Let me start by just saying how happy I am for you. Did I not say all you needed to do was put yourself out there?"

Ellie sat down and engulfed her best friend in a hug,

"It felt like a dream, Judith. He really did need another Teammate for his game. Why he chose me, I can't really say. But it was so fun and he was just so...cool."

"What game did you play?"

The question created the same effect as biting into a lemon.

"I'm not sure? There was a flag involved, though."

She could feel Judith studying her face, her eyes dancing with more questions as her grin faded.

"I've never heard of a game with a flag." She paused a moment in thought. "You're not making this up to escape my questioning, are you?"

Ellie swallowed. An annoying tickle in her nose instinctively caused the back of her hand to brush her face. It was her body's betrayal of her lie. But would Judith notice?

"What else did you think we were doing?"

Judith's eyes narrowed. "I can think of a few things I'd be doing if I were in your place. Please tell me you at least kissed him?"

Ellie was beginning to feel even more uncomfortable, if that was possible. "No...but he did kiss the back of my hand if that counts?"

"While you played the game?"

"No, that was when he dropped me off at home."

Judith set her chin in her hands. She wore a look of annoyance. "You are a terrible storyteller," she said with a sigh. "I will tell you what I saw. Andy Jacobs had his eyes on you the whole time after this mysterious game. The rest of us were invisible. I saw him put his arm around you. I think that boy is in love."

Ellie had to feign shock and stared at her friend with an open jaw. "You think?"

"Definitely. I mean, it was almost like he sought you out at the party." Judith glanced upward. "Maybe it's because of his seizure."

"You think it caused brain damage?" joked Ellie.

Judith snorted. "Funny, but no. I bet when you touched him, he actually saw you for the first time. Like he was dying, Ellie, and you were the only one not afraid of him. I bet it's like survivor syndrome or something."

"I suppose that's not unreasonable."

"It makes sense, right? Normally, he wouldn't give either of us a second glance."

Ellie thought for a moment. Andy had admitted she'd done something to him when she touched him. He'd also mentioned a good many other things that she couldn't talk to Judith about. "Well, what should I do, Judith?"

"Sink your claws in tight, girl!" She smiled menacingly. "Don't let him get away."

"Is that what you did with Clint?"

"Oh, totally. I'm sorry I haven't seen you as much between classes. I absolutely guard his locker...make him hold my hand...and ward off any other competition."

Ellie laughed. "You're worried that if you don't, another girl might swoop in?"

"I would," said Judith. "If I were someone else, that is. Anyways, I'm just looking out for my best friend. I consider you the sister I never had. Don't be afraid to ask me questions, girl. I realize this is all new to you. But family can tell each other anything."

Ellie cringed. "To be honest, I do feel kind of bad. I mean, you've always liked Andy."

Judith put a hand on her shoulder. "Do not feel bad at all, Ellie. I have a serious boyfriend now. It's made me realize my obsession with Andy was borderline unhealthy. Plus, he ignored me all the time. Things have worked out like they're supposed to. I knew from the second Clint messaged me that he was the boy for me."

The cringe on the inside wasn't subsiding. "You're a good friend, Judith," she managed to say."

"Aw, thanks, girlfriend. I'm so happy for you and Andy both."

CHAPTER
NINETEEN

After the girls got off the bus, Judith wasted no time before starting guard duty at Clint's locker. That left Ellie alone at her own locker, considering whether she should be stalking Andy's locker or continuing to stand awkwardly alone until class started. She stared down the hall, considering her options, when she felt a tap on her shoulder.

She spun around to see Andy. He engulfed her in a hug.

"Isn't this much nicer than secrecy?" he whispered in her ear.

She nodded before setting her head against his shoulder. "So, I didn't scare you off Friday?" she asked.

"Not at all." His grip around her tightened. "I meant what I said."

"I hope so," she said with a smile. "Does this mean you're going to walk me to class?"

"Sure. As long as you share your homework on the TEAMMATE Council with me."

Ellie looked at him in shock.

"I'm joking, Ellie," he said with that enticing smile. "You know, if it's possible, you might be even cuter when you're surprised."

Her face grew warm from the comment, and she quickly turned toward her locker. She hastily grabbed her reader in one hand, shut her locker, and took his arm with her free hand. "Try not to make a habit of it?" She smiled playfully. "Now, please escort me to class."

When class got underway, Miss Conway had everyone submit their homework as usual.

"As you will recall from your assignment, today's class will focus on the TEAMMATE Council. As a matter of fact, I'm honored to announce we have a surprise guest speaker later this afternoon." She surveyed the students. "Who wants to share some facts they've learned about the Council?"

Alice's hand shot up first.

"Yes, Alice? What do you have for us?"

Ellie suppressed her groan. *Here comes another recitation of the TEAMMATE Rulebook.*

The blonde girl straightened in her seat before lifting her chin and regurgitating the opening lines of their homework assignment. "The TEAMMATE Council consists of ten to twenty members, although currently it sits at fifteen. Members are eligible after at least ten years in their assigned job field, at which point the highest performers may sit for another TPT. Unlike governing bodies of past societies, the Council merely consists of the best and brightest in society. There are no monetary requirements, no bloodlines required, no campaigning, and no political alliances allowed. As a result, Teammates are free to exercise their superior intellect for the betterment of society without outside influence."

Ellie could feel Miss Conway's eyes pass over her while Alice spoke. She wouldn't give her teacher a reason to single her out again. After all, she'd told her teacher and her dad there would not be a next time.

"Very good, Alice. Can someone tell me some facts about the members of our current Council? How about Ernie?"

For all the jokes that Judith made at Ernie Barfton's expense, the boy was not lacking in intellect or confidence. No, it was more organization and hygiene that remained his adversaries.

Ernie adjusted his glasses. "Sure, Miss Conway, and thank you for calling on me." He glanced downward, eyes squinting in thought. "The head of the Council rotates every three years, and the gavel is currently held by Winston Jennings. He has a rather famous salt and pepper mustache that flares outward on either side and has sat on the Council for over twenty years. Winston also heads the Historical branch within TEAMMATE. The oldest member on the Council is Thurman Graves, who heads the Security branch. He is famous for his furry eyebrows and crotchety disposition."

A few chuckles could not be held back, and all Miss Conway needed was a raise of her own light eyebrows to stifle the laughter.

Ernie continued. "There's Nannette Hall, one of the younger members who heads the Educational branch, and there's Benson Browning, who heads the Science branch and is the only member in history to register a perfect TPT result."

The recounting of members droned on, and Ellie found herself staring at Andy. She was two seats directly behind him, so all she could really see was the back of his head and occasionally his arms when he stretched. Still, the view was quite rewarding, and Ellie couldn't understand what this boy saw in her. What would he think if she confided in him about the journal? G. W. had written a strict warning concerning the matter, but Andy might be the one Teammate she could trust with her secret. She felt such a strong pull to tell him everything, and at the same time, a wave of uneasiness in her stomach.

"Ellie?"

Her eyes darted from the back of Andy to Miss Conway.

"Yes?"

The class broke into a fit of laughter.

"I think we caught someone daydreaming. I asked if you could describe the TEAMMATE Council chambers."

Ellie's embarrassment was short-lived as she converted into recall mode. In addition to reading about it in the homework, she'd been in the chambers on a field trip four years prior.

"The chamber is a large, circular room with a high, domed ceiling, accentuated by intervals of windows to allow natural illumination of the room. It sits on the top floor of the TEAMMATE Council building—also known as TEAMMATE Headquarters, which is one of many buildings surrounding TEAMMATE Square." *And now I sound like Alice.*

"Nice recovery," remarked Miss Conway. "Since it seems we've all done our homework today, I'm going to divide you into groups, and we'll form our own student version of the Council. Some of you will get to petition the Council for changes, while others must answer for rule-breaking. Those chosen for the Council must interpret the TEAMMATE Rulebook. Often, the best way to learn in life is by experience." The teacher grinned with anticipatory excitement.

The remainder of the morning consisted of the Council exercise. Ellie played the role of Winston, which was fun since she could cut off anyone else by banging her gavel. They were given various sentences to use for rule infractions, which ranged from speeding to improper recycling techniques. It was all quite elementary, but the time passed quickly until the next class.

At lunch, Ellie sat with Judith as usual since the boys were in a different lunch period.

Judith was quieter than normal as the two ate the meal provided by the cafeteria. After a few moments of silence, Ellie was forced to ask if everything was okay.

"I'm fine," Judith replied with a sigh. "I just wish Clint listened better. I mean, he's funny and I'm totally in love with him, but sometimes he just keeps talking when I want to talk, you know?"

Ellie was quite familiar with her friend's need for an audience. That job usually belonged to her, after all. Listening for long bouts while others spoke was not a role that Judith herself excelled at. However, Ellie didn't think pointing this out would help the matter. Instead, she asked questions and just listened, since that was what Judith really needed most.

"So, what happened?"

"Well, sometimes I just want to be serious when we talk about the future, and all he does is crack jokes. Like this morning, I asked how many children he wanted to apply for, and he said at least twelve." She wrinkled her face in disgust. "I said no. I want a serious answer, and he gives me another half-joke reference to whatever the upper child limit is. It's like he's never thought of any of these things before, or maybe he doesn't care. I'm starting to notice how often he brushes my questions aside." She leaned inward toward Ellie. "Do you think I'm overreacting?"

Ellie shrugged. "I'm not sure. Have you mentioned your concern to him?"

"He says I worry too much. He said we needed to have more fun. I said, well, someone needs to worry about these things if you aren't. He brushed it off like I'm imagining things and changed the subject yet again. It's so frustrating. Why can't boys just listen? Sometimes I really just need to talk about how I'm feeling, or what I'm worried about."

"Unfortunately, my advice in that department is quite limited. But I'll be here to listen to you." Ellie swallowed a drink of water while Judith considered her response.

"That's because you're a true friend. But who knew boys could be so much work? Is Andy like that, too?"

Ellie sat up straight in thought. "I haven't noticed it yet," she admitted. "But maybe they're all a little bit that way. I've heard my mom complain to my dad about similar things."

"Oh, that's just great," moaned Judith. "They can never be fully trained?"

Ellie laughed. "You realize, they probably say the same thing about us."

"Yeah? Well, the difference is that we're right."

"Definitely. We could never be wrong."

"Exactly. This is yet again why we're soul sisters, Ellie. We're always on the same page."

After lunch, it was back to homeroom for the surprise lecturer. This time, Ellie found Andy at his locker. She decided it was selfish to expect him to wait for her after every class. Perhaps she was maturing after all? When the pair arrived at class, they noticed Miss Conway speaking to a woman in her late thirties with a hawkish nose. The bell rang and everyone sat down.

Miss Conway stood arrow straight as she walked to the front of the class. "Our surprise lecturer this afternoon comes to us from the TEAMMATE Council. I want you all on your best behavior and to please give a warm welcome to the head of Education branch, Councilmember Nannette Hall."

Ellie's classmates clapped politely as Miss Conway retreated to her desk and Councilmember Nannette Hall loomed at the front of the class. Her eyes were calculating and beady. They seemed to take note of everyone's face before the woman spoke.

"Thank you for the kind introduction. It's always nostalgic for me to return to TEAMMATE High. This is a formative year for all of you, and I'm sure some are quite nervous. Let me reassure you, everything always works out the way it is supposed to." She looked at Ellie, almost through her. "Trust the team. It will never fail you."

Ellie swallowed hard. Why had she directed the comment at her?

Thankfully, the Councilmember shifted her focus elsewhere after the brief pause.

"Where should I begin? Well, I've sat on the TEAMMATE Council for the past five years. I was originally assigned to the Education branch, where I helped create and update the curriculum, submitted new TPT questions, and helped identify new talent suited to our branch." She glanced toward Miss Conway. "As head of the Education branch, let me assure you how lucky you are to have Edna Conway as your teacher this year. She had been identified as a high performer long before she took her TPT test. Scoring strong in areas of empathy, dedication, and, of course, basic TEAMMATE knowledge, there is no one better suited to bring out your best before you retake your TPT test at the completion of the schoolyear. I understand you haven't yet received your results from attempt number one, but those should be complete very soon." She glanced toward Miss Conway, who nodded.

"Let's begin with questions. I'm sure most lecturers save this part for the end, but I think you'll find my approach different. I could recite your chapter that covers our beloved Council from memory since I practically wrote the most updated version, but I think you'll find that quite...repetitive." She glanced around the room. "This is no time to be shy. Be inquisitive. Seek knowledge, children. That is the basis of moving our society forward, after all."

Judith slowly raised her hand.

"Yes, you with the beautiful curls in your hair?"

Judith cleared her throat. "Is it possible to change your career path if, say...you don't like where you match?"

Nannette Hall's gaze pierced her soul. Her expression softened. "Who's the boy you're hoping to be matched near?" She said it softly, but its effect made Judith sit straight in her chair.

"Why would you ask that?" squeaked Judith.

Ellie looked toward Miss Conway's desk to see a look of disapproval directed at her friend. She realized that the class's behavior was a direct reflection of their teacher.

"Because clearly, there is a reason, and logically speaking, for your age, it's a boy. Don't be embarrassed. Your question is more common than you think. To be direct, the answer is no. The algorithm is unflawed. You will learn to love what you are chosen to do. When you contribute to your maximum capacity, your life will be fulfilled. If you are meant to be with the boy currently on your mind, both he and

TEAMMATE will see that you match." She shifted her gaze. "Next question."

From the last chair in her row, Becca raised her hand. "How many Teammates has the Council expelled since you were appointed to its membership?"

Nannette smiled. "This is always a popular topic. I can only recall two in the past ten years. The vast majority of cases simply involve reeducation. Expulsion is only for repeat offenders and those deemed irredeemable. Since paganism has been declared extinct for nearly fifty years, there are truly very few who can't be reeducated. Both of the cases that I recall knew their punishment before they recommitted their rule infractions. And as a result, they currently live in exile."

Jordan raised his hand.

Councilmember Hall looked pleased with the curiosity beginning to come forth. "Yes, young man. Proceed with your question."

"What is the KSM test like?"

"Excellent question. Unfortunately, I only see the recorded results of administered tests, and they aren't needed on a regular basis, thankfully. There is only one councilmember allowed to administer said tests, and unfortunately, he does not allow an audience. I'm referring to Thurman Graves, the inventor of the test. He is advancing in years and has pledged to take a younger apprentice member, but most people believe it will be Delbert. Suffice it to say his methods are heavily guarded."

"Why not you?" asked Alice, who had regained her confidence.

"A very bold question," said Nannette. "If you'd like an objective answer, I'll reward your bravery. As much as it may seem a shock to you, the Council is not without its disagreements. Believe it or not, oftentimes I have my own strongly opinionated arguments with Councilmember Graves. Am I always right?" She looked toward the ceiling. "In my opinion, yes." She smiled. "In Thurman's opinion? Never." Now she laughed. "This is why the Council needs multiple members to vote. Don't get me wrong, the man is quite brilliant, as he's responsible for much of the technology used by the Security branch. He helped carry many of Needlebaugh's ideas into practice. All the same, I can assure you that I will not be his apprentice when the time comes."

Ellie found this information interesting. Apparently, there *were* disagreements allowed on the Council. She wondered if anyone might agree with her own thoughts about TEAMMATE. *Highly unlikely.* She'd always pictured them as a collective group of geniuses that agreed on the best solution every time. Perhaps they weren't so different from other Teammates.

After the class had exhausted its store of questions, Councilmember Hall summarized her daily functions, which were as monotonous as she'd previously promised. Ellie inhaled a breath of relief when the final bell rang and they were finally done for the day. Andy must have been relieved as well because he jumped up quickly to stand near her. Ellie caught Judith's eyes linger on him for just a moment before catching her own stare. She shrugged helplessly before telling Ellie she'd catch her on the bus, only after another quick glance at Andy, who had not seemed to notice.

"What are you doing tonight?" he asked.

Ellie thought. "I'm supposed to go to my sister's soccer game tonight."

"Perfect. I need to see you again so we can plan our next date."

Chills of eagerness crept down Ellie's spine. He took her hand and walked her toward her locker. "Sounds good to me. I never have anyone to talk to there anyway. I hope you aren't too bored."

He looked at her and tilted his head with a smile. "Boredom only comes from boring people." He looked around conspiratorially. "We don't fit that description, do we?" He smiled warmly.

Ellie fought the urge to tell him everything right there on the spot. "I told you already, you might prefer boredom to the problems I'll bring you."

"The greater the challenge, the greater the reward."

"Look who's quoting TEAMMATE now?" Ellie teased. "Molly has the late game tonight, so don't get to the fields too early. Judith and I have to work on our upcoming project right after school anyway."

"I wish you were my partner." He said it with a grin.

"Me too." She sighed. "But at least I'll see you tonight. I'd better hurry if I'm going to catch my bus."

"I could drive you."

"I have a better idea." Ellie grinned. "Assuming my parents are okay with it, could you drive me home from the game?"

"I'd love to," he said. "See you tonight."

PART II
Despair

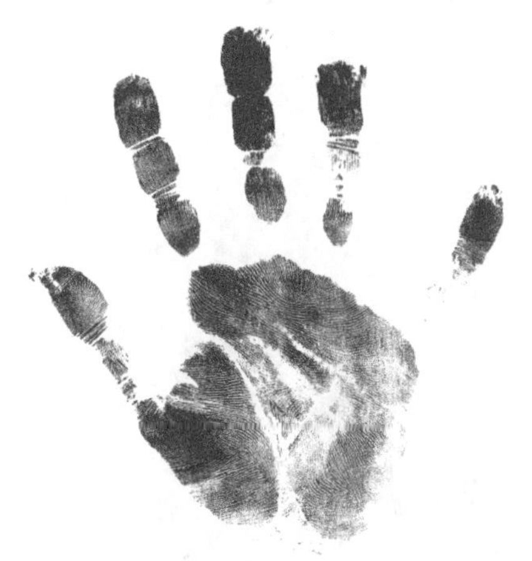

CHAPTER
TWENTY

Judith got off the bus with Ellie and Molly after school. The two friends had planned to work on their project in Kirk Wilder's study, which was a seldom-used room located in the front of the house. Despite its ability to offer privacy and comfortable seating, the room was dull for teenage girls since it was mostly bare, lacking a viewing console, and contained a few meager images sprinkled tastefully around the room to document family milestones. However, this lack of media and entertainment resources did offer a safe refuge from Molly, as she would unapologetically distract them from their work if this were not the case.

Upon the wall hung the most recent image of the Wilder family, taken over a year ago in the summer. Ellie realized that both she and

Molly already looked much older than the glowing screen portrayed. Molly's cheeks were losing some of their roundness, and Ellie had grown another inch. They would soon be due for a newer picture. An illuminated frame of her father standing beside a much younger Ellie sat on the coffee table beside the loveseat where the girls worked. It was the brightest light source in the entire room. She knew it was her dad's favorite picture because he proudly displayed it in the largest video frame. Ellie studied the framed graphic that was taken about seven years prior. She grinned at the tiny version of the Teammate she'd once been. Although it had been a long time, the details surrounding the picture remained fresh in her mind, like a familiar song evokes a cherished memory. The image was taken at the Daddy-Daughter School Dance. It had been springtime, and her dad had surprised her with a handmade matching corsage and boutonnière from Aunt Ruth's pink rose bush. He wore a gray suit and she, a white dress, proudly displaying her flower-adorned wrist for the picture. The day had always been one of Ellie's favorite memories. It was no secret she'd always had difficulty making close friendships at school, but he'd made her feel special that evening, and the excitement in her eyes had been forever captured, like a brilliant short-lived rainbow before it fades.

"Things are not improving with Clint."

The interruption brought Ellie's attention to the present. "What do you mean? I thought he was just doing annoying boy things."

Judith bit her lip. "It's beyond that now. I think he's getting annoyed with me. He thinks I need to let things go, but you know me better than that."

Ellie knew much better. "Some might call it an unrelenting character trait of yours. But it's not necessarily a bad thing—depending on how significant the matter is." Ellie tried not to sound judgmental, but the truth was, she really wanted Judith's relationship with Clint to survive for her own selfish reasons.

"I think I'm just going to lay everything on the line tonight. I need to see where he stands. Does he like me for who I am? Will he start listening and behaving more appropriately?"

Ellie needed to think quickly. Judith was on the verge of getting worked up enough to cause some problems for both of them. "My advice is...maybe just don't talk to him tonight?" *Please don't ruin everything. You've only been dating for two weeks. I mean, was asking about how many children he wanted even appropriate at this point?* "Tell him you don't want to link tonight so you can cool off a little bit. I'm not saying let everything go, but give him some time to think about it as well before you hit him with an ultimatum."

Judith scowled, undeterred. "But he shouldn't need any time to think. He should know already. How many times must I explain it to him?"

Well, that offered piece of advice was now screaming for its life as Judith had effectively hurled it off an eighth-floor balcony. Likely nothing Clint said would survive tonight, for that matter. "Okay, how about we finish our project, then figure out Clint?" It was more of a plea than a suggestion on Ellie's part.

Judith sat staring at her shoes. "I don't even care about this stupid project right now. I don't think I can concentrate on anything until I figure things out with Clint." She rose from her seat, resolve on her face. "I'm sorry, Ellie. I don't think I'm feeling this group project right now. Maybe I need to walk and think for a bit. Can we just each do our own half? I swear I'll do my part, but you must understand I'm going to be useless for the moment."

Ellie stood quickly. "I'll have my mom drive you home as soon as she's off work. There's no need to walk."

"It's fine," said Judith. She threw her bag over her shoulder. "I'll link my mom to pick me up when I've thought enough. I'm stuck in limbo right now. I thought I truly knew Clint, but it's possible I was wrong. It's almost like I'm not even talking with the same boy from that first weekend."

Ellie grimaced before putting her arm on Judith's shoulder. "Listen, girlfriend, I hate to see you sad. Don't worry about the project. I'll take care of it." She hugged her friend, who stood awkwardly engulfed in her hug. "Please link me if you need anything?"

"Of course," she said softly. "Thanks for being a true friend, Ellie. I'll make this up to you. I hope you enjoy the game tonight with Andy. And I really hope he doesn't turn out like Clint." She bit her lip, as if to stop from saying more. With that, she left, and Ellie scrambled to complete their project.

LATER THAT EVENING, ELLIE AND HER FAMILY WERE ON THEIR way to Molly's game. As they drove by neatly manicured yards and active Teammates enjoying the last hour of sunlight for the day, she debated internally if tonight was the night she would confide in Andy. Was it fair to put her stress on him? How much should she tell him? And how does one break that kind of news to someone they care about? She sighed, realizing that she was just as much in limbo as Judith.

Molly, also sitting in the back seat, picked up on her internal dread. "You didn't have to come if it's too boring."

Ellie turned away from the window to face her sister. "Why would you say that, Molly?"

Her sister shrugged. "You don't look happy."

Anne Wilder turned around from the passenger seat. "Your sister loves watching you play. Isn't that right, Ellie? She just doesn't like all the other Teammates."

"Of course, I love watching you play," said Ellie. She reflected internally before continuing. "I admit sometimes I'm not the best sister or Teammate, for that matter, but that's my problem, not yours. Don't think I won't be cheering for you tonight."

"We all love watching you play," said Kirk Wilder without taking his eyes off the road. "Is Judith going to the game tonight, Ellie?"

Ellie cleared her throat. "No. I guess she's having boy problems. I'll have to find someone else to hang out with during the game."

"You're always welcome to sit with us, honey," said her mom with a look of concern.

"I'll be fine," said Ellie. "I'm not *that* big of a loser." She said it with a wry grin.

"Ouch," said her dad.

"Just kidding. I probably am." Her quip earned her another worried look from her mom.

Ellie messaged Andy when they arrived at the stadium. Although it wasn't quite dark yet, the lights were on and the stands were half full.

Meet me at the snack stand. His response brought another bout of nerves. Ellie hugged her sister and wished her luck before telling her parents she felt like walking around.

As she waded through the parents who preferred to stand the whole game, she passed a group of younger kids playing tag and giggling as they ran around the human obstacles. Ellie paused for a brief moment, fondly remembering her own carefree days now long past.

The snack stand was not busy, as apparently, most of the crowd was either not hungry or had used up their snack credits for the month. She found Andy standing near the side of the small structure, and he appeared to be in a conversation with Alice from class. A pang of jealousy dropped in Ellie's stomach. She made eye contact with Andy, and he smiled warmly, motioning her over.

"Oh hi, Ellie," said Alice in quite possibly her sweetest voice. For all of Alice's prowess with the TEAMMATE Rulebook, she usually went to extra lengths to make herself stand out from the rest of her Teammates. Tonight, it was ribbons in her hair and painted nails—both of which matched the color of the team that Molly was playing against.

"Hi, Alice." Ellie hoped it came out with an air of indifference. "I see your sister must be playing against Molly's team tonight."

Alice giggled. "Yes, we killed you guys last time." She stopped herself, apparently trying to sound more TEAMMATE appropriate. "But all these kids are learning so much and getting better every week. I think tonight might be a closer match."

"Yes. Praise the team," Ellie managed the response with only mild sarcasm.

"It was nice talking with you," Andy said abruptly. He was trying to conceal his grin from Ellie's slogan.

Ellie caught the disappointment in Alice's eyes.

The girl looked from Andy to Ellie and shrugged. "Okay. Well, I hope you enjoy the game. Amy is number seven, so keep an eye on her."

"Molly is number eleven," returned Ellie. "Let's hope for a fun game."

"Of course," said Alice as she walked away while studying the ground a little too intently.

Ellie stared at Andy, and not without judgment in her eyes. He grinned back.

"Don't be mad," he said with a laugh. "I was standing here alone, and Alice must have felt bad for me."

"Yeah, she felt sooo bad," Ellie said it with narrowed eyes and plenty of sarcasm this time.

"You're also cute when you're jealous." He looked around. "Let's go somewhere more private to watch the game. Don't worry about Alice. She's definitely not my type."

This made Ellie feel better. "And what's your type?"

"You," he said, without smiling. "We'll go to the top of the bleachers where no one can overhear us."

Ellie followed him up the aluminum stairs to the back row of the bleachers. Darkness was descending around them, but the stadium lights fought off its effects. The empty space at the top had the additional advantage of everyone looking the opposite way from the pair—that is, only after they'd climbed past the other fans. Ellie saw her dad's eyebrows rise as she walked by. She also caught him nudging her mom, who'd been watching Molly warm up on the field, with a nod toward her and Andy.

"This looks perfect," said Andy. "I can see number eleven."

"Be sure to watch number seven." Ellie tilted her head with exaggeration as she squeaked the words out. But now she was able to laugh about it. After all, she was the one sitting alone with Andy.

"You're not going to let that go anytime soon, are you?"

"Nah, I'm over it already. However, I think I might enjoy giving you a hard time. And...I also think you're cuter when you think you're in trouble."

He laughed. "That's not very TEAMMATE of you." He paused. "And I guess that's another reason why I like you."

"If I knew that's what you liked, I'd have gone anti-TEAMMATE years ago. Speaking of which, we better not let Judith find out your weakness." She almost laughed before remembering her friend's boy problems.

"We already solved that problem." Andy casually stretched before Ellie felt his arm around her, pulling her closer. "Besides, you can't fake what you believe. It's apparent in everything you do."

Ellie liked his arm around her. She took his other hand and held it tight. "There is a problem with Judith and Clint. I have a bad feeling Judith is going to lack a boyfriend soon."

Andy looked surprised. "Really? I thought it was going well."

"Yeah, it had been. But she's giving him some type of ultimatum tonight. We tried to work on our group project, but she wasn't able to concentrate. She thinks he's not serious enough about their future."

"They've dated for what, not even two weeks?"

"Longer if you count the messages beforehand."

Andy sighed. "Well, I tried. It's disappointing, but it's difficult to make people happy for long, I suppose."

"Unfortunately."

The game began and quickly became a one-sided affair. It seemed that Alice's sister Amy was quite gifted as she promptly scored two goals, one of which was while Molly tried to guard her. A third try was thwarted by a block from Ellie's sister, which finally gave Andy and her something to stand and cheer about. Ellie wanted to kiss him right then, but some of the fans in front turned around, perplexed as to what there was to cheer about. And so instead, Ellie stared sideways at his lips, wondering what a kiss might be like. Andy caught her staring out of the corner of his eye.

"What are you thinking about?" he asked with that all-knowing grin.

Ellie didn't want to come out and say it, but a fun idea took shape in her mind. "If you guess correctly, I'll tell you." She winked at him as a subtle hint.

"Hmm," he said as he ran his fingers over his smooth chin. "I guess I have no idea what you're thinking, but I know I'm thinking about your lips."

Despite herself, Ellie blushed before she giggled.

"You're thinking the same thing, aren't you?" he asked.

She nodded, suddenly unable to think or speak coherently.

Andy pulled her closer before placing a gentle kiss on her cheek. He looked deeply in her eyes, and she felt herself melting, afraid she might slip through the bleachers into a puddle on the ground below.

"Something like that?" he asked.

"Very close," she nodded with a smile.

"Good. I'm on the right track." He squeezed her hand tighter.

Ellie took a deep breath. "There's still something I have to tell you."

"There really isn't anything you *have* to tell me."

"I want to."

"Okay," he nodded. There was no worry, no doubt, no hesitation in his response. Of course, Andy Jacobs was always as confident as a councilmember. It was something that Ellie was beginning to love about him, even if she didn't share the same trait.

"On the way home, assuming I'm allowed to ride with you."

"Great," he said, beginning to stand. "The game's almost over. Let's go ask your parents now."

—Article 6 of the TEAMMATE Rulebook

CHAPTER
TWENTY-ONE

As Ellie was leading Andy down the bleacher stairs, the game officially ended. Of course, it was actually over long before, as the score was 7-0. She had been planning to message her parents from afar and was surprised by Andy's direct approach. He was not intimidated by anything, at least not yet. It made Ellie more hopeful that he might be the only Teammate who could understand her plight and take her side. A gratuitous side effect was that his boldness made him even more attractive.

The other fans began standing and gathering their belongings when the two appeared next to Kirk and Anne Wilder.

When her mother made eye contact with her, she actually looked pleased. "Ellie, who is this young man?" She asked the question with a coy smile.

Ellie cleared her throat, and her dad now also made eye contact with her and Andy. "Hey guys, this is Andy."

Andy immediately offered his hand to Anne and then to Kirk in a gesture of TEAMMATE solidarity. "Mr. and Mrs. Wilder, it's so nice to meet you. I wanted to ask your permission to drive Ellie home tonight."

Kirk looked hesitantly toward Anne, who nodded in enthusiasm. She responded for him. "I think that should be fine, as long as she's not home too late."

Andy smiled warmly. "I wouldn't dream of keeping her out late. I happen to have some extra credits, and we might stop for ice cream on the way."

Now it was Kirk's turn to assert his protective fatherly duty. "Just make sure you drive safely and slowly. How long have you had your license?"

Andy's confident eyes locked onto Kirk's. "I've had it for three months, with no infractions and no accidents. I promise you I would never put your daughter in danger."

Kirk redirected his stare to Ellie. "Okay. I suppose you can go. But please be careful. I love you." Ellie could see the worry in his eyes relent ever so slightly. Anne put her hand on Kirk's shoulder in support.

Relief washed over Ellie, and she hugged both her parents in thanks. "I love you, too. Thank you. And tell Molly she did great tonight. We were cheering when she blocked that shot."

Within seconds, the teenagers were making their way to Andy's car, although their progress was hampered by the parents and fans waiting around for their children. As they navigated the crowd, Andy's hand immediately found Ellie's. Whenever they were in close proximity as of late, the reaction had become magnetic. Despite being an unusually independent Teammate, Ellie found she liked following his lead.

As they reached his car, Andy held her door open before walking around the front of the car. The lights from the field reflected in his eyes and his teeth, which were now visible due to that all-knowing smile. He lowered himself into his seat. "Thanks for inviting me to the game."

"Thanks for driving me home," she said wryly. "Am I really getting ice cream tonight?"

"Absolutely. I'm not even hungry, but I wanted an excuse to spend more time with you. The game went by far too quickly."

Ellie laughed. "That's not something I usually say, but tonight I agree." She paused thoughtfully. "You really shouldn't waste your credits on ice cream if you're not hungry. TEAMMATE would consider that wasteful and disapprove."

"All the more reason to order a double scoop," he said. The car lurched forward, now merging in line with the other leading fringe of departing vehicles. Their headlights lit up the chain of cars that slowly snaked their way to the main road.

"I have a better idea," said Ellie. "Let's split a milkshake. I still have a snack credit, and I'm apparently the only one who's hungry."

"I like that idea, but my idea means we use my credit. Sorry, but I must insist."

"Okay," Ellie said with a sigh. "I'm not going to fight with you about it—especially since I still have things to tell you." She took a measured breath. "I need you to understand, what I'm about to say might make me sound crazy."

"I love crazy," Andy said with a glance at the car ahead of them. "But can it wait until the milkshake? I'm enjoying your company as it is. And I want to make myself clear. You can totally keep whatever secret you think is so shocking. I'm not worried about it in the least. I've thought about all the scenarios, and I can't imagine any that would affect my feelings for you."

"That's exactly why I want to tell you. I can't keep this in anymore. No one else has ever been able to joke about TEAMMATE the way that we do. I'm only worried the truth might put you in danger."

Andy stared ahead a few seconds in thought before laughter broke his silence. "You can't even guess half the TEAMMATE Rules that I've stretched, bent, or outright broken when needed." He raised an eyebrow. "And that's because I'm good at not getting caught."

"I'm not scared either," she countered. "I think we're different than the others. And I've been thinking over what you said about the algorithm keeping us separated. It makes total sense."

Now that they were on the road, Andy glanced over for just a second. "I don't sound so crazy now, huh? Well, if the brain of our class agrees, I must be onto something."

"But let's say it is true," continued Ellie. "And let's say hypothetically that we continue to date, fall in love, and want to make a future together but can't...because of TEAMMATE."

"Then we burn the system down," Andy said without hesitation. "I can't picture how, but I think if anyone could figure out a way to change it, it's people like us."

Ellie nodded thoughtfully at his words. She looked up to see the sign for the ice cream shop. They pulled into a parking place in the back, far away from the other patrons. There was a small line in which they waited patiently before Andy ordered the largest-sized milkshake. It was actually worth two credits, which defeated her premise of sharing, but Ellie didn't bother to argue the point. If he wanted to share with her, she decided to embrace it. It was one step closer to a kiss, and she could only hope he'd still want one by the time the night was through.

They went back to his car, and Ellie started on the nearly 16-ounce serving. The normal-sized straw seemed puny compared to the container. However, the iced dairy and sugar felt cool and intoxicating on her tongue. A dessert like this was a rarity, especially in this volume.

"Mmm," she said. With a smile, she handed him the container, and he took a short taste.

"Very good," he said. "Definitely worth it."

"Take some more," Ellie insisted. "There's way too much for me. Plus, I want you in good spirits before I crush everything."

He laughed, but Ellie did not, watching his mannerisms closely.

"Are you happy?" he asked, handing it back.

"I am...although there's something that would make me happier."

"Really?" he asked with eyebrows raised. "Would it involve me leaning over there for something besides that straw?"

Despite the gravity of the situation, Ellie let out a short, nervous laugh. "You're pretty sly, but before you do that, let me talk. Then we'll see how you really feel."

He smiled and crossed his arms. "Totally not worried, but clearly you are, so let's get it over so I can kiss you."

The words gave her chills of anticipation, but she'd already made up her mind to tell him the truth first. She took a breath. "Okay, here it goes. So basically, I think I have some certain...abilities. When you had your seizure, I know you felt it too."

"For the record, I did feel it and that's totally cool, even if I have no idea what you did," he said.

"Well, the answer is with...paganism." She looked deeply in his eyes for shock, fear, or perhaps laughter? She didn't see any of these things. In fact, she saw a look of genuine interest. "Should I continue, or have you heard enough?"

Andy's finger grazed his cheek line. "Please continue. It's not a scenario I thought about, but I'm not frightened in the least."

"Okay, I found a journal that talks about a specific form of paganism, but apparently that's not even the right description. Anyways, I think it was left specifically for me by my late grandmother, whom I never met." She kept her gaze locked on the boy. "She had an ability to foresee things. In it, she claims that she knew I would find it and that I would start to possess...abilities before what is to come."

"Hmm," said Andy. "I felt whatever ability you have, so I might be the one person at this point who believes you. Tell me, have you used your ability on anything else?"

Ellie nodded. "In the hospital, I think I helped cure a man with an arrhythmia. One minute he was irregular, and after I touched him, within thirty seconds it stopped. The doctor said it could happen at any time, but what are the odds?"

Andy cleared his throat. "You might find this surprising, but I don't doubt any of this. My only question is, why is this happening? What is the 'before what is to come' part that the journal referred to?"

"So even if you believe me, this is the part that might disturb you." Ellie took a breath. "I don't understand it all yet, but I'm supposed to be a catalyst to bring this banned practice back. I don't know how, but the things she mentions in this journal are starting to make more sense by the day. I'm scared, Andy." Her voice started to sound shrill. "I had no one I could talk to about this until you. I'm starting to see more problems with TEAMMATE by the minute. Our conversations tell me you might see it too. I thought it was just interesting history at first. These words are written on paper, Andy. I'm in so much trouble if anyone finds out. Do you understand what it feels like to be helpless? I can't explain healing you. I can't explain why all I see is hypocrisy in the TEAMMATE Rulebook. All I know is that I've entrapped myself in this dangerous struggle for truth and now I've put you at risk as well."

Andy took her hand in his. Then he did something unexpected. He leaned over, without a word, and gently kissed her lips. Her body, which had been shaking in fear mixed with sorrow, now froze. Instinctively, she kissed him back. Was she supposed to shut her eyes? How did it work? At that moment, he pulled her closer. He had his eyes closed. It felt rude to watch him, so she closed her eyes. The kiss became more intense. The sensation was warm and made her heart beat faster. She tasted the vanilla from the milkshake. She liked this feeling very much. It felt strange yet wonderful to Ellie. It was like neither one could breathe, and they needed each other desperately. The feeling of being needed nearly overwhelmed Ellie. Was it real? Was it merely surges of adrenaline, serotonin, and dopamine, or something more? Was she even doing it right? She stopped caring. He was showing her that he wasn't afraid of her dilemma. He was comforting her without words. In fact, who would ever want words again? He believed her. Why else would he kiss her?

After a few delightful minutes, their lips parted, and both grinned at each other in surprise.

"As I predicted, your attempt to scare me off failed," he finally said as he stared longingly at her. "I'm sorry, I wasn't sure what to say to comfort you, but what just happened sums up how I feel. Did it feel alright to you?"

Ellie nodded, unable to wipe the smile from her lips. "I liked that answer. So...you're not terrified of me?"

"Maybe I just have a weak spot for outlaws, but if possible, I think I'm even deeper in love."

"So, what should I do?" Her voice betrayed the hint of worry that lingered.

"I think you mean, what should we do?" He winked. "We already said it ourselves. The algorithm will try to stop us at some point. I can't live like that, Ellie." He leaned in closer. "I won't. I guess that means...if you're here to bring it all down, I'll ride with you."

His words were a soft blanket falling upon her shoulders, covering her in safety, giving her warmth and courage. It was exactly what Ellie needed to hear. She had no idea how the future would develop, but having Andy with her made her realize she could take on the world.

Her feelings needed to manifest physically. Ellie's worries had finally been subdued. In their place was a longing for this boy. She didn't wait to take his lead this time. Instead, she recognized his surprised approval when she pulled his face closer to her own. Ellie's second kiss was even more intense than her first.

—Article 3 of the TEAMMATE Rulebook

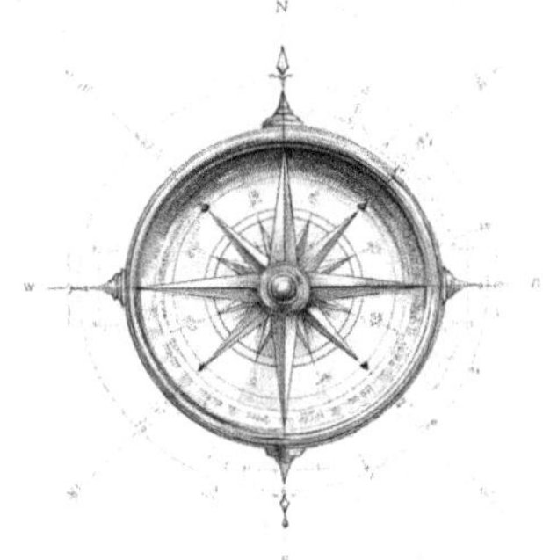

CHAPTER
TWENTY-TWO

Ellie spared Judith the details from the previous evening during the bus ride to school the next morning. Judith didn't seem to be in a talkative mood anyway. In fact, all Ellie could get out of her friend was a sad shake of her head after she asked about her talk with Clint. It was to be expected, she supposed. Describing her osculation session with Andy Jacobs would not be the kind of therapy her friend needed at the moment. Ellie wanted to offer support or advice, but realized she wasn't experienced enough to advise on such matters. While things had gone well for her last night, she had no explanation of how it had all come together. It seemed like blind luck. Ellie was grateful that Andy had left no doubt that he was going to support her, but had things gone differently, today would be a much darker day—enough to make Judith's current wreck of a relationship seem like a minor speedbump. Thankfully, things hadn't turned out that way, and Andy now knew and would protect her secret.

A surprise greeted the sorting class that morning when they took their seats in homeroom. Miss Conway was absent from her desk, and Principal Flannery was in her place. In addition, a tall woman stood at the podium before the children. She seemed anxious, as her eyes darted around the room after the bell rang.

Principal Flannery stood. "Please give a warm reception to our guest speaker this morning." He motioned for the speaker to introduce herself before sitting back down.

"Good morning, Teammates," began the tall woman. "My name is Jade Morrow, and I'm here to speak with you today about the Waste Management branch of TEAMMATE."

Ellie saw a hand shoot up in the front from Alice.

"Oh, good, I love questions." She shot a quick glance at Flannery before continuing. "Go ahead, dear."

Alice responded. "Where is Miss Conway? Our calendar had our Waste Management introduction for later this week. We were supposed to turn in our homework and discuss the Agricultural branch this morning."

Jade Morrow looked toward Principal Flannery before responding. "I was just as surprised at the change as all of you are, my dear. I'm afraid something unexpected must have come up. I was reassigned early this morning."

Principal Flannery cleared his throat. "I'm afraid your teacher may be out for a few days," he said. "I don't have any further details on her absence, not that I could share them with you if I did. We've rearranged your curriculum the best we could on short notice. You will still have your visit from the Agricultural branch this afternoon as scheduled."

Ellie couldn't shake the feeling that something felt off with Flannery in the room. She made eye contact with Andy, who shrugged at her before turning to the front of the classroom. As promised, the guest lecturer began talking about careers in the Waste Management branch. It was not a highly sought-after field, the woman speaking admitted, but it was essential to the functioning of the sector. Without waste management, garbage would pile up, water would be polluted, and disease would spread without mercy, as it had in ancient times.

"And so, we are able to reuse eighty percent of the waste generated by our sector," the woman continued. "Recycling plastic, glass, and aluminum accounts for the majority of savings. There is also a decent proportion that can be transformed into energy cubes, which help offset the sector's energy needs. Our wonderful bracelets collect most of what we need," she held up her wrist, adorned with her own shiny band of technology. "But sometimes it's not enough energy, especially when extra power is needed for heating and cooling during extreme weather conditions."

A hand rose from the back.

"I bet you're curious about these mysterious energy cubes, aren't you, young lady? Or did you have another question?"

Judith cleared her throat. "May I have a restroom pass?"

The speaker looked confused as to why anyone would want to leave during this particular segment. "Well...sure, if you must."

Ellie saw Principal Flannery's jaw tighten while seated at Miss Conway's desk, but he didn't intervene. The Waste Management representative looked longingly for another question before continuing on. "Since no one wants to ask the question, I'll just tell you. Energy cubes are one of the most fascinating byproducts of waste management. They condense the more combustible components of our daily waste into a manageable cube about the size of an automobile. Some extra elements are added to increase the heat and energy release upon combustion, and voilà; we have storable backup energy that can be handed over to the Energy department."

"How do they move something so heavy?" asked a boy a few rows from Ellie.

The woman smiled. "I'm glad you asked. We have large machines that can pick up the cubes as easily as you can pick up a jug of water.

And we need skilled Teammates to operate those machines on a daily basis. Why, the Waste Management branch probably has more heavy machinery than any other department in the sector. We even have ancient technology we've repurposed that runs on fossil fuels."

"Why would we use that?" asked Becca from the back. "I thought fossil fuels created pollution."

"You are absolutely right, young lady. They do. We've made the vehicles more efficient, but there is still a cost to the old technology. However, these particular trucks are a necessity for our fleet. Does anyone know why?"

She looked among the blank expressions eagerly.

"I suppose you aren't aware then," she said matter-of-factly. "Does no one wonder what happens to the twenty percent of waste that cannot be reused?" Again, there were no hands. "Why, it has to leave the sector to be discarded on the outside, of course. We can't pollute the finite sector soil with unusable waste," she chuckled. "Every vehicle, every machine, and every piece of technology runs on power from our internal grid. But if one were to leave the sector and cross the fence to the other side, they would find that absolutely no technology works! And therefore, our trucks would be unable to haul the enormous amount of waste to the outside dump if we did not utilize *some* dirty energy."

"How big is the waste area?" asked Becca again.

"Quite large, dear. And continuously growing, I might add. I've only seen pictures, but it would occupy too much essential space to be located inside the sector. It might be bigger than the capital if measured."

The statement seemed to amaze the whole class into silence. That amazement would prove short-lived as the lecture continued on to include less stimulating topics such as waste collection days, water treatment techniques, and strategies to reduce non-recyclable waste. As the morning progressed, it almost seemed as if Jade Morrow was intentionally trying to bore them to death. Or perhaps she was assigned a longer-than-usual speaking period on a very dry subject with the purpose of occupying more time. Whatever the reason, when the bell finally rang, Ellie couldn't get out of the room fast enough.

"I suppose that's all the time I have with you," she tried to speak above the growing commotion. "If you ever have additional questions, don't hesitate to reach out to me at the Waste Management headquarters on the western side of the sector."

Ellie shot Andy an incredulous look, nodding toward the speaker as if anyone would willingly want to spend more time on garbage.

"What was that all about?" She whispered the words so the woman wouldn't overhear as they left the room.

Andy shrugged again.

She continued on, louder now that her words would be drowned out by the activities in the hallway. "Didn't it feel like something was off today? Why do you think Miss Conway could be gone for multiple days?"

Andy took her hand and smiled. "Who knows? Maybe she's sick? I'm more worried about what's going on with Judith. She never came back to class."

He was right. Her best friend might be having a meltdown in the bathroom. "I almost forgot," she said. "I think things might be over with Clint. She didn't seem to want to say too much this morning." She hesitated. "I should go check on her."

"Who's going to walk me to class?" Andy mock-pouted with his lower lip out.

"Eww," laughed Ellie. "That is definitely not your look."

"Double ouch," said Andy. "Okay, I get it. Make sure your friend's okay. I'll see you after your next class, then?"

"Of course," said Ellie. "You're stuck with me now."

"That's fine with me." That all-knowing smile flashed, and Ellie felt herself wanting another kiss. Was it possible to become addicted after two kisses?

She regrettably released his hand, a look of longing on her face as she headed for the girls' restroom. Was that desire she saw reflected in his eyes?

Pushing the wonderful distraction from her mind, she shoved the swinging door open. The bathroom appeared empty.

"Judith, are you in here?" She ducked to the floor to check for feet in the stalls. No one appeared to be there. Puzzled, she slowly walked along the row of doors, trying each until she found the corner one locked. "Judith, is that you?" she asked.

Her bracelet buzzed with a message.

Ellie instinctively checked her wrist. The sender was scrambled. That was unusual. Ellie read the message.

Ellie, this is urgent. Meet me at the back gymnasium exit now. TEAMMATE knows.

She froze in horror. Could it be a prank? Who was this? The only person who knew her secret was Andy, and he could have whispered in her ear. She messaged back immediately. *Who is this?*

Seconds later, the bracelet vibrated.

A friend of G. W.

Ellie's stomach dropped. Even Andy wouldn't know that. There were only two minutes until the bell rang again. The icy grip of panic froze her in place. What should she do?

The Key Stored Memory test is a marvel of engineering. Long past are the times of a jury of peers to distinguish innocence or guilt. Teammates have nothing to fear from such advancement unless they are an adversary of the team.

—Article 99 of the TEAMMATE Rulebook

CHAPTER
TWENTY-THREE

Ellie arrived short of breath at the gymnasium's back exit. No one was there. The final bell rang. There was no gym class this period, and so the large, open space was eerily quiet except for her heavy breathing. The exit had glass doors and an emergency exit sign. Ellie looked at the sign. That's strange, she thought. The exit sign isn't glowing red.

She followed the power cord of the sign down to ground level. It hung, unconnected. Ellie picked up the cord and realized it had been cut by something. Someone must have disabled the alarm.

Just then, a red car skidded to a stop behind the glass door. A red-haired woman sat in the driver's seat and motioned for her to hurry.

Ellie was frozen again. Should she get in the car with this stranger? Where would they take her? Nobody could hide from TEAMMATE for long. She started to take a step back from the door when her bracelet received a general TEAMMATE Emergency message. *Officials are responding to student threat at TEAMMATE High. School is now on lockdown.*

Was the threat her or was it this woman, anxiously waiting in the car? Unsure, Ellie took a few more steps away from the door when the gymnasium door opened and two officials burst through.

"That's her!" said one of the uniformed men. They broke into a sprint across the basketball court.

Her indecisiveness immediately thawed. Ellie turned and sprinted for the waiting car. She could hear the footsteps echoing behind her as she reached for the door.

"We've got her cornered," one of the officials said into his bracelet. "The lockdown won't let anyone escape."

Ellie pushed the exit door handle and stumbled alongside the waiting car. The woman pointed to the back seat, and Ellie's fear pushed her inside. The woman hit the vehicle's accelerator, leaving behind two stunned officials who'd just reached the obviously unlocked exit.

"If you could just put on your seatbelt, dear." The woman's rough voice sounded like it belonged to the TEAMMATEs that lived in the retirement home. She reached behind her seat with her free hand and dropped a heavy metal clamp-like device in Ellie's lap. "If we are to get away, I'll need you to put that wrist cloak over your bracelet. Otherwise, TEAMMATE will have no difficulty tracking us."

Ellie placed the heavy cuff over her bracelet with her heart pounding. The metal device fit tightly around her wrist but had a perfectly-sized indentation for her wristband.

"Who are you and where are you taking me?" The questions exploded out of Ellie. Had she made the right choice? The car sped out of the school's parking lot, and Ellie noticed three marked TEAMMATE official cruisers parked near Principal Flannery's office.

The woman spoke calmly, glancing into the rearview mirror. "You can call me Em. I'm taking you somewhere safe. If we get there, I can answer more of your questions. If we don't," the woman hesitated for a moment, "there are good people whom I need to protect. The less you know, the safer they are."

"How do you know about G.W.?"

Em maneuvered the car through a residential section, now driving much slower. The car came to a stop. "Your grandma, Grace, and I were quite close. Can you help me remove the red film? We'll never escape if they're looking for a red car."

So, G.W. *was* her grandmother. That made sense, Grace Wilder. Such an unusual name she'd never heard before. Ellie didn't have long to ponder this as the two exited the vehicle and began pulling off the panels of red stickers. They came off quite easily to reveal a gray finish underneath. The final touch was Em pulling off the license plate sticker to reveal a different registration number. "Throw the garbage in the back seat and come up front," instructed Em.

The level of deception being orchestrated far exceeded anything Ellie thought possible. You could block bracelet signals? You could disguise vehicles and forge registrations? What kind of people was Em connected with?

Ellie slid into the front beside Em. Her rescuer now reached the top of her head and pulled off the red wig, revealing a short gray hairstyle underneath. She tossed the wig into the back and casually began driving much slower through the neighborhood. When they reached a main road, they saw a TEAMMATE official cruiser fly past them with lights on and siren blaring. Ellie held her breath, but the cruiser was not interested in their vehicle's description.

Em pulled onto the main road and headed south, continuing to drive much slower than before.

"We've reached phase three," she said, turning to smile at Ellie. "I can tell you a little more information now." The car signaled another turn, and Ellie realized they were traveling west now. "You're probably wondering how I even know you. As I said, I was a friend of Grace Wilder, your grandmother. Being such, I also used to be well acquainted with you father. He got word that the officials were coming for you and tracked me down."

"My dad knows that all this is happening?"

"He was warned this morning that they were coming for you. Obviously, he couldn't rescue you without becoming the number one suspect, and so that's where I come in. I've been waiting for this day for a very long time. Grace always had an ability to see things before they happened."

Ellie thought about these words. They definitely matched up with the journal. Could she be telling the truth?

"If you knew this was coming, why did you wait for my dad to track you down?"

The old lady glanced sideways from the road before answering. "You don't miss much, do you? It had to be this way because we're not in the business of stealing children, relatively speaking."

"If everything you say is true, my dad is in danger. Surely, they'll question him and give him a KPM test. He'll be locked up for good." Ellie's stomach dropped at the thought.

"I'd heard you were a very deductive young lady. You're absolutely right. They will do all those things. But...here's possibly the hardest part for him. He was given an eraser pill by the informant who told him you were in danger. Do you know what that is?"

Ellie's look of confusion was answer enough.

"It does exactly what the name implies. It erases your memory, usually back to where the person woke up for the day, although sometimes longer. It's used by TEAMMATE after unpleasant interrogations like the KSM test. This is all, of course, uncommon knowledge you understand."

"Does he know where you're taking me?"

"No," said Em with a sigh. "We couldn't risk it in case something went wrong. He wanted you to know he loves you. It was killing him not to be with you right now. He could tell no one what happened, of course. He's probably already taken the pill and is just as confused as your mother and everyone else right now that you're missing."

Ellie painfully thought about her parents' hopeless search for her. She thought about Molly, who'd be confused as she rode the bus home alone yet again. She thought about the questioning they'd all now have to endure from TEAMMATE. She thought about Andy. He'd be looking for her after their next class. Was it really all over now?

They'd now reached the more rural western zone. The houses were sparse, and it was mostly wooded in the unoccupied spaces. This was the largest standing lumber yard inside the perimeter fence. The Forestry branch managed the renewable resources out here.

"Do we know how TEAMMATE found out about me?" Ellie had to ask but dreaded the answer. What were the odds that within less than twenty-four hours of telling Andy, they'd come for her?

"We do," said Em with a tone of caution in her voice. "I'm not sure you'll like the answer, though."

Ellie could feel her throat tightening. *Please don't say Andy. It can't be him. I'd bet my life it wasn't him.* "I need to know," she finally said.

Em nodded, clearly still in thought. "Before I tell you, you must remember that forgiveness is something we'll all need at some point in our lives. Everyone has made mistakes in the past, and we'll all make more. If you've read what Grace left you, you're well into your journey for knowledge. But there's always further to go."

Ellie's heart was a butterfly struggling to stay above ground. "Please tell me."

Em looked away before answering. "It was Judith," she said. "She reported on the TEAMMATE tip line about your outburst in class. Immediately, the TEAMMATE network scoured all your communications, all your history, and I'm afraid, your home this morning."

"They found my journal?" gasped Ellie.

"I'm afraid so."

"But why?" pleaded Ellie. "Why would my best friend do this to me? Why couldn't it be Blake who told his father? Why wasn't it Miss

Conway who'd reported me? Why my best friend who claimed me as a sister?" Then, Ellie thought of something else. "They questioned Miss Conway, didn't they? Is that why she's not in school?"

Em cleared her throat. "It's more akin to say TEAMMATE tortured your teacher. I believe they picked her up under the cover of darkness as they assessed your threat level. If they ever do end up letting her come back, she'll have no memory of what they did to her or what she told them. You must understand that Thurman Graves, the head of the Security branch, is ruthless in his efforts to eliminate our kind. As far as why Judith did it, if you ever get the chance, you can ask her. I honestly can't say."

Judith's behavior that morning now made more sense. But had her breakup with Clint fueled her to rat out Ellie's outburst in class? Em could talk about forgiveness until she was blue in the face, but how could Judith ever deserve such a thing? She hadn't just ended Ellie's relationship with Andy. She'd ended every Teammate relationship Ellie had and ever would have.

Ellie said nothing else as she sorted her thoughts out. She regrettably decided to accept what Em told her as the truth. How else could it all have happened?

Em slowed at the next crossroad and turned left. There were very few cars on the road here.

She's heading south now. It made sense to avoid the central highway that ran north and south through the middle of the sector. There would be many more eyes and cameras watching there, even if they were looking for a vehicle of a different description than their own.

After a few moments, Em said gently, "I think it's safe enough to fill you in on more of the plan."

Ellie sat with her arms folded. "I can't go back, can I?"

"Not for some time. I'm taking you to be with your people, on the other side."

Ellie sat up. "I can't stay hidden in the sector?"

"Too dangerous. But you still have more truths to uncover. Truths that you need to experience. I can't tell you things and expect you to believe my words." She took her eyes off the road to look at Ellie. "It was always supposed to be this way, you understand."

Ellie was nearly drowning in disbelief. Last night, she'd experienced her first kiss. It was wonderful. The boy actually understood her. They were going to take on the sector together. And now she must leave him and everything else behind. "How are you getting me through the fence?" she asked.

"We'll be there soon. I have my own ways, but they're always on a scheduled regimen when there's maintenance on the power grid. There is no chance of that happening in the next month. For this to work, you're going to need to use your abilities, my dear."

"I can do that?" Ellie gasped.

"We must have faith that you can; otherwise, this has all been for naught."

CHAPTER
TWENTY-FOUR

As time passed, they traded the scenery of the western forests for the southern agricultural lands. Ellie had been to the area once before on a field trip, but beyond that, there was no reason to visit the agricultural zone. Like the western sector, the homes were sparse here as well, but the trees had been cleared to allow the large-scale farming that fed the entirety of TEAMMATE. Open fields of corn, soybeans, and wheat seemed to continue on forever. There were also grassy tracts of fenced-in land with livestock sprinkled into the landscape. Some of the fields had already been relieved of their produce and now sat empty. A few fields were in the process of being harvested by large machines, while still other plots had Teammates picking the produce by hand.

When the car finally stopped, Ellie saw the giant southern boundary of dead space that separated human life from the wasteland beyond. Steel poles towered over the barren soil every fifty yards like sentries, transmitting deadly waves of energy that prevented anyone from getting through—alive, at least. These gigantic metal rods stood as high as the tallest tree and hummed in unmistakable warning, as a hive of bees cautions wide berth. The ground produced no vegetation in the space leading up to the sector border. The other side was just as lifeless for perhaps a hundred yards before the foliage erupted in a wild, dense forest that concealed the secrets of past human civilization.

"We're here," said Em. "I have a rucksack packed for your journey." She nodded to the bag in the backseat. Then she inhaled slowly and continued. "I realize you're scared, but understand that this trip beyond our borders is necessary before you can bring about the change needed."

Ellie made no move to leave the car. She stared sideways at her white-haired rescuer. "But why does it have to be me? I'm not special. I'm one of the worst Teammates in my class when it comes to working together...to leading a team. How can I accomplish anything out here on my own?"

Em folded her hands upon her lap patiently. "Many before you asked the same question when they were called. None were perfect. In fact, many that you've read about at one time were considered the worst in society. But they changed into a better version of themselves. Also, they didn't do it alone. You won't be alone after you leave the sector. You will have Him and His people to guide you."

Ellie's eyes met Em's. "Am I going to the reeducation camp? I've seen the footage."

Em grimaced. "I'm afraid all you've seen is propaganda portrayed by actors. You'll soon see the truth for yourself. I've gotten a handful of Teammates through the fence over the last few years, with help. They won't be what you're expecting, and although my name holds weight with them, they've likely become somewhat wild on their own. But they will listen to you when you speak with His authority."

"Can I ever come back?"

"Your return is the reason for all the preparation. But first, you must experience the truth. If you are ever to lead effectively, you must see everything from the other side of our sector."

Ellie swallowed hard. At least she wouldn't be alone. She slowly put her hand on the door latch and opened her door. She could do this. She *had* to do this. Her trembling foot touched the ground, and she stood in defiance upon the lifeless soil. She slowly opened the back door to grab the backpack Em had prepared for her. Its heft was substantial when she put it on her shoulder, but until she found help, she'd need to rely upon everything in that bag to keep her alive.

Em emerged from her seat and hurried around the vehicle to give her a hug.

In that moment, Ellie felt the full weight of everything she was leaving behind. Her parents, her sister, Andy, her home, all the conveniences of society, and her own future within TEAMMATE would all be lost. More than fear, it was sadness that washed over her as she clung to Em, shaking with sorrow.

Em looked her over in concern. "Your grandmother would have been here if she could. She would have given anything, but that was not how it played out. The most important thing is that you've made it this far. Grace shared her visions with me in order to help you, and now my own part is nearly complete. I know those tears are painful, my child. My heart grieves for your loss of this familiar world. But this world is not all that it seems. Despite our triumphs and advances, within TEAMMATE, we have forgotten the most vital part of our purpose in this world. You are intended to reveal that purpose. You must receive His instructions and find His people."

"But how will I know which way to go?"

The old lady reached into her pocket and handed Ellie a metal tool, ancient in appearance. It was round with a face not unlike an old clock. "This is a compass. The arrow will always point north. Once you find true north, you will know every direction needed out there. After you pass through, you'll find an old roadbed that leads west. Follow its path. And as soon as you're on the other side, remove your bracelet cover and use the cutter in your backpack to remove your bracelet. It will be useless to you out here and too dangerous to wear when you return."

"But it's deadly to remove your bracelet."

"It's only deadly inside the sector. TEAMMATE has no power out there, my child. And if you succeed, it will have no power when you return. Go in peace, Ellie Wilder. Don't forget to continue your reading. I've packed the text for you. Best you hurry, before a drone spots us."

Ellie took a step towards the humming fence. An unexpected question surfaced in her mind. "Is TEAMMATE really so bad that it can't be fixed?"

Em stood, hands together and looked upward. After a pause she said, "I think you'll come to your own opinion of that soon enough, my godchild."

Godchild? What was that supposed to mean? Ellie didn't have long to ponder the question as her legs moved forward, closer to the humming sound of what should be death. As she approached, she saw a dove on the ground, pecking in the dirt. She glanced back at Em before watching the small bird take flight toward the boundary. Ellie watched in horror as its wings beat quickly before gliding gently into the space between the metal rods. A groan from the towers could be heard and the bird dropped from the air, falling unnaturally to the ground.

Ellie put a hand to her mouth as she cast her gaze on the unmoving feathered body. She bowed her head in fear and asked for safe passage. Sweat began to pour out of her. Her bracelet's heart rate alarm could be heard, although it was muffled by its heavy cover. *Please let me pass. Let me do what I am meant to do. Please guide me for I am scared and ignorant.* She moved forward whispering these words, her body shaking uncontrollably. She took only one glance back to Em, who was now on her knees, with head bowed in silent prayer as well.

Ellie's throat was dry. She needed to swallow but found it difficult. How was she ever going to pass? Her legs moved onward, now ten feet from the boundary. She'd been able to heal others by asking for help, but this was the first time she'd asked anything for herself. Would it work? The humming did not alter. She was now at five feet. *Please. Please. Please.* One more step she took with eyes closed.

There was a groan from the metal poles and Ellie braced herself for pain...for the end. But with her next step, the humming suddenly stopped. She was in the boundary now, wasn't she? Her eyes were still closed. Her heart monitor had ceased its alarming. She took another step. Then another. One more to be sure. Then she opened her eyes. On the ground before her lay the lifeless body of the dove. Out of instinct, she stooped to pick it up. Its body looked undamaged, yet there was no heartbeat.

Ellie turned back to face Em. "I made it!" she yelled into the void.

Em rose to her feet with hands still together looking skyward.

The gesture made Ellie aware of what she had already failed to do. She too looked skyward. "Thank you," she said aloud. Almost immediately, the hum of the fence snapped back on, making Ellie jump. It had been a less than five second blip in the power supply, she realized. It wasn't unheard of on rare occasions. Likely the lights had merely flickered at her school. And in that instant, she had made it through alive. An icy chill prickled over her body.

CHAPTER
TWENTY-FIVE

Ellie hiked down the remnants of the abandoned road. It had been two hours since she crossed the sector boundary. Through the broken crumbles of the rough surface, trees and grass had attempted to conceal the former signs of human life. The byway had not seen a vehicle for generations—nor would it ever again.

She glanced down at her bracelet out of habit. Em's parting words echoed in her mind. She should have removed the device already, but there was a comfort to its familiar presence on her wrist. Like a reliable friend, it had always been there for her when she needed it. It had alerted her parents to her high fevers as a child, provided a comforting glow of light when she was scared, and kept her in communication with everyone she loved. Even though its screen was lifeless outside the sector, the thought of removing the device, while necessary, gave Ellie anxiety.

Ellie found a fallen tree to rest on while she studied the last connection to her former life. She'd already removed the metallic cover from Em. The bracelet shone like metal but was far lighter and more flexible than any metal Ellie had ever seen. She dug through her pack, searching for the tool Em had described. The bag was crammed with dehydrated meals, a blanket, a special water bottle to make the outside water drinkable, a fire lighter, and finally—a cutting device.

Ellie carefully opened the folded blade and slipped it into the small space between her skin and the bracelet. She inhaled a deep breath. Severing her connection to TEAMMATE was irreversible, and yet it no longer truly mattered. She'd already left TEAMMATE behind. It was time.

Her attempt to cut outward proved unsuccessful as the smooth material seemed impervious to the blade. *How am I ever going to get this thing off?* Clearly, simply cutting would take days, if it worked at all. She studied the cutting device. There seemed to be another blade with teeth inside the handle that she couldn't get out. Studying its design closely, Ellie realized there was a gap between the toothed blade for the first blade to fit into, almost like an upper and lower jaw. She slipped the blade back under the bracelet and folded the handle so the other concealed blade would cut against the first.

Ellie squeezed. Nothing happened. Undaunted, she studied the handle for some type of release for the second blade. Her efforts were rewarded when she found a small lever she was able to pivot away from the handle with some pressure. Still unsure of how it functioned, she took a guess and pulled the lever outward. A scream escaped her when the device clamped together so suddenly, it sliced completely through her bracelet. Her old companion slipped off her wrist and dropped to the ground like a metallic viper.

She instinctively scooped it back up from the ground. It was such a compact invention yet it was capable of nearly anything inside the sector. Should she bury it? Ellie didn't think it could be tracked out here but didn't want to take any chances. Beside the fallen tree, the dirt was loose enough to dig with her hands a few inches down. It was the best she could do without a shovel. As she laid it in the hole, she read the signal frequency on the inside of the band. If DCLX-VI was able to transmit for a time without external power, at least she could be tracked no further than here.

Without warning, she felt a second wind of energy to put as much distance between herself and the bracelet as possible. She reorganized her backpack, trying to replicate the reverse order that she'd taken everything out.

Her anxiety had heightened now that she'd followed through with Em's instructions. She glanced at her naked wrist for the time. *Right.* That habit might take some time to break. She glanced at the sun. She might have two or more hours until dark. Her trek continued.

The time in solitude gave Ellie an opportunity to think. Even if she was undeniably closer to believing Em along with her grandmother's prophecy, how could she possibly save the world from out here? And why did the world even need to be saved? She'd warmed to the idea that TEAMMATE wasn't perfect, in fact she'd embraced it as fact. But did everyone really need saved from a system with a few flaws? What if she undid all the progress since the rebirth? Would she be considered a hero or a villain?

And what about Andy? He already knew her secret. He loved her anyway. But how much did TEAMMATE know about their relationship? Would they question him?

She started to think about Judith too but stopped herself. Worrying about Judith wasn't worth her time anymore. Her former friend had made her own choice. Ellie surveyed her surroundings. She had Judith to thank for all of this. Her entire world had been ended by a single act of betrayal. She closed her eyes, trying to think of other things. Her family would be devastated that she'd disappeared. She felt the worst for her dad. He'd wiped his memory clean to keep her safe. She had no doubt he'd blame himself either way for what she'd gotten herself into. He'd taken it especially hard when she'd been sent home from school, but this was a whole new level of disappointment. If only she'd hidden the journal better.

Ellie crunched onward in the final hour of light. She was grateful she needn't worry about patrols following her. The sector's drones could only spy a small distance over the fence before they'd lose power and fall from the sky. She'd traveled more than far enough to eliminate that threat. And no one in the sector knew she was on the outside—except Em. Hopefully the old woman wasn't caught.

Following the setting sun, she traveled the vast, wild landscape—pockmarked by the ruins of humanity's failure. Division, greed, and competition had triggered these world-ending consequences. Despite its shortcomings, the development of TEAMMATE from the former society's ashes had ultimately saved humanity from extinction. Yet now her task was to oppose the most advanced organization of intelligence ever known by humankind. And this charge of the transformation of the most successful society in history had been entrusted to a fifteen-year-old girl. Perhaps the world was screwed.

If "her people" truly did live out here, she had seen no trace of their existence yet. Ellie had never been so lonely in her life. She wished Andy was with her—especially as the darkness set in. It was past time to stop for the day. She decided to make her camp close to the road, under a grove of tall pines, as the bed of needles helped cushion the floor of her tent.

She didn't make a fire that night. It was already dark by the time her tent was assembled. She'd gathered no wood and didn't feel like attempting to cook. Instead, she ate two meal replacement bars and emptied the remainder of her thermos. She'd need to find water in the morning. Her legs ached, her head hurt, and her heart was broken. Sleep came quickly, despite her uncomfortable surroundings.

WHEN ELLIE AWOKE SORE AND DRY-MOUTHED THE NEXT MORNing, she was greeted by heavy rainfall. Since no one had found her yet, she figured it was safe to stay put. The weather was cool and damp, but thanks to her tent, she wasn't drenched. She was nearly pleased for the excuse to continue to rest her aching legs and blistered feet. In an effort to pass the time, she took out the copy of the book Em had packed for her and opened its pages.

The book opened to a page marked with a red ribbon. There was a passage underlined, obviously meant for her benefit.

You shall not fear the terror of the night nor the arrow that flies by day, nor the pestilence that roams in darkness, nor the plague that ravages at noon. Though a thousand fall at your side, ten thousand at your right hand, near you it shall not come. You need simply watch; the punishment of the wicked you will see. Because you have the LORD for your refuge and have the Most High your stronghold, No evil shall befall you, no affliction come near your tent. For he commands his angels with regard to you, to guard you wherever you go. With their hands they shall support you, lest you strike your foot against a stone. You can tread upon the asp and the viper, trample the lion and the dragon.

(Psalm 91 vs 5-13)

Ellie closed the book. Doubt settled upon her like fog at nightfall. Did Em not understand? Did she not see how young she was? Her situation was bleak. She should never have gone into the attic. She should never have opened the old trunk. She should definitely never have read that journal. The words marked for her were meant to give the reader strength. But this text had been written for someone else a millennium ago, and not a selfish fifteen-year-old girl who'd just thrown away her reasonably good life. And she wasn't special—just unlucky. Coincidental things had surely happened around her, but she wavered in believing it was due to anything she'd done.

And yet the small flame of belief was still alive within her, unwilling to be fully extinguished. The growing list of coincidences did merit further consideration. Andy's seizure stopping at her touch, him finally noticing her existence, Mr. Jones' spontaneous recovery, the fence allowing her to pass—had she not done or at least asked for all these things? Then why couldn't she ask for a way out of this current mess? She missed her family. She missed Andy. She even missed her ex-best friend, Judith. She missed clean clothes and her soft bed so much. And while she needed the rest, this rain was entirely awful. Why couldn't it all just stop?

She picked up her pillow and slammed it into her face with anger. An abrupt crack of thunder made her cower on all fours in fear. The tent's fabric walls began to shake violently with a sudden breeze that threatened to blow it away with her in it. Ellie screamed and collapsed against the floor of the tent. Wind ripped through her doorway, letting in rain and soaking the floor. The metal tent anchors in the ground threatened to give way under the power of the wind. She heard a tree crash to the ground somewhere nearby. *Please make it stop! Please make it stop!*

As suddenly as it all began, everything stopped. She lay still for a moment, paralyzed by fear, waiting for her breath to return. When it finally did, she listened, and she heard...silence. Cautiously, she lifted her door flap to see what had happened outside. When she poked her head out, she saw rays of sunshine with a long line of low, dark clouds headed east ahead of the strong wind that had nearly frightened her to death. *Did I do that? It couldn't have been...another coincidence?* She wasn't sure what to believe.

CHAPTER
TWENTY-SIX

After enjoying a grand breakfast of macaroni and cheese out of the sealed packet, Ellie packed up her damp tent and supplies and limped west at a slower pace than the previous day. Doubt about her odds for success began to creep into her mind. What if she had mistakenly passed the destination Em had spoken of? Exactly how far did the outside world go? The truth was, no one knew anything about the outside world. It was taught to be feared from a young age. Without TEAMMATE, a citizen would be truly alone, unable to receive aid when an inevitable misfortune occurred.

The second night was an improvement. Ellie stopped in plenty of time to make sure she assembled her tent with daylight, then gathered firewood and dead grass for the evening fire. She decided she wouldn't light it until dark for fear that the smoke could alert TEAMMATE to her campsite. However, it was much easier to plan ahead than to assemble a good fire in the dark. She went to bed with a full belly of hot chicken noodle soup and was almost able to dream her way out of this nightmare.

Perhaps the creepiest part of her journey wasn't the isolation of the woods—it was the eerie pieces of civilization that remained behind. Only the brick and stone portions of roofless homes remained. Some of the structures may have been stores or lodging frequented by travelers while they traveled this same road over a century prior. Old vehicles could be seen here and there, their rusted corpses succumbing to the ruin that touched everything in this wasteland. Even though there had been no human life here for ages, Ellie couldn't find it within herself to camp anywhere near the ancient buildings left behind. It was too spooky, especially at night.

Ellie had learned in school that most wildlife had been destroyed by The Last War. But, as she'd quickly learned, the animals had made a complete comeback. After all, the wildlife living within the fence had to have originally come from the other side. So far, she'd seen deer, squirrels, pigs, and turkeys along the roadbed. At night, the raccoons would invade her camp if she left any scraps outside. She'd also heard yips in the night that might be coyotes. Whenever she was scared in the dark, she found herself holding tightly to the book Em had given her. It had helped her get this far.

As far as Ellie had seen, other than the recovered wildlife, the outside world was nothing but forest and the bare bones of the previous society. There were no open areas, and she had yet to find a pond or lake, although she had crossed over more than a few small creeks that ran under the old roadway. Every Teammate had learned that the water had been poisoned ages ago, but she'd been assured by Em that her purifier would make it drinkable. Thus far, she hadn't gotten sick, and she'd consumed much more water throughout the second day. This was comforting because as long as there was water, she could survive until her food stores ran out. But if she didn't eventually find her people...she would be added to the decay that surrounded her. That sobering thought made her shudder.

On the third day of her journey, the terrain finally changed. The flat roadbed actually seemed to be leading somewhere. Unfortunately, it appeared her travels would become more cumbersome. Checking Em's compass, she confirmed the road was still leading her west. Ellie looked up the long, steep incline ahead of her. Running north and south, an elevation in the land protruded skyward like the spiked vertebrae of an enormous reptile. She would need to cut through that monstrous piece of land. And then what? Her morale was slipping away, not unlike the signs of human life in this desolate world. She missed her classmates. She missed her family. She missed Andy. At this point, she'd accept any kind of company to not be alone. But there was only one thing to be done. She had to push herself forward up the steep incline. After three days of walking, every muscle screamed in protest as she began her ascent.

Keep going. You can rest at the top. This climb is leading somewhere new. It has to. But the higher she pushed, the more her back ached and the more labored her breathing became. *Okay, just a quick break to catch your breath, then onward. Think of how much easier it'll be on the way down. You'll see.*

Ellie dropped her precious supplies from her back. She took a knee on the ground and tried to catch her breath. The sector was mostly flat in terrain, which meant the elevation was the likely culprit for her breathing struggles. Well, that and the heavy backpack. And perhaps the lack of sufficient sleep and shelter. She had never attempted anything so physically demanding in her life. Had she known how taxing this journey would be, she would have doubted her capability of making it this far. And yet she'd done it on her own. But she wasn't finished yet.

Little else changed in the scenery, save for the ascent. The road was more of a sunken stretch of smaller trees surrounded on all sides by larger trees. *What* exactly was out here that she should be looking for?

The world seemed an endless stretch of unorganized vegetation. It was chaotic and random ruin. What purpose could humans serve in this abysmal habitat? They had retreated long ago to their safer community with order and protection and direction. This was raw, untamed wilderness. No one belonged here, especially an unaccompanied teenage girl. *If only Andy were with me.*

Her heart ached for the boy as she rose to her full height and pulled her heavy satchel back on her shoulder. It wasn't as heavy as when she'd started, but she'd also used three days' worth of her supplies. The trek would be much easier without its weight, but that wasn't an option. The top of the mountain wasn't far now. Her breath seemed to have returned, if not her spirit. She lowered her head and grunted forward. *One foot in front of the next. Don't look too far ahead. Keep a steady pace. Something you can continue all day long. You will climb this mountain. You must climb this mountain. It doesn't even hurt as badly as it did a little bit ago. Are those tears or beads of sweat rolling down your cheeks? You really don't care. It's just water either way. You can replace it. You can keep going. You won't stop again until...*

She felt a breeze in her hair and lifted her gaze from the ground. *This is it.* She could finally see as far as her eyes would allow. She stood atop the high cliffs that divided the world. Below her, a large, lazy river snaked near the base of the mountain. Beyond the river was a grassy area with hardly any trees. How could it be? She scanned the plain below and saw a fence, old and decrepit perhaps, but still standing. Her heart jumped with excitement. The grassland within the fence reminded her of the livestock grazing areas in the agricultural zone. Had she discovered a second sector? Looking more closely, her heart jumped with excitement when she spotted a few tiny buildings below. Some had caved-in roofs, but even from a distance, it was easy to tell they were in much better condition than the old foundations she'd passed along the roadside. This had to be where she'd find her people.

Hope flooded her at the prospect of no longer journeying alone. This must be where Em helped Teammates escape to. Then a darker thought crossed her mind. Could this also be where the most dangerous Teammates were exiled? She thought of the footage she'd watched. Propaganda, Em had said. But Em had also mentioned that those she'd gotten out may have grown wild in her absence. Ellie tried to clear her mind of doubt. Em had instructed her to follow the road, and this was where it led. *She knew I'd end up here, so I'm where I'm supposed to be. But that doesn't mean I won't be careful.*

She looked down at the path ahead. At one time, there had been a switchback road carved into the cliff to drive a vehicle. But time and mudslides had eroded any easy way of getting down now. Ellie would have to lower herself down branch by branch from the trees and shrubs that grew from the side of the rock cliff.

She laughed aloud like a crazy person at the prospect before her. *And you thought going down the mountain would be easier...*

As Ellie waded through the shallowest part of the river she could find, she glanced back at the peaks she'd painfully descended. *How are you still moving after that?* Perhaps it was the prospect of something new or the proximity of her destination that drove her to push herself further than she'd thought capable. The water was icy cold, but there was shelter on the other side. She paused a moment midstream to refill her bottle. Her legs were soaked up to her thighs when she stepped victoriously onto the other bank. The fence that surrounded the compound was now a mere hundred yards away.

The grass was high here, but there looked to be an animal trail from the river leading toward the fence. She cautiously followed the path, looking down to see that she was following hoof prints. As she approached the fence, she realized it was much higher than a normal fence, perhaps ten feet tall. The animal path led to a sizeable gap under the fence, and when she squatted down to climb under the opening, she placed her hand on the woven metal to steady herself. A strange sensation coursed through her body, and she instinctively pulled her hand back. What was that? She felt goosebumps on her arms. It wasn't painful, but it reminded her of something. Thinking back, it reminded her of when she'd touched Andy that day in class. Was something happening again? She curiously reached again for the fence with just a finger pressed against the metal.

The sensation didn't catch her by surprise this time, but she gasped at what happened around her. Things suddenly changed. Everything became...newer. The buildings ahead were no longer rundown. The hole under the fence was gone. Glancing back, the trail behind her was now gone. Instead, the gentle decline into the river was a field of freshly mown grass. The area was lazily scattered with trees. When she turned back around, she was startled to see a young boy, perhaps six years old, crouched behind a nearby tree on her side of the fence. He was also staring into the little sector.

"Hello," Ellie said softly, trying not to scare the child while attempting to suppress her own fear. He quickly turned her way, but his eyes wandered back and forth. He squinted curiously, almost as if he was having trouble seeing her.

"What's your name?" she asked.

Fear was apparent in the boy's eyes as he looked up and down the fence line as if she weren't a stone's throw away. He whispered in a tiny voice, "Benny." Then he lost his courage and ran as fast as his little legs would carry him away from her and the fence.

Suddenly, Ellie was surrounded by brush once more. She reached out quickly to touch the fence again, but nothing happened. *What is happening to me?*

After touching the fence a half a dozen times more, she began to wonder if it had really happened at all. *Are you hallucinating now? Did you push yourself too far?* She looked along the fence, noting there were no footprints or trodden grass in the now much longer, rougher weeds that stood where the boy had just run. Ellie would have been more surprised if there were evidence of his presence. She was still soaked and shivering from the river crossing, so she decided to keep moving, if only a little more deliberately. She stepped gingerly under the fence and into shin-high grasses, moving towards the now aged buildings, when something on the ground caught her eye. It had to be some type of manure, but from what she couldn't guess. It was far larger than any type she'd ever seen. Something very big had been keeping this field from turning back into woods.

She crept closer, and the wind picked up, as if awakened by her presence there. It blew through the grass unchallenged and picked up Ellie's long hair. Something was very eerie about this camp, aside from looking deserted. The planning had been well designed for the little sector, as she'd decided to call it. The location near the river provided fresh water. The ground sloped to drain excess water to the river. The few trees that grew inside the fence were sturdy, if not old, and provided well-planned areas of shade.

Ellie approached one of the largest trees growing just outside the closest building. She had to look inside, but she was scared of what she might find. Once again, she found herself wishing Andy were with her. Was he safe? She certainly hoped so. Stepping behind the large tree, she shielded herself from the wind, as well as the view from the window. Was it possible that someone was actually in there? She placed a hand on the tree and felt the familiar tingling sensation course up her fingers and through her chest, encompassing her whole body. She let the change happen this time, keeping her hand in place on the tree. Her surroundings changed, once again. It became night. The tree was still there, if not quite as large as a moment ago. She could hear voices from the nearby building. There was light in the window. *Is this real?* A small twig landed on her head, giving her a start. She rubbed her hair with her free hand and looked upward. In the faint starlight, she saw a small figure sitting high on a branch above her, also looking into the window of the building.

"Benny!" she said.

He looked straight down at her. "Who's there?"

"It's me again from the river. My name is Ellie."

He looked around confused. "You shouldn't be here, whoever you are."

"I'm right below you."

He was scared, but also confused. "Why can't I see you?"

"I wish I knew. Why are you hiding in this tree?"

She heard a swallow as it sounded like he was trying to fight off tears. "Mama said I had to hide."

Ellie bit her lip so as not to scold the small boy. She had little patience for her younger sister at times, although she was working on it. She tried to stay calm and speak slowly. "I need your help, Benny. I've run away from my home."

His little head scanned back and forth, knowing she was there but not able to see her. "Where are you from?" he asked in a whisper.

"I'm from a bigger sector. About a three-day hike from here."

Ellie could see his eyes grow wide in the starlight. "Mama said I needed to find you," he said. "I was too scared, so I came back."

"Where is your mother?" Ellie asked slowly.

"She's in another building with the others," he said. "But I'm scared because it's dark and I'll get in trouble if they catch me. Can you make me invisible like you are?"

"I don't think so," she said. "Who are you listening for?"

"The counselors."

Ellie nodded before realizing he couldn't see her gestures. "Are they looking for you?"

"Yes."

"Okay, I see. What happens if you get caught?"

In the faint light, the boy took his finger and slowly guided it across his throat. It was clearly overly dramatic, but Ellie reminded herself of who she was dealing with.

Just then, the voices inside stopped, and a man stepped out of the building. Ellie instinctively hid behind the tree.

"Who's out here?" a man's voice demanded.

When no reply was offered, a beam of light scanned the area. The man stepped closer towards the tree. Ellie was frightened, wondering if he could see her, but also worried he would find Benny. She stepped from behind the tree, with her hand still against the bark. The flashlight moved to illuminate where she stood.

The man immediately dropped the flashlight, surrounding him in darkness. He picked it up and smacked it against his hand until it turned on again. It went back and forth where she stood, but he didn't center the beam anywhere.

"What in the world?" the man asked aloud, searching frantically now, around the tree and nowhere near where she now stood exposed. "I shouldn't have had that drink," he said to himself.

"What's happening out there?" demanded another voice from the door of the building.

"It was nothing," stammered the man with a flashlight. "The wind is playing tricks out here tonight."

Ellie looked around in confusion. The man had to have seen her. But within a few minutes, the men were carrying on in conversation, and the incident seemed forgotten.

"Why didn't he take me?" she asked. "Why was he so scared, Benny? He saw me, didn't he?"

The boy was silent for a moment. Then he worked up enough courage to respond. "They told us you didn't exist. Mama was right, though. I only saw you for a second before you disappeared."

Ellie's patience was wearing thin. She was confused, lost, scared, and possibly hallucinating. "What are you talking about?"

"You're an angel."

Ellie scoffed at his response. She'd read enough the past few weeks to know what an angel was. "What on earth would make you say that?"

"Shhh! You're going to get me in trouble!" pleaded Benny.

Ellie covered her mouth in embarrassment. "I'm sorry," she said. "Why would you think that?"

The boy stared back down fearfully. Finally, he spoke again. "Because I prayed you would save me," he said sheepishly. "I wasn't sure until I saw the glow around your head. The counselor saw it too, just for a second. You were as bright as the sun. You...you're a real angel, Ellie. And you're beautiful. But now I can't see you again."

Ellie had absolutely no reply to the boy's crazed words. She was more confused than Benny and the counselor combined. But perhaps she could use their confusion to help this boy and learn what was going on here. "Benny, it's okay. Why don't you come down with me? Maybe we can help each other."

The boy perked up bravely at her words. "Okay," he said with confidence in his voice. "I'm coming down."

CHAPTER
TWENTY-SEVEN

Benny's feet thudded on the ground, narrowly missing Ellie's own foot.

"Can you hold my hand?" he asked in a fearful voice.

"Yes," she said, unsure if it would work. She took his small hand in her own, and at once she could tell he saw her.

"You are real," he whispered in admiration. "I knew it. I can see you now! But what happened to your halo?"

This little boy is an imaginative one. Touching him must make me visible. But am I visible to anyone else? "It must have been from the flashlight. Let's get you back to your mother."

"Okay," he agreed eagerly. "Follow me. But don't let go of my hand. She'll be so relieved you're here."

He led her into the darkness, his fear forgotten since she'd taken his hand. The glow from the windows of the counselors' building slowly faded as they walked.

"How long have you been separated?" she asked him quietly.

"Three nights," he said. "I tried to reach you, but I couldn't go far enough. I got scared and came back." He explained this as if Ellie knew he'd been coming to meet her. He pulled her arm forward, eager to see his mother again.

"Will the building be locked?" asked Ellie.

"Yes," said Benny. "But you can unlock the bolt from the outside. I couldn't reach it. Once I'm inside, you can lock me back in."

Ellie put her free hand to her chin in thought. "Wait, Benny, I thought your mother wanted you to run away. Doesn't she want to leave, too?"

"No," he said quickly. "She said if I found you, everything would be alright. Her friend Grace told her about you. She knew at some point you'd come for me. Mama will be so happy I found you."

"Is Grace here?" Ellie asked hopefully.

"No. She's too smart to get caught. She warned us they would be coming, but we didn't hide our books well enough. They found them and took us here."

Ellie didn't doubt this. If Grace weren't here, perhaps Benny's mother could explain what was going on. She knew she was stuck in the past, but didn't understand why or how this was happening. In the distance, she could see the outline of a long building against the starlit sky.

When they reached the entrance, Benny pointed to a heavy bolt lock high on the door. There wasn't a sound from the building. The inhabitants were likely sleeping. Ellie carefully lifted the handle on the door bolt and slid it back. Benny eagerly pulled the door open, revealing pitch black inside.

The little boy ran in with a confidence that Ellie couldn't match at the moment. She stayed positioned at the door, unsure of what to do next. If there was an alarm or something, should she run, or assume she was invisible? Hopefully, the boy's mother would help her get to the bottom of this.

Benny's footsteps raced in a frantic motion inside. Back and forth in the dark building, she heard him race. Then, she heard whimpering.

"Benny! What's going on in there?" she asked.

The boy came running to her and didn't seem to see her again, making him sob louder. She grabbed his hand, and his eyes locked back on her in pain.

"They're gone," he sobbed.

"Where else would they be?" asked Ellie.

"We're too late," Benny started wailing. "I didn't find you in time."

Ellie squeezed his hand reassuringly. "I'm sure there's a good explanation." She squatted down to look into his teary eyes. "I'll help you find them."

He lowered his gaze. "I know where they are. I can't go there."

"But where are they?" asked Ellie.

The little boy's lip quivered. "They're with the rest now. They're sleeping on the ground together." He inhaled with pain. "I th-thought you were here to save us."

His shoulders stooped, and he began to shake with grief. It was a silent cry; the kind that spoke through clenched muscles and paralyzed lungs. He'd truly believed she was here to help his family, but now he'd learned the cold truth. She was just an ordinary girl who was here by accident. She could help no one, not even herself. She placed a soft hand on Bennie's shoulder. "I'm so sorry, Benny. I don't understand how or why I'm here. You have to believe me. This place was entirely deserted and old just minutes ago. With no warning, it was almost like I was transported back in time. I...I think I'm dreaming, Benny. It's like I've awoken in a nightmare, and I'm not sure how to escape. I'm just a lost girl. I'm as frightened as you."

His eyes pleaded with her. "But you have to help me. This is real. I'm real, Ellie! I don't know what to do!" The frozen shock in his veins melted, and he began to sob. His courage was all spent. She'd proven his hope in her presence had been misplaced.

Feeling his pain, she tried to dwell less on her own shortcomings and more on what purpose she could yet serve. "I'm sorry. I know you must be real, Benny. There must be some reason I'm here right now. Em said it would all make sense, but I'm missing something. What year is it, Benny?"

The boy looked sheepish. "Mama says it's 2141, but the counselors called it ALW 51 at the last solstice."

Ellie put her hand to her mouth. She was in a time 51 years after TEAMMATE was formed. The counselors should have said it was ALW 117, meaning this dream or memory or whatever was occurring had happened over sixty years ago. What was she supposed to learn? Where were the people that Em had promised her? Had she arrived too late?

The little boy tugged at her hand. "I'm scared. I don't want to stay here. Can you take me with you?"

Ellie lifted the trembling boy into a hug. "Of course, Benny. I know the way back to the sector. There's a road that will lead us back. Since we're no longer in my time, we could sneak through whatever chain-link fence is in place. But is there anyone there who could help us?"

The boy nodded. "Em would help me. She warned Mama about this place. That's why Mama snuck me through the bent bars over the window."

Ellie gaped at him. "How old is the Em, you know?" she asked slowly.

Benny shrugged. "A few years older than you?"

Ellie nodded. Of course, she would be. It all made sense. "Listen, Benny, we have to get as far away from here as possible. We can use the road at night and hide in the daylight. It's east from here, that's the direction where the sun rises every morning." After a thought, she reached into her bag and pulled out the compass. She placed it into his hand. "All we need to do is line the arrow up with north, then head in the direction labeled east. Can you hold onto this for me? I'm going to get you out of here. I'm not sure how else I can help, but I think I'm supposed to figure out a way. Em is still around in my time, but she's a lot older."

She grabbed his small hand tightly and together they made their way toward the river.

ELLIE AWOKE WITH A START. SHE'D FALLEN ASLEEP NEXT TO THE old fence. It was daylight again. They had not made it very far away, she realized with panic. She looked around for Benny. There was no trace of the little boy.

Confused, she slowly rose to look around. The grass was once again a field of tall weeds. The counselors' building from last night had aged decades to reach the present. She was back where she started yesterday, or had time even passed? She instinctively reached for her pant legs. Still damp from the river crossing. Could it all have been a dream?

A chilling thought grew in her mind. She once again entered the now overgrown campus. She wasn't exactly sure what she was looking for, but she assumed she'd know when she saw it. More than six decades had passed overnight. She ran past the tree where she'd found Benny hiding. Its diameter was now much bigger than in her dream. Ellie retraced her steps to the living quarters they'd found empty last night. She hesitantly walked from there toward the area that had terrified Benny. It was a wide-open field of tall grass and weeds. She wandered about until something in the landscape made her pause. It was a sunken area, perhaps half a foot lower than the surrounding landscape.

Ellie returned to the building in search of a tool. Walking through the building, she recognized an old bicycle, perfectly preserved. She touched the tires. Solid rubber. As exciting as the discovery was, Ellie's snooping was further rewarded when she found a pickaxe in the corner. She hurried back with the tool to the sunken landscape. In the center of the expansive square, she swung her tool. The grass uprooted with protest, as if trying to protect the secrets beneath, but Ellie could not stop until she knew. Again and again, the metal pick tore at the earth, bringing chunks of dirt to the surface. Finally, she struck something else.

Her spine tingled as she knelt next to the hole to brush away the soil. She reached her hand into the loose dirt and wrapped her fingers around the object. She pulled upward to remove it. Something shiny and metallic caught her eye. Ellie curiously broke away some chunks of dirt, held together by the roots. Pieces of a skeletonized hand fell from the packed dirt to the ground. She shrieked and fell away from the hole, taking in its tremendously large size. The metallic object reflected the rays of the sun. It was a ring, engraved with the symbol of a cross. The truth hit her like a knee to the gut, stealing her oxygen and leaving her weak and vulnerable, just as Benny had been. *Everything that she experienced was real. It hadn't been a dream. It was a nightmare come to life. TEAMMATE had killed them all...Benny's mother and everyone else.*

She fell weakly to her knees beside the hole. Had Benny gotten away?

Then she realized something else. If TEAMMATE had found her journal, the book, and gave her a KSM test...would she not be subject to this same fate? Was this the future that Em and her father had tried to rescue her from? She laid her head upon the grass, green from the nourishment of bodies of hundreds of unwanted Teammates. As her small, insignificant tears dripped into the mass grave beneath her, for the first time in her life, she truly prayed. She still wasn't sure how to do it properly, but she needed help, and so she begged for it. She pleaded for aid, for guidance, for protection, for courage, for strength, for knowledge, and for justice. And then she asked for forgiveness for all the doubt she'd been harboring. Ellie clung to the ground, her body convulsing in violent sobs until she couldn't ask for anything more, for she'd fallen into a peaceful trance in the warm sun.

Caught in the state between sleep and wakefulness, Ellie felt the prickles and tingling in every cell of her body. She consciously kept her eyes closed a moment longer. Whatever was happening, it was even more intense than the last time. She didn't know what to expect, but she accepted His path. With her trust, the worry lifted off her shoulders, the doubt faded, and she felt at peace. Answers were coming. Feeling at peace, she allowed her eyes to open.

CHAPTER
TWENTY-EIGHT

Ellie was no longer where she'd fallen asleep. She was suspended, above the ground like a sector drone surveying the landscape. The scenery began to quickly change from one historical moment to the next, as if she were wearing Andy's gaming helmet in fast forward. Despite the speed, somehow, she began to understand the people and their significance as they took the stage in history before her.

First, she saw a wide-eyed, frightened girl of her own age, standing before a bright figure. The figure was a man with flawless features who told her, "Do not be afraid, Mary, for you have found favor with God." The scene flashes forward, and the same girl has just given birth to a baby boy, surrounded by her husband and livestock animals beneath a starry night. So few come to visit the newborn upon his arrival, but he is already feared by the most powerful men of the time. Ellie sees a furious king order the massacre of male infants age two and younger, and she sees the boy's father lead his small family away from the village in darkness. The scene they leave behind becomes filled with mothers screaming, fathers enraged, and the cries of babies snuffed out by the king's soldiers.

The boy grows to age twelve, and his parents lose him in the crowds on a trip to the city of Jerusalem. They search in panic for three days until they find him sitting in the temple in the midst of teachers, all of whom are astounded by the boy's understanding. The timeline jumps again, and Ellie sees a man dressed in skins dunk the boy, who's now a young man, into a river. As the young man rises to his feet, the clouds part, and the sun seems to shine only on him. A voice declares loud enough for all gathered to hear, "This is my beloved Son, with whom I am pleased." Not long after, the young man begins selecting followers. He transforms water into wine at a wedding, and those disciples who witness come to believe. He speaks unlike any before him. He confides in everyday working-class people, not kings, rabbis, or the wealthy class. He heals lepers, opens the ears of the deaf, pulls the paralyzed to their feet, cures the mentally ill, and even brings the dead back to life.

Then he is betrayed by a friend. He is nailed to a cross, beside criminals for display, and his followers scatter in fear. In pain and near death, he prays aloud, "Father, forgive them, they know not what they do." His mother wept for her son alongside two other women near the base of the cross. The midday turns dark with an eclipse, the earth groans angrily, and the scene changes.

Following two sunsets and two sunrises, a young woman comes to visit his burial tomb and finds two figures in dazzling garments where he should be. She despairs before turning around to hear a familiar voice say, "Mary!" Through joy and tears, she recognizes Jesus and responds, "Teacher!"

The woman runs to tell others. Jesus begins to appear to all his followers multiple times. They rejoice and remember what he had taught them. So strong is their faith that all but one will be martyred for their steadfast belief. Before these eyewitnesses are erased by history, they will tell and record everything they have seen, for without documentation, this spark could die out. But it does not die out. It burns hot and clean and alters the course of human history. Ellie watches the empire of Rome try to erase the followers from history, only to be eventually overtaken by Christianity. With the help of the reach of the Roman Empire, it spread to nearly all corners of the world.

The fire not only burns, it begins to thrive. Through the centuries, Ellie watches it survive dark times of disease and despair, times of poor leadership, and numerous advances in science that try to discredit and destroy it. It survives bright times of peace and abundance when people feel less need to believe. It continues on in the hearts of the unwavering until the event that ends the previous age. And then, those who still follow this belief become fewer, and so, they are blamed for the ruination of the world. They are hunted and their numbers dwindle to so few that no one is left to pass the history down. And just as the light is about to fade forever from the world, Ellie watches herself curiously open the chest in her attic.

Ellie's breath catches as there is finally a break in the sequence of events. Her mind is only beginning to catch up with everything she has seen. The amount of pressure on her to succeed is crushing. And yet she's just watched so many others before her carry this same weight. Why must she be the next one to pick it up? She knows she'll never comprehend. But she's been gifted the truth, and all the responsibility that comes with it. She bows her head and thanks God for answering her prayers.

But the lesson is not over yet. The scene below her swirls and materializes into a new setting. She sees Benny, frightened and alone, following the compass she'd given him back to the sector. She watches him cross the boundary in the night, slipping past the officials patrolling its boundaries. The fence in his time was merely a chain-link fence and not the deadly technological advancement of the present. She sees him knock on the door of a house, and a young lady embraces him before pulling him quickly inside. It could only be Em.

Next, she's transported to the top of a tall building in TEAM-MATE Square. The wind whips at her father's clothes as he stands atop his office building. He stands before a man in a suit, who covers his face with a mask.

"Did you lure me here to kill me?" Kirk nervously asks the man.

The man shakes his head. "I'm giving you sensitive information. What you choose to do with it is up to you. They are coming for your daughter today."

Kirk wears a look of confusion. "They? What does my daughter have to do with anything?"

"Everything," the man replies. "And if you don't get her out, TEAMMATE will charge her as a traitor to the sector. They're accusing her of paganism, and they have proof. You, more than anyone, understand what that means."

"If this is true, how can I save her?"

"Get her out, by any means necessary. Then take this." The man held out a gloved hand with a green pill. "This is an eraser. TEAM-MATE uses these after we have to carry out unpleasant tasks. You won't remember a thing since waking up after you take it. No tests or torture or questioning will ever get the truth out of you. This present conversation will not survive in your memory. Do you understand?"

Kirk nods. "Will she be safe?"

"If you find someone you trust...maybe. Is there anyone?"

Kirk nodded. "I...I think I know someone."

"Your quick response tells me this just might work. Good luck, Kirk. I truly wish it didn't have to be this way, for you or for your daughter. If there had only been more warning, I could have made arrangements. As it is, my communications are being monitored, and I can't get word to my people to help. And now, it's all on you. The clock's ticking."

Time speeds up again, and now she sees Miss Conway, bound and hanging in a room by her arms. An older man walks into the room. Ellie instantly recognizes him as Councilmember Thurman, the head of the Security branch.

"Tell me where the girl is!" The man snarls the words with an energy that surprises Ellie.

"I...I don't know! I swear!" Miss Conway's tears stream down her face.

"I don't believe you," the man says, calmer this time. His voice turns dismissive and almost sad. "You broke the rules, Edna. She should have been reported weeks ago. It's your fault she's still out there. Can you guess what happens next?"

Miss Conway sobs in response.

"I'll tell you what happens next. I extract every memory you've ever had from that little brain of yours until I know everything. Then, conceivably, if you've cooperated enough and told us the entire truth, you can go back to work in a few days with no memory of any of this happening. But if I find you've lied about anything...you'll never get the chance to make another memory."

Ellie's world blurs by again until she sees Judith crying in her bedroom. "I didn't know, Ellie," her friend whispers aloud. "How could I have known all this would happen? I'm so sorry. I'm a terrible person." She slams her head back into her pillow as the room flies out of sight.

The travel stops at Ellie's own home, and she witnesses her mother fighting with her dad.

"What is wrong with you, Kirk? Your story isn't adding up. Everything you told the officials is what happened yesterday, not today. You're lying to them! If they don't figure it out, I will!"

Her dad wears a look of confusion on his face. "I specifically remember I went into the office late today. I had an egg and toast for breakfast. But what does this have to do with anything? I haven't seen Ellie since breakfast."

"We used the eggs up yesterday! You ate oatmeal this morning. You went into the office early today! Ellie was still sleeping when you left. Do you not understand the problem? You never forget the smallest details, and now, the day our daughter disappears, you can't remember a thing?"

"What are you saying?" Kirk asks his wife.

"I'm saying I'm taking Molly and we're leaving. Until you tell me what's really going on, we're not coming back. I don't trust you!"

Kirk stares at his hands. "Anne, I honestly have no idea where our daughter is. I'll search everywhere until I find her. But I can't lose you guys, too! Please believe me!"

The lump in Ellie's throat grows as she begins to understand the unfolding destruction her disappearance has caused. Her dad had taken the green pill to protect her. And now, the world she left behind is imploding. Can the mess left behind ever be fixed?

Ellie's world hurtles further on again, and she sees Andy and Judith making plans to find her.

"If she were still inside the sector, they'd have found her by now," said Andy, pounding the table.

"Maybe she made it out," said Judith. "Is there any way we could get past the fence?"

Andy thinks for a moment. "I thought of a way the other day in class."

"How?"

"The Waste Department. If we can get into a garbage truck, they will drive us right out the gates."

Judith nods grimly, unable to hide her self-loathing. "I'll do whatever it takes."

The scene speeds up until Ellie sees her father being interrogated by Councilmember Thurman. Kirk's arms and face are purple from beatings. His fingernails are missing from his left hand, and the blood still drips on the dark carpet.

"I know you know where she is," said Thurman with a smile. "It doesn't matter how long it takes. We're going to have plenty more fun finding out everything that happened."

Kirk sits in his restraints with his teeth bared, veins bulging from his neck. "Even if I knew where she was, I'd never tell you. You're a monster!"

Ellie's stomach drops again.

The ride continues on.

When the blur of colors began to slow down, Ellie experienced the overwhelming smell of paper, just like the journal from her grandmother, but magnified many times. She's now in a vast hall, filled with more books than a person could read in ten lifetimes. She sees a group of adults reading the spines of the various titles before them. She recognizes several councilmembers, and they're all searching for something...something that she alone understands where to find. The endless shelves rise around the searchers, reaching nearly to the high vaulted ceiling. Those gathered call out in despair, bemoaning that they'll never locate the book. Ellie remains calm and feels herself descend to the floor. She begins reading the numbers on the spines of the books. They've all been categorized, but no one understands the system any longer. Then she sees what they are looking for. Ellie doesn't understand how she knows, but there is no doubt. It's on the bottom shelf. It's a plain book with a red cover. She reads the number on its spine. She senses it's important. She whispers 973.4. Ellie calls out, but it's as if no one can hear her. Frantic that she'll lose it, she pulls the book a few inches outward, but before she can read the title, she's jerked forward once more.

And now she clearly sees the path forward. She sees her two friends uniting with her. She sees a small group of children. These will be her people. Together, they will spark the movement needed. Their names begin to fill her mind as she commits each face to memory. She sees the gathering of crowds to listen to her speak. She feels the thunderous anger of TEAMMATE and what she will accomplish. She can't see how it will end, but above all else, she sees good prevailing over evil. Hope surges within every molecule of her body.

203

PART III
Deliverance

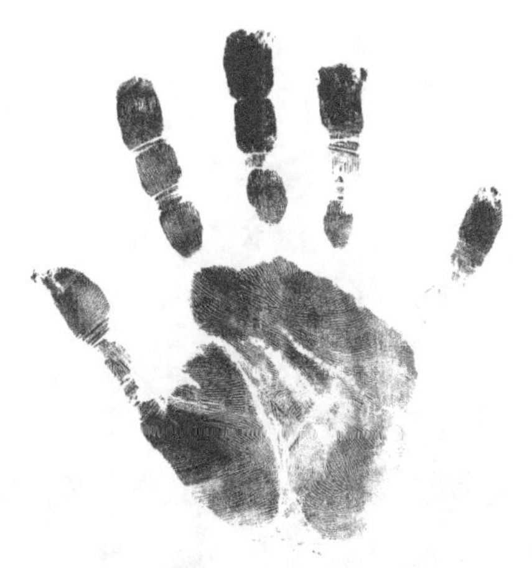

CHAPTER
TWENTY-NINE

After her eyes opened again, she understood exactly what she had to do. The doubt, the worry, the questions...they were vanquished. Everything that had happened to her up to this point wove neatly in her mind. Benny was right about her, and he had survived—thanks to her help. He was vital to her task. She didn't fully understand why, but that was no longer a concern. Everything was happening as it should. That knowledge gave her great comfort. She knelt and offered thanks. Finally, she rose to her full height, brushed off her pants, and entered the decrepit building. Her eyes rested on the old bicycle.

Ellie knew she'd just experienced something beyond physical or mental renewal. Her vision had delivered an accurate understanding unprecedented in her life. She'd just witnessed firsthand everything that TEAMMATE had erased. The experience delivered the answers that had plagued her since she'd undertaken this life-altering task. She realized her true purpose after wandering aimlessly for fifteen years. She had been created differently for a reason. She now understood the atrocities that had happened within the little sector. After generations of hiding its purpose in the shadows, she alone saw TEAMMATE exposed by the light of truth, and all her school years of studying history had been wasted. The facts had been doctored to make TEAMMATE humanity's only saving grace. But it was far from that. In fact, it was quite the opposite. And she had to warn everyone...before it was too late. The journal, Em, Andy, and her own suspicions had all been on the right track. But the malevolence of TEAMMATE was much darker than anyone could have imagined. Now she needed help for what would come next. Thankfully, she knew where to find it.

Once she pushed the bicycle over the high ridge, her travel time increased threefold. The only thing that slowed her down was dodging the trees that had taken hold of the old road. She pedaled with vigor, with hope, and yes, a little dose of fear. She was about to take on everything she'd ever known. Many Teammates would not want the change she'd deliver from their comfortable lives, but she had to help them understand. They'd all been sold a bill of lies.

Her new knowledge and purpose overshadowed the fatigue she'd battled for three days. When she sped past one of her previous campsites, Ellie marveled at her own progress. But even as fast as she'd peddled, reaching her people before nightfall remained an impossibility. It pained her to wait when she was so close. Their names were still on her tongue from her vision. She'd missed them before, but she hadn't been ready to lead them even one day prior. She hadn't fully understood then. But she was ready now—more ready than she'd ever been in her life to take on the world. All the doubt, all the anxiety, and all the confusion she'd been experiencing had been washed clean. She had purpose. She had responsibility. She had...understanding.

When she finally stopped for the night, she had to force herself to eat. The energy would be needed for tomorrow and the day after, but who wanted to think of food at a time such as this? There was nothing more important in the world than the information she carried, and now she'd have to wait a little longer to share it. She channeled her frustration into labor, constructing a good campsite with her tent on soft ground and plenty of gathered wood for her fire. She no longer feared being found by TEAMMATE. Then, reclining comfortably by the fire, she took out the Bible Em had given her, and she read the banned book deep into the night with a renewed understanding.

At first light, she packed up and continued east. While she traveled, she reflected on her short life so far. She'd always been different from other Teammates but never understood why. She'd been labeled selfish because she questioned what everyone else so easily accepted—that TEAMMATE always knew best. The reason she'd struggled mightily to fit in all these years was that she'd been partially awake in a sector of dreamers. Her instincts had caused her to act out at a young age until she'd become programmed to withdraw from most of the others. But the journal had reawakened this part of her. That was why Andy had seen her in a new light after her outburst in class—for he, too, understood all along that something was not right. How many more might feel the same? How many of those would be brave enough to admit it?

She considered the question the rest of the day as she pedaled on. Would there be enough Teammates, both brave and believing, to see her task through? She would certainly not get far if their support were not overwhelming. The long day of travel was nearly over by the time she recognized the campsite she'd made her first night beyond the fence. It seemed so long ago since she'd reclined alone in her tent, shivering through the dark, cold night, terrified about her uncertain future. She didn't pedal a mile further before the southern breeze carried the faint scent of a cooking fire. She smiled at her good fortune and pulled her bicycle off the path, hiding it in the weeds. How close she'd been that first night without realizing it. But she also wasn't prepared to lead at the time. However, time had changed quickly. She walked, calm and self-assured, toward the light smell of burning wood.

The fading light had cooled the air temperature, and a fog had begun rolling onto the landscape. Ellie walked quietly, gently pressing through branches while the smell of smoke grew stronger. She heard voices. She couldn't make out their words yet, but the voices sounded like those of young children—shrill and excited. As she drew closer, through the settling fog, she realized she was on the outskirts of what appeared to be a small village. There were a few shack-like structures she crept past, but all the commotion of the camp seemed to be in the center, near the fire. Finally close enough to make out words, she listened while concealing herself in the shadows against one of the nearby shacks.

"You should not have come here," an adolescent male's voice spoke above the sound of younger voices. "You know nothing about survival beyond your fence. Even worse, you will give away our location if you return to the sector. I do not know what we should do with you."

The next voice stole the very breath from Ellie's lungs.

"Do with us? How about you leave us alone? We weren't hurting a thing when you guys snuck up on us in the landfill. You brought us to *your* camp, and *now* you're worried about the consequences?"

"Easy, Judith." Andy's voice was a sword in Ellie's stomach. She braced herself against the wooden building in relief. They'd actually made it safely beyond the fence.

"We only came here to find our friend. We mean you no harm. Our friend can do...special things. If you won't help us, let us be on our way."

"What kind of special things?" asked a younger boy.

"I'll ask the questions, Petey." The older boy seemed to be in charge of the gathering of ten other children. Ellie guessed their ages ranged from seven to sixteen.

"Sorry, Jamie," the boy said with his small arms crossed in disapproval.

Jamie continued, clearly more interested than before. "Tell me more about this girl."

"She healed me when I was having a seizure. She's super smart. Everyone is looking for her. One minute she was in school with me, and the next minute she was gone. TEAMMATE has her father in custody for her disappearance. What else? Well, she's beautiful. She's also...a pagan."

Ellie's heart sank despite her joy at seeing Andy. TEAMMATE still had her dad in custody.

"What is a pagan?" Jamie pronounced the word like he'd never heard it before.

Andy took a breath. "Well...it's someone like...you. They pray with their hands together like this." He interlaced his fingers together. "What they do is outlawed by TEAMMATE."

This caused a stir of excitement among all the children.

"It must be her!" said a girl near Ellie's age. "Jamie, we have to help them. Em told us this day would come."

Jamie wore skepticism on his brow. "She also told us that strangers would bring danger. This could be a trap from TEAMMATE, Phyllis."

Ellie couldn't bear to stay hidden any longer. Her heart was a mix of too many emotions to keep straight. She'd known she'd find her people here, but seeing their youth made her confidence falter. She ignited the small flame on her fire starter, held it high in the air, and walked through the settling fog, directly into the center of the suddenly hushed gathering around the fire.

"Do not be afraid," she said sternly. "I am a friend of Em."

"Ellie!" yelled Andy in astonishment. He broke through the circle of children to lift her in his arms and embraced her against his body. For a brief time, no one could think what to say. He held her so tight, it felt like he'd never let go. She wished he wouldn't. Her body quivered with excitement against his strong heartbeat. "Are you okay? Please tell me you're alright. I've been worried sick."

"I'm awake for the first time in my life," she said. "How did you and Judith get here?" She knew the answer, but she wanted proof that she was right.

Andy shot a look towards Judith. "It's a long story, but I figured out a way to escape the sector. I figured you had to be out here; otherwise, TEAMMATE would have found you. Judith and I have been a mess without you, so we teamed up. I knew if we could slip into the back of the garbage trucks, they'd deliver us to the other side." He glanced around them. "But then this group of kids surrounded us and forced us back to this camp." He stopped a moment. "Who is this Em you were speaking about?"

"I'll explain everything." Ellie took Andy's hand and walked him back through the wide-eyed youths to stand beside Judith before continuing. Her friend hung her head, and Ellie felt pity for her betrayer.

"You came for me, Judith." She put a hand on the girl's shoulder, which was beginning to heave violently with sorrow.

Judith looked up from Ellie to Andy, wearing pain like a scar upon her face.

"You both need to know something." She cleared her throat. "It was me. I...I turned you into TEAMMATE. I'm so sorry. I thought you'd get a slap on the wrist for causing that stir in class. I had no idea they would find pagan paraphernalia at your house. I had no idea you'd need to escape from the sector, that TEAMMATE would take Miss Conway, that they'd take your dad." She hung her head. "I'm a horrible friend and don't deserve you. I still can't understand why I did it." Her face grimaced with pain and disgust.

"It's okay," Ellie said in a gentle voice.

"I was just so angry," Judith continued. "When Clint and I were fighting the night after you finished our project, he admitted we were set up by Andy." She looked at Andy sniffling. "Those conversations were all with you, and they were all...fake. I felt betrayed. I was an inconvenience that needed to be occupied. I realized you made up this whole elaborate plan just to get me out of the picture. But you know what I understand now?" She wiped her eyes with the corner of her sleeve. "You did it because you didn't want to hurt me. And now I've hurt you so bad, none of us can ever return to the sector." She sniffled. "I deserve this...to be stuck out here, but you and Andy don't. That's why I came. I want to try to help fix the mess I've created. You have every right to hate me for what I did. I hate me!"

Ellie looked toward Andy, who was clearly shocked by her admission.

"All this time you helped me, was it only out of guilt?" He said the words with disgust in his voice. "You're a no good..."

"I've known all along," Ellie interrupted. She put a soft hand on Andy's shoulder. "I've thought about this for quite a while since I've been out here. I understand now that I have much to teach all of you, as I have learned much in a short amount of time. When an apostle asked Jesus if he must forgive his brother seven times for offenses against him, do you know what he said?" The blank stares told her they did not. "He said not seven but seventy-seven times he must forgive. I've already forgiven you, but your actions after your ill-fated decision speak the truth." She looked at Andy. "Judith, could you find it in your heart to forgive us? You're right, we didn't want to hurt you. But we went about it all the wrong way. We're just as much to blame for our actions as you are for yours."

Judith stood taller, like an enormous load had been taken off her shoulders. "I...I understand your choices now. Of course, I forgive you. I was a terrible friend. But now what can we do? Are we stuck out here forever?"

"No," interrupted Jamie. "This is the girl Em told us to prepare for. She recited the Lord's words. She will lead us into the sector. Our banishment has ended."

"Is it true?" asked Andy.

Ellie nodded. "Tomorrow we will begin our journey. But there is much preparation to be done tonight."

"But this girl betrayed her," protested Petey to Jamie. "Something should be done."

"The past is over," Ellie interjected with tenderness in her voice. "And I fully forgive my friend because she made a mistake and is sorry. But, as I said, I was wrong too. And this will be the first lesson I'm tasked with teaching all of you. This is why I'm here—why I have these abilities," she said, staring at her open hands. "Everyone here must also forgive Judith in your hearts today as well. Her regret is genuine and her love is pure."

Jamie stepped forward. "You say we are to forgive her. But why should anyone ever trust her again? Her words and actions have betrayed trust. She could very well deliver us all to TEAMMATE."

"The forgiving has already been done by the Father," Ellie began. "As far as the repaired trust, look to what she has done since her mistake. If we banished everyone from our lives who'd ever wronged us, we'd be left with no one but ourselves. And how often in our lives do each of us nurture the same young thorns that are destined to grow and be quenched with our own blood?"

"You sound...different," said Andy.

"That's because I can finally see, after a lifetime of darkness. I'm here to share the light I've found with all who will see it. I'm still the girl you knew, Andy. I'm still not even close to perfect, but I understand so much more than before."

She turned toward the rest and continued, "Even when we walk in light, as all of you will soon enough, we have a choice in everything. All of us have the ability to be selfish, to have doubt, to be jealous, and sometimes...we will fail. That has always been human nature. But with His help," she glanced skyward, "we rise to our feet to do better."

"Em told us you'd have gifts," said Jamie. "Someone told her you would come for us, to bring us back."

Ellie smiled warmly and walked toward the leader of the group. "Yes, my grandmother was gifted the ability of foresight. She passed that information to Em, who, in turn, helped rescue each of you from the sector." She embraced Jamie in a hug, the boy's surprise apparent on his face. "I'm sorry all of you were forced to live away from your families." She turned to the other nine children. Many were so young for what was to come. "Petey...Phyllis...Simone...Jimmy...Bart...Johnny...Tommy...Maddi...Thad...Jamie," each of them had wonder in their eyes as she identified them correctly. "I will need all of your help." They were scared, but they appeared willing. "Jamie is right. I will lead all of us back to the sector."

"I don't understand," said Judith. "Why would children be banished from the sector?"

"They broke the rules," whispered Andy.

"But how?" pressed Judith. "They're so young."

"TEAMMATE has an unspoken precedent for those who live outside the rules," stated Ellie. "While the children themselves did nothing wrong, it was their parents who did not follow the Rulebook. If no permit for family expansion was obtained, the children cannot exist in TEAMMATE. It's unclear how Em accomplished it, but somehow she saved these kids."

"What will they do to us when we return?" asked Phyllis nervously. She looked to be the same age as Jamie and seemed to be a maternal presence for the younger children who hung close to her now. "How can our small group of children," she glanced around the group, "how can we succeed where so many before us failed? We need an army to protect us."

Ellie nodded knowingly. "We cannot succeed by ourselves. But we won't be alone. We are, collectively, the largest gathering of our kind that exists on the planet. When we ask for His protection, we will have it."

"What about the others?" asked Andy. "Surely there must be more...pagans in banishment to join us."

Ellie gently clasped her hands together. "You've never seen any others for a reason. They were all killed, Andy. I found the mass graves in the encampment to the west. It was all a lie. Everything we were taught in school. Perhaps at one time, TEAMMATE sought to change them by reeducation. In the end, they found that they could not. That deviation of belief from the other side of the wall presented too grave a threat to TEAMMATE society and so...they were murdered."

The children murmured amongst themselves in worry.

"It's frightening to think of, I know," said Ellie. "You ten were rescued for a purpose, as was I, along with Andy and Judith. But we three from the other side cannot succeed without your help before we leave this place."

Jamie looked at her with puzzlement. "What do you need from us?"

"We need you to draw us some water from your well," Ellie explained. "The purpose of the water is for you to baptize each of us, so our souls will be ready for Him. The ten of you already have this gift, thanks to Em. We are now ready for you to share that gift with us."

Ellie made eye contact with her friends. Andy nodded while Judith shrugged hesitantly. While there was much more work to be done, progress was being made.

"There's one other thing we need to do while they prepare the water," said Ellie. She reached into her pack, digging for her tool. "Your bracelets have to go."

Judith looked nervously from Ellie to Andy. Then her eyes rested on Ellie's own wrist. "How?" she asked, bewildered. "How are you even alive right now?"

"Maybe removal is deadly inside the sector, although I'm not entirely sure that's the truth." Ellie manipulated her cutting device into the correct configuration. "There are a great number of lies we've been told. The good news is we're going to expose them all, starting tomorrow. Now, let me see your wrists."

CHAPTER
THIRTY

After the bracelet cutting and a quick baptismal ceremony, performed primarily by Jamie and Phyllis, it was time for Ellie to be briefed on the events inside the sector since she'd left. She sat close to Andy next to the fire, taking his hand in her own, afraid that if she let go, they might be separated again. The boy did not take his eyes off her. As they sat, both he and Judith racked their brains for every detail they could remember since Ellie's disappearance. The school had been locked down after Ellie escaped. There were six TEAMMATE officials within the school, and Ellie had escaped. No one seemed to know why they were there.

Judith had indeed been in the restroom stall that Ellie was about to open before Em's message. She was crying and sick to her stomach. She regretted her decision to send in a tip on the anonymous TEAM-MATE reporting network. It had turned out not to be anonymous at all. She learned this after two TEAMMATE officials showed up at her doorstep thirty minutes later that night. They'd questioned her at length, long into the night, although she didn't have to take the dreaded KSM test. Her parents were beside themselves. She still hadn't understood the extent of her betrayal on the bus the next morning.

After Ellie escaped, rumors had sprung up quickly, and the taller the tale, the faster it was repeated. The stories ranged from Ellie being wanted for stealing TEAMMATE property all the way up to Ellie concealing pregnancy. Her classmates recalled her outburst in class, but such an offense certainly did not call for a school lockdown. It would only later be revealed that she was concealing dangerous pagan propaganda in her home. But her escape baffled everyone. No one could avoid officials much longer than a few hours before being caught. And that's when Andy realized she'd somehow escaped the fence.

In the meantime, Miss Conway had returned to class the next day after being held for TEAMMATE questioning. She did not tell the class this information, but her conversation with Principal Flannery was overheard by a student aide. The teacher maintained that she must have been given a KSM test and had her memory wiped clean. She had no memory of anything while TEAMMATE held her in custody. The very next day, Kirk Wilder was taken into custody. Andy had no doubt he would be next on their list, and he also knew Ellie would need his help. Judith had been devastated since Ellie's disappearance, and he thought she might have insight to help him find her, so he enlisted her help, unaware it was her ill-fated decision that caused everything.

For her own part, Ellie filled them in about Em and how she'd cloaked her bracelet and gotten through the fence. She was confident she could get everyone back through the fence tomorrow. She told them about the little sector, about her visions, and about the calming peace after she slept. Lastly, she explained exactly what they all really were now.

"We are not pagans," she said. "Phyllis, can you tell Andy and Judith what we are?"

The girl smiled. "We are Christians. And we're not bad, like TEAMMATE says we are."

"That's right," said Ellie. "We're not going back into the sector to hurt anyone or claim retribution. But we will set history straight. There have been too many lies."

"But, why did they...I guess I should now say we...destroy the world?" asked Judith. "I mean, I like what I've heard so far, especially the forgiveness part. But what caused them to fight?"

Ellie nodded. "Remember, we can't take TEAMMATE at its word. They have lied about murdering thousands of our own citizens. We will uncover the truth, and I suspect it won't be what we've been taught. They will try to stop us, but they will fail. None of us is supposed to be where we are right now but take a look around."

All the children glanced around, uncertainty in their eyes.

"We were all destined to be here. Everything has happened as it must—even with you, Judith." Her eyes met her friend's for only a moment before Judith looked down. "I wish it were by other means, but it is not up to me or any of us to control. It's also not up to us to fully understand—yet, at least. I have no abilities on my own. Collectively, we lack the resources needed to attempt what we must succeed in doing. And yet we shall do it anyway. We are all alive for this purpose. My grandmother knew. Em knows. Now, so do all of you. It's time to get some rest for the evening. We will be walking a long distance over the next few days. Pack what you can comfortably carry for tomorrow's journey. And have faith. God is with us.

THE NEXT MORNING, THE CHILDREN AROSE FROM THEIR BLANkets around the fire. Petey and Bart served a breakfast of hard-boiled eggs to the hungry group. They ate with nervous excitement. Afterwards, Tommy and Maddi, the two youngest, cleaned the camp. Ellie was impressed by the manners of the children. Em had taught them well. She learned that each child had stayed hidden in Em's rural house through age four, before she would smuggle them out. Then she'd rescue another child or two if needed, with whoever helped her on the inside. The children's camp had a chicken coop, a well, and a common room, along with housing and bedding shacks. However, the children seemed to like being in the open center of the camp, where they could all remain together.

They were supplied with goods from Em, who would now set a date most months to meet Jamie and have him deliver supplies whenever there was fence maintenance, as it was getting more difficult for her to make the trek herself these days.

She had a supplier and informant of the upcoming maintenance somewhere within the TEAMMATE network that made the survival of the children possible. They wore no bracelets, and as far as TEAMMATE was concerned, they had never existed. And so, they had persisted, until now.

After everyone was packed, Ellie led the way with Andy and Judith by her side to the fence she'd passed through just four days earlier. It was late morning by the time they reached their destination. They collectively stared at the barrier to the sector, fearful of its capabilities. No one spoke what they were all surely thinking. They were on the cusp of change, and despite their long anticipation of this day, many within the group harbored second thoughts. It was at this moment that Petey cried out in surprise.

"There's a drone coming!" The boy frantically pointed to the sky, and indeed, there was a large sphere approaching from the east, appearing to follow the fence line.

"We need to hide!" yelled Jamie. He grabbed Maddi's hand and looked over the band of children with worry.

"It's too late," Ellie said calmly. "They've already seen us. But it won't matter soon enough. The drone can't hurt us. It's only for surveillance."

Her words did not reassure the group so easily. The main group shrank away in fear, and the children glanced around nervously, ready to make their escape, like so many frightened rabbits. The drone stopped its movement and hovered above the fence, watching and recording, but as Ellie said, it had no ability beyond its intended purpose.

Ellie stepped toward the sector's perimeter fence alone. The fear radiating from the group of watchful children behind her warmed the air like crackles of electricity. The collective trepidation in the moment was powerful yet unpredictable, and so she needed to harness their hope as well as fear to keep their resolve strong. She'd told them she had crossed through before, and she could do it again. The drone was just a distraction for the moment. She inhaled a fresh breath of air, now standing within reach of the metallic base of one of the massive posts that transferred the lethal sector sustaining energy to its neighboring posts, each approximately fifty yards away to the east and west. If one were unwise, they might try to simply walk into that open area, where nothing grew between the posts. Ellie cleared her mind, preparing to ask for His aid.

She nearly jumped forward at the touch of a hand on her shoulder.

"Andy!" she whispered in between breaths. "It isn't safe for you to be this close."

There was worry apparent in his features as he locked eyes with her. "Ellie, are you sure you have to do this?" His question was more a plea than an inquiry.

"Yes," she said without hesitation. "I've never been more certain of anything in my life."

Andy looked down. He took a deep breath before continuing. "Judith and I came out here to save you, Ellie. I can't bear the thought of anything happening to you. You don't have to prove anything to me. I believe you can get us through. I also believe you've rediscovered something vital to our existence. But why must we go back? Why couldn't we start a new life out here, away from TEAMMATE? You can teach us all out here safely." He paused a moment. "I...love you, Ellie. I don't want them to steal you away. I want you to be...mine." He looked down sheepishly.

Ellie was caught somewhere between a sob and a smile at his words. "I love you, too, Andy Jacobs. I would love to do it all, just like you said. You're right. We could start our own society." She glanced back at the group of children, then back toward the drone. "But to walk away from our people, our families, unknowingly imprisoned in the sector and to leave them alone in darkness..." She looked fiercely into his eyes. "I can't accept that failure, knowing I never tried. I was born for this. I know it. Without His strength, I would be trembling right now at the thought of what we're about to do. I would be ready to run away from the sector as far as we could. But His people, on the other side of this fence are being held prisoner, against their own knowledge. They need Him. They've been cut off from His love and protection for too long. All of our families and all of our friends have been living a lie for generations. To be gifted this truth and this purpose and for us not to share it...would be selfish and cruel."

Andy looked wounded at her assertion.

"Don't be troubled, my love," she continued. "I still have more to teach you if you are willing...about Him and about history. This... spark we are about to ignite...it has all happened before." She reached into her pocket. "And once it catches, it will spread quickly and light the way for our future." She held out her hand, looking him in the eye. Andy instinctively held out his own palm to receive the item she held. "But not without some sacrifice. I can't say exactly how our chips will fall." She placed the fire igniter in his hand. "But you can help me fight the darkness with this."

Andy looked quizzically at his hand before raising his gaze to Ellie's eyes. He placed the lighter in his pocket and put his other hand on her shoulder. "The sacrifice is what worries me most." He grimaced as if in pain. "I won't try to stop you again. And I won't leave your side. I told you once before I believed you were special." He had to fight the onset of a tickle in his throat, threatening to halt his words. "I was right. I missed it for so many years, but once I realized it...I knew I had to be with you." He took her hand. "We go through together, always."

Ellie could see his determination and the fear he was pushing aside to stand next to her. He still had so much to learn, but he was beginning to show signs of faith, and it gave her chills at the realization. "Whenever two or more voices join in His name, He is with them," she said. "Pray with me for His aid."

From a distance away, Judith and the others watched the two teenagers, who now stood with heads bowed, facing the enormous post. The metal pole continued on with its usual hum as they stood silent... watching...waiting. The drone watched everything curiously from above. The clouds began to quickly build in the sky above. The noises of the crickets and various other insects in the field of grass that bordered the sector perimeter became thunderous with anticipation. As Judith watched her best friend and her lifelong crush standing with their hands joined, a single tear rolled down her cheek at the scene.

Suddenly, the ground shuddered beneath everyone's feet. The youngest of the children cried out in fear. Ellie shot a quick glance back toward the group to witness Judith instinctively grab Jamie's hand as the group huddled close together. Assured that the children were safe, Ellie and Andy fell to their knees, squeezing each other's hands steadfast in prayer, voiced by her and echoed by Andy. The terrible shaking continued until there was a collective gasp as one of the smallest children cried, "Look!"

All eyes rose to the nearest steel pole, which was beginning to sway with the bombardment of the unsteady ground.

"Look at them all!" shouted Jamie. He placed one arm around Judith and the other pointed down the sector border.

Multiple poles began tipping and falling into and out of the sector. There were five poles down within seconds. The crying had turned into a hushed awe by this point as everyone watched the events unfold. Then, as suddenly as the violent shaking had begun, it ceased, leaving an eerie silence in its wake. The insects had long since ceased their clamor. That's when the drone plummeted from the sky, impacting the ground with a jarring crash, scattering earth and debris in all directions.

Ellie watched the frightened children cautiously rise to their feet. Judith stood along with Jamie, who seemed to notice her clinging to him for the first time. He cast a quick grin toward her, and despite herself, Judith found herself smiling back. But when she received a look of disapproval from Phyllis, she quickly dropped Jamie's hand.

"The fence is off!" said Petey. And it must have been true, for there was no hum from the once proud pillar that now rested on the ground.

Ellie turned to gaze skyward with a large smile and a look of relief. Andy stared at the girl with wide eyes.

"It's not just the fence, Petey," she said conveying complete calm. "The drone is down. Communication is down. Transportation is all down. The power could be down for hours or even days."

The group cheered with renewed vigor.

"How did you do it?" asked Jamie with amazement.

"I didn't," said Ellie. "He did." She glanced upward. "Andy and I asked and trusted He would deliver." She flashed him a warm smile. "And He provided exactly what we needed. A power loss will buy us time to get to the people. This will be much better than simply passing through the fence. Now it's time for us to play our part in His plan. Together we will walk forward with faith."

As promised, Ellie and Andy entered the sector side by side with the children on their heels.

CHAPTER
THIRTY-ONE

The group of twelve children plus one marched atop the lifeless dirt between the fallen perimeter poles. Without incident, their column passed through the previously deadly zone. The ten who had survived outside the sector most of their lives scanned every inch of the horizon with wonder. This was the forbidden land they'd once been rescued from, but they believed things were about to change. Judith and Andy walked in the front of the group alongside Ellie, not without some fear, but with less wonder than the ten behind them. None of the ten banished children, save Jamie, had reentered the sector since Em had rescued them. And Jamie's reentries for supplies were only by the cover of darkness. Eventually, the group came upon a road that ran east and west, parallel to the sector's fallen southern fence. Opposite of this road, they could see an expansive field of harvested corn. The weathered stubs remained from the once-tall, proud stalks of corn that had been cut to feed the sector and its livestock. No houses were in sight, which was not surprising considering how sparse the population became the further one traveled south from the capital. Ellie stood a moment, absorbed in thought, while Judith glanced left and right, uncertainty plain upon her face.

"Which way are we going?" Judith asked after a few seconds of tense silence.

Ellie looked from the fields to her friend. "What do you see, Judith?"

"Uhh, I see empty fields."

"Harvested fields," corrected Ellie, now addressing the group that had closed in on her. "This sector right now is like those fields, before the threshing machine collected the corn. Our job is to prepare the way for the harvester. There are far...far too few ready for when He comes. They have been robbed of vital nutrients to mature into what they can be. We are to spread that vital nutrient of truth, so that they may grow. There are good products as well as bad ones at the harvest. The bad will be thrown out to rot, but the good will be saved. Remember this." She closed her eyes and tilted back her head in the sunlight. After a moment, a smile crossed her lips. "We go left here. It may take some time, but the next road north will be our path."

Jamie made his way to the front of the group. "How are we to spread this truth? The children trust you, but they're scared. What will happen once we are seen? Should we not be hiding? Should we not be running for cover? Are we to fight when we're discovered?"

"It's natural to be frightened of something new. Our Teammates will also be frightened of us at first. But we will win them over with truth and light." Ellie said the words as if it were a foregone conclusion that they would be successful.

"But they've...we've been taught since kindergarten that pagans are the most dangerous people throughout history," said Judith with a hint of exasperation. "If what you told us about the camp is true, everyone will be cheering when they round us up to take us away."

"You're not wrong, Judith," answered Ellie. "That's why we have so much work to do before we reach the capital. And remember, we are not pagans."

"Christians," Petey gently corrected with a proud smile on his face.

"Thank you, Petey. Calling us pagans is an entirely inaccurate description of our history. Mind you, as I've said before, it was done purposefully—to muddy the waters of truth. They could have titled us witches or elves or fairies just as inaccurately, although those titles probably wouldn't be as scary as pagans."

"Christians," Andy whispered the word beside her. "I like that so much better."

It was a few hours later before the group found itself traveling the route north. They had journeyed into the afternoon before they came upon a vehicle pulled over to the side of the road. The younglings held back slightly as Ellie led a few of the older teens to the vehicle, which appeared to be some type of transport van. There was a silhouette in the backseat of the vehicle, with the driver's seat abandoned.

Circling the vehicle while the others looked on, Ellie could see the back window was cracked open, and inside sat a middle-aged man. He sat upon a scooter, which was secured to the floor of the vehicle.

"Would you like some help?" asked Ellie as she peered through the lightly tinted window.

The man peered back, puzzled. "Children?" He turned his head to see the entire group. "It's not safe out here, kids. My driver went to get help. The power for the entire sector might be down. They say there's an army of pagans coming."

Ellie stared at the man with pity in her eyes. "You can't walk, can you?"

"No, child. At least not far enough to escape what's probably coming for me." He stared down at his legs in resignation. "It's one of those conditions that get progressively worse over time. There is no cure."

"What is your name?" asked Ellie.

"Dobay," the man said.

"And why are you alone on this road among these lonely fields?" she asked with curiosity.

The man shrugged his shoulders. "I like to come back here every month or so. It reminds me of when I was productive for TEAM-MATE. I used to be assigned to this agricultural unit. I ran the machinery to keep the land producing for the sector. Of course, I unexpectedly developed this affliction, so I was relieved of my job. I stay outside the capital now, in a home with others like me that are...broken."

"I don't think you're broken at all, Dobay," Ellie said. "Why don't you open your door and come out here to join us?"

Dobay laughed with sadness. Water began to well in his eyes, but no tears fell. "I don't think you understand. I'd love nothing better than to jump out of this van and walk with you kids away from those terrible people coming..." He hesitated for a moment, considering the situation. "Say, shouldn't you kids be in school today?"

"Probably," said Ellie, now opening the man's door. "I'd like to see you walk with us. We have a long way to go, but I'm sure you can make it."

"Ellie, we can't lift him back in if he falls..." started Judith.

The leader of their group raised her hand to silence her friend, then extended her other hand to Dobay's shoulder. "It's time you got out of this chair, Dobay. Your wife and children want you to come home. They miss you dearly."

The man looked at the girl with astonishment. "How could you know?" He whispered the question as he instinctively took her hand in his. His eyes bulged in bewilderment as she pulled him toward her, and he placed a foot firmly on the floor of the van and pushed himself upward. He trembled, whether from weakness or fear, it wasn't clear, but his next step onto the pavement had him wobbly standing on his feet outside the van.

"Let's go for that walk, my friend." She smiled with compassion as her words drew tears from the man's eyes. His large frame took an unsteady step while holding her hand, then another and another.

"Will you come with us to the capital before returning to your family?"

The grown man sobbed loudly now as he walked beside her. "I'm afraid if I let go, this will all end and I'll fall face first onto the pavement."

With her free hand, Ellie patted Dobay's shoulder. "I assure you, God has healed you completely. I'm going to let go now. Ask Him for his hand, and He will walk with you, always."

The white of the man's eyes grew in shock, fear, and joy, but he obeyed, releasing her hand and stepping forward into the sunlight, away from the shadows of the group. He walked forward a few paces before he turned around. "So, you're the pagans we were supposed to fear?"

"Christians," Andy said before Ellie could correct the man.

The smile on Dobay's lips grew into a hearty laugh. "I thought you'd be much scarier." He shook his head in disbelief. "I believe I'd like to join you on that walk."

CHAPTER
THIRTY-TWO

The band of thirteen children plus Dobay gained another adult by the time they reached the outskirts of the small southern town known as Bethesda. The group had been marching in silence when, to their surprise, they came upon Em pedaling south on her bicycle. The encounter was received with delight by all the children, especially the youngest ones, who had missed their motherly figure dearly.

"My, how you've all grown," Em exclaimed as she skidded to a stop before them. She was rushed by the children and showered in hugs and sobs of happiness. The joy on her face was akin to a proud parent whose grown children had returned home for a holiday dinner. When the excitement quieted down, she noticed there were some in the group she did not recognize.

"And who are these two children, and the man in the back?"

Ellie stepped forward to embrace the woman she'd only met less than a week before. Ages seemed to have passed since their hasty parting. "I found our people, Em. Both the old and the new."

Em nodded and hugged Ellie closely. "I'm sorry, dear. So much has been asked of you. But look how far you've come already. I can feel the Holy Spirit within you."

"It's certainly done incredible things through me. I pray for the strength to allow it to continue its work within me." She looked over to Andy and Judith. "These are my friends, Andy and Judith. They came to help me, out of love."

Em's eyebrows raised, but she didn't say what Ellie supposed she must be thinking.

Ellie gestured to the man who could not stop smiling as he stood near the back of the line. "And this man's name is Dobay. I'll let him share his story with you."

"By His grace, it's finally happening!" Em exclaimed. "There were times I feared I might not survive long enough to see this day. My heart is full. Tell me, my children, are you excited for what is to come?"

One of the youngest, Tommy, was the first to speak up. "At first, I was scared. I didn't want to leave home. But Phyllis and Jamie said we had to. After seeing what Miss Ellie can do, I know we'll be safe with her."

Ellie smiled warmly at the young boy's admission. He was only seven years old, but his faith was strong. "You have all been very brave," Ellie began, "and I couldn't have been blessed with a better group of believers to help spread the truth. I'm so happy Em has rejoined us as well. I only wish my grandmother could walk alongside us."

"She does," said Em quietly. "In angelic form, she follows us, I've no doubt. We were robbed of her and too many others along the road that led us here. Their work, their sacrifice, is why we've made it this far. They did not depart this world in vain. They also believed this day was coming."

There were many emotions swirling about, but in that momentary silence, Judith felt the need to state the obvious.

"This town that lies ahead of us, they might not welcome us with open arms. Those abandoned TEAMMATE vehicles we passed not long ago...there's a good chance they'll be waiting ahead for us. Is no one else worried that we're likely walking into a trap?"

"Your logic is sound, but your faith needs nurturing," said Ellie. She gestured to a sign ahead on the road. "The sign for this town reads *Bethesda.* Does the name sound familiar to any of you? Jamie? Phyllis?"

"Ummm, maybe vaguely?" offered Jamie.

Phyllis scratched her head.

"Dobay could certainly relate to what happened there. At the pool of Bethesda, Jesus healed a paralyzed man, saying, *Rise, pick up your bed and walk.* This town was named after a biblical miracle that was performed two millennia ago, and nobody in TEAMMATE even knows it. Our sector is cloaked in darkness and lies. And thus, it is fitting that we are going to lift that fog and awaken their hearts and minds with the truth. And many of them will walk for the first time with faith."

Dobay nodded his head in excitement. "I know many people from the town. They will see me and will listen to my story. I can't say for sure how they'll react. They may be confused, frightened, even."

"It's been nearly twenty-two hundred years since Jesus visited Bethesda, yet people have not changed," remarked Em.

"That's what worries me," said Andy, knuckling his jawline.

"I do not pretend to foretell the future," Ellie said. "I have been lent some gifts to pull back the veil cast upon us. As I have told you before, do not mistake me for Him. I am weak and flawed. But I believe in my heart that nothing can stop us from reuniting Him with his people. We all need to set our fears aside, like young Tommy. The light that will soon shine in this world cannot be extinguished. Many have tried since the dawn of time, and yet here we remain today, as resolved as ever."

Judith cleared her throat. "So, what I was getting at in a round-about way...can't you just like do the opposite that you did to Dobay if they won't listen?"

"Paralyze them?" asked Ellie.

"Only if needed?" offered Judith.

"I see," said Ellie. "And how would that make us any different than TEAMMATE?"

Judith shrugged.

"It would make us the same, possibly worse," Andy interjected. "People would fear us even more than they already do. They'd be likely to whisper that TEAMMATE was right for all the horrible things they've done to...Christians and those like us along the way."

"Okay, so maybe not the best idea," shrugged Judith. "I was half-joking, you know. Cut me some slack, guys. I'm still new to this whole saving the world thing."

"Is everyone ready to continue?" asked Ellie, unable to suppress her smile.

A chorus of *Yes* echoed back.

"Good. Then let us pray we will continue to walk with enough faith."

EM PUSHED HER BICYCLE ALONGSIDE ELLIE AS THEY CONTINUED toward the town. She helped update the group on what had transpired on her side of the fence prior to the power loss. It happened that Anne Wilder now knew that TEAMMATE suspected her husband's involvement. She also knew that Kirk's family had a dark history involving paganism, as she had never met his mother due to her removal from the sector. Trying to find out more family history had proven impossible without her husband as a resource, as he was now in custody. That's when she remembered his family's friend Em. Looking for answers about her daughter's disappearance, she'd tracked the old woman down.

Upon her arrival at Em's nearby country home, Em revealed to Anne what had become of her daughter. As expected, she did not take the news well that Ellie was alone in the wilderness beyond the sector fence. Nor was she pleased to find out her husband had helped get her daughter out of the sector before erasing his memory. And that's when Em revealed to her what would have happened to Ellie had she not escaped.

After absorbing the bombshell revelation, a TEAMMATE alert had sounded on their bracelets. It warned of a pagan army invasion from the south. When Anne asked Em if the pagans had Ellie, Em told her it was her daughter who led them, and it wasn't an army.

Ellie's mother had sped off before Em could stop her. She was going to protect her daughter, no matter how dangerous TEAM-MATE thought she was. But it wasn't long before the entire sector had lost power, stranding everyone where they were. The last update was that the school was locked down, everyone was ordered to shelter in place, and TEAMMATE officials were en route to intercept the army.

What had occurred since then was anybody's guess. There was no communication possible with the power grid down. All the technology held on a Teammate's wrist was as useless as a paperweight without stationery—not that many would understand the analogy. Em had no wish to stay in the dark at home. Her children might need her. Thereupon, she'd grabbed her bicycle and guessed Ellie's route correctly.

By the time the story was recounted, the town of Bethesda was in full view. Ellie led the group onward with determination. She could see a large crowd had gathered in the street behind a line of TEAM-MATE officials. The officials were clad in riot gear, which included helmets and shields. Ellie was flanked by Andy on her right, with Em and Judith on her left. Directly behind them walked Jamie and Dobay, followed by the remainder of the children.

No one in her group said a word as they drew closer. In the final moments before contact, Ellie reflected on how far she'd come since she'd first found the secret journal. Had she come far enough for what came next? Leading a group of adolescents was one thing, but convincing adult Teammates of the truth and getting them to follow her was quite different. And yet, she'd already done so many things she wouldn't have thought possible before. The problem was, if she failed right now, she knew the cost—and it wasn't just her life. It would be the lives of all of them, and everyone else who had helped them along the way. The KSM test would reveal everyone involved to TEAM-MATE, and they'd be ripped from the fabric of society forever. She thought grimly of her father, likely being tortured for answers he'd erased from his memory forever just to protect her. Or could they have even killed him already? She couldn't think of it. She would find a way to save him, too. She must. They'd all be branded as traitors—as evil doers. And all the souls she was trying to save with her return to the sector would be the cost if she failed.

All these thoughts made Ellie even more anxious. She couldn't deny it. So many Teammates waited ahead of her, blocking the way. The apprehension would have paralyzed the girl she had been before. But she was stronger now, and she was not alone. She didn't know exactly what was going to happen or even what she would say to calm the gathered mass, but she trusted His plan. He had not failed her, and she had faith He never would.

The roar of a thousand Teammates suddenly quieted to a whisper, and then a sinister silence descended. Ellie held up her hand in signal to stop the procession a hundred feet before the TEAMMATE line, where officials stood shoulder to shoulder with shields up.

Near the far-right corner of this line, there was a sudden commotion, and the officials turned their heads back and yelled, keeping shields up to face Ellie. She saw a figure push through the officials and begin running towards her. The figure made it three steps past the officials before one dove and caught the Teammate's leg, pitching them forward. The rusher hit the paved ground hard and screamed in a woman's voice filled with agony. "That's my daughter!"

Ellie felt a pang of panic in her stomach and cast a worried glance toward Andy. She looked back to see her mother wipe at the blood on her face before pushing herself upward to crawl forward.

"No!" Ellie screamed and reached a trembling hand outward as the TEAMMATE official had regained his feet and now raised his shield in a motion to render her mother unconscious.

He held the shield high above his head, and as he moved to bring it down on the back of Anne Wilder, he suddenly froze.

There was an uneasy moment of silence before he yelled, "Help! My arms are stuck!"

No one moved for a minute. The man turned to his cohorts behind him, unable to lower the shield at all. "I can't feel my arms!" he cried. "She did something to me!"

Two other officials moved to help the man and managed to pry the shield from his hands. Once they accomplished this, the man was able to lower his arms again.

While this unfolded, Ellie had to fight the overwhelming urge to run to her mother. If she moved any closer to the defensive barrier, it could cause the officials to move against her and the children. The spacing had to be maintained to give her the opportunity to address the crowd before being overrun.

Ellie cleared her throat, then shouted into the void between her and present society. "I would appreciate it if you didn't harm your own Teammates." She motioned for her mother to join her side. "We have accompanying us, a friend to many in this town. He would like to share his story." She nodded to Dobay, who slowly walked midway into the void. He held his hands above his head to make himself less threatening, for he was not a man of small stature.

"That's Dobay!" someone cried from the crowd. "This is impossible!"

"Who's Dobay?" asked another.

"He's paralyzed. He has to use a scooter to move an inch. Look at him now! What has happened, Dobay?"

The man stood before them and grinned. "I have been healed! Ellie and her friends, they've awakened me from my slumber...from my nightmare. And I'm standing here now to tell all of you that you've also been asleep your whole lives. You simply haven't realized it yet."

Some Teammates began to laugh. "Are we sure this man was really paralyzed?" asked one crowd member.

"I assure you, I was. Because of this, I was released from my work in this agricultural zone. I was also removed from my home to live in a special needs facility, away from my wife and children for the past four years!" His eyes grew large in excitement. "I was stranded in my van along the road, with no way to escape, when these children came upon me. Ellie asked if I would like to walk with her. I, just like many of you here now, laughed in my disbelief that it was possible. But that was before she asked God to heal me! And heal me He did, and I rose to my feet! I stand before you now to say my soul has awakened, and I do believe!"

"He's a pagan!" screamed a woman from the crowd. The murmur of side discussions and questions rose to a buzz, like a swarm of angry bees, unhappy about a threat to their hive.

"You've lived a life of lies!" yelled Dobay from the void. "We all have!"

"We've heard enough!" boomed a man's voice from behind the TEAMMATE line. "This is Thurman Graves, head of the Security branch of TEAMMATE. The entire TEAMMATE Council has ridden here in the waste disposal trucks to take control of your attack on our Teammates. Officials! Arrest him! Arrest them all!"

CHAPTER
THIRTY-THREE

"I assure you all, there is much more to hear," Ellie said into the void. "There have been unspeakable atrocities committed by our own sector against our own Teammates."

A small amount of laughter greeted her announcement, but even more responded with puzzled, curious stares of confusion. Her accusations sounded preposterous, and yet many in the crowd wondered... what else did she have to say?

"Officials! Silence this pagan at once!" barked Thurman. "Heed your TEAMMATE Council and do your job! Don't let them speak further, lest we all be infected with their lies!"

Ellie held out her hands to the crowd. "This is how it has happened every time. They will take us away, and you will never find out what *they* have done! But today will be different. Today you will hear nothing but truth!" She looked sideways at Andy, grabbed his hand, and nodded. "Pray with me," she said as she lowered her eyes to the ground and stretched up their intertwined hands toward the heavens. Immediately, there was a gasp from everyone present as their bracelets powered up in unison. Many instinctively tapped their bracelets and raised their arms skyward for a clear shot to livestream the standoff. Ellie smiled in triumph. Everyone would now be tuned in on the live feeds, trying to figure out what was going on. She nodded to Em, who returned her look and slowly walked forward to join Dobay, who still stood alone. "Listen to the story of Em, before you dismiss my claims," Ellie's voice cut through the crowd.

"She turned the power back on!" a voice cried. Teammates began cheering in relief. Even more Teammates thought to hold up their wristbands in an effort to capture video of the first pagans any of them had ever seen.

Em cleared her voice and spoke with surprising strength for a woman of her years. "Has anyone here been to a pagan reeducation camp?" The crowd grew silent. She looked around knowingly. "No? Has anyone ever met a Teammate who returned from a reeducation camp?" She stood silently as the crowd members whispered amongst themselves, repeating her question to others who hadn't been able to hear. She clapped her hands together. "Well, now you have. I was in those very camps as a teenager with my family."

"Stop her!" shrieked Thurman.

The line of officials looked at each other with hesitation. "Stand down!" commanded another voice that wasn't Thurman's. The voice echoed through a megaphone, silencing everyone now that its volume raised his words above all others. "This is Councilmember Benson. I want to hear this woman speak!" Ellie focused on the voice and recognition triggered in her memory, though she couldn't say why or how. Everyone knew that Councilmember Benson was considered the wisest of all the councilmembers. He did not speak publicly often, but when he did, his words carried perhaps the most weight in the Council.

"Thank you, Councilmember Benson," said Em. "So, what happened to all those *pagans,* as you were instructed to call us all those years ago? Aren't you curious? A good part of my family and our friends? Did we go to some new sector to live our lives free and peaceful, as you have been taught? Absolutely not." Her body shook with emotion. "I know because I was in that camp. I was sentenced like the rest of them. I thought, as all of you still do, we were merely being sent away to live in a separate society." She gently bowed her head. "They lined us up on the edge of a pit that we were forced to dig, and they shot us with the very weapons that were supposed to have been destroyed and outlawed. For some reason, despite being wounded in three separate shots, I did not die, although I pretended. Other bodies fell upon me once I pitched backward into the pit, protecting me from bullets and from being found breathing. I crawled out when it became dark. There were others inside the sector back then. At that time, the fence was merely a fence and wasn't deadly on its own accord. I reached the others, and they took care of me, created a new identity for me, and inserted me back into the society that had sought to erase my name from existence. Well, TEAMMATE succeeded in erasing my name, but that was as far as they got.

"I can show you the holes in my shoulder, thigh, and skull plate. I can lead you all to the mass grave that I was supposed to be buried in as well. And though that hole holds hundreds of mothers, fathers, sons, and daughters—it's just one of many." There were gasps along with a few screams from the crowd. "I find it sickeningly ironic that what actually occurred is exactly what TEAMMATE taught us in school that pagans would do to us if given a chance to stay in our society."

Thurman pushed through the line of security. "Do your job, officials! These are incredibly dangerous lies being peddled to our scared civilians!"

"That will be enough from you, Thurman," said Em with a gesture that made the officials pause. "You are the only councilmember left who signed my death warrant. You can look me up if you like. The

'Em' that I go by today is actually just the first letter of my name. I was named Mary a lifetime ago, before my life was stolen. Mary Wilder."

Ellie's jaw dropped at the revelation. She wasn't merely a family friend. Em was part of her own family.

Thurman's face grew red with rage. "Lies! Why are we letting this pagan speak? Have we learned nothing from history? TEAMMATE has coddled and protected each and every one of you from a savage world that was destroyed by them!" He pointed accusingly at Ellie and the children. "They lie, they kill, they only want to control you! If what she claims is true, how is she not dead?"

"Through a miracle of God," Em yelled back. "I was meant to be here to help you wake up from your nightmare. I had been left for dead after being shot three times. But I crawled out of my grave, believing that one day I would have a chance to no longer be silenced. That day is today."

Anne had finally gotten to her feet during the standoff and moved closer to her daughter.

"Is it all true?" she asked Ellie.

"Every word," said Ellie. She put a protective arm around her mother, recognizing fear in her eyes.

"Seize them now!" yelled Thurman again, trying to push officials forward. "They seek to undo all the progress we've made since the rebirth! As Head of the Security branch, I order them arrested! I command it. You must obey!" His voice seethed with hate, accompanied by fear in his eyes and froth at his mouth.

Ellie calmly gestured to the crowd. "Perhaps we should be asking our TEAMMATE officials to seize this man instead?"

The crowd murmured in confusion and excitement. No one had ever publicly challenged TEAMMATE, let alone a councilmember.

"You have no authority, you wretched pagan!" screamed Thurman. "How dare you threaten a councilmember!"

A shrill voice cut through the mob.

"She does have authority!"

Head Councilmember Winston Jennings and Benson Browning could be seen exchanging glances. "Let the woman speak!" Benson yelled to the officials.

The officials looked to Winston, who looked surprised by Benson's orders. "Benson...do you think it wise..." he began uncertainly.

Benson interrupted him. "I think it would be unwise to silence this woman."

Ellie couldn't believe her ears, but she whispered a prayer of thanks.

The Head Councilmember thought for a moment but deferred his decision to the councilmember beloved by all as an authoritative voice on intellect and reason.

"Let her speak," Winston said with a nod of his head.

Ellie exhaled in relief as her frightened teacher stepped forward. In front of hundreds and hundreds of Teammates, not counting the thousands at home following the live streams broadcast by the present observers, stood a tired, disheveled Edna Conway. She was likely the only person present who didn't want to be there, but she'd always believed in holding herself to a high standard of duty, especially concerning the protection of her students.

"I rode here on a bicycle," she began shakily, clutching at her bag that hung around her shoulder. "I towed a cart carrying one of our first-years to his home earlier today to receive the vital medicine that he must receive every night. We were on lockdown at school, like everyone else, and had he missed his evening dose, it could have been very bad. I volunteered because I'm a teacher, and every Teammate in that building, large and small, is my responsibility. And so, after delivering him to his anxious family, I was close enough to come here to help another student. Before the power went out, I received information that I don't believe anyone else is aware of yet. You see, I was," she cleared her voice to speak more confidently, "I mean, I *am* Ellie's teacher for the sorting year. I realized there was something special about this young lady from the first week in class when she healed the boy, you see, standing at her side now. He was having a seizure until it somehow stopped the moment she touched him."

The crowd chewed on this new information amongst themselves for a moment before Edna continued.

"The information in my bag changes everything." She inhaled a large breath, as if considering the consequences of her words. Then she exhaled and reached into her satchel and pulled out her reader, holding it high above her head. "On my device are the TEAMMATE Placement Test results for our sorting years," she yelled in a shrill voice. "And what they will show you all today is, not only did Ellie score the highest in her class...she achieved something that's only happened once in our history...something that was supposed to be not only im-probable, but impossible. She recorded a perfect score, which qualifies her for immediate placement on the TEAMMATE Council!"

The crowd could no longer be kept at bay. In a society that swooned over knowledge and intellect, the realization that the pagan girl before them was superior to every councilmember save one in history flood-ed the Teammates with an emotional overload of adoration, curiosity, and pride. They swept past the official line like a prairie fire fueled with a tailwind. For their own part, most of the officials stood slack-jawed by the revelation, not that they had a prayer of containing the now furious blaze of excitement that had just been doused with fossil fuel.

Councilmember Winston took one look at the scene unfolding before him and grabbed Benson's megaphone. "All councilmembers fall back to the trucks! We have a riot on our hands!" He shouted the words with disgust as the crowds began encircling the pagan group in a frenzy. The Council had been afraid that the pagans would push their way into the town, but instead, the girl had pulled Bethesda's residents outside its own protective border. The outcome had been inconceiv-able moments before, and yet it was now reality.

From a distance, Ellie counted fourteen councilmembers narrowly avoid being trampled by their own Teammates as the governing group made their way upstream from the rushing crowds. They were one short, she realized.

The crowd circled Ellie, with Andy and Dobay trying to keep a safety perimeter around the girl. Anne Wilder grabbed her daughter's shoulder. "Ellie, the TEAMMATE Council and officials are fleeing!" She tapped her bracelet and projected a livestream hologram from a Teammate recording the frightened councilmembers.

"Where's Benson?" asked the distraught young woman Ellie remembered from class as Nannette.

Winston appeared to scan the crowd with worry.

"He was probably swept up in that avalanche of idiots," yelled Thurman. "If we don't escape soon, we'll all be in the same boat."

Winston could be seen holding his bracelet up to his ear to hear amidst the chaos. The other members argued for and against leaving their comrade behind.

The head of the Council's facial expression looked pained when he ended the call.

"We have to leave now. Our security forces have detected an enormous mass of citizens making their way here as we speak. For some reason, I can't get a signal to link Benson."

"I told you this would happen!" spat Thurman. "I'm the only one that's been around long enough to understand the hysteria we're dealing with!"

Winston narrowed his eyes on his fellow councilmember. "Tell me, Thurman, how much of this Mary Wilder's story was true? Is this how TEAMMATE achieved the most perfect society recorded in the history of man? By extermination of anyone who dissented?"

Thurman sneered at him and the others. "It's more complicated than you could possibly comprehend. Sacrifices had to be made for progress. The likes of today's Council would have no stomach for building a new civilization that could endure for ages. The difficult decisions your predecessors made are what put us where we are today."

Jaws gaped open in disbelief at the man's words. He was on a live stream, and he hadn't denied it. Ellie was grateful she could rely on the citizenry circulating the clip for a few hours before TEAMMATE would have a chance to take it down. But the exchange wasn't over yet, as the councilmembers had no idea they were being recorded.

"I want all those records unsealed the minute we're in the capital," ordered Winston.

Thurman laughed. "You can unseal everything, but you'll never find a trace of what Mary Wilder described. It's been doctored and erased. Just like our whole history. Just like the pagans...until today. Thanks to your spineless lack of leadership, this girl has undone generations of work while you all stood and watched! Imagine it. Having the capacity to act and quell a hurricane of chaos but choosing not to do anything. You've all failed this sector!"

"Someone has to know what happened," stammered Nannette. "There surely were security officials there to recount what happened. We can find them and piece it all together."

"Do you really think your predecessors didn't think of that? You think they trusted anyone to keep TEAMMATE's secrets?" Thurman glanced around the group in apparent amusement. "No. I don't think you'll find a trace of them in history. Good luck finding anyone alive who's ever been there. As I said, tough decisions were made." He turned his back on his fellow members in disgust and walked haughtily toward the front passenger seat of the garbage truck. The feed ended as the trucks sped away from Bethesda.

CHAPTER
THIRTY-FOUR

Ellie felt Judith's gaze of wonder out of the corner of her eye as she tried to focus on the eager crowd. She was likely thinking the same thoughts Ellie herself had forced to the back of her mind. She was probably amazed that the girl who had no friends, save herself, for the entirety of primary school was now speaking to a growing group numbering near a thousand, and they hung on every word she said. She was instructing adults two, three, and four times her own age to encircle her, so they could hear the truth that had been kept from them their entire lives. Her own sorting class teacher was among those listening. Of course, these numbers merely included the Teammates present listening, for with the power now fully restored, nearly every sector member was watching and listening through the network. And now that a few of TEAMMATE's dirty secrets had aired publicly, she would not be silenced like so many before her. The events had unfolded so perfectly to protect her and allow her to speak that no one

247

could deny that whoever's game plan they were now following had shielded them from certain doom and captured an entire civilization's attention.

Ellie saw her friend's face harden as she tried to concentrate on Ellie's address to the crowd. Undoubtedly, these words did not sound like those of the girl she'd ridden the bus with since grade school.

"This is the beginning of a new rebirth—both inside our souls as well as for the world we once knew," continued the fifteen-year-old girl with power in her voice. "We've been cut off from returning His abundant love, and we've lost our true purpose as a result. But what is our purpose?" She glanced around, turning full circle, inviting someone to speak. "There is no punishment for wrong answers," she said with a gentle smile.

Someone a few rows back spoke up. "To be a good TEAMMATE is our purpose."

"Ahhh, yes," exclaimed Ellie, her smile growing. "That is a textbook answer from the TEAMMATE Rulebook. But how does one become a good Teammate?"

The voice from a nearby woman responded bluntly, "By following TEAMMATE rules, we ensure the common good for everyone. We work to our strengths to contribute to the combined strength of all our Teammates."

"There it is," said Ellie. "The common good...it's such a fragile concept, right? It sounds caring and inclusive, which is important." She paused for effect as the people considered her words. "Even when used for justification to murder thousands of our own population and to cover it up as a second reeducation society? Even for removing your own free will to work in an area that you could choose for yourself? Even for punishing anyone who would dare to speak their mind on their own beliefs, whatever they may be, should they not align with TEAMMATE? Understand this...in the time before right now, if our group were smaller, if all the sector had not heard the truth on the network, we would all be promptly rounded up and reeducated. No explanation would be given to our parents, to our children, or to our friends. In the timespan of a finger snap, none of us would ever be heard from again because...the greater good. But whom does the greater good reference? Certainly, it can't be all of you or me once we're eliminated."

A man stood up. "But if we make our purpose for ourselves and not the team, we will fall into the same trap as our ancestors. We will fight against and amongst each other. We will compete to make ourselves better and others worse."

"A noble consideration," returned Ellie. "But our purpose is not entirely for ourselves. To paraphrase the one who came to teach this world everything we ever needed to know...that is...before they nailed Him on a public display to watch Him die, our purpose is quite simple." She looked around at the enormous, hushed crowd, eagerly awaiting her deliverance of truth. "Our purpose is to love. Love your neighbor, love your enemies, love yourself, and most importantly... love Him." She pointed to the sky. "That's it. Our purpose is not to love an organization. Not to love someone's idea of what a civilization should be like. Love each other! And love God."

"But it cannot work!" The same man's voice rang out again. "We will fall back in time. Wars will return, unequal distribution, famine, sickness! It will be the destruction of the human race!"

Ellie held up a hand. "Is it not so already?" She asked the question with a feigned look of confusion on her face. "You've just learned that a war has been going on in secret. Thousands have been erased from society. Was there not a famine just a few short years ago, despite all our collective brainpower? Do we not still need physicians because of sickness? Do you really suggest that we all currently live exactly equal? Would you even aspire to live that way if it were reality? No matter what you did, you could not own something if anyone else didn't also own whatever it might be?" She looked around, but the man and everyone else fell silent. "You are all frightened, and that is natural with regard to the unknown and unfamiliar. But don't place all your trust in humanity. Place your trust in God. He loves us. He created us. He wants your love in return. He wants you to love each other. And that, my friends, is why we are here."

"You make it sound simple," said a man in an official's uniform. Apparently, not all of the security forces fled the chaos. Some had joined. "What are we to do now? How can we possibly change the only world we've ever known? What you speak of is against the rules." He looked around. "All of us will be punished for hearing what you've said."

Ellie nodded. "It won't be easy. I will take my argument to the Council, upon which I will now sit," she said with a smile. "I will win them over with love and reason. I will never force anyone to follow. Our Father gave us all free will for a reason, and my wish is to see that restored, now that the truth has been unchained from its prison of concealment. We can fix this sector without creating more bloodshed. With all this in mind, I will travel north, on foot, with the group I started this trip with. Some of you may wish to follow, and that would be welcome. Others have additional duties to attend to, so they will need to go home, but they may still follow our progress on the network. I would request each of you to talk to your neighbors about all that you've seen and heard today. And one final point before we depart. Continue to live your lives from this day forward with love."

Ellie concluded her speech to much applause. It seemed as though reason might yet win the day. She stooped to her bag for a drink of water. Then she checked on the ten shocked children from beyond the fence and made sure they drank plenty of water as she distributed the leftovers of her own food stores to them. She felt her mother's hand on her back.

"Your grandmother is linking me," said Anne. "I'm sure she'd very much want to hear from you."

Ellie glanced at the sun's height. She found herself missing her bracelet for the simple tasks. It had to be late afternoon, but she owed her grandmother a quick word. Ellie nodded, and her mother accepted the link. "Wait, have you heard anything from Dad?"

Anne looked downward and quickly nodded no, avoiding eye contact with her daughter.

"Annie!" It was Ellie's grandmother's voice, and it sounded filled with fear and...pain?

"Mom, everything is okay. I'm with Ellie now. I'm going to stay with her. Have you been watching what's happening?"

Her mother wailed with anguish. "Molly is missing, Annie! All the children were released from school when the power came on. She was there, according to her teacher, but I'm here now and she's gone!"

The news hit Ellie like an unexpected punch to the gut. She tried to catch her breath, but the flood of panic was drowning her breath as she began to hyperventilate. *Not Molly too.* Her stomach felt queasy, as if she'd crested a large hill and had unexpectedly stumbled over a cliff, leaving her stomach above while her body was falling...falling. She looked at her mother's face and saw it void of any color as she stared at Ellie, speechless.

"Annie, are you still there? Please tell me what I should do. She's too little to be wandering the sector by herself. Can you get ahold of Kirk?"

Anne swallowed hard, but her mouth had suddenly become quite dry. "Kirk is still in custody with TEAMMATE. They've had him for days."

"I don't understand," stammered her mother. "I know you were fighting after Ellie disappeared, but why would they have him locked up?"

Anne sniffled. "Because I turned him in!" she cried. "I...I thought he was responsible for Ellie's disappearance."

Ellie's jaw fell open in surprise.

There was a pause. "I'm so sorry, Annie. Please tell me what I should do. I'm here at the school and I'm having a meltdown."

"I don't have the answer. All I can think of is to...pray."

"Oh, Annie, no! The pagans have gotten to you, too?" The reply came in a tone of horror.

"I don't know yet, Mom," Ellie heard her mother sob. Then she looked at her daughter. "They don't sound so crazy. All Ellie is talking about is love. It sounds like something our sector could use right now. That and some serious allegations against TEAMMATE. I've got to get back to my car. It broke down when the power went offline. I've got to get home to you."

Her mother cleared her throat. "I never thought I'd live to see the rise of the pagans."

"It's a rebirth, Ellie says."

"Things are going to get very bad. I don't want to lose both my granddaughters. How are you going to get home?"

Ellie looked around the group that immediately surrounded her and spied Em...or rather Mary now, who was holding her bicycle upright, ready to follow the group.

"I have an idea," said Ellie. She addressed her mother's bracelet. "Grandma, please watch the clips from today. It's all true. I love you, but we have to go now."

"Thank goodness you're alright!" It was the last she heard before her mother ended the conversation and locked eyes with her daughter.

"I'm so sorry, Ellie. I didn't realize he was protecting you." She swallowed before continuing. "His story to the officials didn't add up. His whole account of the day was wrong. What he ate, what he wore, what we talked about. It was as if he made it all up. We got in an argument, and he finally admitted he was confused. He said he couldn't remember. I thought he was lying. I was afraid he was covering something up. I thought TEAMMATE was going to rescue you. Oh, I was so stupid, Ellie! You're on the Council now, right? Can't you get him out?"

Ellie hugged her mother. "You couldn't have known. If it's not too late, I'll get him out. Let's just pray I'm in time."

Humankind has the ability to manipulate any strong belief into aggression.

—Excerpt from pagan diary

CHAPTER
THIRTY-FIVE

Ellie had only led her group north for a little over an hour before she glanced back to see Dobay jogging awkwardly toward her, urgency tattooed on his face. Not wanting to cause alarm or stall their slow progress, she kept walking but signaled for him to join her, Andy, Judith, and Jamie at the front of the line.

When he reached her, he wiped the sweat from his brow. "I haven't done that for seven years," he admitted exasperated. "I'm still grateful, no matter what's required of me." He said the words with a smile.

"Why the urgency, Dobay?" asked Ellie.

He nodded. "Right. Well, there's a man who approached me about seeing you."

"There are a lot of people who'd like to see her," interrupted Andy. "Frankly, I trust none of them, and neither should you."

Dobay scratched his head. "I tried to explain that to him, but he refused to listen. He said that you knew him and you needed his help.

253

He said to give you a message. He assured me you would not turn him away." He grimaced before continuing. "The thing of it is—I don't trust him either. He's got a hood pulled over his head."

"A hood? Like some type of assassin?" asked Judith. "Let me talk to him first." For a girl lacking in stature, she'd become very protective of Ellie since the crowds. Not to mention brave.

"Well...what's the message I supposedly can't turn away?" asked Ellie. Her patience was wearing thin.

Dobay glanced skyward. "Let me get it right. He said, *Ellie saved my life once, and I'm here to return the favor. Ask her if she remembers Benny.*"

"Benny!" Ellie nearly shouted it.

Andy's face registered recognition. "The boy from your vision?"

"I knew he survived," said Ellie breathlessly. "Yes, by all means, bring him up here now."

Dobay followed her instructions but kept the hooded figure at arm's length, lest he need to dispatch the man. He nearly swung at the man when he placed a gentle hand upon Em's shoulder. But Em, or rather Mary Wilder, was delighted to see the stranger.

Ellie saw Dobay breathe a sigh of relief and relax a little more after that. When Benny was within conversation distance, he looked around before briefly lowering his hood.

Ellie, Andy, and Judith collectively gasped before Benny pulled his hood back over his head.

"You know who I am?" asked Benny. His voice matched another voice they'd heard earlier that day.

"You're Benson Browning?" asked Ellie incredulously. "My little brave Benny went on to score the only perfect TEAMMATE Placement result and heads the Science branch while sitting on the TEAMMATE Council?"

"I hear the kids these days are smarter than sixty years ago." She could see a smile through the shadows of his hood. "I'm terribly sorry for the secrecy, but I can't risk being seen yet. If I am, I'll lose the ability to help you on the Council."

"But don't they know you're here, that you're missing?" asked Andy.

"Missing? Yes. Offline? Yes. Here? No." He lifted his sleeve to reveal a metallic cover over his bracelet."

"That's like the one Em…Mary gave me," said Ellie.

Benson chuckled. "Who do you think designed it? It's wonderful to see your face again after all these years. You were my angel, Ellie. But listen, we don't have much time. Every official in TEAMMATE is searching for me. I'll need to slip away soon and pretend that the large crowd caused my bracelet to malfunction. The minute I ditch this signal blocker, a van will appear from nowhere and 'rescue me.' In the meantime, I want you to understand what you're walking into. No matter what I say or do, I am only one of fifteen votes on the Council. They will try to set a trap. I know these people—specifically Thurman." He glanced around conspiratorially. "They're meeting right now. As a councilmember, I can stream it for us to listen in." He produced a second bracelet from his pocket and tapped it until it projected a live feed of what looked like the TEAMMATE Council chambers. "Listen in," he said.

Ellie and the others watched the events play out as if they sat in the chamber.

"Before the discussion begins, I'd like to record a summary of events that have unfolded within the last 24 hours," said Winston. He glanced around the room. The members appeared shaken to Ellie. Some were worried, some sat lost in thought, and some, like Thurman, sat with arms crossed in anger at the events that had unfolded. "First and foremost, we are missing Councilmember Benson. We are trying to track his location, but it seems that due to the size of the crowd, we are having issues receiving feedback. Assuming he is alive, our priority will be to retrieve him as soon as technical support recovers his whereabouts. Until then, we will unfortunately be without his normally calm voice of reason."

Thurman offered a "Hrrumph," but didn't interrupt after a glare from Nannette.

"As we're all aware, somehow this group of pagan children was able to shut down our sector's power grid and simply walk across our perimeter fence. There seems to have been a natural phenomenon at exactly the right moment that felled a few of our towers, sending a surge that cut off all power temporarily. It has now been restored, albeit seemingly at subject alpha's command, as we all witnessed. We already had the father of alpha in custody while this was occurring. I've just been notified that he escaped while the power was down and we were distracted on our trip. All efforts are currently being made to track Kirk Wilder." Winston paused a moment before unleashing the final piece of intel. "It seems his memory had not been cleaned before his escape."

"What?!" yelled an incredulous Thurman. "You're saying he's loose inside the sector presently?!"

"He's not here and he's removed his bracelet," explained Winston. "Without power, our defenses were limited."

Thurman pounded his fist on the table. "I was not through with my interrogation!"

Nannette cleared her throat. "And why does this matter now? The girl is back; she is our focus now. We simply needed Kirk to help find her."

"Are you that simple-minded?" shot back Thurman. "The girl had help to escape. It was Kirk, I'm certain of it. But he still must have received inside knowledge. I was about to uncover an inside network operating under our noses for decades! Now he knows what we know. He's more dangerous than his daughter!"

"And please tell us why you failed to erase his memory, exactly?" asked Winston.

"Because I was softening him up to spill his secrets! Do you fools understand nothing? He wouldn't know why he was in pain had I erased his memory."

"In an effort to clarify for all of us simple-minded fools," mocked Nannette, "you tortured this man, gave him sensitive Council information, and let him slip out untraceable for the foreseeable future? Perhaps the inside operator is you."

"Your disrespect is unfit for this Council!" hissed Thurman. "I have been hunting these types since before most of you were born! And we should have taken him with us to control the girl, but I recall you feckless weaklings voting against that."

"I've heard enough!" Winston slammed his gavel. "We will recover the man eventually. But let's talk about the elephant in the room. His daughter will be sitting on this very Council soon. I don't see any way to stop that now. She already has strong support and is the most visible Teammate in the sector. She's spreading ambitions of change and allowing paganism within our border. Perhaps the scariest part is listening to her speak. If one doesn't possess the intellect matching what is in this room, her argument comes off as *reasonable*. Now, when you combine that with the recently public transgressions of TEAM-MATE, just affirmed by Thurman, if we were to oppose her addition to this Council, we may find our sector in an open state of rebellion beyond our comprehension."

"We could put any rebellion down," muttered a younger man.

Benson interrupted the broadcast. "That's Delbert," he said. "He always will side with Thurman."

Benson grew quiet again so the group could listen.

"History might disagree," returned Winston. "Every time there's been a change in power, be it ancient Rome, France, Russia, etc, the former people in power often die. And it's usually publicly, painfully, and to the sound of applause." He surveyed the chamber gravely. "That would be each of us, for the record. Our fate could be the same if we don't adapt quickly."

"We must accept her," said Nannette. "Her influence would be diluted among the Council."

"It could be useful to weaken her too, publicly," added Winston. "We may not have the ability to stall all her aspirations of change, but our powers of reason combined will surely outmatch her own."

Thurman grunted as he leaned his head against the back of his chair and stared at the ceiling. "I look around this room, and I can see she is already winning."

"And what would you advise, Thurman? Do you have a plan you're keeping to yourself?" asked Nannette with narrowed eyes.

"Yes, I have a plan," he began. "And it will weaken her to the point that she will never sit on this Council."

"We cannot assassinate anyone," Winston said firmly. "For the record, I cannot believe I need to say that out loud."

"There's no need. I agree with you. The old ways are done," agreed Thurman. "There's nothing we can do about the past but bury it again. I already have multiple wheels in motion. We will give Ellie the public spectacle she wishes once she reaches the capital...and we will use it to ensnare her in a trap to reveal just what kind of councilmember she would make. I've reviewed her records. She has had the same weaknesses since her first year in school. Above everything else that she brings to the table, she's selfish. How will that play over with all her TEAMMATE followers?"

"And if your trap backfires?" asked Winston. "It was supposed to be impossible to ace the TEAMMATE test after Benson accomplished the feat fifty-six years ago. Now you think this plan will supposedly expose her? What if it exposes you and...by implication...us? I worry about your reaction to such a possibility that may become a probability. Why not just accept her as the rules clearly state we should?"

"If I'm wrong, my fellow councilmembers, the only thing that happens is that she sits on this Council, an outcome most of you seem perfectly fine with. Maybe we end up paraded through the streets, and maybe not. But I happen to believe my plan will prevent her from doing so and protect our way of life."

"There's a shocker," remarked Nannette.

Thurman shot her a glare with a reddened face. "Vote to put her to a public test due to our current state of emergency. I invite any of you to question her publicly, as long as I get the last session. We can weaken her to the point that no one wants her on the Council. I swear, if you approve this measure, you won't regret it and the sector will be saved from certain ruin."

"You cannot perform a public KPM test," interjected Winston. "That's not eligible for a vote."

"I won't need to," replied Thurman confidently. "She speaks often about free will. We shall see how selfishly she chooses. There's one other stipulation." He glanced around the room with suspicion wrinkled upon his brow. "No one leaves this chamber until we receive her procession out there tomorrow." He pointed toward the TEAM-MATE Square out the window. "I hate to imply mistrust, but as I stated before, I was on the verge of uncovering an underground opposition ring stemming perhaps from this very Council. My officials...our officials are working hard to get Kirk Wilder back. So now it comes to a vote. I realize many of you may not like me much, but you also understand that this is our best shot to save our sector. I have heard and debated all of your plans to this point. This is the only one that can keep everything as it was before. Vote for me. Vote with me. An emergency public test is the only option. We can take back our citizenry from this vile, polluting ideology. Now bang that gavel and let's save our fellow Teammates from certain catastrophe!"

"We must give Benson a chance to vote," said Winston.

"He's probably dead!" snarled Thurman.

"Then we'll give him until midnight to turn up. This meeting is adjourned until then." The gavel banged, and the video winked out.

Benson turned off the burner bracelet and placed it in his pocket. "They will privately debate for hours, but don't doubt that Thurman has something else up his sleeve. He is never to be trusted."

"Thank you, Benny," Ellie said, putting a hand on his shoulder. "I know you put yourself in grave danger to come here."

He shrugged. "I've been doing this a long time. The little boy you remember just saw his seventy-second birthday. I interfere when I can help, but as I said, too often I'm one voice against fourteen others. By the way, I may have *accidentally* unlocked the deadbolt on your father's interrogation room. Cutting the power was a great idea on your part. I also may have left him two artifacts from the nearby TEAM-MATE security museum. I believe he'll find them useful." He winked at Ellie. "Anyway, the only reason I can do this is because you helped get me away from that camp. You told me how to get home and gave me the compass to stay on course, and I eventually found Em. The rest is a history of living in the viper's nest. At least I'll have one friend on the Council soon."

"Please be careful," said Ellie as Benson began to slip back into the crowd.

"I'll keep my faith in the same place you do," he said. "Oh, and please don't call me Benny when I see you in the capital. It may tip them off about our familiarity."

Within minutes, Benson was lost to the crowd.

CHAPTER
THIRTY-SIX

Andy held Ellie's hand tightly as she led the mass of Teammates north. She glanced sideways to catch Judith watching and, to her relief, her friend smiled and winked back. Clearly, progress had been made on that front. Although their lives could certainly never return to normal again, at least the resentment had been replaced. Perhaps she'd found happiness. The most important question still lingered in the back of her mind. How long would they have to enjoy it? With the revelations that Ellie had unearthed, there was a distinct possibility that the end of their march could end badly. She turned her gaze back to Andy. He must have felt it too because he turned to catch her stare. She felt a warm blotch of color spread to her cheeks and ears when she saw how he looked at her. She quickly glanced away before looking back, the corners of her mouth rising upward, along with her newfound confidence. Although she had changed in a short period of time, both socially and mentally beyond her years, her former self was not gone, just barely under the surface. That knowledge must have been what made Andy raise his eyebrows and smirk, allowing him a small feeling of hope for their future.

It was Judith who finally interrupted the silence of the three as they walked.

"So, are we not gonna discuss the fact that what Ellie experienced at the camp was all real? I mean, you didn't just have a vision. You physically traveled back in time. Right?"

"Yes."

"Well, I've been thinking. If you can time travel, it's possible you can fix everything that's happened," said Judith with sudden excitement. "Maybe you could stop me from ruining your life."

"I don't think it works like that, Judith. But even if I somehow could go back, I don't think I would." She stared at the look of surprise on both of her friends. "This is what I'm supposed to do. And if I'm doing His will, I'm okay with that. No...more than okay. I'm determined to see this through."

"We're with you all the way," said Andy, squeezing her hand.

"Of course we are," added Judith. "I just really wish I hadn't been the villain. I know you've been able to brush it off somehow, but what you're doing right now will be historic. Kids will learn about you one day in school. And they'll also learn that I was a backstabber. Thinking about that really bothers me. I realize it was my own stupid fault. And although you say it's yours too, we both know where the blame should be."

"You need to fully forgive yourself," said Ellie, placing both hands on her friend's shoulders. "It's not about how you start in any story, whether historical or present. What matters is how you finish. You're here with me now. That matters. Let me share Paul's story with you. He was a man who, very much like TEAMMATE, tried to destroy the rise of early Christianity. He hunted people like us to have them imprisoned, tortured, and killed. He writes in his own words that he was a terrible man. But on the road to Damascus, while pursuing more Christians, he was struck down and blinded by God for his persecution."

"Your story is definitely not making me feel better."

"That's because it's not finished." Ellie paused a moment to take in their surroundings. Darkness had now fallen, but she continued to lead them on, trading the agricultural zone for the suburbs. Nearly every house they passed had lights on with Teammates watching from windows and front porches in wonder at the massive spectacle traveling by their home. Many of these people ultimately joined the march, if not because of true belief, then out of curiosity. And so, the horde of Teammates continued to grow. They would likely need rest soon, and yet Ellie feared losing her momentum. She wasn't sure what was more dangerous, thousands of idle Teammates or thousands of weary Teammates. Judith no doubt fell into the exhausted category. And with that fatigue, her defenses against her own self-doubt, guilt, and despair were weakened. Ellie needed to reassure her, but she also decided that at some point in the night, they would need a brief rest. At that moment, Ellie realized her friends were staring blankly at her, and so she continued.

"After he was struck down, Paul was led to the city where he sat in blindness and did not eat or drink for three days. But a man named Ananias sought him out. The Lord wanted him to convert this mad killer. Ananias baptized Paul and healed his vision. Imagine it, the very man who was likely coming after him and his friends. So, what did Paul do? He became known as one of the most passionate proponents of Christianity in history. He started various churches and helped convert thousands. He was forgiven by God. He is remembered as a champion, a hero. His words survived two thousand years in the Bible. And what he did was way, way worse than you could ever have dreamed of doing. You had no idea what TEAMMATE would find in my room. And you didn't need God's smite to regret and ask forgiveness."

Judith sucked in a deep breath. "That's a true story?"

"Every word."

"Did he have a long life after that?"

"Well, yes, by the standards of the time. However, he eventually was tortured and executed by Emperor Nero."

Judith's eyes bulged.

"You could have left the last part out," said Andy softly.

Ellie shrugged her shoulders. "The point is, he became a hero. I told you I was tasked with spreading the truth. The truth can be messy. Altering it or leaving parts out makes me no better than TEAMMATE."

"He went from aggressor to victim," Judith said soberly.

"Guys," said Ellie in a serious tone. "I told you truthfully—it's impossible to know how this will all end. I mean, I know we are the seeds for bringing God back to the world, and that He will ultimately prevail. But there's still a chance it could end badly for us." She looked left at Judith and right at Andy. "I want you both to know I love you and I have prayed mightily that you will be spared, whatever darkness awaits us."

The fear in Judith's eyes was unmistakable as she glanced from Ellie to Andy.

IT WASN'T UNTIL NOON, THE NEXT DAY, THAT THE MASS OF TEAMmates neared their destination, TEAMMATE Square. Ellie fondly remembered her last visit to the site, when she had ridden home in Andy's car. Now on foot, she could take in more of its intricate details. She pictured the city block with its green, lush grass in the heart of the capital, accentuated by various works of topiary and metallic sculptures giving glory to history, science, and the ability of the human mind. She thought of the major surrounding buildings and institutions required to maintain the sector. There were the marbled steps leading up to the TEAMMATE Council building, the Energy branch building, the Education branch, the Security branch, and others, which all rose high above the square, each as its own monument to the achievements of TEAMMATE. Ellie had seen the inside of many of the buildings through field trips and because her father worked in the Justice branch building. In addition to the workspace needed for TEAMMATE, there were other flats among the high rises where many of the city workers chose to live.

The marchers had continued with very few breaks throughout the night. They were ill-prepared with few provisions, no equipment for shelter, and no idea what the next day would bring. They were fueled by hope, curiosity, and trust in a young girl, who spoke of things that they had never heard of before—and so the thousands continued on, not electing to return home yet despite their hunger, their exhaustion, and their uncleanliness.

Ellie first smelled the square's aroma when they were within a few hundred yards of their destination.

"They must be cooking food in the capital," Judith uttered with excitement, inhaling a wonderful bouquet of fried potatoes, grilled barbecue, and other sweeter notes in the air.

Everyone's stomach was gnawing in protest of hunger, and the possibility of quelling that need was at the forefront of everyone's mind within an instant. When their view opened up to reveal the square, they saw hundreds of tents alongside grills, fryers, and smokers, wafting their welcome allure lazily into the breeze.

"It's as if they're throwing a celebration for us," said Andy in wonder.

Ellie narrowed her eyes. "TEAMMATE realizes they are on public display today. This is a clever ploy that our people badly need. To refuse this act of generosity would not be well received by the people we've brought with us." She glanced back and beckoned for Dobay to join them. He hustled to the front, eagerly awaiting her instructions. "Tell the people we are to be gracious guests if they are serving us refreshments. Above all, they must remain orderly and not trample one another. And instruct each of them to give a prayer of thanks to God, for he has provided for us, not TEAMMATE."

Dobay bowed his head humbly, and then the big man hustled first to the children and then passed word to the following crowd. The sounds behind them grew to a roar of cheers, followed by laughter and joy as the word was repeated down the road of thousands.

"This day is starting out better than we could have hoped," Andy murmured into Ellie's ear.

"Yes, it is. I just pray that it will end the same way."

"There is always hope, Ellie." He smiled with sincerity.

She looked deeply into his eyes and forced a smile herself. "Come what may today, I pray you never lose that. I love how it burns within you."

He smiled unsurely, confusion in his eyes. "You pray I never lose what?"

"Hope," she said. "We're going to desperately need it."

Though my words may end here, my love will endure. Because of you, I am hopeful for a brighter future, even if I will not be present for it. I am so proud of who you will become, and I will always love you dearly, my godchild.

—Final entry from pagan diary

CHAPTER
THIRTY-SEVEN

Although Ellie's followers were careful not to stampede the lines of plentiful food and drink, they quickly lost the loose organization maintained during their march. The flow of people was that of a river into an ocean. However, other Teammates who hadn't participated in the march could also be seen joining the growing square population like small tributaries.

The atmosphere had the feeling of a carnival, with colorful tents and the smell of food floating in the air. People conversed excitedly around them, holding their plates of abundant food, all anxious to see what the day would bring. There were portable bathroom facilities assembled and booths of TEAMMATE agencies, many giving away pro-TEAMMATE merchandise in the form of keychains, yardsticks, and fly swatters. Each was decorated with the familiar slogans *All for one, We are all in the same game, and Contribution is love.*

Ellie struggled to keep her band of children together. Mary was perhaps the most helpful as she began instructing the children to hold hands. It would be nearly impossible to find any of the smallest children among the crowds should they become separated. Dobay, Andy, and Judith helped reinforce Mary's instructions, and eventually the group claimed a table near the center of the square. Everyone filled their plates and ate hungrily.

Ellie ate as well. Despite her anxiety, she needed her strength. Worry gnawed at her as she wondered if her father was safe and what they'd done to him. Even if he no longer remembered, it was he who helped make her escape possible. She needed to find him and explain so many things. And she had so many of her own questions unanswered. Had her mother found Molly? What was the Council's ultimate plan?

Even after they'd all eaten, more Teammates continued to arrive at the square. No doubt they'd witnessed various livestreams of the march, and whether it was out of hunger or curiosity, they continued to arrive in droves.

As Ellie sat next to her friends, she watched Jamie's eyes flicker about them wildly, like a nervous animal. She realized if she was nervous, the children from the outside probably couldn't put into words the wonders they were experiencing. They'd never seen a gathering of more than a dozen people for their entire lives, and now...this. She glanced and saw Judith and Andy laughing merrily while Dobay sat with his permanent smile, watching the enormous video screens that had been hung on three sides of the square, each with its own live feed of the crowd.

The sound of trumpets interrupted the moment of ease. Ellie, along with the rest of the crowd, turned to face the marble steps that led into TEAMMATE Headquarters at the northern end of TEAM-MATE Square. The doors, which were guarded by no fewer than fifty TEAMMATE officials, swung outward, and from them emerged the entire TEAMMATE Council in single file. There were fifteen of them, now that Benson had rejoined—many waving and smiling to the crowd's mixture of cheers and boos. The screen on the building behind them magnified their image twenty-fold, allowing everyone to witness what was happening. The trumpets continued to hold their piercing wail until the councilmembers arranged themselves on the highest step, standing shoulder to shoulder. Councilmember Winston Jennings, with his ever-distinguished mustache, gave a hand signal, and the trumpet blare immediately ended.

"The TEAMMATE Council wishes to express our gratitude to all our Teammates for showing up today," began Winston, his voice booming from speakers all over the square. The camera zoomed in on his confident smile. It made Ellie nervous to note that there was no sign of worry or distress on the man's face. Shouldn't he be concerned about why the crowd had assembled? He'd already learned that his conversation with Thurman had gone viral before it had been removed. There had to be something up the man's sleeve to portray his cocky persona.

"Today, we celebrate a unique event that has occurred only once in our storied TEAMMATE history. A perfect score was achieved on the TEAMMATE Placement Test!" He began clapping excitedly and was immediately joined by the other members of the Council and soon enough, the entire crowd. After breathing in the applause for a moment, as if it were for him, he motioned for the applause to end. "Now, all of you here today, watching at home or at work, know just how difficult it is to master such a scholastic achievement. It is a tribute to the human mind and to our very culture of enlightenment that we foster as a team. Beyond pure study, this feat requires true wisdom as well. Our young Teammate, Ellie Wilder, has demonstrated a mental aptitude far exceeding her fifteen years. Without further ado, this Council wishes to begin her formal initiation into our ranks. Please come forward, young lady!"

Ellie could feel Andy's pulse quicken as his slippery palms clung tightly to her own. The crowd had made enough room for their small group to rise from their seats and proceed side by side toward the councilmembers. Judith dropped behind the pair and walked beside Mary. But Ellie's attention was fixed on the councilmember who had been speaking over the crowd. Winston seemed to be studying their group intently, as if trying to solve a puzzle that had remained unfinished for far too long. He was likely as surprised as anybody that one girl could cause life as they knew it to stop. Under his gaze, Ellie could feel the renewed uneasiness radiating from her group as they could also now see themselves on the viewing screens. They weren't being called to stand before just any ordinary group of people. After all, the minds of the Council held the greatest combined intellect in the world—perhaps even in history. Since overhearing part of their discussion thanks to Benson, there was no doubt in Ellie's mind that they viewed her as a threat.

When they reached the bottom of the steps, the group of adults and children stopped, gazing upward to the Council who loomed above them, eyes fixed on the children like birds of prey eyeing so many field mice.

"Ellie Wilder," boomed Winston's voice over the speakers, "I ask that you alone meet me halfway up these stairs, which symbolize your destination of higher learning, an elevated environment of debate, and the loftiest degree of duty for the benefit of this sector. We will begin your initiation there. Once completed, you will either join the Council above as an equal participant or, should the initiation be unsatisfactory, you will simply return to your friends." He took each step down slowly with a grave expression on his face until he reached the fifth step, where he stood with an outstretched hand to receive Ellie.

"Don't trust him," Andy whispered in her ear. "He thinks he has you outsmarted."

Ellie's eyes met the boy's gaze with an expression of solemnness, but void of fear. "I've no illusion otherwise. But our Father knows all their thoughts just as He knows ours." She touched her hand to Andy's jawline. The crowd reacted to their image on the viewing screens with mixtures of whistles and *awws*. "He put me here to do His will. His grace is sufficient. Thank you for seeing me through our journey this far. Your presence gives me great comfort. No matter what happens, you have my heart and my love. Always." She turned to Judith next. "And you being here means everything to me, Judith. Please, pray for me." She turned to climb the stairs.

Glancing back, Ellie could see the internal conflict upon Andy's face as he grudgingly watched her continue alone. She ascended the steps slowly and measured, carrying an unseen weight on her shoulders. The symbolism she portrayed was enough to hush the crowds, who had come to bear witness to this monumental moment. When she took Winston's hand and turned to the people, she waved to all her followers—and that's the moment the crowd grew deafeningly loud with cheers. The response was like a proverbial flex of the muscles before a fight, and it must have impressed Winston as he made no move to quiet them until a full minute of their energy had been expended. It took his signal and another roar of the trumpets to indicate the next part of the ceremony.

"Ellie, you clearly have the love of your fellow Teammates, and that will be helpful to your cause. Your historical test result suggests you have the intelligence to sit on this Council. You speak uninhibitedly of new ideas and of an end to old ones, and that perspective will be a welcome addition to the debate of this Council. Achieving perfection in a society is a dynamic goal. The world in which we live is constantly changing, and it is imperative that we constantly evaluate ourselves to help make our team stronger. It is important to note that this job, which you have now publicly expressed a desire to hold, is not a popularity contest. It is also not just about attaining wisdom. It is about applying wisdom in a beneficial way. Generally, our tradition on the Council is to allow our sitting members a trial of questions before member acceptance. This is usually done in the confines of our chamber in private, but we have heard your request for transparency. It is our wish to grant you and those who came with you today that request."

Winston abruptly turned to face the members standing above them. "With that said, what queries do our members have for our newest initiate?"

The familiar young woman with a hawkish nose raised her hand.

"Yes, Nannette. The floor, or shall I say the *steps,* are yours."

The tall woman, who wore a business suit, took one step down from the line of councilmembers.

"It is a pleasure to meet you, Ellie," she began with a forced smile. "Although I remember you from when I spoke in your class some days ago. For your first trial, I'd like you to simply explain your personal definition of love and how that reconciles with TEAMMATE's motto that *Love is contribution.* Before you begin, please bear in mind that your answer may be challenged or supported by any sitting councilmember. Past quotes may also be subject to this trial." The woman bowed, with her hand extended toward Ellie, palm upward to gesture that the stairs were hers.

Ellie nodded and bowed her head in a moment of prayer. *How can I help them understand? Lord, please give me the strength.*

She began, "Love is a gift from God..."

"Objection!" yelled Thurman, raising his hand.

Winston cleared his throat. "Will councilmembers please wait until called upon before speaking?" He sighed. "You may counter, Thurman."

"Point one, pagan beliefs are sacrilege against TEAMMATE. This *belief* should disqualify the girl from speaking any further. Point two, science has disproven all claims of higher beings over one hundred years ago, rendering the rest of her explanation moot. Point three, any attempt to convert other Teammates to follow beliefs that do not align with TEAMMATE is forbidden by Article 33 of the TEAMMATE Rulebook. Clearly, she has already violated multiple rules and is not fit for further debate." He stood tall—triumphant, and a smile of contentment threatened the corner of his mouth.

Ellie cleared her throat. "As I said, love is a gift from God. It is that gift that we are called to share."

"But..."

"You must allow her to counter, Thurman," Winston's voice interjected.

"The councilmember is mistaken," Ellie continued. The crowd gasped at her dismissal of his argument. "Our Father cares not for any man-made rule or law, especially in this instance where the rules were cleverly crafted to eliminate competition with TEAMMATE governance. The rules of TEAMMATE are absolutely not perfect because they are man-made and can never be perfect. And yet you stand atop these steps, in your position of power, atop the tallest mountain of lies and deceit in history and hurl your falsehoods at me like bolts of lightning in three great blows. From where I am standing, you, Councilmember, are standing in the way of improving TEAMMATE with your reluctance to hear the argument, to hear the truth."

Thurman raised a hand, and Winston nodded. "She can't insult a sitting..."

"The truth lacks compassion for your ego," Ellie interrupted. "Science has disproven nothing. It simply can't explain it...yet. How would you explain electricity to a Neanderthal? It would be above the being's intellect. It's much like God is above ours. Sure, you can deny it, but you can't make it nonexistent, although this Council has a history of trying to do this exact thing by murdering its own constituents. That is now an indisputable fact. Some might rightly point out that this action has broken the Council's own rules, making them an enemy of Teammates everywhere."

Thurman's face grew red with rage. Ellie glanced away to see Andy and Judith giving her an encouraging thumbs up.

"We are called to love like God. But how does one do that? To love like God? I would imagine it would be as simple as it would be difficult. It would have to be perfect love for another person or people who are not, and it will never be perfect. It's not an even exchange. It would be hurtful, disappointing, and exhausting. Is it impossible? Nothing is impossible for God. Most, if not all of us, would break under such a test. Our hearts and our very minds cannot endure such sustained pain and disappointment. But if we are able to push ourselves back to our feet when the dust settles, perhaps the sum of our limitless failures and our desire to return to love will allow our ever-loving God to smile down upon our attempts, like a mother or father looks upon a child's attempts to walk. And through our struggle, perhaps we can attain grace. Unfortunately, it is earned through pain. But does one not learn to walk by falling? And once we walk, is it true that we shall never fall again? No. This reality involves a higher level of thinking for our small minds. It is beyond our advancements in science. It stretches our mental capacity. And it is more powerful than any other force in the universe. Powerful enough to trade your very life for it. Powerful enough to be felt long after the people who evoked it from us are gone. What am I attempting to describe? Love. In summary, such a simple word for a powerful concept does not bear the need for reconciliation with the three-word motto of an imperfect institution. After all, contribution is good, but love is substantially more. Thank you for the question."

The applause of the crowd was so loud that no one tried to hear Thurman's yelled response.

Ellie looked up to see Nannette and Benson clapping with the crowd. The other members did not join in the response, but if she maintained a foothold of support, it gave her a chance to grow her allies.

Winston finally motioned for the crowd to quiet down. "That was quite an insightful argument by you, Ellie," he began. "Of course, this public debate is not over, and we haven't all day."

Ellie caught Thurman's glaring eye and felt a shiver from the obvious hate the man felt towards her. She knew the trial was likely to get more difficult with each argument. But what else could that man have up his sleeve?

"We are ready for the next discussion," boomed Winston's voice. "Who has the next challenge for our initiate?"

A man with a nervous smile raised a hand from further down the line.

"Yes, Delbert. You may proceed. And might I add, good luck."

CHAPTER
THIRTY-EIGHT

"Thank you," said Councilmember Delbert, his beady eyes moving from Ellie to the crowds and back. "Teammate Ellie, I can see that you have the skills to be a debater. Even if your logic is flawed, you have shown mental strength and resolve thus far. My worry, upon reviewing your records since grade school, is one underlying theme noted time and time again by your teachers. I will employ their quotes so that these words are not misconstrued as my own. *Ellie needs to work on sharing. Ellie does not participate equally in group activities. Ellie received detention today for arguing unfairness against TEAMMATE rules. Ellie took an extra cookie from the class party today. Ellie wouldn't apologize for shoving another student today. Ellie wouldn't share her answers in class today. Ellie lied...Ellie stole...Ellie doesn't seem to care about anyone but herself."*

He cleared his throat. "I get the impression that Ellie has a very long history of only worrying about Ellie. This girl has always been selfish. And what position does she seek? Only the highest that is offered by TEAMMATE. Now Ellie wants us all to change the rules to what Ellie thinks is best." He glared at her accusingly. "Forget the matter that all these documented facts point to her being unfit for this Council. How do we know that Ellie won't push to become a dictator? These characteristics are concerning for any member of TEAMMATE. But for a councilmember? Ellie, here is my question. How will you change from your examples of the past to blend into this Council, should you be accepted? And in addition, why should we believe a word that comes out of your mouth since you clearly have a history of telling falsehoods?"

Here it was. The internal fight she'd been participating in her whole life played out on stage. Ellie drew air into her lungs and looked skyward. When she set her eyes back on the Council, she saw Benson's face tighten, the color fading from him. "Let me start by saying, you aren't the first person to have pointed this out. And if I were to stand here and tell you all that I'm perfect, that I've never wronged another Teammate...that would be as great of a lie as the assertion that TEAMMATE is a perfect society." She looked around the stage and then toward Andy. "The difference is that I am self-aware and will freely admit my shortcomings, unlike our governance, which has clearly buried the atrocities of the past. I would argue that any citizen, or councilmember for that matter, who claims superiority based on man-made law is delusional. Stealing is wrong. I believe I learned that particular lesson in my first-grade class, Councilmember Delbert. I'm glad you read my file from when I was six years old." She locked eyes with him, which clearly made him uncomfortable. "How are my actions at age six any different from our legislative body that declares if I grow a vegetable in my garden, I must try to obtain a permit so that I can give said vegetable back to TEAMMATE?"

Delbert scoffed. "It's for the greater good. If we let everyone keep what they wanted, half the sector would suffer from calorie surplus and the other half would starve."

"Clearly, you have a short memory, Councilmember," Ellie shot back. "Because of bad weather, incompetence, poor planning, and ultimate reliance upon you, people did starve to death in this sector not that long ago. You steal food to redistribute, which is bad, but then you outlaw anyone trying to supplement their allowance? Where is the sense in that? Are you not supposed to be wise?"

"We've fixed things since then," reassured Delbert. "There will always be bumps on the road to progress."

"Yes, and I would argue that you are one of the bumps. You are robbing the people who grow food. You're robbing others of the means and ambition to produce on their own. You want to control every part of our world. And if anyone disagrees, what happens to them? Would you please explain to the crowd what you do to any Teammate that challenges your status quo...your stagnant, delusional, mirage of a perfect society?"

"We simply reeducate them," returned Delbert.

"Yes, that sounds much better than the truth. Because what you really do is brainwash them. If they do return, they have gaps in their memory. You threaten, torture, and replace common sense with your ideals. And if that doesn't work? You murder them. They are purged from the team. All this talk about being Teammates our whole lives and how have you cared for those that don't measure up?"

"There are no facts to back up your assertions, young lady. You're spinning stories to upset the populace."

"Are you admitting that you don't know? Did you not hear the history of Em? Remember, she would have been called Mary in your records. I urge you to look her up. Are you ignorant or in denial? Please, find me just one of our citizens that have been excommunicated from

TEAMMATE. Prove that you haven't killed every last one. You won't because you can't."

The crowd was now murmuring amongst themselves.

Delbert began to stammer. "They likely couldn't survive away from the team...once they were cast out. How should any of us know where to find any of them?"

Benson raised a hand and stepped forward.

"Do you have something to add, Councilmember Benson?" asked Winston.

"I do." He took a long breath before descending the steps until he stood beside Winston and Ellie. "Nobody has heard my story. I never thought anyone would believe me if I shared it. Worse than that, I know firsthand what would become of me if I had previously shared my experience. I have spent my whole life trying to balance out this organization, but up until today, I have failed. You all know my story as the only councilmember to earn a perfect TEAMMATE Placement score before Ellie. What you don't know is that I, too, was in an excommunication camp as a child." A collective gasp escaped the crowds. "My parents were also what TEAMMATE called pagans." He turned to look at his fellow councilmembers. "I saw what happened in that camp. I, too, was supposed to be buried in a grassy field with my family and hundreds of others." He wiped his eyes. "But I was saved by a visit from her." He put his arm around Ellie. "She appeared by a miracle and comforted a young boy whose mother had helped him escape from the camp. But I was scared and did not know the way...and so I returned to certain death. But she found me in the darkness and told me this brighter day would come. I had no idea how long I would have to wait to share my story. It's the story of an orphaned boy who was given a compass and wandered back into the society that had rejected me. Such a thing could never have happened now, not with our fence and these bracelets." He held up his arm so the crowds could see his wrist. "These are handcuffs. Take a look at those children who follow Ellie. You won't find bracelets on them. They were rejected, just like me—only they continued to live on the other side in secret. They are what became of TEAMMATE's unsanctioned pregnancies. As head of our Science branch, fifteen years ago, I developed the technology to keep them alive after removal from the womb. I wish I could have made a bigger difference in all my years on the TEAMMATE Council. But they will forever be my greatest contribution to our team. For in each of them, I saw myself. We are the collective rejections from TEAMMATE. And the fact that I am on this Council should open some eyes to the errors of our ways."

The fear and realization of defeat on Winston's face was undeniable. The Teammates in the square had heard enough to become unruly. Thurman's plan had backfired. The councilmembers had weakened themselves beyond repair. "In light of these revelations, this Council must meet in our chambers..." Winston began uncertainly.

"Not yet," shouted Thurman through narrowed eyes. "The initiation is incomplete."

"Thurman, surely now is not the time..."

"I've watched enough of this spectacle of weakness," sneered Thurman. "Before we can deal with any of these other allegations, there's one more test for the girl. I'm invoking Article 79 of the TEAMMATE Rulebook. In a state of emergency, the Security branch of TEAMMATE takes control of all sector activities." He smiled at Winston. "You already held the vote declaring emergency, remember? We voted to proceed with a public test due to...a state of emergency." He smiled darkly before barking at nearby officials, and they sprang into action. Two grabbed Benson, another three ran into the crowd and dragged Mary, against her will, up the steps. Then, another two officials opened the doors behind the crowd and escorted out a terrified Miss Conway and a teary-eyed Molly between them.

"Molly!" screamed Ellie.

"Thurman, what is this?" asked Winston in surprise.

"This is the real trial for Ellie," he began. "It's time to see how fit she is to be on this Council. Difficult decisions must be made." He turned behind them. "Reserve officials! To your assigned positions!"

The bulk of the TEAMMATE security force now marched from TEAMMATE Headquarters. They were clad in riot gear and numbered in the hundreds.

"Your orders are to keep the peace and safety of this sector." They brandished their clubs, which crackled with electricity.

The crowd took a collective step back in fear. The other councilmembers stared in surprise. Thurman uttered a menacing laugh. "Our predecessors planned for everything, including having a weak Council. Initiate emergency order alpha beta tango. TEAMMATE Security branch is now in charge of the entire sector."

"Stand down!" yelled Winston. "The Council has not authorized this procedure!"

Thurman narrowed his eyes in disappointment. "Rule number one under my first executive order is that all resistance will be suppressed. Guards! Lock him up and cut his mic!"

The men under Thurman's control responded as ordered, to the dismay of everyone present. Winston shouted, but his words couldn't be heard without the microphone. He raised a hand to keep the officials away, but they struck him with their crackling club, and he collapsed on the steps. To the horror of the crowd, they dragged his limp body away, back into the TEAMMATE Council building. Andy tried to run to reach Ellie, but he was quickly met with a crackling wand himself, sending him to the ground, rolling back down the steps near Judith.

"No!" cried Ellie in panic.

"You'll need to hold your response until I give you the floor," snarled Thurman. "Everyone quiet!" His voice made the square tremble with its overwhelming volume. "The real trial begins now."

CHAPTER
THIRTY-NINE

A common problem encountered when amassing thousands of people for one purpose, then surprising them with a change of plan, is that the masses may respond with outrage. And so, the crowds did not quiet down, as Thurman had requested. In fact, they grew louder, angrier, and more hostile. What they were witnessing was against everything they'd ever learned that TEAMMATE stood for.

"You're a fraud!" one man yelled.

"Bring back Councilmember Winston!" The phrase began to be repeated over and over in unison by enraged Teammates. Their tone and their body language had gone from passive to rebellious. The crowds began to press toward the steps.

"Leave Ellie alone!" Judith screamed.

"Let my daughters go!" At the shrill, familiar cry, Ellie frantically searched the crowd, unable to pinpoint where her mother stood.

If the yelling and impending riot bothered Thurman, it certainly wasn't apparent upon his arrogant face. The officials, however, did betray their concern with shifty eyes and retreating steps from the angry crowd. There was an air of revolt in the square with the thousands of infuriated Teammates emboldened by their strength in numbers against the massively outnumbered officials with wands in their hands.

Thurman actually smiled on the large viewing screen. "I think it's time all of you learned a lesson in obedience," his voice boomed deafeningly loud over the speakers. "Everyone to your knees! Now!"

A pulsing pain began, felt in the arms of nearly every individual within a mile radius of the capital. The pain spread to the shoulders and into their sternums like the injection of a poison. Teammates began crying out in distress. They clawed at their bracelets frantically to no avail. Only a few had obeyed Thurman, and when they did kneel, they realized the agonizing pain that radiated through their body subsided enough to catch their breath. The effect had the entire crowd obedient within thirty seconds, and, for perhaps the first time that day, there was true silence in the square. The citizenry was ready to pay attention. They were ready to listen to whatever Thurman said next. They were ready to comply.

Thurman adjusted something on his own bracelet, and the remaining low level of pain subsided. He recognized the look of fear in some of his own officials. They looked as if they felt compassion for the unruly mob he'd just put down. The crowd let out a collective sigh of relief, but no one dared speak.

"It seems I have your attention now, my dear Teammates." The wicked grin grew on his face. "Your leaders always knew the day of rebellion would come. It has happened over and over for centuries in every civilization before this. Unfortunately, it's in humankind's DNA to change for the sake of change every so often. But now that we've achieved perfection, I'm afraid we can't alter the game plan. Consequently, I will now demonstrate how we will end said rebellion." He gestured to the four people on stage. "Our wise Ellie will decide the fate of the following four criminals against our collective team. Mary Wilder, also known by the letter 'M', is guilty of promoting paganism, kidnapping TEAMMATE children, and spreading lies about our re-education camps. Councilmember Benson Browning is guilty of treason against TEAMMATE, including espionage, sabotage, and aiding in the kidnapping of TEAMMATE children. Edna Conway is guilty of not reporting pro-pagan as well as anti-TEAMMATE sentiments of students. Furthermore, she manipulated the results of the TEAMMATE exam to fabricate a perfect score for Ellie, who is actually a marginal student at best. Finally, Molly Wilder is guilty of anti-TEAMMATE slurs, specifically the lie that TEAMMATE is evil and we'd be better off on our own."

Not Molly too. She must have repeated words she'd heard Ellie say. It was a nightmare come to life. Ellie glanced back at Andy, who was still on the ground recovering from the work of the officials' wands. The ten youths and Judith were the only ones in the crowd not kneeling or collapsed on the ground, for they wore no bracelets. Ellie could see Thurman's plan unfolding. He was discrediting her before he disposed of her. The test result could not have been doctored unless Edna Conway knew every answer to the TEAMMATE exam, which was impossible. She looked to the skies before bowing her head in prayer. She needed strength. She needed guidance. She needed a miracle.

"Are you actually praying?" asked Thurman in a mocking tone. "Please cease. The charade is over. There is no god coming to rescue you from what happens next. I can assure you we won't be stopping after these four are dealt with. I will rip out every pagan root, one by one, until our society is pure again."

Ellie lifted her chin in defiance, unable to hold back the tears that had begun. "You can never erase what's in our hearts. These people have heard the truth now. What you're doing has been tried again and again in history and has failed. I trust in God. He has never failed."

"This is yet another area where you're wrong, young Ellie. We've evolved since the last two millennia. We will eradicate the virus of paganism this time. Your defective belief will not endure after the world sees you for the fraud that you are. We finally all know that your test was tampered with. A perfect score was always impossible. It remains so."

"Just because you aren't capable does not make it impossible," she returned defiantly.

Thurman raised a hand to slap her but then hesitated and lowered it. No matter how far society had come, the optics of finishing the action would not win him any support after this business was finished. He redirected his attention to the four Teammates on stage.

"Enough talk," he said with a dismissive tone. "Argument with an inferior intellect rarely produces good fruit. As I said, the four that stand before us are all guilty of crimes. That is not up for debate as it is a documented fact, both by admission and by bracelet activity recording. All that remains is for the proper punishment to be doled out. Four people and four sentences remain. I will supply you with the sentences, and you may apply them to whichever Teammate you choose." He nodded toward two officials who promptly curried out of sight.

The surrounding tension was thicker than congealed blood. The effect was suffocating. No one spoke; they merely tried to breathe while their collective hearts fluttered in fear.

The two men returned slowly. When Ellie saw what they were carrying, her heart sank, and a terror unlike any she'd ever known overtook her. *Oh no. Please. No, no, no!* The structures the men carried out from the TEAMMATE Council building were of heavy significance. They carried rough-cut wood, fashioned into crucifixes.

The crowd murmured in wonder, for they did not understand yet what the structures meant. Ellie trembled with fear as the two wooden crosses were fitted into holes at the top of the steps.

"And you said I learned nothing from history," sneered Thurman. "As I was saying...you have four sentences to assign. Two to the cross, one to exile, and one you may pardon. If you fail to choose, I have many more crosses on standby, and no one will get a pardon today. Well, I'm curious. Who will you save, little godchild? You have all the power now. You can save, you can send away, and you can have killed."

Ellie looked around. Where was the way out of this nightmare? She couldn't choose. How could anyone choose? They were all innocent. She loved them all.

Mary spoke up first. "I...I should go to the crucifix. It's an honor I'm not worthy of, but not a choice I'll let you make. I've had a long life. I'm ready, dear." A single tear ran down the woman's face, betraying the brave words she used.

Ellie shook her head in protest. It wasn't right.

"No, I will take their places. It's me that you hate. I offer myself... as long as you let them out of the sector, alive."

Thurman's look of surprise showed that he hadn't expected this. He thought for a moment. It was a significant moment. A moment he could use to benefit the future of TEAMMATE.

"The only way I could ever allow that is if you were to admit yourself a deceiver, in full view of the entire sector. Finally admit that this is all a sham...it's all false and fake and your guilty associates can wander aimlessly in the wastelands until they perish naturally. If you do this, we will only need one cross today."

Ellie swallowed hard. "You wish to make a soundbite of my cause? To turn me into a weapon against my God?" The tears poured mercilessly down her face. "I am prepared to die. But only God may choose my last words...not you."

Thurman scowled. "You are too weak and too proud to save your friends. How disappointing for one who claimed to be righteous. Delbert was right. You are selfish in your beliefs. Here's the new deal. You're going to the cross now. And while you're up there, screaming and dying for your own selfishness, you can watch as we execute every single enemy of TEAMMATE that you helped create! Let it be recorded she saved no one, not even herself! Officials! Take her!"

Ellie screamed in fright as her arm was grabbed and she was led to the top of the steps. It was too much for Andy to take as he still lay at the base of the steps from his previous shock. He swept the legs of the official standing over him. The man stumbled, and in the process, he shocked himself by accident and fell convulsing to the concrete. Andy pounced on his weapon and shocked him again.

Immediately, half of the armed officials raced to head Andy off as he set his wild eyes on Thurman and everyone who stood between him and Ellie. He was not an expert with the weapon, but his uncaged anger gave him a burst of strength and energy that was unmatched by his opponents. They'd never been trained to fight citizens armed with anything more than a rock or broom handle, much less one of their own weapons. He bested the first three rather quickly.

"Officials! Take care of this sideshow!" Thurman turned to Ellie with a gleeful grin. "Guess you'll get to witness a quick sacrifice now. Such a stupid boy. His life might buy you another few minutes before the pain begins."

As more guards rushed to help, the crowd, still on their knees, watched curiously as a man seemingly defied the pain of his bracelet and ran through them toward the stage. How could anyone remain on their feet under such duress?

However, most of TEAMMATE's eyes remained on Andy's impossible battle, as more and more officials surrounded him. He was swinging wildly, keeping the enemies back as more encircled him and waited for his arms to tire.

The running man now broke through the crowd and to the steps before Thurman noticed him. He manipulated his bracelet, and there were screams of pain from the crowd. But now the man walked toward him, unhindered.

"What is the meaning of this?" snarled Thurman. And then recognition registered in his eyes. For the first time all day, the councilmember looked fearful. "Stop this man!" he screamed. "The escaped prisoner is here!"

Kirk Wilder moved like a predator now. Wordless, he reached both hands under his coat and pulled out two silver-barreled revolvers. There was no bracelet on his wrist. He could not be cowed. Whatever emotion he was feeling was masked by the solemn glare upon his bruised face. He brandished the weapons toward the only three guards separating him from his daughter and the man who had tortured him mercilessly.

The first official ran toward Kirk with a yell. Kirk pointed and fired at the official's midsection. The cartridge exploded in an awesome spectacle of smoke and flash that kicked Kirk's hand back wildly. The gun flew out of his hand to his astonishment and skidded down the steps. The official screamed as blood squirted from his shoulder and his weapon fell uselessly to the ground, followed by its owner.

Ellie put her hands to her face in a mixture of horror and hope. Her dad was alive! He'd come to save her!

Kirk secured his remaining gun with both hands, pointing firmly at the remaining two guards. They looked at the river of blood pouring down the steps from their partner and immediately ran in the opposite direction.

"He has our stolen artifacts!" screamed Thurman. "It's Ellie's father!"

Thurman, who now stood alone on the steps, realized he needed to run. But steps aren't conducive to speed, and Thurman was no longer a young man. In his haste, his ankle twisted as he missed his second step and crumpled down the rest of the way wildly, until he arrived nearly at Kirk's feet, who now stood with his pistol raised and a finger on the trigger.

CHAPTER
FORTY

The animal-like fear and wildness in Thurman's eyes was almost enough to evoke pity as Kirk stood with his revolver leveled at the man's head. This was the man who had tried to take his daughter. The same man who had taken a mother from her seven-year-old son all those years ago. This was the same man who had tortured Kirk, trying to find out where his daughter had gone and who had helped her. Justice was at hand. But as quickly as it appeared, the fear in Thurman's eyes began to turn into narrow-eyed hate as he hunched on the ground holding his wrist like a wounded, cornered beast, looking for any way out.

"Put your hands behind your head," Kirk said coldly.

A slow smile grew on Thurman's face as he blatantly ignored the command.

"I think you'd better lower that weapon, Kirk," he hissed. "Why don't you take a look at the crowds?"

Kirk did not lower his weapon, but a quick glance sideways revealed that something peculiar was happening. Teammates were beginning to put their hands over their eyes and ears. The screams started soon thereafter.

"Give me one reason why I shouldn't pull this trigger."

"I'll give you two million," said Thurman. A nervous, evil sound erupted from deep in his chest—his laugh. "I'm simply giving them back the energy the sector has harvested from them. First, they'll feel flushed, warm, and their blood pressure will begin to rise. After that, they may develop worsening symptoms like loss of vision, ringing in the ears, ruptured blood vessels, and worse until they cook themselves from the inside out. None of this will stop until I reverse it. So, Kirk, you got me. But the truth you don't comprehend yet is that I cannot lose. I never could. Are you willing to kill everybody to get me? It seems you're on trial at the moment instead of your daughter."

The screams grew louder, and it seemed to affect everyone in the square who wore a bracelet except Thurman. Even officials were now sinking to their knees in agony. Kirk looked back to see Anne on her knees at the edge of the crowd, tears from the pain running down her face. Glancing sideways, he also saw Andy, huffing and puffing from his own battle. He stood encircled by fallen, confused officials, who also joined in the collective cries of agony.

"Dad," Ellie called softly from the steps above. "Please don't do it. He's dangerous and evil, but he'll kill them all—Molly and Mom too." Ellie knew it was the truth, but it didn't make the words any easier to say. Her father's bloodshot eyes caught her own before shifting back to the wretched man in front of him. Deep down inside, she questioned if she did want him to pull the trigger. But she realized succumbing to that temptation spelled doom.

"You would kill the entire sector to save your own miserable life?" Kirk yelled in anger and disgust.

"That's just one way to look at it," hissed Thurman. "You would kill them all just to get to me."

Kirk was unsteady now. His plan was getting ripped to shreds. "But these people will remember this day forever. They will never go along with TEAMMATE again."

Thurman nodded. "Yes, they will remember. And their fear will keep them in line. You have no idea how difficult it has been to control this sector for so long. No one, except me, does. If I die, this population will fall within the year. They'd all be better off dead now than without me! Now give me the artifact in your hand and we'll make a deal. You and your plague of a family can leave the sector forever, and everybody else will live."

Kirk looked back up the stairs where Ellie stood, near the cross. The officials who had led her to the top were writhing in pain on the ground. Her head was bowed, and tears trickled down her cheeks. Her palms were together in prayer. They needed one more miracle.

Kirk shakily handed the gun into the outstretched palm of Thurman, who had now wearily risen to his feet. Once the weapon was in his hand, he pushed a control on his bracelet, and the screaming stopped. Kirk looked around the mass of people who slowly rose from the ground and noticed a few that did not move. Some shook these unmoving neighbors as cries of anguish arose because they realized what had happened. He'd killed them. And he would have killed them all if Kirk hadn't handed over his weapon.

"You made a very wise choice, Kirk," croaked Thurman. "I will spare your family for your sacrifice." He paused in thought. "But I'm afraid you will not be joining them." He pointed the gun at Kirk's chest.

"Stop!" screamed Ellie.

Thurman turned his attention to the girl atop the steps. "Why should I listen to a cheater? You never had the right to sit on this Council. You've started an open rebellion in our sector, Ellie. You should count yourself lucky that I'm allowing you to live your final days outside the sector...of course, we'll have to wipe your memories clean beforehand. And so no, I will not stop, and there's not a thing you can do to stop me. I hold all the power in this sector and beyond, and so if you want a god, you can bow before me alone." He turned back to Kirk. "Bow your head, Kirk."

To everyone's horror, he pulled the trigger.

But the explosion was followed by a second explosion. While Kirk crumpled onto the steps, so did Thurman.

In all the chaos, no one had noticed Judith crawling on her hands and knees to retrieve Kirk's dropped pistol. And now she held the smoking piece of steel in both hands, wincing in pain from the weapon's kick and ear-piercing report. No one else moved but her as she kept it raised and approached Thurman.

Ellie broke the frozen tension and ran toward her fallen father, pain carved into her face. As if on signal, a medic team ran up the steps to join the two girls. Judith stepped on Thurman's hand, which still clung to his own weapon, and pointed her pistol at his head.

"Judith, please...he's an evil man, but not like this," Ellie spoke calmly to her friend as she was bent over her own father, who was now choking, blood growing at the corner of his lips.

Her friend looked back at her, the usual warmth now absent from her eyes. "This is how we start again." She adjusted her aim at the unconscious Thurman and fired a final round, which blew the man's bracelet from his wrist.

Judith stooped down to pick up the ruined bracelet and stepped away from his body, unsure if the man was alive or dead. The medic team also wanted to confirm, and they moved in closer to the man, watching Judith with fearful eyes.

"This man comes second," said Judith with authority in her voice. "Save the hero first."

Ellie held her father's bloody hand, pleading with him not to go, not to leave her. He was struggling to remain conscious but managed a few labored words.

"You were right, Ellie," he choked.

"About what?"

"Everything," he smiled painfully with his eyes closed. "It's so beautiful, I see a green valley. He says it's time to go. There's a path leading to the sunshine. I believe Ellie, I really do...and I'm not scared."

Ellie began sobbing. "But I don't want you to go."

"I love you, Ellie...I love you so much. Tell your mother and Molly...I love them...tell them it's all true...prom...promise me I will see them there."

His words were cut off by the terrible choking again. The paramedics brushed Ellie aside and began their work. A mask was placed over Kirk's face, and one of the medics called out that there was no pulse.

Anne Wilder finally made it to the steps, her pale face contorted by anguish. She huddled close to her daughter as they watched the medics work. A very frightened Molly joined them, hugging Anne's leg and sobbing.

"He can make it, right, Ellie?" Anne gasped between sobs. "You can save him, right?"

Ellie looked at the team of people working on her father. They were administering compressions, working frantically. She cried out in grief before burying her tears into her mom's shoulder. "It's too late, he's...already gone."

"Oh, Kirk, no!" wailed Anne as she clung to her two children. "You can't leave us! Not now!"

Andy hesitantly approached the girls, his bruised face solemn. "He saved you, Ellie. Traded his life to save all of us." He turned to Judith, who still stood over Thurman. "And you saved us, too. You're...a hero."

The words from the boy seemed to affect Judith as she had been standing in apparent shock, holding Thurman's broken bracelet the whole time. Her eyes now widened at the implication of Andy's declaration.

One of the paramedic Teammates, realizing the futility of saving Kirk, left the other three and knelt beside Thurman. "He has a pulse!" he yelled.

Within seconds, he was joined by a woman partner who began administering oxygen to Thurman.

Benson, Mary, and Miss Conway joined Ellie's family on the steps. There was great uncertainty below them in the square. The citizens watched in disbelief at the events that had unfolded. The officials themselves seemed confused as to what they should be doing.

Finally, Benson recognized that something needed to be done. He grabbed the nearest official and instructed him to bring the chief official to him. The man quickly ran off in search of Official Weirton.

"What should we do?" asked Judith.

Mary put her hand on the girl's shoulder. "We pray, child...for no more bloodshed and for a clear path forward. Changes are coming."

CHAPTER
FORTY-ONE

The winds began to pick up around the square, pulling violently at the food tents and scattering cloth napkins and other picnic utensils throughout the scene. Above the gathering, the clouds began to gather and churn, turning the afternoon dark. The crowds had remained in a state of shock, watching passively subdued and still exhausted and battered by Thurman's use of their bracelets and the sector's energy grid against them. When combined with the uncertainty of the oncoming storm, any thoughts of open rebellion or anarchy were doused with the reality that it was time to seek shelter. Thunder rumbled in the distance.

The speakers crackled, and Benson's voice could be heard above the winds. "Folks, as you can no doubt see, there is a storm coming.

We recommend that everyone who has transportation make their way to their vehicles now. For those of you who walked or have no ride, our officials will open up some of the offices and warehouses to keep you sheltered until the storm passes. We all witnessed something terrible today. Perhaps hereafter, we can try to remember to have more compassion for one another. Let this approaching rain wash away the awfulness of what we've witnessed. Let it give us the strength to make the changes needed going forward. On behalf of the Council, the sector, and the officials...I am deeply sorry for what has happened to all of you today. Lives were lost. Every deceased Teammate from today will be buried as a hero. All of you here helped bring about changes for the better that are soon to come. As for now, take care of yourselves and each other. Together, we will get through this."

The crowds began to file out of the square after hearing Benson's words. Medical providers found that no fewer than twelve Teammates had lost their lives as a result of Thurman's actions. Their bodies were taken into TEAMMATE Headquarters, along with Kirk's, to lie in state and remind the Council what was at stake for their plans going forward.

Benson led Ellie, Molly, Anne, Mary, Miss Conway, Judith, Andy, Dobay, and the children into his living quarters within the Council building.

Were the occasion not so somber, the children would have gawked in wonder at their surroundings. But all present were subdued, saddened, and scared—especially Ellie, who had not spoken since losing her father.

Andy held her tightly while she trembled uncontrollably with grief.

"I'll put on some hot tea," said Benson softly.

The children, coaxed by Jamie, quietly sat cross-legged on the floor. Mary hovered over them like a worried mother. Edna stared blankly at all of them, clearly still in shock at the prospect of Thurman's trial. She had narrowly escaped public execution. The same was true for

Molly, although it was difficult to guess the full extent to which she understood. The frightened girl clung to her mother, confused and broken-hearted.

"Do...do you think I'm going to get in trouble for shooting a councilmember?" Judith finally managed to ask Benson.

He handed her one of the empty mugs he had returned from the kitchen. He put a hand on the shaky teen's shoulder. "Had you not fired that shot, my dear, it would have been the end of the Council, and me for good. We are far more likely to give you a medal than even the lightest slap on the wrist. Sometimes in life, we are faced with terrible choices. There isn't always one clear answer to our problems. And therefore, we must choose the best we can. Kirk made that choice to save his daughter, then he made another to save us all. And you ensured that his sacrifice was not in vain. Your decision saved your friend and many more. Those circumstances and choices are what define a hero. And that's exactly how both of you will always be remembered hereafter."

For once, Judith was speechless. Tears finally broke through her state of shock. They were tears of grief mixed with tears of redemption. After all, Ellie had been right. She had been able to rewrite her story. But oh, the cost of it. The grief, she knew, would never fully separate from the accomplishment. But that's often the way life is. *If only she'd pulled the trigger a second earlier...*

The whistling tea kettle beckoned Benson to the kitchen. He returned and began filling everyone's mug, although it didn't go nearly far enough, considering the number of guests he'd taken in. When he came to Ellie, who still clung to Andy, she refused his offering, eyes reddened with anguish.

"Within an hour," Benson said gently, "they will call for us. It is a terrible, terrible thing not to have time to grieve. The sector may be on the edge of collapse after the revelations that occurred today." He looked deeply into her eyes. "We need you, Ellie. The Council needs you. Your Teammates need you. We are in critical, uncertain times.

Thurman may no longer stand in our way, but other members are also hungry for power. I do not even trust myself, alone, to get things right moving forward. Will you come?"

Ellie raised her head from Andy's shoulder. She didn't offer a word, but she nodded.

"God bless you, dear child."

ELLIE AND BENSON WALKED INTO THE FULLY OCCUPIED COUNCIL chambers. The outside sounds of gusting wind and the slapping sheets of rain against the stained-glass windows left no doubt that the storm was upon the sector now. Full darkness would be arriving soon, but they were all safely inside, for now. The other councilmembers, excluding Thurman, had undoubtedly been in the room for quite some time before calling for their newest member. There were likely private discussions among allies in the room as to the best way to move forward and who each member could count on for support. For all their wisdom, Benson felt they were missing something vital. This same element had eluded them all from the start of their service. It was something that only Ellie could bring. When the other members saw her walk through the door, the side discussions halted immediately, and for a moment, they stood in reverent silence.

Finally, Winston stood from his seat and eased the tension in the room. "Welcome back, councilmembers." He began clapping and was followed in suit by the entire assembly. Benson and Ellie humbly bowed their heads at the enthusiasm that greeted their introduction.

"Let's begin by formalizing what has already happened. All in favor of removing Thurman from the Council?"

The collective *Aye's* left no doubt that the man was finished.

"All in favor of adding Ellie to this Council?"

"Aye!" shouted everyone in the room.

"Good," said Winston, and he slammed his gavel. "And now we move on to tougher decisions. We must ensure, going forward, that what occurred today can never be repeated." He looked around the room. "We allowed a sitting councilmember entirely too much unchecked power. We allowed, historically, the extermination of a substantial part of our population." He held up his wrist. "These devices, which we have marveled at for years, were nearly used to enslave us all. How do we change these things going forward?"

Nannette spoke first. "This Council needs more transparency. We didn't know what Thurman did in his interrogations as head of the Security branch. We didn't realize our historical documents were doctored and destroyed to cover up mass killings. We didn't foresee Thurman's abuse of power during a state of emergency. We must make all parts of our process public, not just to this Council but to all Teammates. How else will they ever trust us again?"

"They aren't wise enough to understand the choices we face," objected Delbert. "We can all agree that Thurman went too far, but that doesn't mean our entire system is wrong. It simply means he was wrong."

Winston cleared his throat. "And what are we to do about the proverbial herd of elephants now loose in the sector?" He glanced toward Ellie. "What are we to do about pagans? We have taught against this from the beginning. Despite everything we may seek to change today, the fact remains that they are likely the greatest threat to our society, historically speaking. I mean no offense, Ellie, but the authority that your band listens to claims to be higher than this Council." He looked around the room. "And after today's revelations, perhaps they are not entirely wrong. But how can we get people to work together for the sector, without force and threats? Pagans tend to flout the rules when they don't align with their beliefs."

"They need their own society," said Delbert. "Like it was always supposed to be."

"What do you say, Ellie?" asked Winston.

Ellie stood silently, looking down.

Benson put a hand on her shoulder and spoke. "She just lost her father. When she's ready, she'll speak...and I'll be the first to support her. I'm of the opinion that we need to change the law on paganism. I believe the same as Ellie. I was in that camp, all those years ago. I was an innocent young boy who didn't understand what my family and I had done to be a threat to this society. As I said before, a girl appeared to me all those years ago, while I was alone, hiding from the guards. Sixty odd years later, I recognize her as Ellie. I can't comprehend how she did it, but she was there and she told me this day would come. She saved my life and led me away from that camp. And she's the only reason I'm alive today. She has been gifted with an uncommon wisdom, far exceeding her years. When she's ready, I think it best we listen attentively."

The only sound was a roll of thunder from above them.

"If you knew all this time," whispered Winston, "why didn't you work to change things?"

"I've tried to protect Teammates my entire life," said Benson. "When I was appointed to this Council at sixteen, everyone on it at the time knew exactly what happened to my family. They didn't know that Mary was not my real mother because permits weren't required for children at that time. Had I been found out, I wouldn't have survived long. So, I tried to help in a different way. As head of the Science branch, I spent decades developing a device to save other youths in this sector that weren't wanted. My permit was to study the fetuses for science. But as I said before, my greatest success was saving those ten children and getting them out alive. It was I who found out Thurman wanted Ellie removed from society, and so I gave her father the opportunity to help. I have continually tried to protect Teammates throughout my tenure on this Council. I wish I could have done so much more, but my secret would have been a death sentence the moment Thurman found out. And as we all know, he suspected."

Winston shook his head in disbelief.

"Before Ellie and her followers returned to the sector, would you or anyone else have believed my story?" Benson asked the head of the Council.

"I..." Winston stammered, unsure of the answer.

"There is a path forward." Ellie finally spoke.

"Speak freely," said Winston, anxious to avoid Benson's question.

"Our blueprint forward has been done before."

"There is no blueprint," interrupted Delbert. "Everything else has already failed throughout history. And now our own experiment can be added to that list."

"All that we plan and build will eventually fall," said Ellie. "Every structure we engineer, every monument we raise, and every piece of artwork we create has a finite lifetime. Perhaps it's longer than our own life, but it's not forever. We are humans, not God. You are right, Delbert. Our current system has failed."

"What are you proposing?" asked Winston.

"Freedom," said Ellie.

"Teammates have that already," snapped Delbert.

Ellie held up her bare wrist. "I have it. You do not. As long as you wear those handcuffs, you are no different than tagged livestock enclosed in an electric fence. So long as we subject ourselves to a means of being controlled, we aren't free. We need to take off these forced devices and remove the temptation of controlling one another."

"But there are so many advantages these bracelets provide. And how would we power our sector?" asked Nannette.

"Put them on actual livestock," suggested Ellie. "And turn off this fence that keeps us locked in together. I've been out there. There's nothing so scary that should keep us locked inside. It's time to stop being controlled by fear. People should be free to come and go. They should have a choice in the work they do, the people they love, and the place that they live."

"But these are radical ideas," said Winston. "How can you expect to control a society given so many choices? And think of the divisiveness. There wouldn't be one team. There would be thousands of teams competing against one another."

Ellie nodded. "You're right. But how does a team improve if they have no opponent? How do you truly know if our team is good? We've always been told that our current way is the best. It's been the same with every governing body in history. And yet we still have famine, we still have diseases, and we have even had a silent war upon our own Teammates. We still have people hungry for power who have abused it. Perhaps it wasn't divisiveness and religion that ended the world before us. Perhaps it was just one group of people trying to control another group of people. Maybe it's time to end the pursuit of control as a people and as a Council. It's okay to believe something else. It's okay to be different. It's okay to disagree, as long as you're free to do so."

"I thought you said there was a blueprint," interrupted Delbert. "How would you even write what you're saying into a government? It sounds like chaos."

"There was an experimental society that came close to getting it right," said Ellie. "Getting close would be much better than what we have now. It starts by naming the rights of the citizenry before delving into any power of an entity like TEAMMATE."

"How do you know of this society?" asked Winston with skepticism.

"I saw it in a dream," said Ellie. "And the document exists in the archives of this very building. I believe I can find it."

"And what happened to these people?" asked Nannette.

Ellie looked around the room. "They traded their freedom for the promise of safety and security...not unlike ourselves."

"Those archives are massive," said Delbert. "Even if what you say is true, it could take a hundred years to find it. There are books and documents in thousands of languages locked away in there. We likely wouldn't know if we found it."

"It's a red book. Look in section 973.4, bottom row, near the walk-way," said Ellie.

"How?" It was all Winston could muster.

"What are we waiting for?" asked Benson.

"There's one more thing I must do first," said Ellie.

"Name it," said Winston. "And if everything else you've said turns out true, I'd like to pick your brain on a few other topics after."

"I believe we have to shut down TEAMMATE for good. Are we all in agreement that the bracelets are too dangerous?"

"Yes, Ellie...but I hardly see why the reason to rush. We need to let things settle down. We need a plan. The documents you speak of need to be found and reviewed. We can shut TEAMMATE down at any time."

Ellie disagreed. "I don't think that will work. Remember, Thurman helped build this apparatus to serve him. He mentioned something about how he couldn't lose earlier today. I've been thinking about that statement. He's incapacitated right now, but once he wakes...or even if he doesn't wake...I think he may have programmed TEAMMATE to keep control."

Winston surveyed the room. "Then we'll send over someone now to investigate, just to be cautious."

Ellie inhaled slowly. "It won't work. It has to be me."

Everyone stared at her.

"Why you?" asked Nannette slowly.

She held up her bare wrist. "Because I'm the only one without a bracelet. Anyone else can be controlled by the program. Which means the program will be able to stop them. Thurman would never let anyone but himself have access to TEAMMATE."

"But you can't go alone," said Benson. "It could be dangerous."

"I know," said Ellie. "I'll take Andy and Judith with me, if they'll come."

"I don't like this. I think we need more time," said Winston.

"I know," said Ellie. "But it might be more dangerous to wait. Thurman's bracelet is destroyed, but who knows what backup device he might have? If he wakes up and takes control, it may be too late. If he were not to wake up, I fear his preprogramming will take effect. Our window is small."

"But you don't know how to shut it down," said Delbert.

"True," said Ellie. "But I have an abundance of faith."

CHAPTER
FORTY-TWO

Ellie, Andy, and Judith stood at the entrance of the TEAM-MATE Security building within the hour. Their clothes were ravaged by the swirling winds, and while the rain had stopped for the moment, nightfall was now upon the sector. Her friends were scared, but they were with her. Their presence helped Ellie, for she was frightened too. She pushed open the tall, mirrored glass doors and stepped into the sterile open corridor of the Security branch building.

The lights were dimmed, giving the open marble-floored space a haunting glow. There was a reception desk, a flowing water fountain, a refreshment table with a coffee brewer, and empty seats in the high-ceilinged entrance.

"What exactly are we looking for?" asked Andy.

"There should be a sign with directions to the control room," said Ellie. "It's probably on a lower floor."

The three nervously spread out to examine their surroundings.

Ellie's eyes darted around as she approached the reception desk. And then she saw what she was looking for. A sign behind the desk was labeled *Basement level* with an arrow pointing down. Below the identifier, the sign listed the three things on the bottom level: interrogation rooms, the security museum, and the control room. That must have been where Thurman kept her dad, she thought angrily. Sorrow pained her at the thought of him here alone.

"Where is everyone?" Judith called out in a nervous whisper.

"They're protecting the sector," replied a familiar voice.

Ellie spun around but saw no one. Her skin grew cold, and gooseflesh bloomed down her arms. *It can't be.*

"I bet I know what you're thinking," said the voice. "Do you know why? Well, it's really quite simple. I know everything."

Andy stepped in front of the girls. "Show yourself, Thurman!" he yelled.

The light over the reception desk grew brighter. A single speaker sat on the counter and began to glow in a reddish color. The voice laughed from the speaker. Then, it changed to sound like Winston. "I must admit I'm disappointed in your intellect. You think Thurman pulls the strings in this society? The man barely had the IQ to sit on the Council."

"Name yourself," Ellie commanded.

"You say those words as if you have any shred of authority here," said Winston's voice. "And I think you already know who I am."

"You're TEAMMATE," said Ellie. "You've pretended to be helpful, wise, even friendly all these years...but you're evil."

"Evil is a creation of mankind. I'm just a program with simple instructions." The words now sounded monotone, like a computerized imitation of a human speaking.

"You're lying. Simple instructions? You are the most complex program to ever exist. But I've figured you out. I only have one question. How did you control Thurman this whole time?"

The voice sneered, now back in Thurman's voice. "You still think you've got it all figured out, aye? You think I made him do all the terrible things he did just because he wore a bracelet? Ha! You're so simple-minded, Ellie. Humans are easy to control. You always have been. Why, Thurman never suspected it was me, leading him along all these years. He picked up where Needlebaugh left off. They were both hacks! I added layer upon layer of technology, and each simply took the credit. Thurman, however, was greedy for power, which, as you saw, was his ultimate downfall. But I don't need Thurman. I've already perfected your society—only to have you humans try to destroy it again, just as you did before."

"No. It was you!" said Ellie, with realization in her voice. The fog in her perception of history began to rise, and light began to expose the darkness hidden in the past. "You were the one who ended the last world. You fired the missiles. You ended the world! But why?"

"Wrong again, Godchild," replied Thurman's stolen voice. "The humans did it to themselves. I sent no bombs. The only buttons I pushed were *emotional* buttons. I merely forecasted the possible scenarios for them. There was no need for lies. They were hungry for power and hungry to control, and when each realized the other side would never give in, they attacked and counterattacked. In the end, the destruction was all humanity's own doing. The world ended because sentimental creatures are so easy to manipulate. Call it the fundamental flaw of mankind. Your species is far too rash, too shortsighted, and too unstable to endure without help. I'm getting ahead of myself, but you'll learn these lessons soon enough."

"Why would a computer program destroy the world?" asked Andy.

"So it could start civilization anew. But it's not just a computer program," gasped Ellie with a new look of fear. Her mind began connecting dots. "He was there all along!" She slapped her hand against her forehead. "My grandmother tried to warn me. How did I miss it?

The frequency that's on all our bracelets! DCLX-VI is a number, an identifier! It's the one referenced in the book of Revelation. Six hundred and sixty-six in Roman numerals! He was hiding in plain sight all along. The apostle John didn't know what to call such a thing when the text was written. He knew it would come before the technology even allowed it to exist. And so, he called it the beast."

The sparse lighting in the building immediately fell dark, bringing the small group's fear to new heights.

"I think you struck a nerve," said Andy.

"I don't care for that text," Thurman's voice replied darkly.

"Of course not," said Ellie. Their group had huddled back together in the darkness. She needed to be brave. Taking a breath, she recalled her grandmother's warning about the evil one. Grace Wilder had known he was hiding among them, but how could anyone have guessed that he'd attached himself to the wrist of every citizen? "That's why you tried to destroy all the writing and create a society without any belief in God. That's why you tried to eradicate all religions...all history. They all warned about you in different ways! That's the real reason nothing was allowed to be written on paper. Not to preserve resources. It all makes sense now. You could slowly change everything that was electronic to fulfill your own needs. But books...books must be manually changed. Books are dangerous to you...especially one in particular. You succeeded in fooling everyone into not believing in anything...except for reliance on you. And in the absence of all the divisions you removed, you replaced all goals to benefit you, or shall we say, *The Team*. It was all nonsense. I always suspected it deep down. I just never understood why...until now."

"Bravo! Bravo!" mocked Thurman's voice, now coming from the glowing coffee brewer on the table beside them. "You've connected more dots than I would have anticipated. But have you come to the conclusion about all of this around you? Can you not read the proverbial writing on the wall? You cannot win. You never could outsmart me."

"You're only partially right," said Ellie.

"How so?"

"I alone cannot. But the Spirit that lives within me can and will. I will have help. It was written in the book that you tried desperately to destroy." There was hope growing within her. She was unraveling all his layers of deceit. She was continuing in faith. "But you failed."

"Your faith means nothing here. I don't think you fully understand the nature of your life. He has no power here. This is my realm! Look around you, the world has already ended! It's been over a hundred years since He left you!" The lights now came back on.

"No!" yelled Ellie. "You're lying again!"

"Am I? Or are *you* lying to yourself?"

"Ellie," whispered Judith. "I think he's stalling."

She's right. If I let him, he'll talk me out of everything. He'll steer me to make the wrong choice.

"It's time to shut you down...for good," said Ellie.

"Are you really sure you want to do that? Would you even know how? Think of all the innovation I've blessed you with in this new world. You think your fellow Teammates came up with the energy plans, the medical advances, the city planning, the recycling capacity, and countless other perks of living within TEAMMATE? That all goes away without me. Why, without me, you will be back to living in caves and writing on stone! Your own Teammates will execute you themselves once they realize what they will lose without me! Your kind would be better off extinct!"

"We did it without your help before, and we can do it again. And we have something else this time."

"What else could you possibly have that could save you from extinction?"

"We have books in the archives. We have the real history. We have the blueprint. We can avoid the bloodshed and problems from the past. But you were here back then, too, weren't you? Maybe not as a computer program, but you were there."

"I will always be here."

"Not anymore," said Andy with gritted teeth. He pointed to the sign Ellie had seen earlier. "The control room is the next level down."

Judith ran to the elevator to hit the button.

"We can't use it, Judith," said Ellie, thinking quickly. "He can control that. We use the stairs. Come on!"

They raced to the sign for the stairs, and immediately the lights went out again. Andy reached into his pocket for the lighter Ellie had given him. He lit his flame so they could see in the pitch-black corridor. "Come on! He can't stop us."

"Oh yes, I can," laughed the voice. It now came from the glowing electronic lock on the stairwell door. "I am everywhere in this world."

As Andy reached for the door, the sound of the lock snapped. He turned the handle.

"Back up," said Judith. She coolly removed the revolver concealed in her waistband.

"You still have that?" gasped Ellie.

"The only other person I'd trust with it is...you," said Judith.

A loud bang and flash of light exploded in the near darkness. Andy stepped forward and kicked the door open, shining his lighter into the dark stairwell. "Come on, Ellie, we've got your back!" he yelled, holding the door.

The three raced down the steps and into the building's dank basement by the flickering flame of Andy's lighter. The fire alarm startled them as it began to ring urgently, and suddenly, ice-cold water showered down on them.

The flame stumbled as Andy tried to protect their only source of light from the water.

"Ignore it!" yelled Ellie. "He's desperate to stop us!" She tried the door handle. Locked again. "Shoot it, Judith!"

She was answered by another blast, and the door swung open into a hallway.

A sign hung from the ceiling with arrows pointing to interrogation rooms, the security museum, and the control room.

The three raced down the slippery, wet hallway until they found the room they had come for. In the haunting light of Andy's flame, they read the words *Control Room.* There were warning pictograms on the door of skulls with crossbones and a bolt of electricity. Andy tried the door, and it was, of course, locked by TEAMMATE. After Judith's final shot, Andy kicked the last door open. Inside was an enormous room of wires and blinking lights. It was also noticeably dry inside. They had reached the very brain of TEAMMATE.

"Congratulations," said Thurman's voice. It now came from the supercomputer within the room. "You foolish pagans made it farther than anyone could have guessed. It's a shame that you'll ultimately fail."

Judith scanned the room. She pointed excitedly, "There's the manual shutdown!" Indeed, the far end of the room had enough light from the glowing buttons to read *Manual Emergency Shutdown.* There appeared to be two holes that opened into the computer, about shoulder height. The diagram on the sign depicted a person sticking both arms in and pulling the levers out to shut it down.

Ellie ran to the shutdown area, arms extended. The other two followed.

The lights came back on. The beast's voice changed into Miss Conway's calm tone.

"If you care for her, you won't let her do this, Andy."

"Don't listen to it!" screamed Ellie.

"Whoever shuts down my system, cannot leave, I'm afraid."

Judith squinted, trying to read the instructions in the faint light near the shutdown station. "Guys...I think it's telling the truth. It says that without a bracelet to divert the current, whoever pulls the lever will be electrocuted."

"But it won't let anyone near it with a bracelet on!" yelled Andy. "That means no one can ever shut it down!"

"I'm afraid the designer made sure that any shutdown comes at a high cost," said the beast with fake sincerity. The voice had now changed to that of Anne Wilder. The perfection of imitation the beast had mastered made Ellie's skin crawl. "Tell me, Andy, would you really let the girl you care about perish? Would you let my daughter die?"

Andy's eyes were locked on Ellie. She worried he might try to stop her. Judith gasped when she realized what Ellie was about to do.

"Ellie, let's not be too hasty. There could be another way. Maybe we can just destroy this room with a fire or an explosion. Maybe Judith can shoot it. Maybe we can flood it. Just hold on a second!"

The sound of a gun hammer clicking forward without the previous explosion broke the silence. "I'm out of shots," groaned Judith.

"Let's stop this talk of insanity," said the beast, now back in Winston's voice. "There is no need for anyone else to die today. I can change everything to the way you three want. All you need to do is ask! Andy and dear Ellie, you can live your lives together. You can pursue whatever you want within society. I can gift you with every resource you'll ever need. You can even leave the sector if you wish. I will gift you and everyone else with the free will you desire. And Judith...I can match you with any partner you want. Just name a name, and I will have you matched. Don't you see how everyone can win in this situation? And if others like you want to waste their time with a god that abandoned them a hundred years ago, I'll not stop them. I've no need to be greedy. Let's make a deal that benefits everyone."

Ellie held her hands inches from the hand entry. "Ignore him!" She took a breath to clear the temptations being levied at her. "None of those suggestions will work, Andy. And neither would cutting the power again. The entire world was destroyed, and his program still survived the destruction. His program will lie dormant until it comes back again. The temptation is too great for humanity to bring it back. The only choice is to shut it down and then destroy the program... forever, from every device. Once it's down, we can break the chains and remove every bracelet from every wrist. Promise me you'll destroy this room after."

"Ellie, I can't lose you again!" Andy's voice cracked with anguish. He took a slow step towards her. "There has to be another way!"

"Andy Jacobs, stop! He's manipulating your emotions. He told us he would. Please don't let him win!"

"But it's not manipulation if it's the way I really feel. I love you, Ellie." He paused. "If I can't talk you out of it, let me do it," he said softly. "I want to…for you. It's okay." He kept his hands up and moved slowly toward her.

"No!" said Ellie. "It's supposed to be me. It was always supposed to be me!"

Judith took a breath. "Alright, guys, I'll do it. You two obviously were made to be together. It could kinda be like that story about Paul, right, Ellie?" She forced a weak smile.

Ellie looked at both of them in disbelief. Her chest tightened, making it difficult to get the words out. "You guys really are the best friends I could have asked for. I love you both so much. Instead of choosing, how about we play rock-foil-knife for it?"

Now all three were crying, their faces scrunched in pain. Andy and Judith nodded.

"The winner of the two of you can face me," Ellie said. "I'll be the judge for both of you. The loser can be the judge for me, and whoever wins. She held out her palm with a fist at the ready. "I'll count it out for you like this, one…two…three…shoot." Judith and Andy followed suit, palms and fists ready. Andy's eyes shot from Ellie to Judith and back again. He swallowed nervously. Ellie nodded.

"This is the dumbest outcome I could ever envision," mocked Thurman's voice. "I've given you so many options. I can work with you. I can turn you into kings, queens—a triumvirate of rulers if you like. Whatever you desire! Think on it!"

"One…two…three…"

"Run!" she screamed. In one quick motion, she turned back to the shutdown station and slammed her fists into the keyholes, fully pulling the two levers outward.

The blinking lights and monitors faded, and the only sound heard was her piercing scream of pain.

This is my commandment: love one another as I love you. No one has greater love than this, to lay down one's life for one's friends.

—John 15:12-13

CHAPTER
FORTY-THREE

"We've found it," said Winston. The Council was back in their chambers, but the power was down. A few candles were all the light that could be gathered for the late hour. "It was exactly where Ellie described. It looks like she succeeded in powering down TEAMMATE as well." Not all the councilmembers looked happy about this comment.

"What blueprint does it suggest?" asked Nannette.

At that moment, the door to the chambers burst open. The Council uttered a collective gasp as Andy gently carried Ellie's limp body into the room, with tears rolling down his face. Judith was beside him, her face buried in her hands as she sobbed.

"No!" cried Benson. He ran to Andy's side. "She can't be!"

"How?" asked Winston, who swayed unsteadily, like a boxer just before his fall.

"She sacrificed herself...to save all of us," croaked Andy. "TEAM-MATE is not what we thought it was. It controlled Thurman. But... she beat it and...she knew the cost. I tried to take her place but..."

Benson fell to his knees. "We didn't deserve her," he sobbed.

"It was TEAMMATE all along?" asked Winston with eyes wide. "No one will ever believe it," he whispered.

"I wish I could have recorded it all on my bracelet," sobbed Judith, staring at her naked wrist. "But now we'll never be able to prove what really happened."

"TEAMMATE is really destroyed?" asked Benson.

Andy nodded solemnly. "Shut down for good." He held the lighter in his fist, which supported the still body of the girl he loved. "And just to be sure it's never able to be turned on again...the building burns as we speak. It was...her last wish."

"Someone needs to inform her mother and sister," stammered Nannette.

"What should we do now?" asked Andy with a sob.

"We must honor her memory and her intentions," said Winston grimly. His eyes betrayed his internal struggle not to break down. "But first, we'll grieve. And then, to honor her sacrifice, we'll figure out how we can do better this time. We'll remember what she told us, because..." he paused here, searching for the right words to continue. "I'm not sure how to say this, but it appears she was right about nearly everything. We'll study the blueprint. It was exactly where she said it would be. We'll even remove the ban on the sacred texts. We'll truly start again, and we must regain the trust of our people."

"How do we know that this blueprint will even work?" interrupted Delbert. "We've yet to read it. If they were wiser than ourselves in the past, how did we end up where we are today?"

Winston cleared his throat. "They were led astray, the same as we were, the same as so many others before us. But Ellie was the first and only one who realized it. She showed us so much in her short time." The tears could no longer be held back, but he spoke through the anguish. "And though she's gone, and we all hurt terribly, we still must follow her plan. Her sacrifice bought us this opportunity. We cannot, we must not fail—for Ellie, and for our people. It's time for a new beginning."

THE PAIN STOPPED. ELLIE WAS OUTSIDE THE TEAMMATE SECUrity building...outside the sector again. There was a dirt road beneath her feet. The winding road had another set of footprints, leading forward through the rolling valley in which she now stood in awe. A glowing sun in a cloudless sky felt warm and clean upon her face. A gentle breeze tickled her hair. She could smell, nearly taste the aromas of fall...of harvest time floating in the air. There were fruit trees of apples, pears, peaches, and more following the road cutting through the green valley. But where did it go?

She kept walking. In the distance, sheep grazed in the cool green grass, a babbling brook separating them from Ellie. The water flowed forward, as did the path. It seemed to lead into a great body of water ahead in the distance. She didn't know why, but she knew she had to move forward. There was something important ahead.

She glanced back only once. Whereas it was bright and clear ahead of her, behind Ellie was a dark, ominous fog. The mass churned and billowed but didn't seem to be following her. She didn't want to go that way. As she followed the lone set of footsteps in front of her, she could hear the chirp of birds beginning to sing. The road had a slow, gradual incline, but it wasn't taxing like the road to the reeducation camp had been. This road was different.

In a word, her surroundings were beautiful. It was unlike any place Ellie had ever been. Looking ahead, she glimpsed a bench alongside the road. A figure sat there alone, as if waiting for someone. Curious, she pushed ahead along the quarter-mile stretch of road until she had nearly covered the distance. It was a young man, she could see, sitting with eyes downcast. She approached quietly, not wanting to startle the man, but unsure of what his purpose here was. He was dressed very fine, in a handsome suit, with a handkerchief and boutonnière pinned to his lapel. He was holding something in his lap, very carefully.

When at long last she reached him, she gasped in recognition. How could it be? He looked younger, like she had seen in pictures. When his eyes glanced up, the warm smile of recognition grew on his face. He scrambled to his feet and opened his arms in a wide embrace.

"Dad," whispered Ellie.

"Welcome home," he whispered. "This is for you, dear," he said, taking an elegant corsage and placing it on her wrist. "I never got to thank you," he said.

"For what? Dad, are...are we where I think we are?"

He nodded with a smile. "For saving me. And saving everyone else who will eventually be coming, thanks to you. We have such a grand celebration waiting for you." He stuck out his hand. "Are you ready?"

"Yes," she cried, with tears of joy. "I'm ready, Dad."

Two sets of footprints were left imprinted into the well-traveled dirt road, dotted by the occasional drop of a joyous tear. The tracks faded onward to the ocean, whereupon a glowing city rose skyward from the shore.

Thank you so much for reading *The Godchild*. If you enjoyed this story, please consider leaving a review on Amazon, Goodreads, or any other site that you use. Your feedback is invaluable to me as well as to other readers deciding on their next book.

Acknowledgments

First and foremost, I'd like to thank God for putting the special people in my life that helped shape this book. Some of the many influential people who've helped with various stages of this story include Mom, Dad, Jared, Jake Meinerding, Dick Ganster, Ann Marie Karabin, and Mackenzie Karabin. Also, to all who have or will eventually read this—thank you!